When We Have Wings

Claire Corbett was born in Canada and has worked in film and public health. She has had essays and stories broadcast on Radio National and published in a range of publications, including *Rolling Stone*, *Cinema Papers*, *Picador New Writing* and the *Sydney Morning Herald*. *When We Have Wings* is her first novel. Claire currently lives with her husband, son and daughter in the Blue Mountains.

When We Have Wings

CLAIRE CORBETT

ALLEN&UNWIN

First published in 2011

Allen & Unwin
Sydney, Melbourne, Auckland, London

83 Alexander Street
Crows Nest NSW 2065
Australia
Phone: (61 2) 8425 0100
Fax: (61 2) 9906 2218
Email: info@allenandunwin.com
Web: www.allenandunwin.com

Cataloguing-in-Publication details are available from the National Library of Australia
www.trove.nla.gov.au

ISBN 978 1 74237 556 4

Design by Sandy Cull, gogoGingko
Typeset in 11.75/15pt Granjon by Midland Typesetters, Australia
Printed and bound in Australia by Griffin Press

10 9 8 7 6 5 4 3 2 1

MIX
Paper from responsible sources
FSC
www.fsc.org
FSC® C009448

The paper in this book is FSC certified. FSC promotes environmentally responsible, socially beneficial and economically viable management of the world's forests.

For Sam and Sophie with all my love

ALIS VOLABITIS PROPRIIS

You will fly with your own wings

When We Have Wings

CONTENTS

PART

1

John Wilkins (one of the founders of the Royal Society and Lord Bishop of Chester) outlined the four ways that a man might fly:

1) with the help of angels;

2) with the help of fowls;

3) with wings fastened to his body; and

4) in a 'flying chariot', meaning presumably a device or vehicle powered by something other than human muscular effort.

Wilkins judged the first three rather improbable, and in this he was largely correct. Birds and angels are strangely unwilling to assist humans in flying, whilst attempts to fasten wings to humans are notoriously dangerous.

—Pat Shipman, *Taking Wing: Archaeopteryx and the evolution of bird flight*

Gavest thou the goodly wings unto the peacocks? Doth the hawk fly by thy wisdom? . . . Doth the eagle mount up at thy command?

—Job xxxix

1

FLIGHT

Peri circles above the bay, head down, hunting, wind shrilling in her feathers.

'Luisa! . . . *Luisa!*'

Don't call out again. Cold acid drips into her stomach, eating at her. Hugo twists his head around, restless, as if feeling her fear swelling like a wave way out to sea, gathering power, rolling in. Peri wraps an arm around him, though he's already held tight to her chest in his baby sling.

Salt Grass Bay will be deserted, Luisa had said. *Meet me there. Please. Tell no-one*.

There are others, Luisa had said.

Luisa had sounded worried and angry and so, because Luisa is her friend, her sister, who in the months since they met has told Peri true and important things about their lives, she will meet Luisa at Salt Grass Bay. But Luisa's call, her insistence on secrecy, makes Peri uneasy.

Peri had stepped out that morning carrying Hugo as she did every morning, lying to Hugo's mother and father though she didn't say a word. No reason to think she wasn't taking Hugo to the park. She barely speaks to them, to either of them, anymore.

One more circuit of the bay. Lower. It's not deserted. Below Peri a big grey shape, beached seal, rolls back and forth in the low waves.

Not a seal.

Peri lands heavily, staggering onto the sand. Blood drains from her face, her head, she's blacking out, gently, rolling to her side, don't crush Hugo. An eye blink later she's up again, walking towards what she tells herself is a pile of kelp, what she tries to see as a drowned log, but what she knows is her worst fear made real in the morning light: surf breaking against a woman's body, her wings so sodden the slack-tide waves can't push her further up the sand or drag her down into the sea. She knows those soft grey wings. Luisa.

She falls to her knees by Luisa's head, arching her own wings up and away from the water. Can't get her feathers wet. No time to dry them, not now.

Blood has leaked from Luisa's mouth. Peri tastes bile. Leaning over, she retches past Hugo into the sea.

What happened? Luisa fell—no, she was *wrenched*—from the sky. She's a good flier, this was no accident. Look at her! My sister, older, street-smart Luisa, broken in the surf of Salt Grass Bay. Her skin so, so white, her hair soaking, heavy as seaweed.

Peri kneels there in the cold sea, dizzy and sick, one arm still around Hugo, her other hand touching Luisa's cheek, Luisa's skin exactly as cold as the water of the bay. Peri rinses her mouth, spitting out salt and vomit.

Luisa's chalky skin is becoming mottled blue and red. *How long since you died? Why? Why?* Who would do this? What did she want to tell me? Is that why she's dead?

Peri strokes Luisa's hair back from her cheek, closes her friend's eyes. A moment. She struggles to her feet. The sun is growing stronger as it rises. In an hour or two the beach will be a blast furnace: burning sand, glass water.

The wave of fear that was building out to sea is rushing in now, rearing high above her, breaking cold and heavy, smashing the breath right out of her, holding her under.

If Luisa knows something—*knew* something—that got her killed, then what about me? Oh Luisa, what have you dragged me into? They knew you were coming here so they must know *I* was coming here. If they think I know whatever it is that you found out, I'm dead too. I *don't* know, but that won't help. Bad enough I've seen you here.

Peri scans the horizon, but beach and sky are empty. Fly away, *now*. Fly away home. Where is that, now? Where will I be safe? She looks down at Luisa. She isn't wearing her baby sling. Not surprising. Whoever Luisa was frightened of knew about her implant; they'd have made sure baby Amy wasn't with Luisa when she fell.

Push Luisa out to sea, cover her with sand, give her some sort of burial, don't abandon her here, just another piece of trash tangled in seaweed, like the dying jellyfish clotted along the tideline. It's impossible. She's too heavy and there's no time. And she must be found, not hidden.

Peri's throat burns from the bile she's vomited, closing up so it's hard to swallow. She starts her run along the sand, gulping air. It takes all her strength to run fast enough to get off the ground. No time to climb the cliff to launch from a higher point. Someone could be waiting, if they knew Luisa was meeting me here. *Tell no-one.* I didn't understand why that was so important. *There are others.* What does that mean?

Peri's flying now, Luisa's body falling away from her, shrinking into the sea.

I'm sorry. Luisa. My only friend, my only sister. I don't even dare tell anyone you're here. You got away from those fanatics who kept you, your childhood like a prison sentence in that compound; you escaped to the City, like me. Now look at you.

Luisa would not bother about Peri's body for a minute if it put her own life in danger. What *would* Luisa do? Peri flies higher, banks, turning for home. Not home. Peter's house is not home; it never was. She'll run. No, she'll *fly*.

Where can I go? Peri's thoughts fly, faster than her wings, racing so fast as she tries to work out what to do next that she almost misses the clifftop landing platform at the Chesshyre house, stumbles against the rock wall, beating wings to recover herself, her feathers rattling like something dying, dry leaves in an autumn wind. Gasping for breath, trying to soothe Hugo. Calm. Breathe. Can't fly safely like this. Can't fly at all. She looks behind her: dark spots, other fliers, one or two high overhead, a few in the distance. Are they coming closer? Heart pounding from flight and fear.

A drumming of paws inside the house. A golden missile hurtles to the door. *Frisk*. He rears up and scratches at the doorframe.

Peri slides open the door, listens. The stream in the living room runs loud, the only sound beside Frisk's breathing and Hugo's snuffling. The house is still, the quiet so familiar to Peri. Peter and Avis are not there; knowing them, they could return in a few minutes, a few hours, a few days.

She and Hugo are not safe here. She could have been followed. Should she wait for Peter and Avis to come back? No. Even with them she's still not safe because she can tell them nothing. They don't know about Luisa, they'll be angry with her for lying to them. And anyway, how can they protect her when she has no idea who's killed Luisa or why? Will they even want to protect her? No, they'd dismiss her instantly and she'd be vulnerable and alone. They could betray her by accident if she doesn't tell them what has happened. They might betray her on purpose if she does.

Peri changes Hugo, puts him down in his cot. She hesitates, looking down at him. That breadth across his temples, so beautiful. She leans down, kisses his cheek. He breathes into her mouth, that pure baby breath smelling only of water. Peri straightens. Avis wouldn't hesitate to betray her. She's about to send her own child away, after all, for his safety—so often bad things are done to us for our own good, aren't they, Hugo?—so she doesn't need Peri anymore. And these rich fliers stick together. No-one to turn to. No-one can help.

Peri runs to her room, Frisk galloping with her, tripping her. She kicks him aside. *Get out of the way*. She has to think clearly. What does she need?

Undaunted, Frisk bounds onto her bed while she ransacks the room. Her waistband, the only pack she can carry, has to hold her AquaPad, the water-cloth she carries when she flies, energy strips, a flashlight smaller than her finger. Frisk snatches a pillow up in his jaws, growls, worries at it like it's a rabbit. Peri almost smiles.

With essentials packed, Peri pulls on her skims. These near-weightless flying clothes are indispensable for a long flight; they'll keep her warm and cut drag. The material fluoresces yellow, good for a beginner, outlining her against the sky for her own safety. She really needs camouflage now, but she has no choice. Ruinously expensive, these skims are the only set she has.

Hugo's fussing. She never leaves him alone. Frisk disappears into the nursery; Hugo falls silent.

Peri looks around the room, twisting the thin silver ring she always wears. This room is smaller than Avis's walkin wardrobe but it has double doors opening onto the green courtyard where she used to play with Hugo. The room is, by far, the most beautiful space she's ever lived in, and though it's not *home*—has there ever been such a place?—the loss of it will hurt, like shedding a layer of her own skin. Its narrow length is lit up by paintings and photographs Peter's grown bored with, her bedroom just a storeroom for things he's put aside. She glances up at the photograph of blue dye patterning white beach and green sea by one of Peter's favourite artists, a flier called Andy Silver. No taking *that* with her.

In the central well of the house, Peri looks up to the high gallery where Peter and Avis's rooms are, rooms forbidden to her, the nanny who lives downstairs with Hugo. No stairs, no way up there unless you can fly, those rooms are forbidden to Hugo too. He'll never see them, not now they've given up on him. There must be something they can do for him, all their money and smarts, but no, they just froze as soon as they saw Hugo's test results. I don't understand; I'm the one with no money, no education, I'm not even his mother and I'll fight for him harder than they will.

Avis was the first to recover, the first to decide that the sooner they did something, the happier he'd be. Other families had done the same thing, she said. It's not safe for him here, Avis yelled at Peter. Peri had lain in bed, blood thudding in her ears, as she listened to Avis screaming at Peter in the kitchen the evening after the test results came through. Of course Peri hadn't seen the report. Though she looked after Hugo every waking minute she had no right to know. She tried not to breathe as she strained every nerve to hear. What was wrong with him?

Don't you care? yelled Avis. Would you just look at that drop into the fucking *void* outside the front door? Wake up, Peter! *You* designed this house, it's built *only* for fliers, there's a hundred ways for your son to break his neck. There's nowhere for him to play, nowhere for him to explore, he'll be *walking* in a few weeks, Peter. He'll have to be guarded every second. For years. And we'll have to trust his safety, every waking moment, to that . . . to that *bloody girl*. We can't do it. He needs to be with a non-flier family. Just for a few years, Peter. Just till we can fix him. Till we can make sure he'll be *safe*.

Peri leaps into the air now, powering herself up a few wingbeats to reach the landing, and runs to Avis and Peter's vast sunlit bathroom. She's not supposed to have seen this room. Peri shivers; her own body betrays her, no matter how much she tells herself not to think of the things Peter has done. There's no point thinking about those things ever again, not now she has her wings. Well, Peter certainly never worried about *her* safety. He'd risked her life, many times.

Maybe Hugo will be safe if you send him away, Avis. But he won't be yours anymore. Is he yours, even now, if you can think of doing this? She had wanted to run into the kitchen, to plead *Listen to me*. I know about this. You won't get back the same child you sent away.

But *I'm* here, Hugo. If your mother sends you away, I'll go to Little Angels, maybe they'll send me to the new family, I could still look after you.

The bathroom is larger than Peri remembered, the shower alone the size of her bedroom. There's no bath; instead there's a sunken pool, ringed with stone benches under the water. Moss, green as seaweed, grows springy around the pool; it's soft and tough, soaking up water and steam and all that's spilt: soap, safety dust, perfume, sprays and lotions. It glows the brightest colour in that pale room, except for the bottles of Avis's wing dusts and glitter, which crowd around the sinks in every shade of blue, green and rose. Stalling, afraid of what she has to do, Peri bends over to read the labels on the bottles. The dusts shine back at her, each with its exotic name.

Peri squats on her heels. What she needs has to be here. Opening the cabinet underneath the sinks, she's relieved to find the medications lined up: pressure packs of Aileronac, blue squares of Opteryxin, stacks and stacks of the purple Zefiryn gels. Peri shakes her head. Zefiryn's so expensive; there's enough stored here to pay her wages for several years. Is Avis stockpiling the stuff? Grabbing enough for a few months, Peri hunts until she finds bottles of anaesthetic spray and new skin.

Breathing hard, Peri stands up, slipping the precious drugs into her waistband. She folds down the top of her shorts, rolling the flesh of her buttock between her fingers. There, that's it, that splinter smaller than a grain of rice driven deep beneath the skin. An arrow of rage pierces her.

They put a tracking device in me and *I didn't even know*. How stupid I was. No idea till Luisa warned me. Her family did the same thing to her. Peter and especially Avis didn't trust me. No way to pretend any different—I'm less than a dog to them. I'm *branded. Chipped*. And according to Luisa the device does more than just track; if I fly too far or anytime Peter or Avis feel like it, they can pluck me out of the sky like I've been shot. Poor Luisa. Should've heeded your own warning. Obviously you weren't trying to run away, not yet, or you would've done what I'm about to do. *Bastards*.

Ah, it's good, anger, stops me freezing in fear. How dare they do what they did to me? How *can* they send Hugo away? *Bastards*.

Before she realises what she's doing, Peri swings around, a wing extended, sweeping Avis's dusts to the floor. Bottles shatter, brilliant colours spray, puddle, drip. Geranium Lake and Cinnabar Green melt into Sky Blue Deep and Cobalt Violet, the moss floor glinting with glitter and glass. Peri smiles, imagining Avis's fury. One mess I won't clean up.

Luisa had told Peri where the Flight Check device was likely to be hidden and sure enough, when she got back to her room that day she'd felt around and there it was, the treacherous little thing, buried in her. How they must have laughed, Peter and Avis, putting that in me without me knowing. Whatever she does now serves them right.

When had it been implanted? They'd had a few chances. When she'd had the first operation for her wings? Or earlier?

A soft thud from the living room below. Peri freezes, listens for the rustle of feathers. An intruder? Has someone followed her? Oh god, if they find me up here, what will they do? Cut off my wings, throw me into the sea. Luisa's dark hair, floating like weed. Peter couldn't be back yet, could he? Fliers so hard to keep track of, then they're on you in a rush of wings.

Peri runs to the landing. Frisk looks up at her from the pile of cushions he's knocked over.

'Go on, Frisk, you great stupid thing.'

Peri jumps down to the living room, darts into Peter's workroom overlooking the ocean. One more thing. She scatters slicks across the huge table, flings open drawers and spills their contents. A flash of red, buried in a bottom drawer. She pulls it out, turns the solid rose, her gift, in her hands. *You bastard.* Of course you've hidden it. Luisa had almost laughed at her, she'd almost cried for her, when Peri had shown it to her. *Ah, no, no, no*, she'd said. This is the oldest story, my dear. Don't you know yet what he is, what he has done?

Peri finds what she's looking for, almost slicing her finger off as she grabs it, the blade Peter uses for cutting drafting slicks to size. Her hand shakes. She pulls down her shorts and twists around, spraying her skin with the anaesthetic. A hard spot to reach; she's going to carve herself up more than she needs to. Skin, fat, muscle part like rotten silk. A gasp escapes her as the pain burns. The spray has limited strength but makes the pain seem far away.

Hugo wails, the thin sound tugging at her.

Hot blood runs down Peri's leg. She pokes around in her flesh, like digging for a deep splinter. There. She levers the sliver out, flicks it away. Pastes over the cut with antiseptic new skin.

She flings the dripping knife onto the table, feeling bleak satisfaction when her blood splashes over the soaring design for Peter's newest tower and runs from her leg onto the polished floor. How he'll hate this defilement of his workspace. Let him find the mess in the morning. Least of his worries by then.

For a moment her eyes wander over the drawings, posters and displays on the walls of the workroom as if she's never seen them before. That blue ice cliff on the wall to her left, the church; how impressed she'd been, when she first came to the house, to discover that Peter had designed that. The church had been her homing beacon from RaRA-land, the only landmark she'd known to look for when she first came to the City.

Her first day in the City. She'd had a temporary permit—thank you, Mama'lena—and a determination never to leave, never to be pushed back out into the wilds. Peri rubs the taut skin over her left upper bicep. There, under her skin, is another implant, one she checks compulsively, ten, twenty times a day. Her City permanent residency. Wherever she goes she could be scanned and the permit would confirm she's legal in the City. When she got that, she'd been euphoric for weeks. Can't deport me now.

Hugo's crying. Hurt flares deep in her muscle as Peri runs to the nursery.

He's hungry, he's past sucking on his hands, he's red-faced, bawling. She picks him up, feels his heart, the little life beating against her, calming as she holds him chest to chest, settles him to nurse. He sucks at her breast, staring up into her eyes. Fly, fly, fly. I have to leave you but how can I? *No matter how much Avis hates me, no matter how much Peter ignores me now, I've never thought of leaving you, never.*

She stares at Hugo's beautiful things, the exquisite model earth dangling over his cot. You're going to lose all this too, Hugo.

Can't leave you here alone. Especially not now. Someone might come looking for me, find you instead. One-handed, her other supporting Hugo, she fishes out her slick. Ring Peter, beg him to come home right away.

No answer. *Leave a message.* She hesitates.

Last time she'd left a message it'd been three days.

Call terminated.

She looks at the blank screen. Oh god, didn't even think of it. Drops it to the floor. Have to leave it behind. It could be used to track her. Nothing easier.

Luisa's body, rolling in the low waves.

Frisk pads into the nursery, leaps onto the bench next to Peri, shoves his head under her hand. She strokes his nose, willing Hugo to finish nursing. Hurry, Hugo. *Please.* She looks at the wall clock; every second counts. She looks into Frisk's amber eyes. *I'll miss you.*

Hugo pulls away, smiles. 'Pah,' he says, his eyes widening at the little explosive sounds he makes. 'Pah-*p*ah-*p*ah.' *I'll miss you too.* No. I can't leave you here alone, alone in the house and alone in the world when they farm you out to another family. The only solution is that I stay with you and *I can't*.

I can't do this.

Her head fills up with static. The world around her judders to a halt—no, *she's* the one frozen, while the unthinkable stares back at her, unblinking, from the abyss.

I have to take you with me. Keep you safe. Keep you loved. No-one else will do it.

The world spins again, fast, faster, she's moving like the wind, if she stops everything will stop, she won't have the courage to save even herself, let alone Hugo, she'll freeze, sit here. A sitting duck.

She puts Hugo down on his floor mat, rummages through the nursery. A few more things to pack: absorbent squares for Hugo, a hundred no thicker than her palm; warm clothes for him—his cloudsuit and . . . what else?

What else do you need, little man?

You need me.

That's all, really.

I am everything you need.

She picks up Hugo, wipes his cheeks and puts him in the sling. Where can we go? Nowhere safe in the City. She rubs her upper arm, feels for the implant. That micro-seal of acceptance is priceless, many spent their whole lives seeking it.

But now, for Hugo's sake—well, she might as well dig it out too and throw it on the floor, token of her exile, but she does not.

This is it. After this, no return, no forgiveness. The moment I throw away every single thing I've ever wanted, ever struggled for, this life, the City.

Peri locks Frisk in the house, where he whines and scratches in a seeming agony of grief and apprehension. She walks to the edge of the cliff outside the front door.

'Sorry, little man.' She strokes Hugo's cheek and then, with one step over the edge, Peri lets herself fall.

2

OUT OF THE BLUE

Peri was an extraordinary girl. I don't remember exactly when I first realised that but it was towards the end of that long, wet, stormy summer. Not right away, of course, when Peri—and, more to the point, Hugo—were only names to me, spoken by the shaken man calling me in my home office on a sweltering Sunday morning and my first reaction was *why me?*

The reason was obvious in one way. I was a private investigator, recommended to him for my discretion, experience and wide range of contacts, so why not ring me? But then again, with his baby missing, why *would* he ring me and not the police? I would find out there were many reasons Peter Chesshyre rang me that hot Sunday. One was that I wasn't the only investigator he hired that day. The others had to do with the fact that Peter Chesshyre was a whole different species of client, literally, to any I'd had before. I had no idea just how much I had to learn.

It was nearly midday and I was sitting at my dining table in my shorts, half-heartedly sorting through a few documents. I'd been woken earlier by bloody Sunil, an old mate, now a ministerial adviser, who thought nothing of calling me first thing on a Sunday. 'Twenty-four hours a day, seven days a week, mate,' he said when I grumped at him. 'Time and tide, and the media cycle, wait for no man. Got work for you. Keep an hour or so free Thursday. Brief you soon as.'

Staying at home had been a mistake; there was no breeze and the six-storey block of flats, absurdly named Ventura, was baking. I was sweating and my neighbour Vittorio was away with his boyfriend, which meant the people who camped up on Ventura's flat roof felt free to resume last night's salsa party.

I got up and pulled on a shirt, planning to go anywhere with shade and cool water. I was halfway out the door when I felt my slick vibrate. I was only half listening as Peter Chesshyre introduced himself but the sweat chilled on my back when he explained he'd discovered his baby was missing that morning. He wanted me to come to his house right away.

Peter Chesshyre? The name rang a bell. I ran through my mental files as I exchanged my shorts and shirt for a suit and walked out to the access laneway next to my ground-floor flat. I stopped in front of Ray's folding card table and bought one of his locally famous samosas cooked in a little solar oven.

He smiled, weatherbeaten lines crinkling around his eyes. 'You go for a drive, huh?' he said. Ray kept an eye on Taj for me for a monthly retainer. It gave him status among the other street sellers. No-one else had a car to look after.

I wolfed down the samosa and slid into the car, grateful Ray had already unplugged Taj from the charger for me. Lucky there was even one of those still working on this lane.

'All good?' I asked as Taj brought his lights on.

'Yeah, it's all shiny,' he purred.

'We need to get going, Taj.' The first hours after an abduction are the most critical and these had already slipped by while we all slept.

If baby Hugo's captors intended to kill him, he was already dead and had been dead long before his parents woke up. If he was still alive then other scenarios came into play but they all required me to act fast.

'Hey dude, using me means you finally got a rich client,' Taj observed. 'Makes a nice change. Maybe you'll invest in a better suit one of these days. What took Golden Boy so long to ring you, anyway? Sunday morning sleep-in?'

'I'm wondering the same thing,' I said, putting on my tie but leaving the knot loose. Exactly *when* had Chesshyre and his wife discovered Hugo missing? I glanced at my watch. It was nearly half past twelve. *Shit.*

Rain. A steaming monsoonal downpour started just as I set out for the Chesshyre house. To reach it, Taj had to negotiate an unpredictable route through backstreets, tunnels and motorways towards the old Eastern Distributor. Bitter experience had taught me it was always better to let Taj navigate. City road maintenance was so dangerously haphazard it took all Taj's ingenuity and satellite input for him to drive anywhere safely. It occurred to me, as it did every time I used him, that this first car of mine would also be my last. The City's life did not depend on roads anymore; instead, there were the canals, light rail and, of course, Flight. It struck me Flight was more than just a toy for the rich, a wild extravagance in their excessive lives. It was highly practical.

I glanced at my watch again. One o'clock.

'Not been here before, dude,' Taj remarked as we crossed the EastGate tollbridge over Blue Canals into the exclusive eastern suburbs greenbelt. 'Pricey shops along this bridge but down there it looks like a mini Edge City.'

He was right; below the bridge and along the median strip of the Eastern Distributor clung the plastic scrap tents of those who had to live near their jobs as couriers, porters and cleaners. Rather than struggling to build a shack in Edge City, the squatter satellite cities surrounding the City proper, they set up anywhere that was not actual roadway. Their shanties even extended over the water of Blue Canals, though bull sharks and water police kept numbers down.

'Cool,' said Taj. 'Golden Boy already gave my details to bridge security. Usually takes so long to get into these snobby places.' Yes. Getting through security into these enclaves was time-consuming and inconvenient. Unless you could fly. Another huge advantage of Flight: fliers were literally above security checks, body searches and sniffer dogs, the whole rigmarole, most of the time. Their comings and goings were less monitored than those of us mere mortals.

So why had this flier Chesshyre summoned me? The tollbridge receded and the number of pavement-dwellers on this side of it fell to zero. As Taj purred along these lusher streets, his tyres swishing and sending up fountains of stormwater, it came to me where I'd seen Chesshyre's name before: it had been linked with a picture of rooms stacked one on top of the other like caves in a cliff, rooms with heights and drops, around a central void.

A year or two ago I'd seen reports on a controversial new child-care centre, the first one designed exclusively for flier children. This was why it was a big story. The usual suspects brawled over it: media commentators, academics, politicians, child-care experts, most condemning the separation of flier from non-flier children. A NEW APARTHEID screamed the headlines, while Origins cultists, those extremists, picketed the construction site. There'd even been a legal challenge but somehow the developers got round the anti-discrimination laws, leaving the fledglings, the little fliers, free to live out every child's dream as they darted and tumbled through their aviary, their enclosed sweep of sky.

Kohn Chesshyre Li, the now-famous architecture firm, had been named in all the reports. Was my client *that* Chesshyre? My slick confirmed he was. My eyes glazed as I skimmed the information it dredged up—licences and qualifications, membership of professional associations, articles he'd written for architecture journals, references to his honours thesis. A picture popped up of a church he'd designed, a berg of irregular neon blue.

Then I saw something that made me whistle out loud.

'What?' said Taj.

'Well, what do you know? Chesshyre and I went to the same school. St Ivo of Kermartin's—you've heard of it, Taj.'

'Have I?'

St Ivo's was an elite private school run, in my time at least, by stiff-backed black-clothed seminarians, stern, learned old men (though looking back they could only have been in their forties). I wondered if any of them were still around.

Chesshyre was younger than me, though, so I had not known him there. The real difference between us was that I was the poor boy, or at least the not-rich boy—and let's face it, that's the same thing—picked for a sporting scholarship because I was fast on the football field. But no matter how much glory I brought the school in the mud and blood of the playing field, I never belonged. *Oh gawd*, the rich careless boys drawled to each other if I dared speak to them, *it runs* and *it talks*. *Did* you *know the Chook could talk?* One or two smart kids were my friends because they had to be—they weren't rich either. The school fed on their brains and my speed.

Chesshyre now, he was the real deal, I could see—tall, handsome, rich. Head prefect. Rowed for the First VIII. Now he had wings. Of course he did. Oh Christ, I could feel my resentment, like the old football injury throbbing in my right knee. It was going to be hard to like this man, to listen to him, work for him. But you don't have to like him. Worked for his type before, remember? You're just one of the hired help: get the job done, try not to track mud on their floors. Just find his son. Yes, I've worked for his type many times but never for an actual graduate from my old school, a real live master of the universe even before he got his wings, drawling at me from his Olympian height in that strange flat accent the boys at the school all tried for and the rich ones managed for real.

Chesshyre was rich alright and I knew there were a few good reasons why people like him would ring a private investigator on a case as serious as this. For a start, rich people want to be sure they're calling the shots. They don't want the police deciding what priority to give their case and they don't want arguments over the 'appropriate use of public resources'.

But there could be other, darker reasons. After all, the first thing police do in a case like this is scrutinise those closest to the victim. Too often that's where the answer lies. Chesshyre already told me they thought their nanny, Peri Almond, had taken Hugo. Well, we would see.

Also, you could never overestimate the desire of the rich to avoid publicity. The infamy of a kidnapping brings other dangers in its wake: it gives people ideas and one lot of bad luck usually attracts more. The cabinet minister whose daughters were abducted in the Charon nightclub case found that out for sure. My experience on the Charon investigation, the most notorious I'd ever conducted as a cop, was probably the reason Chesshyre wanted to hire me. After all, it was a kidnapping too.

Taj drove through increasingly wealthy neighbourhoods—Diamond Waters, Aalto Park, Boyd Beach—towards the sea. 'Look at the size of these houses,' he said. The houses were growing larger, block by block, veiled by cascading bougainvillea and hibiscus. 'What are *those*?'

'Those are the fancy engineered cultivars rich people like. That's year-round blooming jasmine and *those* are the infamous fluoro-gardenias. Lily loves them. A rare lapse in taste explained only by their fabulous cost.'

Lily. I looked at my watch—twenty past one. We were making good time on the better roads but still I jiggled my knee impatiently. *Too long.* This was all taking too long. My ex-wife Lily was the real reason I'd wanted to escape my flat. She was fed up with me not answering her calls and I worried she'd resort to coming over. There'd be a scene, same as last time. A quiet scene; Lily's not a shouter. She's trained herself to speak low when she's angry; just as scary as the shouting, really. A few days ago she'd materialised at the door of my flat, wearing her lawyer's uniform, the well-cut grey suit she uses when appearing in court. She'd started by refusing a glass of water. Wouldn't even sit down. 'We need to talk about Tom.'

Oh god, when did we ever talk about anything else? Thomas lived with her and Richard but had been spending nearly half of each week with me.

'Now Tom's started preschool,' she said, 'he's so tired in the afternoons. I think he needs the stability of one home during the week. He's so little, Zeke.'

I had to agree, he was indeed little.

'You know I'm not arguing this for myself. You can see it's selfish to insist he travel between us all the time during the week now he's got the long days at preschool?'

Yes, of course I could see that. She'd won her point. Usually did. She was paid large sums of money to do that.

'Of course he'll see you some weeknights. And weekends. *Some* weekends.' Lily pressed her advantage. 'Richard and I need relaxed time with him too!' Lily laughed, low in her throat. 'After all, we've got the stress of getting him off to preschool and you'll get the fun times.'

Ah, so now having virtually full custody is some kind of sacrifice. Lily's so very good at winning through making her strength look like disadvantage. A powerful asset, that, as lawyer and mother. And she's a very good mother, is Lily.

Lately, she's decided Thomas must be a flier and so she needs my consent to the treatments. Her first tactic, the usually effective one of simply assuming agreement, has not worked on me. So now she's let me know that if I *force* her, she'll take me to court. If I deprive Thomas of wings, I'm guilty of neglect. Hardly an empty threat, coming from her, and I can't keep avoiding the issue. Not even the Origins extremists responsible for the Charon nightclub kidnapping made me feel as hunted as Lily does.

Lily the social climber, who wants to elevate our son to the world of fliers, how astonished she'd be to know the identity of my new client. Meeting a celebrated architect and flier like Peter Chesshyre would be a dream come true for my Lily.

We passed a leafy park where young women with their babies sheltered under rain trees. A fat dove, green as a watered lawn, flashed past my windscreen.

The Chesshyre house was hidden, isolated on its own headland. As Taj eased himself into a carport near the base of a sea cliff, I said I couldn't see any buildings and asked if he'd made a mistake.

'No, dude,' replied Taj as he unsnapped my safety harness and opened my door. 'This is the address.'

'Okay. Stay shiny, Taj.'

After scouting around behind the carport, relieved the rain had stopped, I found a path that cut through tea-tree scrub and then snaked up the cliff face. Waves crashed below, sending up salt spray. I climbed, grateful for the wind from the sea, and realised I was looking forward to meeting Chesshyre, curious to see a real flier face-to-face. Of course, I'd seen them on the news and even here and there in the expensive parts of town but I'd never actually met one. I pulled up, struck by the thought of Sunil's call earlier. He wanted me to investigate some bigwig in a fancy church just for fliers. That was the church I'd just looked up, the one Chesshyre had designed. Made sense. Chesshyre was a famous flier architect, naturally he'd be the one to design an exclusive flier church. And now that Chesshyre had summoned me, Sunil's target would only be my second, not my first, real live flier. Funny. I was being dragged into this new world in three different ways. Just showed how fast things were changing. At least now I'd be more of an expert than Lily, for once.

I stumbled over a stone and cursed, frightened I'd lose my footing and pitch head first from the narrow path into the sea. I hate heights and here I was halfway up a cliff, facing a horrifying ascent. The entrance to the house soared high above me and for the first time I could see the house itself, which, with its angled clear walls, sat like a faceted crystal in its cliff-face setting.

Then I saw it. *Oh god, no.* The only way up there, besides scaling the rock, was a godawful bucket creaking on the rusting cable of the flying fox in front of me.

I heard a rushing; a dark shape blotted out the sun.

A man landed, teetered on the very cliff edge and rocked back and forth, arching his wings for balance: Peter Chesshyre. Over two metres tall in his white shorts and loose singlet, his feet shod in thin blue material, not like any shoes I'd ever seen.

But what riveted my gaze were his wings: great curves of azure, of aquamarine, of navy, of shades of blue I had no name for, running and twisting together like streams of water. *Jesus wept.* The first time I meet a real live man with wings and he takes my breath away.

I stood there, no power of speech, hypnotised by the might of this man's wings, at the strangeness of seeing the shining feathers attached to a human being, of seeing a creature so much more physical and present than any normal human being because he took up so much space. There was simply so much *more* of him.

Bizarre to see a man with wings but also strangely familiar; growing up Catholic I'd seen so many images of men, women and children with wings. We'd prepared for this moment for thousands of years just as we'd designed aircraft centuries before daring to build them. The ideal had always been there. Now, now, it moved in front of me in flesh and blood, bone and feather.

As Chesshyre stepped closer I could smell a sharp forest scent coming from his wings—maybe an oil he used for grooming his feathers? I forced myself to tear my gaze away from those wings, to look into his face. He was handsome in that clear-skinned way of the rich; eyes dark blue, set deep above his long nose and wide mouth. His dark hair glinted with a blue sheen, reflecting his wings.

'Zeke Fowler?'

I nodded. His voice, light, bleached of feeling, was as toneless as I'd expected from an old St Ivo's boy and I felt a rush of hatred for him, for the way he sounded, that had been entrenched in me from the six years I'd endured in that place. Then I recalled why I was there and was ashamed. I might be shorter than Chesshyre, and plainer, with my sandy hair and freckled skin, my thin face and astringent expression. (*You always look sceptical*, Lily used to say. *Professional hazard*, I replied.)

But I still had my son.

Chesshyre shook my hand. His skin was hot and dry, fever-hot. 'You'll have to use that, I'm afraid,' he said, gesturing to the flying fox. Well, it couldn't be clearer that all of their friends and important guests were fliers. 'Meet you up top.' He turned away to the cliff edge.

I'll never forget what happened next. It's an image that still haunts my dreams.

Chesshyre stepped off the cliff. My stomach plunged with him.

I knew what he could do but it was flimsy knowledge that didn't stand up to seeing a man drop out of sight like a brick.

Seconds later I heard the whistle of wind through huge feathers and felt the surf of air past my face as Chesshyre was borne up, wings beating. *And when they went, I heard the noise of their wings, like the noise of great waters.* Don't know how *he* knew but old Ezekiel nailed it. That's exactly how it sounded.

I climbed into the bucket of the flying fox, which was beaded with water from the earlier rain. They sure made no effort to make things easier for non-fliers. This rusting machine was probably used for groceries. The nanny would have had to use it too, I presumed. I pressed the button and clutched the bucket's cold sides, staring ahead as the winch started its loud grinding, willing myself not to look at my shadow rising up the cliff. Gusts of air buffeted me, then fell away to the waves below.

Watching Chesshyre take off as easily as I might step onto an escalator, I felt a jab of envy. Seeing him this close it was possible to imagine that thrill and power. Only for a second, though. Not all the surgery, DNA shots, treatments and drugs in the world could prepare *me* to step off a cliff.

I stared out over blue sea, its slow motion wrinkling, as the bucket scraped upwards. I looked at my watch again. Twenty minutes to two. The odds of finding Hugo alive were shrinking fast. Christ on a bike, this thing was slow.

Big clouds shifted overhead, sailing away on business of their own like ocean liners. Chesshyre stood high above, wings gleaming in the intermittent rays of sun.

The bucket lurched to a halt and I climbed out, shaky with adrenaline. Serve Chesshyre right if I threw up all over him and his gorgeous wings.

The Chesshyre house had a river running through it.

It wasn't immediately obvious. The first thing that struck me was that the place was missing a roof. Walls faded away into sky or dissolved into rising mist. I glanced down but saw no raindrops on the floor. The roof was not missing; its absence was an illusion. That was real sky I could see though; I recognised that ragged cloud breaking up over the ocean.

The other thing that wasn't obvious was security. Still, they must have some; they wouldn't just rely on the unscalable cliff face to protect them, would they?

Walking through the foyer, rubbing my hands where my grip on the bucket had bitten into the flesh, I noticed a rushing, chuckling sound as I entered the largest living room I'd ever seen. The whole eastern wall was one transparent sheet of riverlaminate at least fifteen metres high overlooking the sea. I made a note to fix respectable *per diems*. These people could so clearly afford it.

As I followed Chesshyre inside, I examined the way his wings folded along his back so that, while they were longer than he was tall, they did not, quite, touch the floor. That precise line where feathers met skin fascinated me, that line which marked where human became alien. How could those feathers be him, part of the human being that was Peter Chesshyre? I had to resist the urge to touch them.

I crossed a line of grasses that ran the length of the room and screened a stream, the source of the noise I'd heard earlier. Outside the eastern wall a stone terrace that was part of the cliff face shelved outwards over the ocean. A table and chairs stood there but no railing, nothing to prevent one from falling into the void. Falling into the void was what these people liked to do. Chesshyre would be out there with his morning coffee and he'd get up, say, *I'm just going to stretch my wings*, and step into the air.

No wonder I couldn't see the house until I was directly below it: it was carved right into the rock. The back wall was cream- and red-streaked stone with the other walls and roof sealed to it. Against the stone grew a spotted silvery-white gum with pointed leaves, grass plants tumbling fronds over its roots.

'I had a devil of a job convincing Peter not to put more than one tree in here.' A woman walked through the doorway at the end of the room and came towards us. 'And look how badly that's turned out.' She gave an angry laugh. 'I was worried about *him* turning Wild. Always thought he might be one who had to watch out for himself. A stream here, a tree there, could be dangerous if he pushed it too far. But no. It was *her*. Her! And they say it's a myth.' The final words spilled from her fast and low and vicious.

'You're up,' said Chesshyre, in a tone that suggested she should be in bed or in her room; anywhere but here.

She arched her neck as Chesshyre came up to her, bending his head to kiss her cheek. I was horrified to feel tears pricking my eyes as I watched them in a pose so simple and graceful, as if they'd stepped from a painting of great angels; he bent over her, blue wings sweeping the floor, his head lowered to hers, she poised on tiptoe, reaching, the twist of cloth across her hips the drapery of a goddess. Not fair that mere humans could be that splendid. But that was the point: they weren't mere humans anymore. Chesshyre opened his wings right around the woman, encircling her, then drew them away, folding them down his back.

Chesshyre wasn't just comforting her; it seemed more like he was trying to shut her up. Her face was drawn, her eyes very large with black circles round them. Thin to the point of impossibility, her meagre body looked even smaller compared to the massive white wings that trailed to the floor; they looked as if they must drag her to the ground.

'Avis, this is Mr Zeke Fowler. Mr Fowler, this is my wife, Avis Katon. The designer.' A beat. 'Hugo's mother.'

Avis inclined her head, setting the red crest of feathers in her hair nodding, but her glance was wary. Hostility simmered off her like steam from a volcano. I hadn't heard of her but from the way Chesshyre had introduced her it was clear I should have.

I smiled uncomfortably, disconcerted by the nearly bare, yet elegant, woman in front of me. They can't ever look truly naked with wings but I expected a fashion designer, and distraught mother, would wear more clothes. A bit of something shimmery almost covered her breasts; the same material, now pink, now green, shifting colour as she moved, wrapped about her hips, leaving her taut belly bare.

Avis turned back to Chesshyre. She raised her hands, clenched together, but I could see they were trembling. Her voice was a strand of steel pulled tight. Any moment it would break. 'You know, Lima told me she had a friend whose father went Wild. Of course the family searched and searched but when they go Wild there's no finding them. Then everyone says the problem doesn't exist. They've just fallen out of the sky and the body's never found. But *we* know what happens. We *know*—like the nursery rhymes.' What was she talking about? Was she claiming a Wild flier—whatever that was—had stolen Baby Hugo?

Avis started singing, '*Baby, baby, naughty baby, hush you squalling chick, I say. Peace this moment, peace, or maybe rough wild wings will pass this way. Baby, baby, he's a giant—*'

'This way,' broke in Chesshyre, leading me down a hallway of milky blue glass. Avis pushed past him, muttering something about needing a cup of tea.

I shook my head. She was clearly a little odd and for a second I speculated: did *she* do it? Had she flipped, taken baby on a joyflight, dropped him into the sea? Was I being brought in just to establish a cover-up? I'd seen worse.

Chesshyre and Avis swept ahead of me, their wings like royal cloaks. Chesshyre spoke quietly to Avis, as if she were ill. Some serious problem there. They were being *too* careful with each other. Did one blame the other?

We entered a bright long box—the kitchen, lit by a sliver of window filled with blue. The back wall was intense green, alive, a rustling vertical garden of mosses and ferns. The sea crinkled minutely far below; the sky streamed light into every room. So far, no sign of forced entrance, none of the disorder attending a break-in. Inside job, then.

Avis stood at the sink with a kettle, her hand still shaking, as if she could not remember why she was there.

'Could you tell me *exactly* when you discovered Hugo missing?'

I asked as I followed Chesshyre to the nursery, glad to have the chance to question him separately.

'About two hours before I rang you,' said Chesshyre.

'Really?' I said. 'You didn't know he was missing before then?'

'Of course not,' said Chesshyre. 'We only got up around nine-thirty. After a while we realised Hugo and Peri weren't in the house but that didn't worry us. Not the first conclusion you jump to, you know, that your baby's been abducted. We assumed Peri took him to the park as usual. But as time passed we started to worry. Then, when I had a closer look in the nursery and in Peri's room, I could see she'd taken a few things and I got really concerned. So I started ringing around. To find someone like you.'

'Did you find a note, anything to explain what might've happened?'

Chesshyre shook his head.

'And you haven't contacted the police?'

Chesshyre shook his head again. 'It would be much better if we just get Hugo back as quickly and with as little fuss as possible.'

Chesshyre stood aside to let me enter the nursery first. It was cosy, enclosed like a nest. A stand of branches fretted with coloured sparks stood near the door. This was the one room so far with a definite ceiling, though even this one shifted with clouds and sparkled with artificial stars.

In the middle of the room loomed the white cot shrouded in its net studded with cream roses.

Empty.

I turned away for a moment, looking up at the shelves that ran at shoulder height around the room. They bore the most beautiful objects I'd ever seen.

There was a wooden puppet, lacquered gold and red and green, and jellyfish that rolled in water, round as moons. But what was that white thing hanging down like a patch of frost? I moved closer and it gave off a breath of cool like the air that flows off snow. I brushed it with my fingertip. It did appear to be a square of snow.

What exquisite things these parents had bought for this baby. Hugo had probably been long awaited, long hoped for. It was common knowledge fliers had to try harder than most to have children. Why was he missing?

This was not my typical freelance case: insurance surveillance, fraud or suspicion of adultery. This was like being back on the force, with real pain, real fear, real crimes. This was the fate of Chesshyre's baby being entrusted to me. A sick feeling knotted my stomach. It was not new. This moment had always come, on every important police case. One of the reasons I'd left.

I peered into the cot, where a jumble of colour caught my eye—soft toys, huddled together in white linen. And something remarkable: a stuffed lion curled up in the middle of the other toys, larger than the rest, as big as a medium-sized dog, and of far higher quality. Thick fur shone like silk where the light hit. There was the long golden mane, the broad noble nose, the tufts on elbows and tail, the powerful forequarters and leaner hindquarters.

The toy raised its head and opened golden eyes. It yawned, banner of pink tongue curling back. The yawn finished on a low musical growl. Ears pricked, it got slowly to its feet, stretching back legs and then forelegs, head almost on paws, the way I'd seen real lions do a hundred times in historical nature programs.

'Wow,' I said. 'Didn't know they could make things like you.'

Chesshyre was at my side in an instant. 'How *dare* you,' he hissed, his body shaking till his feathers rattled. 'Get *out* of there!' Reaching into the cot, he grabbed the lion, smacked it across the head, threw it onto the floor. The lion snarled, preparing to spring, but Chesshyre raised his foot to kick it and the lion backed away, turning and stalking, with dignity, through the door that we had entered.

Finally, some emotion from the distraught father.

'Looks so real,' I said.

'Frisk *is* real,' said Chesshyre, striding ahead of me. 'A real lion in all but size. Most genes are the same.'

'Oh.' I must have heard about such things but I hadn't paid attention, any more than I did to any other new plaything for the rich.

I followed Chesshyre into a glass walkway, courtyard on one side, blue air on the other. *Have a temper, don't you? Or is this uncharacteristic behaviour brought on by extreme stress?* While for most people stress intensifies what is already there, there *are* people who change utterly, sand to glass, under severest pressure. I hoped I wasn't dealing with one of those.

'Peri's room,' Chesshyre said.

A narrow box not much bigger than a prison cell, white walls covered in paintings and photographs. Chesshyre gestured to a glass door on the right opening into the courtyard. 'Peri played with Hugo under that tree. You can see she left in a hurry. We haven't disturbed anything.'

At last. Evidence. A pile of clothes lay heaped on the bed, drawers had been pulled out, their contents spilled. Someone had been in a hurry. I inspected the room; besides the art, which must belong to the Chesshyres, it was bare. None of the little knick-knacks so many young women like. Not a frilly sort of girl, then. I turned over the clothes. Sober things: grey and black workout pants and tops. One rose-coloured dress out of the league of the other clothes—had Avis given it to her? No jewellery. No cosmetics. Not even any perfume. Not a vain girl either. What did she care about?

'What has she taken?'

'*Hugo*,' snarled Chesshyre, his voice harsh and deep, cracking the veneer of St Ivo's blandness. He took a deep breath. 'A credit slick is missing but I don't care about that. I just want Hugo back.'

'Any photographs in here? Snapshots of family, friends?'

Chesshyre shook his head.

'*Why* would Peri take Hugo, Mr Chesshyre? What motive could she have?'

'I've been racking my brains. Possibly she was too isolated out here, maybe a bit depressed, I honestly don't know. Even that would hardly explain it.'

'Would she harm him?'

Chesshyre passed his hand over his eyes. 'I don't think so. She was attached to Hugo. Still, you realise you never know what people are capable of.' He walked away into the courtyard.

I continued searching. Nothing behind the bedside table. I pulled back the bedclothes, rummaged under the pillows, peered under the bed. Faint scent on the sheets—a vanishing hint of sweat and something else slightly more rancid. A pillow rustled when I put it back. I felt the pillowcase. Something in there. I reached in and pulled out a few sheets of paper covered in handwriting. I looked over my shoulder at Chesshyre but he had his back to me. I folded the paper and stuck it in the pocket of my trousers.

As Chesshyre turned to cross the courtyard, I cleared my throat. He stopped. I explained if I was to prioritise this job the way it needed, I'd have to drop all my other work.

'I understand,' said Chesshyre, then named a figure higher than my wildest hopes. 'Is that what you had in mind?' His voice was colourless again, all feeling bled out of it. He was already walking away as he said over his shoulder, 'That's if you find him.'

I followed him and found myself back in the kitchen.

Avis poured tea. Steam smelling of oranges rose up. A cake sat next to the sink.

I looked at my watch. Quarter past two. Avis sat down with her cup of tea, then put it on the counter. Didn't offer me one. She must've got fed up with her hands shaking because now she sat on them and stared out the window, her face blank.

'The more quickly I finish up here, the more likely I am to find Hugo,' I said. 'Every minute counts in cases like these.'

Avis burst into tears.

Chesshyre stood next to Avis, running his hands through his dark hair. 'Where to start?' he said, looking directly into my eyes.

I nodded. Parents don't want to get to the point because telling another person, launching an investigation, makes the unthinkable real, solidifies it into the larger world outside the family. Benign explanations are no longer possible.

'As I said before,' Chesshyre began, 'Peri has taken Hugo. We think she's attached to him, that she would not willingly let any harm come to him.' Avis swung around at this and began to speak but Chesshyre clamped his hand so firmly on her arm she winced. 'We are extremely concerned about her state of mind, though. You need to be as discreet as possible in your inquiries.'

I nodded again, annoyed. Still these two were not giving anything away. 'You say Peri's taken Hugo. But *why*? There're any number of possible scenarios. Peri could have been taken too, or lost her life trying to protect Hugo. She could have been working for someone else, a commercial rival of yours, Mr Chesshyre. Have you had any communication, *anything* to explain why she left? Any demands?'

Chesshyre shot a warning glance at Avis. 'No,' he said. 'No demands.'

I noted his glance. There was something they weren't telling me. They were distressed but didn't seem frightened that Hugo would be held to ransom. 'It's early yet,' I said. 'Demands could still be made. For all I know Hugo could have sprouted his own wings and flown away.'

'No,' said Chesshyre. 'There may be a number of possibilities but not that one. I see you know nothing about fledglings.' Abruptly, he left the room as if he'd just remembered something.

Avis was silent. She'd stopped crying and was now arranging everything on the counter in front of her—salt and pepper shakers, jars and bottles—into exact rows calibrated by height and colour. She arranged them all, then started over again.

A soft, heavy weight landed on me. I was so startled I almost fell off my chair. The lion—Frisk—had jumped onto my lap. He thrust his head into my hand. His mane was rough and silky. As he scraped his tongue over my hand, I scratched under his chin. He was heavier than I would have expected, all dense muscle and heavy paws. He raised his head and puffed his breath out at me a few times as he kneaded me painfully with his claws.

'Seems you've made a friend,' Avis said. 'He doesn't normally go near strangers.' She put her head in her hands. 'You'd better take him home with you. I don't think Peter can put up with him much longer.'

I ignored this. She couldn't be serious and I had no intention of leaving their house with a lion, even if it was a small one. 'What do you know about Peri?' I said.

'Not much. She's from some godforsaken *hamlet* somewhere. Hadn't been in the City long. *No* family. *No* friends. *No* boyfriend. *I* don't know.' Avis spat out each word as if it tasted like poison. 'You should ask *Peter*. Anyway, she and I, we didn't have much in common.'

Except Hugo.

'Except Hugo,' she said. 'There wasn't much else to talk about.'

I'll bet. I could imagine the stream of instructions that would have been issued to the girl. I'd seen Avis's type before: control freaks, every minute of every day scheduled. Perfectionists who brought their scary intensity to the tasks of motherhood.

I shook my head, annoyed with myself for letting dislike colour my judgement. I didn't know anything about Avis. I tried to look at her more objectively as she sat there, her chin resting on one hand, reminding me, despite her sullen anguish, of the pictures I used to stare at of contemplative angels. And yet now that I was faced with a real live flier, it was clear these new people were nothing like traditional angels.

The reason was the very wings themselves. They were *huge*. Artists never understood, obviously, just how big wings large enough to bear a human being would have to be.

Chesshyre returned, handing me a slick. Its screen showed a picture of a smiling baby, maybe a year old, held up by a young woman. The child was pretty, with brown hair and a calm ink-blue gaze; he'd kept that angelic look that they get at about six months. I remember when Thomas looked like that, with an unearthly radiance. The line about trailing clouds of glory had made sense to me then.

'This is Hugo,' said Chesshyre. 'Hugo Gyr Katon-Chesshyre.'

I examined the slick. 'Is this the most recent picture?'

Avis buried her face in her hands. Chesshyre made no move to comfort her. He nodded.

'What can you tell me about Peri?' I said. Avis was already upset. I might as well persist now. Things could hardly get worse.

Of course I ought to have known better. A rule I apply in my work is that things can *always* get worse. It's a rule I try to live by too. It's not a rule I've ever been able to disprove, alas. Lily once informed me that I'd stumbled on the first noble truth of the Buddha: life is suffering. *Hell*, I told her, *I was raised Catholic. I know it.*

Chesshyre pointed at the slick in my hand. 'Peri Almond's details are on there.'

'Yes,' I persisted, 'that's good. But what was she *like*?'

'Conscientious,' said Chesshyre. 'Hard-working. *Responsible*. I think she worried more about Hugo's safety even than I did.' Avis flung up her head at that, her nostrils flaring, but Chesshyre shot her a look of such pure rage that she retreated into stone-faced silence. 'She was an athletic girl,' Chesshyre continued. I thought of the clothes on her bed. Yes, that fitted what I'd seen. 'She wasn't a city girl, Mr Fowler. Unsophisticated. Even naive. She was a little overawed, I think, when she came to us. She was nice, you know. A bit . . . reserved, maybe.'

Avis could stand it no longer. 'You don't know anything about her,' she burst out. '*She—was—Wild—*'

Chesshyre loomed over Avis, patting the air in that patronising gesture men use to tell women to calm down. 'On the slick there's information from the agency that sent her to us,' he said. Avis turned away from us and glared out the window. 'We got her from a reputable agency, the best.' He sighed. 'We haven't had a chance to speak to them yet.'

'I'll do it,' I said. 'You should be able to rely on the agency's discretion in this. It doesn't look too good for them.'

I turned the slick over and pressed the rim. The next image was an agency business card: *Little Angels*. Of course. It would be called something like that, wouldn't it? The business card included a catalogue of girls available for work. Peri Almond was listed with the other girls, along with their photos, first names, where they were from and their experience. I looked at the head-and-shoulders shot of the same girl I'd seen in the photo of baby Hugo. A young woman. Very young. 'This is Peri?'

'Yes,' Chesshyre said.

Then I took the gamble I'd been planning ever since I entered their house. 'This is all very well,' I said, tapping the slick, 'but I need your security footage too.'

Avis's sharp indrawn breath told me I'd scored a direct hit. Chesshyre looked blankly at me. I'd been prepared to lie and say that I'd seen a security camera hidden at the entrance to their house, prepared to look a fool if I was wrong, but I was not wrong.

Chesshyre recovered quickly. 'Of course. Of course. But as it only covers the entrance area I don't think you'll find it much help.'

It was half past three by the time I left the Chesshyre house with the security images. Riding the flying fox down the cliff was not so bad now with the shadows lengthening. As Chesshyre walked me down the path to the car, I heard Frisk padding along behind us. He must have his own steep cat path down the cliff.

As I drew near to Taj, Chesshyre stepped close to me. 'There is something I should tell you,' he said. 'I couldn't tell you in front of Avis.'

I looked up at him.

'There is one possible motivation. Peri is very young, impressionable. I said she was overawed when she came to us. Naive. And I think she had—*has*—a crush on me. I didn't take it too seriously but perhaps I should have.'

Chesshyre drew something from the pocket of his shorts and held it out. I took it. It was a paperweight with a real rose embedded in its clear centre. How could each petal have been captured so uncrumpled, so perfect? There was even a drop of water on one inner petal.

'She gave that to me, Fowler. Sweet of her, I thought. But now I wonder, did she have a fantasy going on about me? Convince herself we were in some sort of relationship? If you find her, be aware she might say strange things to you. Who knows what she's told herself about me?

I don't think she would harm Hugo but I do think she's trying to get my attention. That's why I called *you*. I feel sorry for her, Fowler, that's the truth. If she's charged for this, her life is over. She'll be banished from the City for a start. You know the deal. She's young, she's made a serious mistake, but if we get Hugo back safe and sound there's no need to ruin her entire life over a silly girlish crush.'

So I was *Fowler* now; we'd reached that stage fast. As soon as I took his money.

I turned the paperweight over, hoping I was keeping my expression neutral. Even if Chesshyre was trying to lay a false trail, he might also be giving me a key to Peri's motives. The rose, with its velvety, intricate folds, its deep soft red, was the very image of desire. Could explain his obvious marital difficulties. Some might think it a bit early in the client relationship to grill him on whether he'd fucked the nanny but this was a kidnapping: I didn't have the luxury of time.

'Are you telling me that you had a bit of fun with her and she thought it was something more?' I asked. 'And now she might be taking her revenge?'

'I've told you what you need to know,' Chesshyre said.

'I see. Well, let me know immediately if Peri contacts you or you hear of anything else.' *Like a ransom demand.*

'Dude,' intoned Taj the instant Chesshyre flew away into a sky rapidly darkening with storm clouds, 'I've been tampered with.'

'What?'

'Black-winged flyboy. Biggest I've ever seen. Checked me right out while you were up there chatting with Golden Boy. I've scanned but can't find anything.'

'Probably Chesshyre's security,' I said. 'He's sure to have some, especially now. Not surprising he took a look at you. Sure you've been tampered with?'

'No,' said Taj, sounding grumpier than I'd ever heard him.

'Keep your shine on. I'll inspect you when we get home.'

As we drove away I thought about how disorienting it was to meet real fliers for the first time. So disorienting in fact that there was

Frisk, lying along the back seat, where Chesshyre had thrust him, telling me to take him for a few days, just till Hugo was home again of course, that he was a fine beast, worth a lot of money, but that he, Peter, couldn't stand the sight of the creature right now. *Wow. Do you normally get rid of members of your family so casually?* So like the rich, isn't it? To hand you a problem as if it's a favour? I had to admit the large downpayment for my services Chesshyre had given me had also thrown me off-balance.

'*Why*,' Taj said after a few moments, 'do I have a large moggy shedding fur on my back seat?'

'Don't whine, Taj. Doesn't suit the sardonic mode advertised by your manufacturer.'

One problem I worried at as Taj drove home, passing back through the wealthy suburbs, the streets growing narrower and greyer as I neared my flat, the flame and emerald parrots and doves giving way to those drab-winged pests, the mynahs, sparrows and starlings the rest of us have to put up with, was this: *how did we get here?* How did we reach the point where I could see a human as radically altered as Chesshyre? The question was more urgent, more real, now I'd met him.

These changes start so small, almost incidentally. We set one foot in front of another and before we know it we've climbed the mountain and can't even see our starting point anymore. How did it begin? Were our feet set on this path the first time a baby was conceived using IVF? Or was it inevitable from the moment we changed our world with fire, with language, with tools?

I began to think we'd been on this journey from the beginning. Is this what it means to be human, to be jack of all trades, the quicksilver species? In the old stories I'd read as a child, they said Fox is the trickster. Or Raven. The shapeshifter, the joker. Never purely predator, never merely prey. Always vulnerable, always dangerous. But of course it's not fox or raven. It's us. No meaning to being human, no one form. We are everything and nothing.

My son, to take the nearest and dearest example. What steps had we taken to shape him? Thomas has eyes of the purest meltwater green, the shade Lily picked for him from the Infant Inventory. Can't remember its real name, something deliberately bland like the Cochrane Register, but Infant Inventory was what everyone called it—the irreverent nickname for what was nothing more nor less than a catalogue of attributes.

Did our corruption start there? Or earlier, when we'd had him screened for the comprehensive A-list of diseases? I wasn't about to skimp on the best health for my son but I didn't want to choose his eye colour. It's too close, I argued with Lily, to treating our child as a product, with a range of desirable features. But she couldn't see it; we'd screened him for disease, what was the difference?

A history of biotech course was part of police training and they'd talked about the first IVF baby and the controversy surrounding her. I recalled the astonishment of my class that there had been any resistance to such an obviously benign procedure. I was the only one not surprised by the heated arguments over the morality of it.

It wasn't just artificial conception. There was the ever-increasing prevalence of surgery and drugs to enhance appearance and longevity. The distinction between treatments curing people of disease and those enhancing their looks and abilities got harder and harder to find, then vanished. There were the infinite possibilities of using your own stem cells for new tissue and organs. Who was now unmodified except the Origins fanatics? *They* were opposed to tampering with human genetics for any reason, avowing that humans had been made perfect by God; any imperfections resulted from deviating from God's will and we had no right to try to escape the punishments we so justly deserved.

All these advances came at a price and the differences already so evident between the bodies and minds of those with good food, education, work and health care, and those without, were becoming permanent. As the power of the treatments you could buy increased, class divisions were entrenched into flesh and bone, cell and gene, and that gulf, the one my mother and father were so sure they could cross by sending me to St Ivo's, was becoming unbridgeable.

Now this was where we stood—I had met Chesshyre with his wings, and even though we'd gone to the same school, the physical differences between us were so vast we trembled on the brink of division into two species. By the time we noticed the changes it was already too late, the plunge into the abyss taken while we thought we were hovering on the edge.

And who are the rest of us, us *non*-fliers? *The five Rs*, we're called: Retarded, Retired, Religious, Rationed and Regional. In other words, anyone too poor or too old or too disabled for Flight. What these contemptuous words disguise is that we ordinary humans are still, by far, the majority. Too old means anyone over about twenty-five and too poor covers almost everyone else, including those from Rural and Regional Areas—RaRA-land, which is anywhere outside the City. Too disabled is anyone too fat or too stupid or suffering from any other condition contraindicated to handle the treatments and then to keep up the ferocious regimen of physical perfection needed to get you up into the sky and keep you from falling out of it screaming. Believe me, there is no equality of opportunity in the world of Flight.

And so I was one of the increasingly rare people who understood the religious objections of those who believe it's wrong to tamper with the human germline. I have some sympathy with them but where do we draw the line? Almost everyone goes along with altering genes that cause major disease. Who wouldn't, for their child's sake?

Until now I never needed to worry about the modifications demanded by Flight because I couldn't afford the treatments. If this job went well, I'd be able to pay some of the cost and Lily and Richard would cough up the rest. They couldn't modify Tom without my consent. But I didn't want to make this decision.

But what will Thomas say to me when he's full-grown—that I denied him the great dream because of my own limitations, my own inability to accept this new world? My own father was not so selfish; I can still see him picking me up after one of the St Ivo's games, can still see the realisation dawning painfully on his face that in his store-bought suit and his middle-management job and mid-market car he was as invisible to the other parents as I was to their sons. I saw him realise that while he'd thought he was part of the comfortable middle class and as good as anybody else, he'd made the mistake of setting foot in a world where that wasn't true, where he could be snubbed. And he put up with it, for my sake, hoping I might even climb to a level he understood was closed to him. And Lily, smart Lily, she knows this and says to me this thing will happen, my son will move into a world I can never enter whatever I do, and I see the truth in that. But do I have to lose him so soon?

It was nearly five when Taj pulled into the laneway next to Ventura. Ray had already disappeared to wherever he hid himself at night. I needed to eat but Taj complained so insistently about being tampered with that I conducted a thorough electronic and physical scan.

'There,' I said, when I'd finally stood up, stretching out my aching back and knees, wiping my hands on a cloth. 'There's nothing, alright?'

Taj was silent. A car can't sulk but Taj managed it.

'Night, Taj. Stay shiny.'

I was starving and grabbed bread and cheese for myself. Usually I bought dinner from the local street sellers but I was impatient to get to work. The fear that anything I did would be futile tormented me. It'd probably been too late before I'd even received Chesshyre's call. What time limit should I set before insisting Chesshyre contact the police? Forty-eight hours. I'd see where things stood on Tuesday night.

Where could Peri and Hugo be? If Peri had gone to ground in the City or, worse, in the squatter slums of Edge City, then there was no chance of finding her. The only hope lay in understanding why she'd run away and where she might go. Random searches through the City would lead nowhere except to despair.

Yet how to understand her when Avis and Chesshyre had trotted out two different views of Peri as unhinged, Avis calling her Wild, whatever that was, and Chesshyre hinting she was obsessed with him?

I set out water for Frisk, smiling as I pictured how thrilled Tom would be when he saw him. First thing tomorrow I'd have to buy food for the lion.

I sat up late into the night running searches on Peri Almond. Very little turned up but the Little Angels information checked out. She was indeed from a coastal hamlet, a town called Pandanus about six hours' drive away. So far the girl wasn't leaving much of an electronic trail, at least not on databases that I could enter. That can be a real problem with the very young, especially kids from RaRA-land. One odd thing: except for her there were no Almonds in Pandanus. So who had she lived with? Where was she from originally? Did she have family somewhere else?

Frisk sprang onto my lap. I shoved him off. He crouched and leapt back onto me. *Thou huntest me as a fierce lion: and again thou shewest thyself marvellous upon me.* I put one arm around Frisk as I began running the Chesshyre security footage on my desk slick. They'd only given me about ninety minutes of it; obviously they didn't want me seeing more than they judged was necessary. After a few minutes of watching a static shot of the ledge in front of their door, I fastforwarded until an hour's worth of images had sped by, unchanging except for clouds. Then the door opened and out stepped a young girl with a baby strapped to her chest. I slowed the images to normal speed. The baby's face was turned away from me, nuzzled into the girl. But what stopped my breath was her wings. Peri had wings? They hadn't even mentioned this to me. Why? I checked the image of Peri in the photo from Little Angels. In that picture she'd had no wings. I looked at the most recent photo, the one of Peri holding Hugo. She was out of focus, her wings just a dark blur behind her; no wonder I hadn't registered what they were. Out of focus, that would be right. Hugo was what mattered; Peri was not important to whoever took the shot.

In the unblinking gaze of the security camera, a tense, white-faced girl with a baby stepped to the edge of the cliff and dropped out of sight. According to the time code, it was two thirty-seven on Saturday afternoon.

Peri was a flier!

This changed everything.

This changed *everything*.

Weird that Chesshyre seemed unaware of the importance of this, had not even mentioned it to me. Why?

I looked back at the shot of Peri from Little Angels. Definitely no wings. Of course not. Coming from Pandanus, she *couldn't* have had wings. She was nobody, from nowhere, and *nobodies do not have wings*. She must have got them while working for Chesshyre. Could this have any relevance to Hugo's disappearance? But what did it mean?

I ran searches that had not occurred to me before. There she was, a member of one of the Flight Gyms, a fancy outfit calling itself the Blue Air Group. I whistled. Man, was it *expensive*. I'd never looked at how much Flight Gyms cost before but the hourly rate was shocking. Little Tom's treatments were looking more remote by the minute. No wonder the girl had nothing, not so much as a bottle of cheap scent, in her room. With no access to medical records, but going by her membership of the gym, I had to assume she'd made her transition to Flight just under a year ago. Most interestingly, her membership had not yet run out. So, she really had fled on impulse, as the disorder of her bedroom suggested.

I started another new search. For the transition to Flight you need doctors. And not just any doctors—serious, heavyweight medical expertise. Which doctors would have overseen this process for Peri? Peter and Avis and maybe little Hugo too would have to see a family doctor who knew about fliers. Might Peri have seen the same one? I could have kicked myself for not doing more snooping at Chesshyre's; I might have been able to find out that sort of detail. I put together a list of names from my search. After all, there were not so many of these fancy new doctors.

Already it was past midnight. Often I lost track of time while doing database searches. I stood up, stretched, thinking I should call Chesshyre, tell him to turn the case over to the police. My job was impossible. If Peri had wings, she could be *anywhere*. I thought of Chesshyre describing the ruin of Peri's life if she were charged. Well, perhaps I could still help her and Hugo. Give it till Tuesday night, like I'd said.

I ran the few seconds of footage of Peri over and over till my eyes began to close in weariness. Was she angry, frightened? Watching that slight, vulnerable figure, the gentle way she settled the baby, stroking his head, seeing her anxious face, it was hard to believe her motives could be cruel or greedy. *Why are you doing this?* I asked the screen as over and over she shut the door, stepped off the cliff, vanished. Again and again, disappearing from my sight, my understanding.

Finally I dragged myself to bed. My trousers rustled as I pulled them off. The papers I'd found in the pillowcase. Each piece of paper was a short handwritten letter. I settled into bed and leafed through them.

Dear Hugo,

I wrote these for you because I wanted you to know how it was when you were very little. Because you can't remember it yourself. And I was the one who was there with you. Who saw you and listened to you and knew how you were.

Dear Hugo,

I was sitting with you, looking out over the sea. A purple mist came down around us. You pushed yourself up and you flung your arm out, pointing. As if to say, Look, isn't it beautiful. Look!

Dear Hugo,

A flock of parrots, black wings outstretched, flew overhead, screeching. You looked up. Awk! you said. Awk! Your first word.

There were others. I read them all several times but I was so tired my eyes kept closing as I tried to analyse Peri's words.

Chesshyre was clearly not stupid, but like so many rich people he seemed blind to the real world. He and Avis had let a winged girl care for their baby—mostly by herself, probably—while they pursued their own careers. A girl alone in the world, subject to who knows what secret fears. Assuming Peter's cover story wasn't the whole truth, was it possible she'd been threatened by a rival of Chesshyre's? She would've been easy to intimidate in their isolated house above the sea. If she *was* motivated by bitterness over curdled love then we had a real problem. If she wasn't actually crazy, if she was even now coming to her senses, realising in horror the seriousness of her crime, then Chesshyre had done the right thing by calling me. The important thing in that case was to get to her, make her see that it was safe to return Hugo. Then her actions would shrink from something potentially monstrous to not much more than an extended outing with the baby she cared for. How I hoped that would turn out to be the case.

3

THE GARDEN IN THE SEA

'Look at the stars,' Peri said, glancing down at baby Hugo. 'See, we can steer by them.' No way she'd risk flying on a cloudy night. Still too much the beginner for that. She tightened her grip on Hugo. She liked to fly with her arms by her sides, as if she surfed the sky, diving into it. 'What you do with your arms,' Havoc, her instructor at Flight Gym, used to say, 'it's very characteristic. How comfortable are you in the air? Do you throw yourself into it?' Now she flew with her arms around Hugo, keeping him warm. Wonderful that he slept, snuggled into the sling, so used to the feel of her, the smell of her, he could sleep anywhere, as long as he was with her.

Ahead and low on the horizon a pattern of stars fell into place. A spike of happiness pierced Peri's anxiety. Havoc had told her she now had bird navigational abilities infused into her brain but she'd never believed she'd be able to use them. Feared she was one of the ones who'd never really get it. Too old for Flight. Not smart enough, not strong enough. But she was navigating, without understanding how, in spite of her lack of faith. Somewhere near here was the Platform. But how to find it in the dark? Still, she had to rest and they wouldn't think to look for her here. Not yet. Peter probably didn't even remember leaving out the PostCard of this place. Coming here was a gamble but surely the danger of sudden late-summer storms would keep everyone else away at this time of year?

Peri wheeled higher. It should be exhilarating, flying through the night over the waves. The power of Flight itself forced a rhythm into her breath, her heart, calming her from her impulsive escape from Peter's.

Rough salt wind streamed into her: *Breathe in, wings up, breathe out, wings down*.

Something was flying through the sea below her, but its progress, mirroring hers above, was more splendid, triggering storms of phosphorescence, black water exploding into aquamarine tracers. A whole school of something big was whisking the sea into luminous froth, blue bolts scattering light through the dark.

Ahead shone a solitary white light. That must be it.

There was something else. A glow. Peri's belly cramped. Her flight muscles were tiring. Did the light mean someone was there, or no-one? People did not fly out to the Platform on their own. It was a long-haul Flight, a place for parties. It had been built for SkyNation by Peter's firm, which designed the environments for all the SkyNations. This one had proved so popular that it had been allowed to remain, drifting slowly, unanchored to the sea floor. For SkyNation guests, the challenge of finding it had been part of the event. When fliers wanted to visit it they checked its position on the satellite link and then used their navigational abilities, as Peri had, to find it.

Peri flew lower over the sea, grateful for the lift from the slopes of the small waves. The bright light resolved into three separate lights, triangulating the landing area of the Platform. She circled, braking, and beat her wings to cushion her landing. She stumbled, righted herself, grateful that the landing area was covered in the new soft-fall developed especially for fliers. Hugo woke and began to whimper. The whimpers ran together; he was tuning himself up. Soon he would cry and she could not risk that.

Peri found a sheltered bench away from the landing area and hummed a familiar song softly under her breath as she cleaned and changed Hugo. There was nowhere to put the soiled padding so, guiltily, she buried it under loose stones next to the bench.

Peri settled herself. Hugo's feet flexed with tension, waiting, then relaxed as her milk flowed. Before Hugo, Peri hadn't known that babies expressed themselves with their whole bodies, their feet just as eloquent as their hands and faces.

'They'll think I've stolen you, Hugo. But I haven't. I just couldn't leave you. I said I'd never leave you.' She wondered at her own resolve, her determination to do whatever was necessary, a steely will she'd seen in other fliers. At what she'd done to get these wings. The price had been higher than she could have imagined. Did she know herself at all? The problem was that she loved this child in a way she'd never bargained for, in a way she had not known was possible.

This unexpected love had wrecked everything.

Gradually Peri's breathing slowed a little. Her heart still pounded from the exertion of her flight and from her fear of discovery. She listened, hard. All she could hear was the wash of the sea against the Platform. At the edges the water sloshed right over the top of the seawall. The middle of the Platform rose to a flat summit, as if the whole Platform were a low, level-topped hill. The hill itself cast the glow.

Peri knew the place a little, from the PostCard Peter had left when he and Avis had flown out here for last summer's SkyNation. They'd left her and Hugo alone in the house for three days. They were always going away. Fashion shows, conferences, site visits. Hugo was fine alone with her. He'd had plenty of time to get used to it.

Hugo pulled away from her breast. He was still sleepy and pushed at his eyes with his fist. Peri kissed the little hand and tucked him tightly into the sling. Hugo's eyes began to close as he snuggled against the warmth of her skin and feathers. 'My poor little man,' she whispered in his ear.

Time to scout the Platform. The islet appeared deserted but she had to make sure. Peri darted up the hill as fast and as silently as she could, straining her ears for the sound of voices, steps, feathers rustling, the sweep of wings through air.

The glow grew stronger ahead of Peri, among the trees and flowers. There were no buildings. As she drew closer, Peri saw the grass, the trees, the flowers, were not lit up by external lights but gave off their own radiance. Leaf and flower, bark and branch, were outlined with light, rimed with fire.

Of course. Peter himself used plants like these in his garden. They'd been around for a while but were only now becoming less expensive, he'd said. Squid genes. That was it. Squid and jellyfish genes gave this luminescence. The best solar lighting, Peter had said, because you can't make a more efficient solar collector than a leaf anyway. You use the plant itself as a light.

Peri walked through the dark and the suspended, shifting light, frightened of herself and what she'd done, drawn on by the marvels of this artificial island, its trees spangled green and silver, their light swinging in the breeze from the sea. Showers of purple sparks tossed in the wind and radiance was thrown up from the grass. Neon-green moss furred trunks and branches with creases of light. Bowers and groves and terraces were lit by hanging flowers of blue and gold. It was exquisite.

Peri stopped, appalled. It hit her that she hadn't run away at all. *I've run straight to Peter!* This is *his* place. He designed it. I'm walking into his mind—the most beautiful part of it.

The beauty of the Platform underlined the fact she'd lost everything but Hugo. This world, the world of the Katon-Chesshyres, of Flight, was now closed to her. She'd had an insecure footing, her position had been low, but she'd loved it; it was so far beyond anything she had known growing up in Pandanus and now it was over. She had no doubt Peter would hunt her down. *He won't forgive what I've done. He'll take you back, Hugo.*

Unless her desperate plan worked. Then she and Hugo might have a future together. Janeane would help. Janeane had business contacts all over the country. Janeane could tell Peri where to go. Peri would lose herself in another city, on the other side of the continent. And Peri was already transformed into a different creature from the child who'd run away from the Venice. Nothing to stop her transforming further. Hair colour, eye colour, maybe even skin colour. None of these things could be hard compared to what she'd done already. And Hugo would grow up loved by the one who'd cared for him from birth. She'd never let him feel he was alone in the world. He'd grow up believing Peri was his mother; she'd be a *real* mother to him. Not like Avis, who never spent more than a few minutes at a time with him. Peri and Hugo would never be found. They would be safe.

Near the top of the hill there was a bower behind a low bank of rammed earth. Peri laid Hugo down on the soft grass to sleep. As she settled herself, she saw the light in this glade came from pinpricks of blue along the earthen wall. Glow-worms, like the ones in the hills behind Pandanus. The blue lights gleamed at her and Hugo from across an abyss, as if the glow-worms were dust, stars, shining at her from the darkness of space. Worms on a wall, stars in space, what was the difference? Worms and stars were equally beautiful, equally mysterious. Although the worms, being alive, probably had the edge on the stars. Alive. Like her. Except—Peri sat up suddenly—she'd been stupid. How could she be so forgetful? She hadn't taken her drugs.

Groping in her waistband, she fished out a pack of Aileronac. With one split dose in her hand, she pulled her wings as far round her as they would go and pressed the tip of the injecting pen against one wing muscle near the shoulder, then the other. Aileronac hissed into her, delivered by pressured carbon dioxide directly under the skin. Every night, every morning. One or two days' negligence might not matter but she wasn't about to take risks with her regime. Not now, when she was pushing her flying abilities harder than ever before.

Peri replaced the pack and sat waiting for the initial whoosh and dizziness to fall away. Aileronac always felt like a flurry of cold air rushing through her muscles and lungs, as if it made her bigger but airier. As if the drug whipped her up, like wind puffing up a cumulus cloud, increasing her volume but not her weight. Now for the Opteryxin. So bitter, always made her feel sick. Peri rinsed her mouth and spat. No Zefiryn tonight. More use first thing in the morning.

Time for sleep, time to focus her mind, time to review all the day's flying, as she'd been taught in Flight Gym. Havoc, her instructor at Blue

Air Group (they'd called it FlightBAG, of course), had been ex-military. For him Flight was a victory over laziness and inertia, each and every goddamn flight a test of skill, fitness and courage. *Every day you don't fly, you fall.* That's what Havoc used to yell.

It was Havoc who'd helped awaken her new but frozen flight muscles after surgery. She'd been so afraid she'd never be able to move them herself and had struggled for days just to raise them a fraction; it was as if her brain was sending instructions to waxen wings. Havoc had taught her the exercises to establish the pathways between her brain and her wings, had helped her bring them to life.

No-one else Peri knew took such a utilitarian approach to emotions. To Havoc, emotions were an unreliable sensor. You paid attention to what they told you, but if what they told you was wrong you learned to ignore them.

Your evolutionary history has not programmed you to fly, Havoc said. *So your thoughts and feelings are not calibrated for it.* Understanding this was vital if she were to learn to fly safely, he explained. You had to learn to control your mind as much as you learned to control your body. With Havoc, who refused to listen to her fears, who ignored her exhaustion, who barked at her that she was paying a lot of money for him to make sure she learned something, Peri felt she'd taken her first steps towards growing up.

Wouldn't Havoc be proud of her now, seeing how well and how far she'd flown that night? She would never see Havoc again.

It takes more than wings to fly.

As Peri stood on the edge of the sea cliff at Angel Falls it was clear to her how true this saying of the instructors was.

It takes more than wings to fly.

Flight takes all your heart and all your mind and all your body. You have to give it everything you have. Including all your money. That was the part they didn't have to say because it was obvious; everyone knew it. And Peri's wings had cost her so much more than all of that. Sometimes she feared the transformation had taken her very soul.

Peri paced back and forth along the cliff, her wings tightly folded. *Every take-off is optional*, Havoc had drilled into her, *but every landing is mandatory*. Each day that week she'd woken early and walked the path along the clifftop to Angel Falls, known for its steady, consistent updrafts. Each morning she told herself *I don't have to fly yet. I'll study the air currents and watch the parents flying with their little ones.* Each morning she returned to Peter's house, to Hugo, a failure. A coward who still hadn't taken her first solo flight.

No wonder it was called Angel Falls. It was the beginners' launch site, where fledglings dived bravely through the air. Peri heard shrieks of laughter or terror but never once saw a child fall to the cold waves below. The parents, powerful fliers themselves, either caught them or flew beneath, making sure fledgling wings powered their babies back up into the heavy, salty air. *How do they know when to catch them, when to let them save themselves? How do they know the right moment for the child to fly alone?*

This was new knowledge, created for the first time this generation. No ancestral wisdom, no folklore to rely on. Mistakes were rare enough that the drop of a child from the sky was still news, fliers everywhere catching their breath in horror. One slip, one hair's-breadth misjudgement.

Peri raised and stretched her wings high over her shoulders as she had a thousand times before to prepare for this moment. Her wings were heavy. The injections had helped but she had to fly every day for a long time before she grew fully into the new strength she needed. The drugs made her feel sick most of the time. You can feel sick for months carrying a baby, her Flight specialist had joked, why wouldn't you feel sick incubating a whole new self?

Peri's body felt lighter even with the weight of her wings and even though she was more muscled than she'd ever been. Her bones too were stronger and lighter. The effort of Flight narrowed her waist, broadened her chest and shoulders, chiselled her muscles. These wings cloaked her, like massive drapery folded elegantly down her back or arching out from her shoulder blades, but they were alive. She was always hungry. She had never worn so few clothes. The wings themselves were warm and her new metabolism threw heat off her like a fire.

Peri staggered, nearly fell. An updraft of air had caught her wings and almost lifted her off her feet. As it was supposed to.

Peri had trialled her wings many times in Flight Gym. At first, suspended in a harness above an invisible safety net, she swooped through the gym that was broader than a football field. With no risk of falling, she'd experimented with her new wings, feeling the way they opened, angled and curved. Net and harness were taken away and her only security was in knowing every up and down of the air-current program run on the Flight simulation system, its extra-strength updrafts bearing her high above the artificially generated clouds and sky-blue of the gym floor. And there were the instructors, the strongest fliers she'd ever seen, who could come to the rescue in the blink of an eye, the flap of a wing. Still, no-one escaped injury; there were always fliers nursing bruises and broken bones and she'd limped around with a bandaged ankle and taped-up wing feathers more than once.

It was disheartening to be such a slow learner. The new fliers, the athletic little six- and seven-year-olds, spun through the gym like swallows. As they grew more skilled, and cockier, they even staged mock aerial battles. They had no doubts about the bird abilities encoded into their brains: they could navigate by stars or by polarised light and colour gradients in the sky.

While Peri dreamed of true Flight, part of her wanted to stay in Flight Gym. The best practice time was at night with sham stars glowing above, the floor dropping away so that the gym's boundaries seemed to disappear. She could dive fast, cushioned by darkness, the tips of her primary feathers outlined in fluorescent safety dust as other fliers wheeled by, their wingtips brushing hers, their wings drawing arcs of electric blue and green against the dark. Moments at a time had felt like real flying.

But here on the cliff edge she faced real Flight, here the lift was not programmed, here the airs were unpredictable. Here she was clumsy, a novice eagle, and shared the air with its true masters, the gulls, the swallows. How would they react to her intrusion? Would they try to drive her off? Not long ago a pair of eagles had attacked a young flier over the desert. The eagles grappled with the flier, one of them clawing at her, entangling itself in her hair and feathers, and high above the desert floor they'd tumbled, plummeting, head over tailfeathers, as fighting eagles do. On the news the flier wept, saying she thought she was going to die.

Today Peri would die. Her brain told her this over and over. Ignore it. Havoc says ignore it. Brain's doing what it's supposed to but it's *wrong*.

How many fliers died on their first flights? As many people as used to die in their first two years of driving a car, Havoc joked. Peri was seventeen. There'd been others like her at Flight Gym, some even in their twenties, who'd got their wings after they were grown. Unlike children, who could slot Flight in as one more developmental task, teenagers and young adults had to make flying their obsession. *You can live*, bellowed Havoc during one especially frustrating lesson, *or you can fly. If that's a choice for you then you're not a flier.*

Peri's specialist said: *Two thousand hours. Two thousand hours in the air to become a bird.*

Peri stepped up to the edge of the cliff. She must let go. She must be prepared to die.

A gust of air rushed over the cliff. She staggered a step, unfurled her wings and ran forward. As she leapt off the cliff, she knew she'd done it at the wrong moment. Dropping as if she'd been shot, she beat her wings hard, harder, harder than she ever had in Flight Gym.

There—is—no—future—in—this.

Her chest and back muscles hurt so much she could barely breathe.

Flying was too hard. If she ever made it to the ground in one piece she'd have to get her wings cut off. She could not live the rest of her life with the burden of these wings and not use them. It'd be worse than being crippled; she'd given up her old life for this new one, this new life that only made sense when she took to the air.

The downbeats slowed her plunge.

Where was the ridgelift, rising air compressed against the side of the cliff—and warmed by the thermal collector of the rock face—which should be rushing upwards and taking her with it?

Where, where was it?

The wind fell away from Peri like a scream.

Breathe.

Breathe in the rhythm of Flight.

Strength began to flow back into her flight muscles, the pain subsiding with the warmth of her effort.

Breathe in, wing upstroke, breathe out, wing downbeat, breathe in, wings up and angled so the wing surface is smaller, breathe out, wings *down*.

Down is the power stroke.

Down and *down* and *down*.

Down with a big wing and *recover* with a small wing. *Down* with a big wing and *recover* with a small wing. The mantra of Flight Gym.

It's like rowing through the air, said Havoc. *You've got to angle the upstroke like a rower 'feathers' his blade. Down with a big wing and recover with a small wing.*

At last. *There* was the ridgelift, catch it, board it, like a wave rising under you from the sea, don't miss it, don't let it rush past and drop you, don't let it blow you back over the top of the ridge into the danger zone of lurking rotors and low lift.

Peri was in the proper rhythm. And now the ridgelift was rising faster and pulling her with it and it was even better than her dreams of flying as a child; instead of flapping her arms, all that effort, now she was beating her *wings* and they were bearing her up. Higher and higher she was rising and the lift was rising, speeding and delirious as an express train and she was past the height of the cliff edge and rising fast, there was no ceiling, no limit to joy, the sphere of crystal endless on every side, no boundary, oh yes, *this* was new, and she was so high now she could soar, angling her wings just so, the study of eagle and albatross paying off, their manoeuvres starting to become second nature—although she still had to think about it, that's why it was so dangerous, it wasn't knitted into her muscles yet, but she felt it all begin to mesh together seamlessly, like dance steps, don't think about it too hard, let it flow, but precisely, the angle of the wing, the curve of her body.

Oh my god, exulted Peri. I am flying!

I—am—flying!

Peri was concentrating too hard to be distracted by the dazzling glitter sheeting below, light falling, sluicing over her wings like rain, air so blue she could taste it, pure as snow. It was beautiful but she wasn't looking at it. Instead she was *in* it in a way she had never been in the world before.

Here it came, the glide, sliding down a long easy curve in the sky. The air was three-dimensional, she was sculpting it into shapes, peeling off long curves, slicing spirals. Now she beat her wings again, soaring upwards. If she flew high enough she would have time to look around her. She set her wings to curve her into a rising gyre. There was a layer of rinsed white cloud just above her. Tufted, spread across the sky like a fleece flung onto a table. Fly below it or above it but don't stay in it—without the horizon line, you can't keep your wings level.

Mist filled her mouth, her nose, her eyes as she rose through cold cottonwool. *You walkin' in the white room now*, Havoc would have reprimanded her. *You don't want to be walkin' in the white room. Never know what's in there with you.* As soon as she was clear of the cloud she checked her wings against the horizon. Dipping and rising, she followed the contours of cloud screening her from the sea below. She drove forward, pushing herself. How fast could she fly? A question that could never be answered in Flight Gym.

Her muscles trembled with nerves, with effort, with exhilaration, as she tried to make sense of her sector of sky, its oceanic depth, its fast-motion changeability, how different cloud, blue bowl of sea, cliff looked from above, from different angles, different heights, but she couldn't fix it in her mind, it ran like water, all senses, streaming around her.

She had never seen the sky in all her life before.

How high could she fly? What was the limit? She was already so high the earth was no longer real. Only her in the sky. Every spiral pure joy.

This was Flight.

The true thing she'd struggled so hard for. It was for this she'd risked and endured so much.

It had to be worth it.

Her flight went on and on, she flew with the utter effortlessness of a dream, her wings never tiring, but into her flight there came the sound of a voice. Just a whisper, cutting through the air sharper than any shout. There were no other fliers up there with her on her first flight. The sound threw her off-balance, she lost her concentration and spiralled down into darkness, she hadn't been flying nearly long enough for it to get dark but she was falling now, she was going to hit the ground . . .

Peri woke, gasping with fright. It was dark, as dark as her dream. Still deep night. How long had she slept? Hugo snored faintly next to her. Before Hugo I never knew a baby would snore.

She listened, her chest tight. The voice whispered, paused, moved away down the western slope of the hill. He'd passed her and Hugo but he'd be back soon, when he found no-one on the other side of the hill. No answering voice. Who was he talking to? Someone far away. Peter? Peter, questioning whoever he'd sent to hunt her; he'd be at home, up late, of course he couldn't sleep. Already, I've stayed here too long. Her heart thudded so loudly in her ears she was frightened it would give her away.

He'll kill me right here, dump my body in the sea, grab Hugo.

Take a deep breath. Only one place to go. One place Peter doesn't know about. Janeane. No-one in the City knows about Janeane.

Behind Peri rose the highest point of The Platform, the lookout at its eastern edge facing in the opposite direction to where the voice had been heading. She bundled Hugo into his sling, praying he wouldn't cry. He didn't fully wake as she fastened her waistband and crept to the lookout, each noise making her jump.

Silence. A rustle, wind through feathers. Was he coming back? All she could do not to run.

The rest of the night, flight without pause. No resting. He must not follow me. Can I do it? I have to. Feathers rustled unbearably loud in the still air. Is he *really* looking for me?

No railing on the lookout, the turf just ended, hillside dropping away sheer. Haven't heard anything; is it possible he doesn't yet know I'm here? Hope hammered her until her chest hurt. One chance. *Don't wait. Move.* Launched into the air, the *churr* of her feathers as thunderous as a hundred doves taking off. Up, up, up.

Peri soared a thousand metres above The Platform before daring to come about, heading north and west, the moon sinking in her eyes. She wished she could get above cloud but there was only cirrus, sketchy and remote, wisps glinting in moonlight; cirrus was high altitude—those ice threads didn't even start till you were over six klicks. At least they promised good weather.

There's the Platform below, the fake islet sending up its glow into the night; *finally* I'm leaving Peter's world, my life from now on will truly be lived in unknown territory.

She looked over her shoulder. The sea, almost still, purled over itself like a rumpled silver-grey shawl under the moon. The sky fell away all around, empty and quiet.

Peri flew without stopping, willing the darkness to extend another hour, another minute, racing against dawn. Have to reach Janeane's before the sun rises. She knew, from the moment she'd found Luisa, that she'd need Janeane's help, but she hoped her ruse of flying to the Platform first would confuse pursuers. The sea was not the City. It wasn't RaRA-land. It wasn't anywhere. Too bad she couldn't just keep on flying over it. Wish I could've planned the flight to Janeane's better. Warned her. Made sure of getting there under cover of darkness.

Soon, the sun would rise behind Peri but already its light shot the clouds through with colour, lightening the darkness ahead. Not far now, not far. Push hard. So strange to fly over this country, which looked both familiar and alien, to see it from the air, the way she never thought she'd see it, the morning bringing it to life below her, colour licking over the hills like flame. She'd have been happy never to leave the City. This was only the second time she'd approached the Owls in darkness. The first time it had been nightfall. She'd been very small. Three? Four?

That morning, almost her earliest memory, she'd woken crying from her nightmare as she so often did. It always started the same way: trembling with cold, her hair knotted by the freezing wind. Ahead stood dark towers spotted with light and between them flowed lines of light and beyond them lay dark plains sprinkled with light. Warmth, softness, held her: *Don't move. You must not move. You'll fall. Wait.* No more warmth. She couldn't move, her arms and legs were numb. She'd been excited by the light and the dark and the cold but now a cooing and whirring surrounded her and she was so afraid, closed in by a whirl of feathers and they came closer, suffocating, then bursting above her, a grey storm. She was alone. *Whooosh-whooosh-whooosh*, the sound fell down to her from above. *Whoosh-whoosh-whoosh*, a turning rhythm; she could not twist her neck to look up to see what it was. She must not move. *You'll fall.* The edge. Don't move. Dark brightening. The edge closer. Light brought terror. *You'll fall*. Cold metal underneath warmed, then burned. The grey feathers had flown away. Left her. They didn't wait. She couldn't see, light burned her eyes, her skin. *Don't move. You'll fall.* Nothing but light. At first stretching out into the warmth then crunching into a ball as the sun grew stronger. The light pinned her to a point on the edge of the world. *Wait*. Nothing beyond the wall of sun. Peri woke with tears on her cheeks. *You'll fall*.

The strange woman who woke her up that morning put her in a car and they drove for a long time. 'Are we going to see Mummy?'

'We're going to see your new mummy.' The woman bought her lunch but Peri couldn't eat. 'Poor little mite.' The woman shook her head.

As darkness fell, they drove down a winding dirt road, passed through a gate, the sign reflecting their headlights: *The Owls*, in rusting letters, next to a metal owl with glass eyes. At the farmhouse the little girl hesitated in the doorway, between the dark and the light. Two women looked at her, one smiling, the other all sharp angles, but it was the smile that frightened her. It was blurry, unfocused. It wasn't for her. Not really.

The smiling woman was called Bronte. 'Your foster mother,' said the woman who'd driven her there.

Tears started down Peri's cheeks as Bronte hugged her too tight. She struggled free. 'Where's Mummy?' Bronte was not her real mother. She felt wrong, too dry and thin. She couldn't comfort the little girl. Like she hadn't enough herself to give anything away. Her smell was wrong too, like something abandoned in a closet. You couldn't say that but it was real. Had Bronte ever felt anything for her? Peri's own fault, a belief down to the bone; she'd messed it up from the beginning.

There below was the farm, there was the farmhouse, every minute she could see the old place more clearly as the sun rose behind her. She banked, came around again; she could land in the patch of rough grass in front of the verandah. A figure was already out and about, moving among the banana trees. Peri dipped lower. Janeane. Must be. Janeane and her eternal bananas.

'Aunty Jan, Aunty Jan, wait!' Peri used to call as she tagged after Janeane.

Janeane showed her stands of the special banana trees she grew. 'Never eat from these trees, see?' she said. 'You never eat *any* bananas unless I give them to you, right? Or you'll get very, very sick. You could die.'

'I won't, Aunty Jan.'

Now the figure came out of the trees, looking up at her as Peri swooped over dry paddocks drowning in gold, flooded by the risen sun. The figure was raising her arm. Peri waved.

A flash, brighter and colder than the melting coin of the sun. A loud crack, the fall of a dead branch.

Aunty, don't shoot!

Peri folded her wings, fell like a stone.

4

LITTLE ANGELS

I woke early from broken sleep. Monday morning, forty hours since Peri had fled. Too long, too long. Peri was a flier. She could be anywhere and the circle of her possible locations widened with each passing hour.

It was only just light when I stepped outside to take Frisk with me on my early-morning run. Street sellers setting up their stalls before dawn, still rubbing their eyes, rubbed them harder when they saw a lean sandy man run past them with a lion on a lead improvised from a piece of flex cable.

When I rang Chesshyre he said he'd heard nothing and then said he had to go, he had an early briefing. I interrupted to ask him how Peri got her wings and why hadn't he mentioned them?

'Fliers are normal to me,' said Chesshyre. 'I don't mention wings any more than I point out that someone has two arms. It's hardly a secret; you saw the security images.'

'But Peri's not one of you. She's a *nanny*.'

'She wanted wings. We paid her well.'

'I would've thought winged nannies wouldn't be too popular. I mean, she's just flown away with your baby.'

'We thought otherwise,' Chesshyre said. 'I thought it would be useful, essential actually, to have someone who could keep up with Hugo once he fledged. You'll find a few other families like us.'

'I need the name of her doctor, then. The one who oversaw her transition to Flight.'

Chesshyre said, 'No idea. I took no particular interest in her transition.'

My ears pricked up. Surely this was a lie. There must be something at stake in this question.

I feigned innocent incredulity. 'Surely you recommended someone to her? You'd know all the best specialists.'

Chesshyre gave a hollow laugh. 'I said we paid her well. I didn't say we paid her well enough to use *our* specialists.'

This answer was just plausible enough to give me pause. It hadn't occurred to me there might be a range of treatments for Flight, from premium to third-rate.

Chesshyre couldn't wait to finish our conversation. What was his hurry? For the first time I wondered if I was not the only person looking for Hugo.

After arranging an appointment with Mrs Harper from Little Angels, it was time to get down to the tiresome task of finding the Katon-Chesshyres' doctor. I began calling each number on my list in turn, routing my call so it looked as if I was ringing from Canobolas-Gerschenkron Pathology. I said I had test results for Hugo Chesshyre and Peri Almond to send through. After four blanks I struck gold. I might've known; Dr Eliseev's practice looked to be just about the most fashionable and expensive on my list. Then I called the personal assistant service I occasionally used and got them to make me an urgent appointment with Dr Eliseev.

In order to interview both Harper and Eliseev, I had to take my first trip into Flierville, the fancy district taking up most of the City's old CBD, now remodelled for fliers.

As I walked to 80 Metre Road, the station nearest to my flat, I wondered what it meant that there'd been no ransom demand. If Hugo was kidnapped for money his chances of survival were slim but if the crime was driven by passion then Hugo's fate was frighteningly random. He was as likely to fall victim to bad luck as to evil intent.

At Central Lines, the City's major rail hub, I had to change to the light rail, which took me to the Point, the only stop within walking distance of Flierville. On my way from the Point towards Flierville, I paused to watch the fliers, intrigued to see the dark shapes high above me all entering Flierville in a clockwise direction. Fliers approaching the airspace above Flierville looked as if they were flying around a roundabout in the sky visible only to them. They circled like a flock of gulls rotates above a tower, and every now and then one dropped down. One flier with showy pale wings missed the dropout point, then arrowed down after coming around the circuit again. Did Flierville have traffic rules known only to fliers?

Ahead rose an uneven edge of green, the trees lining the famous (or infamous) Ring Canal circling the entire district like a moat. Some had said it isolated Flierville, so two narrow footbridges spanning the canal were built. Others said the canal was an ingenious solution to the rising harbour; the water was diverted and at the same time gave Flierville a unique identity. Sightseers loved to look down through the water over the drowned buildings and streets just as much as they enjoyed seeing fliers going about their business in their towers.

Larus Marinus Bridge was deserted when I stepped up onto it. The barrier gate slid open when I swiped my slick, having extracted my personal details and, outrageously, a fee. *Welcome to Flierville, Mr Ezekiel Fowler*, said the barrier gate.

I headed for Little Angels, wondering why the streets I was walking along appeared so unreal. Then I put my finger on it. Flierville did not feel like a theme park because of the Ring Canal; it seemed artificial because it was the wealthiest place I'd ever seen. Where was the garbage? The crumbling buildings? Everything was too clean, too quiet, too new. There were no signs warning of repairs begun years ago and abandoned. No ancient notices detailing interruptions to basic services and expected resumption dates that had never been honoured. No derelict public works. No bicycle-riding vendors and their tiny mobile market stalls that whizzed around the City selling everything from fresh eggs or cups of chai to paper-thin slices of sun-dried vegetables and meats and even flier energy strips, just one of which had enough kilojoules to keep an office worker going all day. No constant jangling of bicycle bells, no chants of street sellers or squawking chickens or shrieking kids, not even the tinkle of monks' bells. I'd have expected to see their white and saffron robes in Flierville, but rich people are famously stingy and a monk can't spend all day begging for his or her meal.

This was the one place I could be certain Peri wouldn't have gone to ground.

The streets were so still but how busy the air above me was with darting fliers silhouetted against the burning sky. I had to be careful. Everywhere I was reminded this place wasn't intended for me. Streets and alleys fell away, sheared off at the end over horrifying falls into concrete gorges. The first time I was confronted with the unfenced drop at the end of one of these streets, I found myself nearly stumbling over a sheer urban cliff below which twenty-storey buildings soared up to greet me, their roof gardens bright with flowers and vegetables and trees. I had to sit down on the kerb quickly, hoping I wouldn't be sick.

Someone yelled behind me and I ducked, nearly flattening myself against the ground. Seven fliers in bright clothes zoomed low over my head and to either side. They'd plunged from the building behind me and now swooped along the edge of the drop just in front of me.

I swivelled my head to the left to watch them veer and half run, half fly up the clear ramp next to me which I hadn't seen till I was virtually upon it. The way they bounded along it as it curved up, up, up into the air made me dizzy and I had a sudden violent imagining of running up the incline after them and jumping into the blue. Now that I knew what the take-off ramp looked like, I realised I was seeing them everywhere, jutting out at different levels from roofs and the sides of towers. I'd assumed they were decorative but no, they were runways and landing pads.

The fliers leaping off the ramp in front of me dived towards the towers below. Their bright clothes made them easy to track and

I watched them fling themselves onto windowsills and ledges, then launch themselves into the air again. They seemed to be improvising, snatching at any sign or beam or tree branch and using their momentum to swing them into the next part of their lurching trajectory, as erratic and looping as a butterfly's. They swung by one hand from a streetlight or ran up the smooth side of a building for a few steps, then they'd leap into the air again. These fliers were playing, athletically, exuberantly, using the whole of Flierville as a gigantic jungle gym, pushing themselves to the limit of their ability to manoeuvre safely, now high, now low, now vanishing sideways into a narrow gap, now whooping and bellowing as they plunged from the highest towers.

Reeling with vertigo, I watched the coloured dots till I couldn't make the fliers out any longer. Then I looked down at my slick, which had in fact run a warning about the drop-off from this street but I'd been too busy gawking to pay attention.

Though Little Angels was smack in the middle of Flierville, in an antique eight-storey building that breathed the scent of old money in its clean sandstone, in the worn granite treads of the steps at the entrance, in the handrails made of real wood leading up the marble stairs, its director, Mrs Harper, was not a flier. She was one of those bullet-proof women of well-off middle age, with the low confident voice, the gunmetal hair and ropes of gold looped around her neck and wrists, setting off her black clothes. I knew her type. Sool her lawyer onto you as soon as say good morning.

'Hello, Mr Flower,' Mrs Harper said. 'Mr Chesshyre mentioned to me that you would be calling today. I'm devastated to hear that there's been a . . . difficulty.'

Mrs Harper didn't sound devastated. I extended my hand, sure her dismissive screw-up of my name was tactical. People like her were masters at making others uncomfortable, keeping them off-balance. '*Fowler*. Zeke Fowler. Registered investigator.' Her handshake was non-committal. I handed her my slick.

Harper studied it. 'The Charon nightclub case?' she said, eyes widening. 'The political kidnapping?'

I nodded.

Harper was looking at me more warily now. I'd had my brief episode of fame, or notoriety, in the never-ending serial drama of true crime and she was just the type to respect that. It'd been one of the top news stories most days for months: the twin teenage daughters of a cabinet minister taken from the Charon nightclub, my eventual discovery of them, brainwashed into living in the central Origins cult compound in RaRA-land under the personal 'supervision' of the cult leader, His Incandescence, the Most Serene Trinity Jones himself. After that followed the uncovering of links between the cult and a number of businesses, some of which were donating money or otherwise closely entwined with the Opposition. On and on the scandal went until even I, the head of Taskforce Advent, couldn't hold all the threads in my head at once. We'd rescued one daughter, who was still undergoing rehabilitation, with her parents caring for the child that she'd brought back. The other daughter was still lost, her father powerless to force her back from the wilds of RaRA-land.

'You know why I'm here,' I began.

Harper did not react. She was not about to do my job for me.

Then followed fifteen minutes of skirmishing about Peri. Harper confirmed Peri had not had wings when she began work for the Katon-Chesshyres. She refused to speculate as to how or why she'd obtained them except to observe that good help was hard to get, many staff received 'generous benefits' and I had no idea of the demand for the 'right kind of girl'.

But *why* was Peri *the right kind of girl*?

I swiped through the pages of the Little Angels catalogue Peter had given me. 'I see from your listings that Peri had virtually no experience. Also she's from RaRA-land. Why do you give her to one of your best families, who then reward her so handsomely she ends up with brand-new wings?'

Mrs Harper shifted in her seat. At last, I was starting to make *her* uncomfortable.

'Do you know of anyone else who has got themselves wings this way?'

'Mr Fowler,' said Harper, 'I would not be party to such arrangements, if indeed they exist. Who knows *how* she got them?' She gave me a shrewd glance.

'You hire someone with no family, no connections, from nowhere. I see you've got a few other girls from RaRA-land too. Why? Not enough poor girls in the City?'

'Plenty,' said Harper. 'But girls from RaRA-land have their uses.'

'What do you mean?'

Harper sighed. 'They come from *RaRA-land*. They've only got temporary work permits. Their employers have to keep renewing them. Or, rather, we organise that on their behalf.'

'So they're easy to get rid of.'

'It's more that their incentive to perform is continuous and goes beyond the purely monetary.'

'But why Peri? Why the Chesshyres? There must be a reason.' I stared at her. Hard. A minute passed. *I can outwait you, lady.* I don't embarrass easily. Another minute. There it was. She was going to speak. She'd decided she had to toss me at least a morsel of information to get me out of her office.

'Yes,' Harper said finally. 'Yes, there are some things training and education won't get you. She was willing to do something for them. Something they were prepared to pay well for.'

'*What was it?*' I said through my teeth.

'She agreed to nurse the baby.'

I blinked. 'Nurse him,' I said. 'With milk, you mean?'

'Yes,' said Harper, 'that's exactly what I mean.'

'How?' I said.

'The usual way.'

'I mean, how—'

'Oh, *that*,' said Harper, waving away the question. 'A few injections. It's nothing.'

'I see. And you'd know which doctors are willing to do this?'

'No, I wouldn't. Assuming a doctor was involved at all.'

'Of course,' I said. 'I didn't mean to suggest you would know any doctors unscrupulous enough to carry out this procedure on such a young girl without consent from parents or a legal guardian. And said legal guardian is, in this case, the government. In the person of the Minister for Child and Family Services.'

What a pleasure to see the self-possessed Mrs Harper gape at me. She was so stunned she left it too late to try the outraged *I don't know what you're talking about* routine.

I'd seen there were no Almonds in Pandanus and guessed Peri was a foster child, a ward of the state. Harper's expression was telling me I'd guessed right. There were no parents to look out for the poor kid, to object to her being used as a milk cow. The absence of protectors in Peri's life had made her useful to Harper.

Harper paled, then reddened, but I was smiling; this was my first real break in this case.

Harper recovered quickly and stood up. 'I'm sure I've taken up enough of your valuable time today,' she said, ushering me to the door. 'Thank you *so much* for taking the trouble to speak with me. I wish you the best of luck finding that poor child. After all, that's what matters, isn't it?'

As I left I wondered which poor child she had been referring to.

Outside Little Angels, in the intensifying heat under the deep summer shade of mango and avocado trees, I checked my watch. Time was passing; it was now eleven am. At least I had something to show for my interview with Harper. I now knew which of my contacts to use in following the lead she had given me.

I rang Cam but her number had been diverted to a co-worker. 'I'm sorry,' said the co-worker, 'Cam's unavailable today. Departmental business. She will check her messages at lunchtime.'

I thanked the colleague and sent Cam a message.

I stared at the fliers looping like swallows over and between the towers as I waited for my takeaway coffee from the Daedalus Cafe. The air vibrated with the rush of wings. A tour group appeared around the side of the roofless building in front of me, floating there in the middle of a concrete ravine, a flock of giant butterflies outlined in pinks and yellows against the dark buildings. As a gust of wind rattled the trees I could hear their startled shrieks of laughter as they were blown sideways.

It was alarming to be around so many large flying creatures. Out of the corner of my eye I'd see a huge shape zoom past, hear the whirl of sound, and my heart would lurch, adrenaline surging into my blood before I could register the form as a flier. What ancient panic were the fliers triggering in me?

I headed for my next interview, absorbing as I walked more of the strangeness that was Flierville, which was so much more overwhelming, even frightening, than I'd expected. Everywhere I looked, craning my neck till it hurt, I saw adaptations for fliers: landing platforms, open balconies and entrances high on the sides of buildings. These towers were half open to the elements, with enormous windows and double doors ajar so that the fliers could arrow directly into their executive suites. Did these towers even have lifts? Their occupants just flew straight to their floor. Maybe there'd be a solitary goods lift, powered by the solar collectors which made up the paint and glassy surfaces of these buildings. All towers had wind generators; the landing sites for the fliers were well away from these. I supposed tangling with even the smallest wind generator could be lethal for a flier.

My stomach lurched at the sight of knots of fliers standing around casually on the edges of platforms and balconies without railings, like the one at Chesshyre's house, sipping their coffee or tea and chatting forty, fifty, sixty storeys high in the air.

An especially remarkable tower soared up ahead of me, dripping with greenery. It looked like a roofless weathered ruin crumbling unevenly back to the ground, its sides streaked with verdigris and startling veins and smudges of gold. I'd thought using metal-fixing bacteria to grow a patina of real gold on your tiles or roof was vulgar but I was wrong. Here were architects who knew how to use them. The deep glow of its green and gold was as pleasurable to the eyes as a pure hit of coffee or chocolate is to the tongue. This was the Newater building, built two years earlier by Kohn Chesshyre Li.

A young flier passed me, heading for the Wings of Desire salon on the ground floor of the Newater tower. Meeting Avis should have prepared me for the sight of this virtually naked yet chic woman, clad only in a few bits of strategically placed fibre, who stopped abruptly at the salon door and fished out a comb. Right there she preened her wings, as she might have freshened her lipstick. As she twisted to get at some hard-to-reach feathers, the muscles of her arms and back moved under her skin.

Only fliers were dressed, or rather undressed, in this way. The luminous skin around me was not titillating, because there was no trace of shame or its twin, brazenness. They were not daring you to look; they were as oblivious as statues. *In naked Majesty seem'd Lords of all . . .*

Other fashionable young fliers were entering Wings of Desire, which looked both clinical and luxurious with its hard pale surfaces smeared with brilliant drips and sprays of colour. Clients settled into reclining chairs and unfolded their wings, draping them over padded frames so that the technicians could get to work. One young woman with white wings perched as if carved from marble while each feather was outlined in sparkling dusts by a crowd of attendants wielding tiny airbrushes and pots of paste and powder. The process would take hours and by the end she would be spectacular. Perhaps she was a bride. An assistant bustled over and the dazzling smudges on the walls and floor were wiped up and brushed away.

So this was the world Peri Almond had aspired to. According to Harper, she'd become a wet nurse in exchange for wings. She hadn't *exactly* said that, I reminded myself. *Careful, Fowler. Don't jump to conclusions.*

The question nagged at me. Why would Peri take baby Hugo? Running away with Hugo did not fit with her desire to be part of this world. Understanding her motive was my key to finding her. Avis had twittered on about Wild fliers. Had the treatments turned Peri Almond Wild? I looked up 'Wild fliers' but the references I could skim quickly were anecdotal, mostly hearsay along the lines of 'my neighbour's brother-in-law disappeared after taking too much Zefiryn'. There were a few blurred images snapped from far away in failing light; the Wild appeared to colonise the same shadowy recess in the minds of fliers that Bigfoot traditionally laid claim to in the rest of us. I thought of the security footage, Peri's pale, anxious face, the gentle way she stroked Hugo's hair. She didn't *look* Wild. Time to examine the next piece of my puzzle.

Risky, going behind my clients' backs this early in the game. It showed how little I trusted them.

Dr Eliseev ran his fashionable practice with six other doctors in the largest building in Flierville, a soaring needle of a tower. Huge ice-blue letters glowed right down the side of the tower: *Diomedea*. Once inside Eliseev's waiting room, I looked it up. Well, there it was, the biggest of the big pharma, working at the cutting edge of research on Flight. Of course Eliseev would work somewhere within its embrace. A slew of current articles swept across my slick, everything from technical journals describing clinical trials to mainstream news stories on improvements in treatments. The most recent was an item on upcoming hearings for the company as it sought listing on the pharmaceutical benefits schedule for a drug called Zefiryn. I had no time to read more before I was received by Eliseev in his rooms.

Eliseev, a non-flier like Harper, was younger than I'd expected, fit-looking, with thick fair hair fading to grey at the edges. Quite properly he wouldn't tell me anything about his patients but his face went white when I told him Peri and Hugo were missing. He struggled for composure as he said, 'They've told me nothing of this.'

'No,' I said. 'They're keeping it quiet.' I kept my voice and gaze steady, not wanting to betray how curious I found his reaction. What I'd said had clearly upset him. Why?

'I've been told Peri was used to wet-nurse baby Hugo,' I said. 'Would you know anything about that?'

'Of course not,' Eliseev snapped. 'No responsible doctor would be party to a procedure like that on such a young girl.'

'I presume you're saying that you *are* a responsible doctor then?'

Eliseev's expression hardened. He stood up, obviously intending to cut the interview short but I didn't cooperate. Instead I leaned back in my chair and gazed around his office, then entered a few notes into my slick. The worry lines on Eliseev's forehead deepened.

'Can you tell me anything about Peri's transition to Flight while working for the Katon-Chesshyres?'

He shook his head, still waiting for me to leave his office.

'Can you tell me anything about fliers turning Wild, Dr Eliseev?'

The lines on Eliseev's face relaxed a fraction. He said, 'There is someone you should speak to. I'll give you contact details for Flight Specialist Dr Ruokonen.' So this was *his* way of getting me out of his office. Offering me another, better doctor. A specialist.

I tried once more. 'Do you have any idea why Peri took Hugo? For god's sake, at least tell me whether you think he's in danger.'

Again, Eliseev looked stricken. He said in a near-whisper, 'I have no reason to think baby Hugo is in danger but speculation is pointless.'

From Eliseev, that rated as a monologue. I ground my teeth: he knew something, he bloody well knew something, but he sure wasn't telling me.

He was at the door, waiting to usher me out.

'Thank you, Dr Eliseev. You've been a great help.' He looked rattled by that, as I'd intended. He hadn't been *any* help and yet his behaviour, even more than Harper's, convinced me the Katon-Chesshyres had something to hide. You're just another lackey to the rich, I felt like snarling at him as I left. Just another tool like me and Harper, a little further up the pecking order, that's all.

Eliseev followed me out of his room. 'Mira . . . *Mira*.' He snapped his fingers at a middle-aged woman in a pink blouse at the reception desk.

The woman looked up, startled. 'Dr Eliseev?'

'Dr Ruokonen's details for Mr Fowler here. Schedule two fee.' Before the woman, Mira Kahdr according to her security tag, had time to respond, Eliseev disappeared back to his room. Mira held out her hand for my slick. Eliseev was extracting his revenge, I supposed, by charging me for a long consultation. Too bad. That expense was going straight back to Chesshyre.

Mira's lips set into a line. Was Eliseev's rudeness habitual? I'd assumed he was taking out his annoyance with me on her. Sometimes it was useful to pressure people like him, especially when they were used to respect.

'Good day so far?' I said.

Mira looked up, rolled her eyes.

'Guess it'll be a long one,' I said.

'Always is,' Mira sighed. 'Probably till nine or so.'

'Dr Eliseev works long hours, eh?'

'Well, you know fliers. Busy people. Here you go.' Mira smiled briefly as she returned my slick.

I stared at a small personal slick near Mira's work screen, cycling through images of a girl with two long plaits. Eleven, maybe twelve, wearing an expensive-looking maroon and gold uniform. What sort of sacrifices was Mira making to send her there? I made a mental note of the uniform colours, the motto on her badge. *Per Ardua ad Astra*. Jesus, show me a school that didn't have a variation on *that* motto.

'Your daughter?' I said. Mira nodded. 'Yeah, it's hard working long days when you've got kids.' I pulled out my slick, leaned over and showed her a photo of Thomas. In spite of herself, she looked.

'Sweet,' Mira said. 'You're seeing Dr Ruokonen about him?'

'Yes.' As soon as I'd said it, it became true. Ruokonen would be my expert guide to the world of Flight, useful not merely for this case but also in my dilemma over Thomas. 'Is she any good?'

'Oh yes,' said Mira. 'The best.'

There was one more person I needed to see in the centre of the City.

'Ah, there you are,' said Henryk as if he'd found that elusive parcel bomb he'd been searching for. I followed him into his old police station, a heritage-listed stone confection with crenellated roofline sitting on the edge of the *other* CBD, the non-flier one situated around Central Lines. Just spending the morning in Flierville had recalibrated my vision, making the rest of the City look shabbier. Usually I didn't even notice the kampungs of plastic sheeting and packing cases cobbled together under the light-rail stanchions but now they impressed themselves on me as if I was seeing them for the first time.

As I mounted the steps into the station, my eyes still on the kampung, I saw a woman in a suit usher her neatly uniformed daughter beyond the periphery of the slum and vanish into its depths. You didn't get to live in *this* kampung, also called Central Lines, without a good job. These were the aristocrats of the slum-dwellers, with valid work permits and even permanent residency.

Central Lines would be so easy for a runaway to disappear into but then it struck me I was still not truly imagining Peri's situation—the thought hit me with such force that I pulled up short for a second. *Of course*. I'd been thinking of Peri's wings as a complicating factor in the case but now I realised they were the biggest advantage I had. Yes, Peri could fly, but the one thing she could *not* do was be inconspicuous. She could not disappear easily anywhere in the City and she could not melt into the kampungs or Edge City at all.

Henryk, walking ahead of me into the cooler stone corridor of the station, looked tall and hard-edged in his funereal suit, his dark hair cut more precisely than usual, every line more distinct against the world. He looked tired, older since I'd last seen him, the frown lines between his eyes suddenly permanent.

'Haven't seen you since your last promotion,' I said. 'Superintendant. Local Area Command. I'm impressed.'

'Give it a rest,' said Henryk. 'That just means my persecution comes from a higher place. Never realised how much wear and tear

Deakin used to save me. Thought he was such a prick when I was but a humble crime manager. So, to what do I owe the honour?'

'Ha,' I said. 'Looking sharp despite that Crown of Thorns. How are you?'

'*My* Crown of Thorns is regulation. Standard issue and up to code, thank you. I look like an undertaker because I've spent the morning waiting to be hauled into the minister's office for ritual castration, along with no fewer than two assistant commissioners and the deputy. I work for the force. How bad *could* I be? I need a decent tenant for my investment property and a long holiday.'

The undertaker crack reminded me. 'I've got a good one for you,' I said. '*Millions long for immortality who do not know what to do with themselves on a rainy Sunday afternoon.*'

Henryk smiled. 'Yes. *This existence of ours—transient as autumn clouds. A lifetime is a flash of lightning in the sky. Rushing by like a torrent down a steep mountain.*'

It was our old game, a grim game we'd played when we'd been cops together. Find as many sayings about death as you can. Death is always standing right there, just behind your left shoulder. I guess like so many cops and doctors we'd hoped a jocular familiarity with death would take some of the sting and terror out of proximity. Can't say it worked for me but Henryk favoured the Zen approach so maybe it helped him.

'Yes, it is, my life is definitely rushing by like a torrent down a steep mountain. Henryk, I need a favour.'

'Of course you do. When else do I ever see my ex-colleagues?'

I ignored that jibe as I always did and followed Henryk into his office.

'Speaking of which, how's Wilson?'

'Loving the freelance life,' I said. Wilson was an IT technician who'd worked for us. 'I don't see him. No-one sees him. I don't even speak to him. He never leaves his room. I just message him when I need him.'

'Boy's a bloody *hikikomori*,' said Henryk. He sat down. 'I can grant you one wish. And ten minutes. Use them well.'

He took out his slick, looked at a message, put it away. Almost immediately he took it out again, put it away again.

'Urgent?'

'Every second of every day.'

I thought of Sunil calling me early Sunday morning: *twenty-four hours a day, seven days a week, mate*. 'Yeah, yeah.' I mimed hammering a nail into a cross.

Henryk laughed. I came around behind his desk and looked over his shoulder at his screen. Messages rolled in for him without pause. 'Jesus wept,' I said. 'Would you see if there's anything on a Peri Almond? Especially in relation to a nanny agency called Little Angels. Can you cross-reference with CaFS yet?'

Henryk made a face. 'Sure I can. And look, there's a pig flying past my window right now.'

'I'm guessing that's a no.'

Henryk almost smiled. 'Nearly got you. Theoretically, with permission we can access CaFS records, but in practice it's usually not worth the trouble.'

As Henryk spoke he searched databases I could not access. I outlined the case. When I described the footage of Peri fleeing with Hugo he raised his fine dark head and narrowed his eyes. 'Hope you know what you're doing, Zeke. Shouldn't you hand this over to us?'

'C'mon, Henryk, I wouldn't endanger the kid. No, there's something about this family. They wouldn't cooperate, not yet anyway. But if I don't get anywhere by close of business tomorrow, I'll make sure they notify the police.'

Henryk grunted, his concentration back on the database. 'So, what's the hourly rate these days, mate? Nice fringe benefits? Well, what do you know—the girl's not a shareowner. Surprise, surprise. Not on the electoral roll either. Underage?'

'Seventeen,' I said.

Henryk looked up. 'Mind you, so few people in RaRA-land bother enrolling to vote anymore. Then they wonder why they're ignored and their lives are shit.' He looked at the screen again. 'Hmm. No tax. No bank records, no real estate, no licences to fish, hunt, drive or own a firearm. Got a low profile, this girl. Oh wait. Fuck me dead.'

'What?'

'She didn't just have a work permit. She'd been given permanent City residency!' He fixed his gaze on me.

'No,' I said. 'No fucking *way*. Let me look at that.' Peri's residency was as astounding as her wings.

'*Nobody* gets permanent residency,' said Henryk.

'Anything else?' I asked.

Henryk shook his head. 'This residency business—someone this girl knows has serious clout, Zeke. You said the family wouldn't cooperate. I know about that. Fliers are a serious pain in the arse to deal with. Fortunately I don't have to, most of the time. I've got Senior Constable Durack for that.'

'Durack? *Mick?* So, he's been promoted too.'

'More than you know, mate. Can fly now. O'Hanlon calls him the Archangel Michael.' He checked something on his slick. 'Durack, you there?'

'Durack. *Wings*. Why?'

Henryk snorted, got up. 'Walk with me.' I followed him into the corridor. 'You don't know? Thought the private sector was always at the cutting edge. New MOs to keep up with. Fliers assaulting non-fliers increasingly popular. Rob them. Or worse. What could be easier? They take some girl up high, poor thing can't fight back, she's got to get back to the ground in one piece. Sometimes they just grab non-fliers, dump them somewhere. Sometimes we find them. Sometimes we find them too late.'

'Why would they do that?'

Henryk raised his eyebrows. 'Forgotten the first law of human behaviour already? Why do people do anything? *'Cause they can.* Don't you follow the news?'

'Sometimes.'

'Yeah, after the circus around the Charon case, I'd give it a miss sometimes too. Amazing those Origins nutjobs haven't set fire to themselves or drunk poison yet. Or put something in *our* water supply.'

'Well, there, you see, you profoundly misunderstand their mission,' I said as I trailed Henryk through the squad room. 'Which is to outbreed us all and be the only ones left standing when the global pestilence sweeps the world as they're certain it must. They'll survive because they alone have stayed pure according to God's will.'

Henryk said, 'So we *do* need to worry about our water supply then, in case they give God's plague a helping hand.'

We entered the tearoom, that room too well-known from a dozen workplaces, with its eternal handmade signs threatening retribution for those who didn't wash their own cups. Ah, the cup fatwa. Didn't miss that. There was a training calendar, a poster for a charity run and a photo of an actor who looked a bit like the commissioner, warding off a horde of zombies. Underneath someone had printed: *The commissioner negotiates a pay claim with the Police Association.*

A group of men and women, detectives and uniform, many of them familiar faces, were milling around, grabbing something to eat, drink. Shift change already? A few sat at the table. I nodded at them.

'Durack, you remember Fowler.' Henryk made himself a cup of tea. His lunch, probably.

'Oh, we are not worthy,' said one seated detective, getting to his feet, bowing. 'The famous Fowler, the avenger of Advent, honouring us with his presence. Oh wait, that's right, you didn't actually *nail* Jones, the big man with the teeny-tiny testicles.'

'It's alright, Lutz,' I said. '*I* think you're worthy.'

One of the women laughed.

Trinity Jones apparently did have tiny testicles—I'd never seen them—or microorchidism, as the doctors called it. As the leader of Origins and thus the poster boy for not interfering with God's handiwork, he suffered from Klinefelter's Syndrome, a genetic condition conferring an extra X chromosome so that his sex chromosomes read XXY rather than XY. He led Origins with an authority, his followers declared, derived from suffering his affliction humbly and penitently. I remained unconvinced. Klinefelter's should make him sterile but I suspected that Trinity, given his momentous beard and muscular though fattish build, dosed himself with testosterone. The image of Trinity, forced to his knees in the rain, flared in my mind as if lit by a lightning flash.

'Uh-huh,' said Henryk, listening to someone on his slick.

Mick shook my hand. His wings shone green-black, like cockerel feathers. The only black flier I'd yet seen and the first one I'd seen in the force. So pigs really *do* fly.

'Hey Fowler,' said Mick. 'How's it going?' He was standing with his cup of tea, his glossy wings creating a bowl of space around him, isolated in the circle of his own beauty. The wings were surreal in that cream-painted room; an element of the divine lighting up this drab place, like going into a public toilet and being startled by a stained-glass window streaming colour.

Henryk turned to Mick, still listening to someone else. 'Any dealings with a flier family called Chesshyre?'

Mick shook his head.

'Fliers,' grunted Lutz. 'Bloodsucking vampires. Might've known that's what you'd be here about, Fowler. Talking to the flash new Raptor with his fancy new wings. Needs a whole fucking tearoom all to himself. With a perch and a bell. *And* a mirror.'

'Give it a rest,' said Henryk, not looking up from his slick.

'Boss,' said Lutz.

'Fucking nuisance when they go bad,' growled a senior detective, throwing his teabag in the sink. 'They hang around the hostels and shelters, preying on poor kids. Claim they're keeping the City free of RaRA-land scum.'

'Let's face it,' said a uniform, 'they *are* scum, mostly.'

'Happen a lot?' I said.

Mick shrugged. 'Enough.'

'Clip their fucking wings,' said Lutz. 'Cut them *off*.'

'It'll happen. They're debating the bill *even as we speak*,' said the senior detective. I remembered his name. Thanit.

Mick raised his eyebrows. 'Amputation's a bit crude, isn't it, Lutz? Don't see you saying the hands of thieves should be cut off.'

'Aw, wings is different,' drawled Lutz. 'Wings are extra. Now, cut off a hand, you're disabling someone. Me, I don't have wings. You're gonna tell me I'm fuckin' disabled? Especially when my taxes subsidise your fucking treatments?'

Mick turned his back on Lutz, covered it by washing his cup.

I thought of the item I'd seen earlier, the campaign to list Zefiryn on the public pharmaceutical benefits schedule. Could see how subsidy for that sort of thing might make people resentful.

I checked my slick. There was a message from Cam saying I could meet her later that afternoon. My best chance of finding the next piece of the puzzle lay with her. As I checked for messages from Chesshyre, two messages came in from Lily. More harassment about the treatments.

Henryk walked me to the front door. 'There was another reason I wanted you to see Mick. Did you notice anything different about him?'

'What, aside from the fact he's now the Archangel Michael?'

'Did he look any different to that flier you met yesterday? Chesshyre?'

'Well, I suppose he seemed . . . bigger. A lot bigger than when I knew him. How did he—?'

'Too right he's bigger. *Raptor* program,' said Henryk. 'The force has to pay for some of us to get wings. Someone's got to do the patrols over the City. Can't deal with fliers if none of us can fly ourselves. So, they set up the Raptor program. Military has one too. Done wonders for recruitment, especially from RaRA-land. The poor suckers don't realise how few are going to be selected for Raptor training. Still, what other chance do they have to fly?'

'I see.' Had Henryk wanted to be on the program? He was too old.

'I worry about Mick,' Henryk said. 'It's not all one way, you know.'

'What do you mean?'

'I mean there are new crimes and we make damn sure there's as little publicity about this as possible—don't want to put ideas in anyone's head—but whole regions of the City are no-go zones for fliers.' He paused. 'Just last week, down south. They'd put up a *net*. Chased him, caught him, pulled out his feathers, set *fire* to him.'

A moment.

'You've been a great help,' I said. 'Thanks.'

'My point is that Mick's solid. I think. Hope I can hang onto him. But some of the others . . .'

'What?'

'Raptor program changes them. Hardly surprising. They make me uneasy and they make the others uneasy. Hard to keep them, for a start. Many become private muscle for flier clients, who pay them three, four times what they get on the force. Pisses me right off—they're modified and trained at public expense and then . . . but what can you do?'

I winced at that as he continued. 'Raptors are targets for non-fliers, so they tend to identify with other fliers anyway. And besides them leaving the force for other jobs, we just lose a lot of them.'

'What are you talking about?'

'We *lose* them, Zeke. They disappear.'

'You mean they go Wild?'

Henryk shrugged. 'Officially no. But it's like the old Scottish verdict: *Not proven*. Neither guilty nor innocent. Not enough evidence. Anyway, disappearances are a particular problem with Raptors, military and police. More go missing than any other kind of flier. The treatments are different, more extreme. From what you've told me about the case, you should be careful. I see why Chesshyre hired you but he'll be covering his bets. He hasn't come to us so that means he's probably got himself some sort of rogue Raptor. To catch yourself a pigeon you need a hawk. And these hawks are very big and very nasty. Do you see what I'm saying?'

I did see what he was saying. Taj's black-winged flyboy was no ordinary security guard. He'd been put on the case before I'd even met Chesshyre.

Outside the police station I rang Chesshyre. Forty-eight hours since Hugo's disappearance. Had he heard from Peri, or from anyone else, about Hugo? Nothing, he said. I promised him an interim report at the end of the day.

'Thank you,' said Chesshyre. He sounded exhausted, even more colourless than when I'd met him the day before. 'Please,' he said, 'you will try to find my son as quickly as you can?'

'Yes,' I promised. 'Of course I will. I'm doing everything I can.'

It was raining as I walked towards the light rail, looking up at fliers navigating the skyscraper canyons. I tipped my head back, staring up at the clouds, rain whirling down onto my face, thinking how long it had been since I'd stared at the sky. As if fliers had colonised it, as if it belonged to them now.

Something flashed into my eyes. The sun sailed out from behind a cloud bank and struck light off a glassy cliff that rose sheer above me. The cliff was not anchored to the earth but set, blue as an ice shelf, between two towers. Rain slid down its sides. Fliers beat their way up to a high arched entrance, their forms showing as distorted slips of colour through the clear walls, like the twists in the centre of old-fashioned marbles. A rope of mist slid over one flank of the cliff, braiding itself into patterns as it fell. The patterns changed constantly. Perhaps fliers especially liked to see the movements of air made visible.

Then I knew what I was looking at. This was the flier church Sunil wanted me to investigate. At least, he wanted me to snoop on someone who was part of it. This was the church Chesshyre had designed, the Church of the Seraphim.

Fascinated, I craned my neck. Someone had vandalised the tower next to the church at street level. In dripping gold letters three metres high ran the words: IF GOD WANTED YOU TO FLY, HE'D HAVE MADE YOU RICH. Not surprising the church had been attacked. When it was built there'd been a City-wide scandal because there was no entrance for non-fliers and that was against the law. Still, the stuck-up bastards went ahead, no-one stopped them and there it was, inaccessible. Sunil had told me the Church of the Seraphim was a cult that believed fliers were the next, more heavenly stage in human development. Fliers were chosen beings, full of grace, above the muck and mire of the earth. They were the future.

I turned away from the church. I couldn't blame fliers for the fact I didn't take the time to enjoy the sunrise or the full moon, sunset, clouds, stars. That was middle age, busyness, numbness. Thomas had made me look at the stars. Once I was carrying him from the street to our flat late at night when he was just a baby and he looked up, exclaiming joyfully, *Bubbles! Dada! Bubbles!* And there they were, pouring overhead into a river of silver foam, glinting on the wind.

5

TROUBLE CHILD

Janeane knelt down, briskly taping up one of Peri's outer primaries. 'Not broken, just bent.'

'Lucky you only nicked me then,' said Peri, leaning forward, her wing spread out along the old couch on the verandah.

'Lucky I wasn't *trying* to hit you,' said Janeane, standing up, brushing the knees of her dark green pants. Her red cattledog pup was watching her from the bottom of the steps. 'Just scare you off.'

'Yeah, you did that real well. Couldn't you see I had a baby?'

Janeane frowned. 'Eyesight. Not what it used to be obviously. Gave me the fright of my life when you dropped out of the sky like that. Jesus, thought I'd have a body to hide.'

'It was safer to drop,' said Peri. 'I had to get you to recognise me, quickly.'

'Yeah,' Janeane said. 'I was doing you a favour, really, warning you off before my neighbours shot you down for real. They don't like prying eyes and most of them aren't as friendly as I am. It's not safe for you. You can't stay here, Peri.'

'I know. But if you want to get rid of me you've got to help me.'

Janeane stared at Peri's outstretched wing, at Hugo, as if seeing them for the first time. She whistled softly. 'Such a skinny little thing. Now look at you. How the hell have you done all this?' She shook her head. 'How'd you even make it to the City? Heard some whinge from Cody a couple years ago saying you didn't work for him anymore, said you'd gone to the City but you couldn't—wouldn't—explain. Good for you, I thought. Where you belong.'

'Mama'lena,' said Peri.

'Don't know her,' said Janeane. 'Know *of* her. Cody has—*had*—dealings with her. Moved on, he said. But why . . . *how* did she help you get to the City?'

Peri closed her eyes. Mama'lena gone. Had she had enough of the Venice, used her connections to smooth her way to somewhere else? Maybe she'd served them long enough. 'It's a long story, Aunty Jan. Anyway, I can't go back to the City. I have to go far away where no-one knows me. Has to be another city. Like you say, RaRA-land's impossible.' Her eyes snapped open. 'So, I need you to help me get to where Ash lives.'

Janeane snorted. 'Far away! Ash's hometown isn't *far away*, Peri. It's off the edge of the known fucking world. Either you're actually insane or . . .'

Or you're in real trouble.

A deep breath. 'I can help you as long as you *don't* tell me what this is all about.' Janeane picked up her rifle and headed down the steps, where the cattledog chased his tail in excitement at her approach. She whistled and he trotted after her.

'These for eating?' Peri picked a banana from the large greenish-yellow hand sitting by the door.

Janeane nodded without turning. 'Be back in a couple of hours,' she called over her shoulder. 'Don't go anywhere. And don't let anyone see you.'

Peri peeled the banana and gave chunks of it to Hugo. When she set Hugo down on the couch, he pulled himself up, holding onto the back. He liked to pull himself up and he liked to cruise, gripping Peri's hand, but she was glad he wasn't walking yet.

'Buh-buh-buh-brrrr,' said Hugo. He stared at her solemnly, his head wobbling slightly. A baby's life might seem carefree but it looked like hard work. There was so much to do: sounds to perfect, muscles to strengthen, hands to get under control.

Peri dug out a Zefiryn gel from her waistband, stripped away its backing, and swallowed the gel with a mouthful of banana. She pulled out her AquaPad, drank, and offered it to Hugo, who sucked water from it eagerly. 'Time to change you, clean you up, little man.'

'Ba,' Hugo said. 'Ba-ba-ba-ba.'

Janeane and the dog were walking up the hill that rose behind the farmhouse. The Zefiryn was starting to work, Peri's eyes focusing with the power of an eagle, the euphoria of such seeing spreading warmth, pleasure through her body. Janeane and the dog disappeared into the sea of banana trees lapping up to the hill's crown. Peri could have counted every hair on the dog's coat, every glossy tatter of the green flags fluttering by the trees, every yellow comma in each hand of fruit. The bananas. The business. The reason I couldn't stay with Janeane, the reason she can never leave. Janeane's lived outside the law for years; she can help me do it too.

With Hugo on her hip, Peri walked down the steps to the rough grass she'd landed on an hour earlier and set Hugo down in the shade of the trees. He crawled over the grass, stopping to pull up a tiny yellow flower. Peri followed him, catching him in her arms and kissing the top of his head; he smelled rich and dry, like a sweet buttery biscuit. She put him down to let him continue exploring. He cooed with pleasure. He liked the grass, the light through leaves making shadows on his hands.

'Fis?' said Hugo, frowning. 'Fis?' He patted the grass. 'Fis!'

So that's who you miss! Frisk. Do you even notice your parents aren't here? Probably not. Peter played with you sometimes, as long as I was there too. But both of them were mostly too busy to look after you. Too busy to play with you. Too busy even to *hold* you.

Peri looked up at the small-leaved trees filtering the sun. Apple trees, no flowers left, no fruit yet, in full late-summer leaf. Drifts of white-tinged pink petals in spring. In the evenings their white domes of blossom glowed as the light faded. 'We lived on tank water, Hugo. That's where we used to wash.' She pointed to a long branch that stuck out towards the house. 'Janeane hung an old canvas bag for a shower there.' The warm water running down Peri's body and the wind blowing over her as she showered was the best feeling she'd ever had. That and the cold creek pooling over stones, its water brown jelly where ripples and bugs wrinkled its transparent skin. She'd plunged her face into the water and let the jelly fill her mouth and eyes. Her skin smelled like rain.

'We could go for a walk, Hugo. See if Janeane has any of her cows left. Or poor old Nutmeg, the horse, he'd have to be dead by now. I used to look after him.'

But Janeane had told her not to go anywhere and Peri was exhausted. Her eyes closed where she knelt on the grass with Hugo. She picked him up and took him into the cool, dark house. Apart from shrinking, it hadn't changed. More cobwebs between each slab of wood making up the walls. There, still with only a curtain for a door, was the alcove where she'd slept. She pushed the cloth aside and went in. Her old bed was still there, covered in papers and bits of old farm junk. She cleared the bed and sank onto it, the old bed now too small to hold her and her massive wings. One wing she folded beneath her, the other she opened out, letting it trail off the bed to the floor, Hugo tucked into her side underneath it.

It was afternoon when Peri woke. Now the house was hot, tin roof popping as it expanded. The heat awakened a luscious smell, a fragrance woven so deep into her brain she was a small child again, waking in that room, seeing the light from the narrow window falling through dust, smelling the glorious scent drifting up from the floor. Linseed oil, soaked into the floorboards. She could hear Janeane moving around the kitchen, the click of the dog's claws as he paced the verandah.

After all these years, Janeane was just the same. Just as incurious, just as uncomforting, just as practical as ever. Peri'd turned up, needing help, clearly in some kind of trouble, and Janeane didn't want to know. The less Janeane knew, the less she could betray Peri. The less she'd be implicated herself in whatever Peri was up to. And Janeane knew she was up to something. Everyone Janeane knew had business it was better not to poke your nose into.

Peri thought about her time at the farm, when she hadn't even realised that she'd been happy. At times, anyway. Janeane used to take her into the bush and tell her all about the birds and snakes they saw and how to check for ticks and how to get them out. She didn't hug Peri after her nightmares; it never would have occurred to her. If Peri cried, Janeane waited for her to finish. Unlike Bronte, who reacted to Peri's fear or anger by getting more upset more loudly than Peri. Bronte suffocated Peri with her own dramas. Peri understood later, caring for baby Hugo, that neither Janeane nor Bronte had a clue how to look after small children. Janeane spoke to Peri as if she were an adult, explaining how she grew the bananas, how she fixed her car, how to handle horses and cows, and Peri worked hard to understand and imitate her.

By the time she was five, Peri fed and watered the farm animals. She could recognise problems with the old windmill by the sound it made. *She's more use around the farm than you are, mate*, Janeane snorted at her sister and Bronte glowered furiously because it was true. Bronte preferred to go into town and stay overnight when she could get away or stay inside the farmhouse, drinking, when she could not.

You're the saddest child, Janeane had said to Peri. *Don't smile or laugh. I don't know, is that normal?*

Even so, that was the happiest time, at the Owls, though Peri knew she was never more than a visitor. As Peri grew older she often thought that she must have remembered things about her mother and father when she first came to the farm at three or four, but those memories, never renewed by being with them, hearing their stories, seeing their pictures, had faded till she had nothing left except her nightmare. The whirl of grey feathers, the burning roof. *Don't move. You'll fall.* The voice her only memory. *Where are Mummy and Daddy, what happened to them?* she asked the woman in the car and Janeane and even Bronte. They said they didn't know.

Peri got up, twitched back the curtain. Janeane looked up from the kitchen table, where she'd been rummaging through Peri's waistband.

'Ah, thanks for bringing that in,' Peri said, holding out her hand. So, Janeane was worried enough to be more inquisitive about Peri's business than she let on. *Shit*, I am way too sloppy, leaving my stuff outside like that. Haven't got the hang of this fugitive thing yet. Still, there's nothing incriminating in there. Why would there be?

'I haven't done anything wrong, Janeane.'

'Of *course* you haven't. It's just . . . the whole of the goddamn City not big enough for you? RaRA-land's too small? No, no, *you've* got to go to the whole other side of the fucking continent. But sure, I believe you, everything's fine. None of my business, really. Except I reckon I'll have half the cops along the eastern seaboard dropping by for a chat.'

Peri sighed.

'So, then. Tea?'

Sitting at the kitchen table on a stool that allowed her wings to sweep to the floor, Peri jiggled Hugo on her knee as she watched Janeane pour boiling water into enamel mugs.

Janeane brought them over, set them down, then sat herself, sticking her long legs straight out in front of her, crossed at the ankle. She looked at Hugo. 'Well, I can see the resemblance,' she said to the baby. 'I first knew your mama when she was just a few years older than you. Always figured her for the maternal type—should've seen how she spoiled my animals—but still, must say I'm surprised.' She frowned at Peri. 'Jeez, how old are you now? Old enough to be a mama, obviously. Still look like a baby yourself, though.'

Peri was about to shake her head. No, you don't understand, Hugo's not—but saying that would be telling Janeane way too much. The fact she wasn't Hugo's mother was exactly the kind of information Janeane most needed not to know. If Janeane got too frightened she might force Peri off the farm with no help from her at all. Or, worse, Janeane might feel she had to tell someone, someone who'd take Hugo.

'Ma,' said Hugo. 'Ma. Ma-ma-ma-ma-ma.'

Peri smiled in spite of herself and hugged him.

Janeane smiled mirthlessly, the vertical lines between her eyes etched deep.

Peri sipped at her tea, keeping it well out of Hugo's reach. She looked around the kitchen, remembering how the adults, Janeane and Bronte, and then Bronte's boyfriend Shane, used to talk around this table and she'd listen as she lay awake in her bed in the alcove, the thin curtain failing to muffle their words. It was Shane who'd spoiled everything; Bronte followed him to his shack nearer the sea, in Pandanus, and insisted on taking Peri. Why? She could never understand. She was nothing to Bronte, just a nuisance.

Peri had wanted to stay at the farm. At Shane's she'd have to sleep in the glassed-in verandah. 'Come with us, Aunty,' she pleaded with Janeane.

'I'm *not* your aunty,' Janeane said through gritted teeth. 'Stop bugging me.'

And that night, as Peri had listened from her alcove, she'd heard Janeane say, 'I can't leave this farm, you know it as well as I do. Got to keep the business going. I'm a pharmer. I've got long-term deals with my clients. I can't just change my mind, up and walk away. I'd have some seriously pissed-off people coming after me. You do know what pharmers do, Shane? I'm sure Bronte's filled you in on our little rural idyll up here in the hills, the industry that keeps this whole region solvent, though you townies like to pretend ignorance. So you know how it works, right? We grow pirated drugs and vaccines in bananas, splice the genes into our crops. We grow them in bananas because they're easy to eat and there's a huge market for this, it's so much cheaper than the legit stuff.'

Much later, living in Peter's house, where she understood she'd begun her education all over again, the education for her *real* life, the life she'd longed and planned for, Peri realised it was painful for Janeane to become a pharmer but less painful than giving up the land altogether. Things Janeane had said to her as they walked over the farm came back to Peri and made sense; Janeane had not wanted to abandon the land. The decaying farms all around them disgusted her. What other work was there for her to do? If she didn't pharm, she'd end up like Bronte.

Peri never forgot the conversation she'd overheard because the worst time in her life began from that moment.

'You don't love me,' she'd said to Janeane. 'You're not my aunty.'

'That's what I told you,' Janeane had replied.

Peri stared at Janeane now as she swallowed her tea. Did Janeane even remember saying that to her?

'Do you ever go to the Venice?'

'Don't start,' said Janeane. 'That hole.'

'I always remember something you said; you said it was a *bit* like Venice: dirty water where you'd expect the streets to be.'

'The hell I did. At least when you left here you started going to school.'

'Yeah.'

Janeane looked at her hands.

Peri set her tea down. 'You know,' she said, 'I was so *happy* when Bronte and Shane broke up. Guess that's why Bronte thought I was a little bitch. I just assumed she'd bring me back here. To the farm. The bush. You.'

Janeane blinked.

The Venice. When Shane finally threw Bronte out, Peri had thought she and Bronte were going to live near the main beach in Pandanus. It was the most beautiful spot she'd ever seen, with its palms on dry mounds of rock rising at the north end, the rock pools on the southern end, and grass fringing the curve of sand. Further back, in the strip of shops across the road, stood the Naxos Cafe, the haunt of surfers and fishermen because it opened early and closed late. Peri loved the Naxos. Janeane sometimes took her there for a milkshake when she visited Pandanus.

But Shane kept driving past the main beach, past the Naxos, the shops and the weatherboard houses, Bronte's and Peri's few belongings rattling in the back of his ute as he turned and bumped down a rough track. After a few minutes he pulled up at a gatehouse. Wire fencing stretched away from both sides of this ruined building, its every window smashed long ago. Peri wrinkled her nose at the stench coming from the piles of rubbish she could see behind the fence.

Peri stared at a sign as they passed: *The Venice Caravan Park.*

The sign, pocked with bullet holes, showed a faded picture of a man in a striped shirt poling a funny-looking crescent-shaped boat. Shane's ute crunched over litter and Peri stared in horror as they passed a row of shacks leaning over a ditch of stagnant green water.

Clothes were hanging in the open areas underneath the shacks and flapped from verandahs. Banana trees pushed up through the rubbish surrounding the stilts supporting the shacks. Women looked up from cooking fires which sent veils of smoke through the Venice and stared as the ute crunched over tins and paper and broken bits of wood.

Shane turned right past a wall of rubbish and onto a muddy track heading towards the sea. When he stopped the ute and they got out in front of a small metal caravan, Peri could smell salt water as well as the rubbish; the stiff breeze blowing off the ocean carried the worst of the stench away. There was a constant shrieking as seagulls attacked the piles of rubbish. She looked around her in disbelief. Bronte had made a mistake, they couldn't possibly live here; but no, Bronte was unlocking the caravan, carrying her things inside.

Ragged children peered at Peri from behind a caravan and with a start she recognised an older boy from her school. Ryan: a bully and a thief. He often stole her meagre lunch, a lunch she'd scavenged herself from whatever was in the kitchen of Shane's shack. Peri's breath felt stuck. She yawned in anxiety, trying to swallow air past the blockage in her throat.

True to form so far in her life, each change left Peri worse off than before. She dumped her bag in the caravan and stepped outside. Ryan came up to the steps, a few of the smaller kids following him.

'Here now, eh?'

'A few nights,' Peri said, pushing her hair away from her face.

Ryan's smile flickered more briefly than the white flashes wheeling and diving over their heads. 'Yeah, they all say that.'

Ryan stood back as Peri came down the steps. He was thin and stunted. His hair was as dry as straw and his clothes were dirty. Peri tried not to smell him or the other little kids who now crowded around her.

'My gang,' said Ryan. 'Water Rats. Show you round.'

By the end of the week Peri's scalp itched furiously with lice and she knew that Bronte was not going to take them back to the Owls. The Water Rats had shown her over most of the Venice. They'd shown her where the communal water tap was and explained she had to line up with her bucket by five in the morning if she wanted fresh water. They had shown her where the women and girls in the park relieved themselves, in the lee of a sand dune on the edge of the filthy lagoon seeping onto the beachfront.

The Rats showed her where they lived: in rusting shipping containers, tents, ancient cars, packing cases and shelters woven out of grasses and branches, shored up with bits of board smeared with seagull droppings. It was hard to believe, but Bronte's little caravan was one of the better places to live in the Venice.

Most importantly, the Water Rats taught Peri to steal food. They showed her where the banana and papaya trees were, where each and every feral pumpkin and sprawling passionfruit vine grew. Mostly the Rats didn't steal directly from shacks or cooking fires. The risk of a beating if caught was too great. *Or they'll set their dog on ya*, Ryan warned. Hungry dogs roamed everywhere so Ryan taught Peri always to carry a sharp stone and how to aim it. Peri became a practised shot; all she had to do was raise her hand to make the dogs veer away from her.

Peri was taller than the other Rats and so much of the stealing fell to her. During the second week the kids led her down to a shack unlike any other in the Venice, hidden in its own little jungle of breadfruit, mango and banana trees surrounded by scarlet wild ginger flowers. It was bigger, sturdier, with a balcony looking to the sea from its second storey. The window gleamed with real glass, unbroken, and the walls shimmered with aqua waves and emerald palm trees. Later she would understand that the unbroken glass in Mama'lena's window meant she was important in the Venice; she was protected.

'Go on,' the Rats urged Peri, snorting and giggling behind their hands. Peri shrugged and moved towards the lowest hanging bunch of bananas. Just as she wrested it free, a hand descended with the weight of a sandbag on her shoulder. As Peri was spun around by a large angry woman, she saw the Rats disappearing over a dune of garbage.

The woman dragged Peri into her shack and hit her hard on the bottom. Peri stared down at the woman's orange and pink dress.

The red sparkly scarf woven into the woman's long black hair glittered as she yelled, 'You a trouble child, ain't you? Don't you know stealing is wrong?'

Peri blinked at her.

The woman patted the heavy silver cross around her neck. '*Well?* Don't you?'

Peri nodded. Satisfied, the woman took the bananas, sat Peri down and gave her a cup of tea and a slice of bread with jam.

Peri stared around the room in amazement. The walls were covered with pictures made from a rainbow of scavenged odds and ends. Some must have been of gods and angels, for they had wings; wings twisted from rusting wire and spangled with broken porcelain. A rainbow studded with butterflies and more angels arched right across the back wall. Peri stood up to examine it. The colours were made up of vivid scraps of plastic flowers and toys, torn pieces of milk carton, cardboard boxes and flattened soft-drink cans, shreds of ribbon from dolls' dresses, blue and pink flakes of shell and shards of green glass, sandblasted by the sea.

That was how Peri met Mama'lena.

Mama'lena made Peri comb her hair to get the lice out while Mama'lena read her a chapter from the Bible. Peri learned this was the price of food from Mama'lena: you had to listen to words from the Bible. It was a price Ryan and the other Rats were not willing to pay but Peri didn't mind. Every day she visited Mama'lena. She liked being read to. She liked having an adult pay attention to her. She even learned to recite Mama'lena's favourite Bible verses back to her. *You one of the few kids in here can read*, Mama'lena commented. *But you can't sing yet. I'll teach you*. And she taught Peri hymns and songs from her village in the Islands. Peri didn't understand the language but she loved the songs. Most often, they would sing Mama'lena's favourite song, 'Isa Lei', until Mama'lena had tears in her eyes.

'*Isa lei*, the purple shadow falling. That's about my home,' Mama'lena would say.

Peri liked the haze in the shack from incense and the cooking fire and Mama'lena's smell of smoke and soap, and she liked the feeling of Mama'lena's warm solid arms when she hugged her. She didn't like the other girl, an older girl of eleven or twelve, practically a woman, who also hung around Mama'lena and hissed *little cow*, *stupid cow* at Peri. Mama'lena scolded her, saying, 'Neveah, leave that poor girl alone,' when she saw that once again the older girl had pinched Peri or pulled her hair. But Peri was not easily dislodged. It would take more than Neveah's jealousy to drive her away.

After a few months at the Venice Bronte banished Peri from the trailer to a canvas lean-to she'd pegged out from the side of the caravan. Most nights Bronte had one man or another in the caravan with her so in a way Peri was relieved to be away from them. But the canvas was flimsy and, with the year turning to winter, the lean-to was hot during the day, cold at night. Peri stayed at Mama'lena's as late as she dared on the nights when Mama'lena was not busy with Neveah.

'Your mama's no good,' Mama'lena would say.

'She's not my mother,' Peri spat.

'Then who is?' asked Mama'lena with a hint of malice.

Peri had no answer.

Peri pushed her empty mug away from her. She put Hugo down on the floor and stretched her arms and shoulders, shivering her chestnut wings which gleamed in the afternoon sun lowering through the kitchen window. Hugo goggled at the aquamarine flashing along their undersides. Did her wings awe him too? Did he wonder where his own wings were? All the people he'd known had wings. Was he starting to see he was different? Her wings were magnificent; *she* was magnificent. She'd become a different creature, like no-one in Pandanus. Would anyone in Pandanus envy her though? Peri thought of her time in Peter's house, with its new marvels at every turn, things that no-one in Pandanus had even heard of, and knew they'd envy her that, at least. Already she'd seen more, done more, than anyone there ever had.

Imagine showing these wings off at the school though, like I used to daydream constantly. Ridiculous. And dangerous. Only Mama'lena would be impressed and I can't visit Mama'lena. I don't even know where she is. Wonder if she has any new girls, any more she's preparing to fly the coop?

Hugo crawled towards Janeane. Janeane stared at the baby as if he might bite her.

'So what gave you the idea?' Janeane said, nodding at Peri's wings. 'Not too many people here would think of that. Still, you've never really belonged here.'

'Look, Hugo,' said Peri, peering under the table. She handed him a biscuit. Hugo sat up and started gumming it.

Peri straightened. 'It was that TV show. *Flights of Fancy.* Moneybags—is he still around?—he gave Ryan's uncle a television. Not just any television but the best, a VaporView, with mist for a screen.'

Peri wondered if Janeane knew Moneybags. If she did, she gave nothing away. Moneybags hadn't lived in the Venice but he often came there to do business. What business it was Ryan did not know. Everybody knew Moneybags and his big green tank that rolled right over the rubbish in its path, flattening bushes, banana trees, even the odd shack. Everybody had stories to tell about Moneybags, of transgressions punished, usually by sudden disappearance, and of services rewarded. To Peri he was a lot like Mama'lena's God—he knew everything that went on in the Venice and delivered justice as he saw fit.

It was for favours unknown that Ryan's uncle scored a television from Moneybags, and on the second viewing night at Ryan's uncle's, among the few assigned space on the shack's rotting porch, from where she could peer through the open window, past the crowd in front of the television, Peri saw the program that changed her life.

Flights of Fancy.

Peri remembered the exact moment she saw fliers, real living breathing people with wings, for the first time. It was in the opening moments of the show when, to dramatic music, the winged hosts of *Flights of Fancy*, Marlon McGuire and Cushla Brandt, landed at that week's location.

Peri stared, hardly daring to breathe. *Don't move.* She'd heard of fliers, but never seen one, never truly imagined a person with wings. Here was Cushla Brandt, on top of a skyscraper, wind streaming her hair, towers rising up all around her with their grids of light, neon signs winking cold blue, hot pink. *I know this. This is something to do with me.* Peri was trying to remember but it was hard to concentrate when here were Cushla Brandt and Marlon McGuire, flying wherever they wanted, *you don't have to wait, you won't fall*, human beings with the power and glory of Mama'lena's angels but better. They were real.

Peri tried to concentrate on what Cushla Brandt was saying. At the end of the series one ordinary person would be raised up to be like them. First you had to prove your worth through challenge after challenge: abseiling, free climbing, ultramarathon, hang-gliding, cross country without map or compass.

Peri felt her way off the porch, her head spinning. Her world had been turned upside down. She was so dizzy with hope she might burst. She should sing and dance her way down the muddy path towards Mama'lena's. Well, why not? She skipped, singing, *I once was lost but now am found, Was blind but now I see.* Now she knew the grace, the exaltation Mama'lena said she felt. Peri had never known true happiness until that moment.

She knew what she had to do. She *had* been blind and *now* she could see, like the person in the song Mama'lena had taught her. She'd been stuck in the dark well of the Venice. Now she'd been shown she was up high under a sky blazing with stars, a sky that would belong to her. She understood something else: her nightmare, the nightmare that had followed her to the Venice, was *telling* her something. She'd come from the City; that was obvious from what she'd seen of it in *Flights of Fancy*. She was from the City. Of course. She was not like the people in the Venice. She was not even like the people in Pandanus. I don't belong here. I've never belonged. Peri thought of the long journey to the Owls. They must have driven all the way from the City. The City, her birthright; the sooner she got back there, the sooner she could get her wings—maybe she could even find her parents. There wasn't much chance of finding them, though, was there? They must have been killed in a crash or drowned or suffered some other tragic, blameless death. They wouldn't have let her grow up this way if they were alive. *Don't move. Wait. You'll fall.* But I will move. I won't wait. Now I know what to do. You can't fall when you have wings.

Mama'lena said God would give her life freedom and meaning. Peri knew Mama'lena was wrong. Wings would give her freedom. You can't fall when you have wings. Peri had a guide for her every waking moment. All her thoughts and actions were now directed towards her transformation. Best of all, Mama'lena approved of Peri's desire. *I will help you. I knew from the first time I met you that you were one of the special ones. You need to know about my church. They all have wings. They have found their way.* The *way. The new way.*

Why don't you have wings, Mama'lena?

Here? I don't need them here, child. They'll be on the other side, waiting for me, my reward.

'So,' Peri said to Janeane, 'I saw what was possible, that real people, even ordinary people if they were really lucky and worked really hard, could get wings.' She laughed. 'You know, the next few years I spent all my time trying to get myself ready for Flight. Running, jumping, diving into the water. I was the fastest girl in my year at school, I was in all the track and field teams, all the team sports. I trained so hard, I used to tear muscles, even a hamstring once. Cracked a rib. The more sport I did, the less time I spent in the Venice. I even took up archery for a term when it was offered by one of our endless stream of temporary teachers. Honing my reflexes, you see.'

Janeane put her hands behind her neck, stretching it. 'Didn't realise television could be so life-changing.'

'Heh.' Peri realised she was enjoying talking to Janeane. Who else could she talk with about her past? To everyone in the City, except Luisa, she had no past, had been born the day she'd first set foot in the City.

'To get your wings, you will have to get out of this here situation,' Mama'lena told Peri often, and Peri would nod. 'But how will you get there?' Mama'lena continued. 'That is the question. You will need a plan. Not just anyone can go to the City. *I* have a plan. *I* can help you.'

Janeane stood. She turned, ducked her head to peer out the window at the sun sinking behind the hill.

'Tomorrow,' said Janeane, 'we'll make plans. Tonight I'll pull together some things you'll need.'

In darkness, Peri awoke, listening. For a moment she had no idea where she was. She strained her eyes into the dark, her ears. A voice. Thin, dry, low. Peri sat up, slowly, trying not to let her feathers rustle. She felt along her side. Hugo slept tucked under a sheet, between her and the wall, his arms flung above his head in the baby posture of utter surrender and peace.

Stealthily Peri stood, folding her wings close to her body, the feathers warm against her skin, their alien softness still shocking. Even now she had to keep reminding herself they were part of her.

Peri tiptoed to the curtain. The smell of their dinner earlier that evening still lingered in the kitchen. Janeane was sitting at the kitchen table, speaking low. No-one was in the room with her. Something rustled as she spread it out on the table before her, consulting it as she talked to someone, could be anyone—a next-door neighbour, a client a thousand klicks away. The police. No, not police. Who, then?

'No,' Janeane said. 'I don't think so. It's not like that. No, no, give me some time, for Chrissake. I'll try but I don't think you understand the situation—' She broke off, looking directly at the alcove. 'Wait a minute,' Janeane said as she stood up, scraping her chair back. Peri held her breath. Janeane folded up whatever was on the table and went outside, closing the screen door quietly behind her. Peri heard her start speaking again as she walked away from the house.

Peri lay down on the narrow bed again. No way of knowing who Janeane was talking to or what she was talking about but she hadn't wanted Peri to hear. Was she going to betray her? Peri lay awake, trying to plan her next moves. She still needed Janeane's help.

Vegetable light, thick and green, fell from the narrow window, dyeing the white candlewick bedcover. Hugo was snuffling and snorting awake. Lying on her side, Peri fed him. The house felt empty. From further up the hill came the dry snapping and crashing of branches. Janeane must be hacking into something up there. Peri should not have slept so late.

'Alright,' said Janeane a couple of hours later, fixing her gaze on Peri. They'd eaten lunch and Peri had washed up. Hugo was on a blanket spread on the floor, playing with a collection of twigs, stones and other things Peri had found for him. Janeane's pup lay on the verandah just outside the screen door, panting in the afternoon heat, his heaving rump rattling the screen. 'Let's talk. I've got most of the information you need. I've even called a few clients and contacts to let them know to look out for you. So they won't shoot at you.' She glanced down at Hugo, who was shaking a dried pod, rattling the seeds inside. They sounded like a little rain shower on the tin roof.

Janeane rubbed at her cheek. 'I don't think you should do this.'

'I know. But I don't have any choice.'

'Hard cases make bad law,' said Janeane. 'Hard choices make bad decisions.'

Peri shrugged. 'There aren't good decisions for me to make, Aunty Jan. Just not-as-bad ones. You have to help me.'

'I'm *trying*,' said Janeane, blowing out her breath in frustration. 'Don't you see that? I'm trying to help you. And the little fella. What you want to do is not sensible, not safe. Poor little thing almost got shot yesterday and I'm your friend, for fuck's sake! I don't even know exactly how many thousand kilometres of baked earth lie between here and where you say you want to go but—how the hell did you even remember about Ash, anyway?'

Peri snorted. 'Why wouldn't I remember Ash? He was only one of your most important clients, and you always used to talk about how exotic he was, how he lived so far away it might as well be a different country, they didn't even have any bananas there, too dry.'

'Huh,' Janeane grunted, leaning forward and putting her elbows on the table. Peri recognised this gesture. Janeane had decided something and would not back down. 'You still haven't told me how Mama'lena helped you get to the City. Or why.'

Peri looked steadily at Janeane. Janeane wasn't going to go any further with this unless Peri talked. Well, it didn't matter now. Why not tell her?

'Mama'lena always had a big thing about how I mustn't be spoiled if I was going to escape the Venice, get to the City. She cut my hair short and gave me a knife and showed me how to use it. She said, *You stab here and pull* up, *like this, see? We don't want anyone looking at you the wrong way. Ryan and his uncle been told to keep an eye on you but you got to look after yourself too. Can't go to the City if you spoiled. You no use if you got a baby like these other young girls. You can't even get a tattoo, understand? You pretty. You worth something. Don't be spoiling yourself. My girls have a good reputation.*'

'Her girls?' exclaimed Janeane. 'Just what exactly was she selling?'

'No,' said Peri. 'It wasn't like that. This is Mama'lena we're talking about. She lives for her church. She has contacts in it. They're all fliers, so they have money. They're powerful, they can get work permits for the City, stuff like that. And she found girls for them, to work for them. They wouldn't want anyone who looked rough, certainly no-one who was tattooed, pregnant, sick, anything like that.'

Janeane glanced at Hugo, a slightly softer expression on her face.

Oh, Peri realised, she thinks I've been sacked for having a baby. Probably to someone I shouldn't have. Good. She's sure to help me now.

Peri paused. What sort of work was she going to tell Janeane she'd been doing? Couldn't risk telling her she was a nanny; Janeane might guess Hugo wasn't hers.

'They can't get good help, you know, it's the old story. Fliers all too rich and spoiled to do anything for each other. The church people knew anyone Mama'lena passed along would be good, you know? Careful. Clean-living.' Peri wondered as she said this how true it was. She only really knew about herself. Neveah certainly hadn't struck her as a good person. 'And,' she added, 'so damn *grateful* to be allowed into the City, not like some of the trash already scraping by there, that they'd be cheap, hard-working and stick around as long as their temporary permits kept on being renewed.'

Janeane inclined her head slightly. 'Wait here.'

Peri waited, watching Hugo mouth the seed pod. He tossed it away, then looked at her hopefully.

'Not now, Hugo.'

His lower lip wobbled.

'Oh, come on.' Peri hauled herself up, retrieved the seed pod and gave it to Hugo, who promptly tossed it away again.

Peri looked around for a distraction. She opened a cupboard. Cups, glasses, plates. She squatted down, opened a lower cabinet and pulled out a small pot. She found a wooden spoon. What was Janeane doing? Impossible to tell what she was thinking. She said she would help Peri but what if helping her meant turning her in? She might think that was the best way of keeping her and Hugo safe or saving her own skin. If that was the case, she should let Janeane think she was staying a little longer then slip away early, get a head start.

Janeane came back, pulled up a chair next to Peri. She flinched as Hugo started gleefully banging the spoon on the pot.

'Bah!' said Hugo. 'Bah-bah-bah!'

'Now,' said Janeane, raising her voice, 'most of what you need I've loaded onto this.' She tapped the screen of the slick in her palm, paging through maps, lists, numbers.

'I can't take that,' exclaimed Peri. 'It can be used to track me.'

Janeane raised her eyebrows. 'You don't think I've got a few of these that are off the grid? In my business? Don't be silly.'

I'm sure you do. But how do I know if this particular one is safe? No way to know.

'Aunty Jan,' Peri said, 'what I really need is to rest a little more. Would it be okay if I stayed a couple more days? Till the day after tomorrow, say—Wednesday?'

Janeane looked as if she was thinking about this but she nodded a little too quickly. 'Sure,' she said. 'I need to lock down a few more things anyway. Some people I haven't been able to get onto yet. Should have it all in place by then.'

That night Peri stayed awake after Janeane had gone to bed. She sat up on her bed, copying information from the slick onto pieces of paper and stuffing them into her waistband. She drew the maps but found to her surprise she was memorising them automatically, just by looking at them, in precise detail. She stared at the numbers and addresses too but memorising them was no easier than usual. So. New spatial abilities were still developing. Would more gifts surface when least expected?

Peri put the slick and her waistband down on the floor and settled on her side. The little room was still hot from the day. The golden length of evening had been so warm that she'd taken Hugo to the creek for a splash after dinner.

Peri closed her eyes, drifting down, warm, seeing the glinting gold-brown creek where she'd floated Hugo through the water. Janeane had sat on the sand, saying nothing, looking up at the brilliant blue of the evening sky, now darkening to azure. A white shape rolled in the water. Luisa. No. Not this pool. Except it wasn't the creek anymore but the Venice's filthy lagoon. You don't belong there either, Luisa. The very last time Peri had gone anywhere near that lagoon was one afternoon when she was fourteen.

One aimless Saturday morning she'd wandered down to the end of the beach, clambered over the tumble of black rocks on the point, skirted rusting bedframes and burnt-out cars on the lagoon's edge.

There was something odd out in the middle of the brown lagoon. Peri stood up on tiptoe to get a better look. Something bright red and green moved sluggishly in the filthy water.

Peri sidled towards the water's edge. She just wanted whatever it was to resolve itself into something obvious. Discarded clothing. A bright green shirt. A red plastic bag.

It didn't.

Peri must have screamed but all she remembered was a long tunnel running in front of her and behind her so that she was far from everything and small, surrounded by blackness except for a round of light ahead, a long way away, a circle of white the colour of fear showing her what she could not bear to see.

A little girl in a green top and red dress floating too far out, too deep in the filthy water. Peri could see a rag doll still clutched in her hand. It was one of the Water Rats, a small, silent girl named Carmel who always had a patchwork of bruises on her face and arms, fresh dark bruises overlapping with older yellowing bruises and sometimes scratches and cuts.

Carmel's stepdad had died not long after that day. An accident. He'd shrieked and hammered to get out as his shack burned to the ground.

How did she know this? She hadn't seen the flames or heard the man's screams. But Mama'lena had. She'd described it quietly, shaking her head sadly over how a sinner would burn, whether in this world or the next. It was only much later that Peri realised Carmel's stepdad's death had been Ryan's initiation into manhood, requested by Mama'lena, approved by Ryan's uncle, maybe even ordered by Moneybags himself, as a favour to Mama'lena. How did she know? Mama'lena's expression, a different swagger to Ryan after the fire.

Don't wait. Go. After she'd found Carmel, Peri wanted to leave Pandanus right away and forever. '*Wait*. You're still too young. No work for you in the City yet,' said Mama'lena. She found Peri a job after school at Cody's SeaChange Nursery. She said, *We have a plan for getting to the City. Not just anyone can go. You need money. They won't let you in 'less you got some. And you need a permit. Can't get past City limits without that. I'll get a temporary permit for you but it'll be up to you to get permanent residency. If you can.*

At last, after working for Cody for two years, she'd finally got Mama'lena's permission and, more importantly, her help, to take the bus to the City. With mounting excitement she'd sat on the bus for hour after slow hour, lurching towards the City. The City that could appear, glittering, around any bend. Long before she could see anything but the endless litter of Edge City, its pirate subdivisions scratched into raw earth, the bus stopped. They waited half an hour. Forty-five minutes. Finally a City official boarded and started moving slowly down the aisle, checking permits. Mouth dry, palms wet, she waited. Would Mama'lena's temporary work permit be good enough? Was it even genuine? At least half the passengers were being forced off the bus by burly guards following the City official. Dejected, they trudged away into Edge City. The official stood over her, held out her hand. Peri hesitated, handed over her permit. The official studied it for a long time. She looked down at Peri, smiled, handed back the permit. *Welcome to the City.*

As the bus rumbled over the last bridge before the City proper, Peri turned her head to the left, searching for the church. Mama'lena told her she'd see the blue star shining in the direction of the sea. Finally she'd glimpsed it, blue gleaming intermittently through narrow gaps in the dark screen of other buildings. She cricked her neck trying to keep the church in view. When the bus reached its depot in the centre of the City, Peri still had a good idea of the direction of the church. Picking up her bag, she set off through the streets, looking about her in wonder. Those big black shapes in the sky above her, going about their business, those were *fliers*.

Finally, finally, after years of being stuck—*don't move, you'll fall*—things moved so fast it was breathtaking. She'd followed Mama'lena's directions exactly. At the church she was taken in, doors magically opened, she was given work, even gifts. She was *special*. It was a dream. It was fate. It was her destiny, the path leading to wings. And the wings would carry her to freedom.

Tomorrow I take Hugo and I take everything I know, the maps in my head, and I fly out of all knowledge. I'll fly over the desert and no-one on this side will ever see me again.

6

THE DEPARTMENT

As I walked to Child and Family Services, Henryk's parting words rang in my ears. *You need a hawk to catch a pigeon.* The Raptor program—bloody hell! Case was tricky enough without having to watch my back, worrying I was being shadowed by the Raptor Taj had encountered. I had to admit, it made sense: hire an investigator to discreetly track Peri, then send in a Raptor for the final snatch and grab. Against a Raptor like Mick, she'd have no chance. A Raptor would attract a lot of attention though, especially in this part of town. I doubted that I was being followed here.

This journey out to Child and Family Services, always known as CaFS, was one I'd made too many times. As a junior officer I'd been assigned to a joint response team, or JRT, tasked with working with CaFS and with Health Services on cases of family violence and child abuse. I'd been so young, only twenty-three, when I was first assigned to the JRT, and even though Cam was only a year or two older than me, she'd seen, to my chagrin, how lost and scared I was. She'd shown me the ropes, explained how the underside of the City really worked, in the hope that the quicker I grew up, the more use I'd be to the team.

Now here I was again. I felt the familiar churning in my gut when I saw the white medium-rise building, its blank-faced floors reminding me of a giant filing cabinet. That's what this place was: in every room, on every desk, were deposited layers of stories, thousands and thousands of them, stories that ended badly, on the whole. I'd had far too much to do with this department in my previous life as a cop. Another reason I'd left. But I could never really get away from it.

I picked up my security pass and took the lift, grateful to get out of the heat. Cam was waiting for me as the lift doors opened and stood on tiptoe to kiss my cheek. A police bulletin would have stated that she was *of Eurasian appearance*. That description would have been misleading, though, as her parents had chosen to give her thick blonde hair that contrasted startlingly with her long black eyes, her brown skin and wide pink mouth. Descriptions based on outdated conceptions of race were not useful now parents could meddle in their children's appearance but the police always were behind the times on this kind of thing. Cam wore a frangipani-print shirt over black trousers, sending the same mixed message as always—colourful on top, with a sober, reassuringly conformist foundation.

I'd never understood how Cam did it. She had a family of her own: a daughter, Dara, and a wife, Marianne. Yet year in, year out, she stuck with this place, working herself into the ground. Being a CaFS case worker was so much worse than being a cop and after twenty years I'd had a gutful of that.

I followed Cam down the hall and through another security door. 'Good to see your usual filing system still working for you,' I said as we entered an office and she shut the door. Her desk overflowed with files and papers, the floor was covered in stacks of files over a metre high, files were piled on the bookshelves and on the little meeting table. I added the stack of files on the visitor's chair to a pile on the floor and sat down.

Cam shook her head. 'If you only knew the dread those files inspire in me,' she said. 'Landmines, every last one of them. There's a dead child in there, or several—oh, they haven't died *yet* but they *will* and so I don't dare put their files away. Any one of those files could blow up in my face. Every day I look at them and think, well, which one is it? Is it the kid who's been reported by the local doctor six times for being underweight, bruised and covered in scabies? The drug-affected newborn who can't stop crying? Or the healthy child whose mother is psychotic and might smother her like she did the previous two—but wasn't convicted—because she can't stand the kid following her around all the time? No way of telling. It's a lottery—no, it's fucking Russian roulette. Except *I'm* not the one who dies. And every time I want to leave at five instead of six, or at six instead of seven, I think, what if that report I didn't follow up is the one?'

I nodded.

'So,' Cam sighed, 'what's your interest in this Almond girl? I looked up her file but there hasn't been much activity on it for some time. There were communications from her foster mother but those stopped about two years ago.'

'That'd be about the time Peri came to the City,' I said. 'The foster mother didn't inform the department?'

'No,' said Cam. She gave a wry smile. 'You know why. She'd be in no hurry to have her carer payments cut off.'

'Hmm. Well, anyway, after getting herself into the City—who knows how—Peri finds her way to a nanny agency, an exclusive one specialising in flier families, and lands one of the best families on the books. Why? Apparently because she was willing to wet-nurse their baby.'

Cam shook her head.

'It gets better,' I said. 'At some point while working for this family, she gets the treatments. She gets wings!'

'Expensive milk,' Cam said.

'Isn't it? Anyway, the real story is that Peri has disappeared.'

'Oh.'

'She's disappeared with the family's baby and I have to find her, Cam. I need to know what's in those files, where she might go, who she might turn to.'

'Disappeared,' said Cam flatly. 'With their baby.' She put her head in her hands for a moment, which was as dramatic a gesture as I'd ever seen her make. '*Shit*,' she said, raising her head. 'If you knew her story. That poor girl. This is terrible.'

If I knew her story. Well, I'd sure like to but there was no point asking Cam to tell me outright. 'One good thing,' I continued, 'is that the family came to me. Not the police. That's why you have to help me, Cam. If they don't prosecute, if they just get their baby back, that's obviously better for everyone. *Including* the department.'

'There is so much headline potential here,' said Cam. She leaned forward, her arms crossed over her belly, as if she were getting stomach pains just thinking about it.

'Yes,' I said. 'It would be a big story and rightly so. Hell, *I'd* read about it. It's got every modern anxiety: wings, no wings, money, no money, the underclass, babies, you can't get good help these days, exploitative rich bastards, everything.'

Cam sighed. 'It'll be the department's fault, no matter what. But her files are confidential, of course.' She waved at a stack to the right of her desk. 'I can't tell you what's in them. And you know we cannot have had this conversation. I'll make discreet inquiries with the foster mother myself as if it's just part of a routine review.'

'Must you?' I said. 'Couldn't you leave it a day? I'd rather she didn't have a heads-up before I get to her.'

'I'm pretty busy, Zeke. It may well take me a day or two to get around to this review. A review that's clearly a bit *overdue*.' As if changing the subject, Cam said brightly, 'Would you like a cup of tea?'

'Thought you'd never ask.'

Cam got up and left the office, pulling the door closed behind her.

I moved over to the files that Cam had so helpfully pointed out. I had to gauge this part of our little dance carefully; I'd have a few minutes but that was all. The uppermost documents, the most recent ones, would probably be the most useful and I started scanning them into my slick. No time to pick and choose; I just had to get as many as I could.

A moment later Cam was at the door with a tray of tea things in her hands. I moved a stack of files and Cam set the tray down. As she stirred milk into the tea, she said, 'How's little Tom?'

'Less little. He's good.'

'How often do you see him?'

'Well, Lily's just renegotiated that. Now it's every second weekend. A few weeks here and there during preschool breaks and the occasional weeknight when Lily wants a night off. Tomorrow night, in fact.'

Cam nodded. 'Must be hard.'

'Yeah. It is, actually. My advice to you,' I said, trying to take a light tone and failing, 'is don't get divorced. It's not worth it. There are good reasons but there are so many bad ones. Being bored and unhappy isn't good enough if you have a child.'

Cam laughed. 'Ah yes, the great adult lie, that kids want their parents to be happy. Jeez, wish I had a dollar for every time I've heard a parent justify their own selfishness that way. Kids aren't concerned with your happiness. That's your responsibility, not theirs.'

'No doubt about it,' I said, calculating how soon I could leave without appearing rude. I couldn't rush this part of my investigation, though, as Cam was likely to supply the only useful leads on Peri.

'So, what's the new man like?'

'If you like a man who's arrogant, condescending, supercilious and patronising—and let's face it, many women do—then he's just fantastic. Thomas dislikes Richard, at least when I'm around. So Richard buys him things and Tom's being spoiled.'

'But other than that he's good.' Cam smiled. How much she wanted to hear about children who were happy, children who were loved.

'Yeah, yeah, mostly. But us splitting up is bad in so many different ways for Tom. He has night terrors, wakes up screaming, *Daddy! Daddy!* And most of the time I'm not there. I used to comfort him. We had a ritual because his terror was always the same: he'd been abandoned in a dark forest. He'd wake up crying and I'd tell him about the path of white stones leading home and I'd talk him down it, describing the trees and the moonlight on the stones. And he'd always say, "You're never scared, Daddy." And I'd say, "Brave Thomas. *We're* not scared."' I sighed, looked at my watch.

'Brave Thomas,' said Cam. She glanced at the files behind me and I was horrified to see tears glittering in her eyes. 'He'll need to be brave. I don't know about you, Zeke, but *I'm* scared.'

'Yeah,' I said. I'd almost said *Me too*. But I didn't. 'Look, Cam, I'm sorry to rush you but I wanted to ask you one last thing: Lily's latest mandate is that Thomas must be a flier. She's demanding I consent to the treatments, even threatening legal action, saying if I deny him the opportunity of Flight then it's a kind of abuse. I assume you'll tell me that's as ridiculous as it sounds.'

Cam shrugged. 'Yes, it is ridiculous, but this is Lily. You can't presume it's an idle threat. She knows how to shop around, find the right judge. The real question is, what do you think is best?'

'Don't know yet. I'll probably never fucking know. If I ever do know, it will by definition be too late.'

Cam was silent as she took me down to the empty lobby. I flicked my security pass onto the reception desk and turned to face her. 'There's something you want to tell me,' I said. 'There's no-one here. Spit it out.'

'There *is* something a bit weird,' Cam said. 'I said there hadn't been much activity on Almond's file for some time and that's true.'

'Yes?' I said.

'Well, we track the movements of all our files, like the police do. Now, someone got that file out two years ago but the records don't say who looked at it.'

'What does that mean?'

Cam lowered her voice. 'What it means is that the officer who passed the file on recorded that it left her desk but the next person who looked at it didn't enter that they had it before it went back to records management. Like all our records, Almond's file is confidential so it's just as well I'm following up with her foster mother; it'll give me a reason for looking at the file, when I'm questioned about it. The ordure is definitely going to hit the solar-powered fan sometime soon on this case. Extreme discretion from now on, Zeke. No more visits, no more calls to my work.'

'If you people are anything like the police you fail to follow protocol all the time: people pull things out, look at them, put them back, can't be bothered to code them into the system, haven't got time, forget or whatever.'

'Of course. I just wonder why someone suddenly thought to look at it after all that time, that's all.' She patted my arm and retreated to the lift.

It was dark when my train pulled into the 80 Metre Road Station, around on the other side of the City from CaFS, and nearer to the CBD. A brief, violent storm hit while I was on the train, the dark blue twilight skies spilling monsoonal rain so heavy that people on the street looked as if they'd been standing under a waterfall and the gutters turned into foaming dirty rivers.

By the time I got off the train the downpour had stopped and the streets were steaming, full of commuters flooding home, all of them as sweaty and hot as I was and most of them wet into the bargain, dripping hair plastered to skulls, soaking clothes stuck to skin.

My favourite Jembe band, with their famous soloist Papa Amadou Mackenzie-Sene, known as PapaZie, resplendent in his traditional blue-and-red-striped smock, was playing on Ventura's low brick boundary wall under a string of pink lanterns threaded through the block's stand of mango trees. PapaZie's little daughter, Kossiwa, was dancing to the music, wearing her brightest pink and gold skirt.

I queued at Murni's warung and bought myself satay sticks as an excuse to stand and listen while I ate. I rarely ate dinner at home anymore. PapaZie gave me a dignified nod as I passed the band, palming a credit slick into Kossiwa's hand. Usually on an evening like this I would've stayed and listened to the band but Frisk would be waiting for me and I needed to get to work on the documents I'd 'borrowed' from CaFS.

When I opened the door I listened for Frisk but heard nothing. I went to the kitchen and opened the fridge to fetch meat for the lion, grabbing myself a beer in passing. 'Frisk!' I called. 'Friiiisk. Come here, Frisk.'

Frisk skidded on the floorboards in his haste to reach the kitchen.

'*Wilt thou hunt the prey for the lion? or fill the appetite of the young lions?*' I said to him as I watched him eat, though eat was not the right word. 'What you do needs another word, Frisk, something like *snarfle*. *Scrumch*.'

Frisk kept his head down, snarfling.

'There's lots in the Old Testament about lions, Frisk. Did you know, my history teacher at St Ivo's told us that one of the main causes of death for travellers in the Roman Empire was lions? *Eating* travellers.'

Frisk did not react to this information.

'Guess you're not about to eat any travellers. Just as well, since I took you running with me this morning.'

Frisk growled as he gorged.

I picked up the comb I'd used that morning on Frisk's mane. Golden and black hairs tangled in the comb's teeth.

'You're magnificent, Frisk, but you've been made safe. Your ancestors ate mine; now we grow by shrinking you. Will the world be full of miniatures? Tiny whales for our aquariums? *Canst thou draw out leviathan with an hook? Wilt thou play with him as with a bird? Or wilt thou bind him for thy maidens? He maketh a path to shine after him; Upon earth there is not his like, who is made without fear.*'

Not only will we bind him for our maidens, we'll take out a patent on him too. Copyright: one small leviathan. Features: 1. Fearless. 2. Unique. 3. Maker of shining paths in the fishbowl.

Beer in hand, I wandered into the living room, Frisk padding after me. I'd brewed the beer myself down in the basement, where my bottles shared space with Vittorio's wine. Every now and then I was woken by one of his bottles exploding.

I surveyed the room. 'Well, Frisk, this place isn't quite what you're used to, is it? Lily didn't like it either. In fact she hated it so much she moved out.' Should've known better than to marry Lily. I had fair warning. We shared the same tutorials in the arts courses of our arts/law degree but she finished the degree and I dropped out of it before the end of first year. So how was I ever going to measure up? I wasn't, not once I went into the force. 'You're still in the law,' she'd say, excited by feeling there was something a bit rough, a bit dangerous about me, but her career soared and mine plateaued; not only was

I not going to be commissioner by the time she took silk but I'd left the force altogether. As you get older, the only real aphrodisiac is money, and her colleagues, like Richard, were far more loaded than I would ever be.

Frisk jumped onto the couch and I lay down next to him. He clambered onto me, rubbing his chin up my arm. He puffed appreciatively a few times as I scratched his strong jaws. I'd learned a puff or sigh was his lion way of expressing affection.

As soon as I'd come in I'd seen the light blinking in the corner of the darkened VaporView. I waved my hand at the screen to bring it to life and sat up to listen, pushing Frisk down onto my legs. Lily. Sure enough, badgering about the treatments.

'Now I'm just mentioning it again because Thomas is at the perfect age and the longer we leave it, the harder it'll be for him and the more expensive it'll be for us. So you need to get back to us as soon as possible. I'm going to make his initial appointment for assessment next month so it's really important we talk about this soon.'

I scratched my head, digging my blunt nails into my scalp. I'd felt a surge of rage by the end of Lily's message. How dare she threaten to make an appointment without my permission? Typical Lily. She knew very well that nothing succeeds like a fait accompli. If I didn't act she would go ahead and once my son was turned into a bird I could hardly turn him back again. I couldn't stall much longer. We spoke so casually of the treatments but what did they entail exactly? I needed more information. I pulled the slick from my wallet with Dr Ruokonen's details and called her office. It was late but a practice assistant was still there. Of course the renowned Flight Specialist was busy but I was told that as I'd been referred by Dr Eliseev they could squeeze me in the day after tomorrow. I had the feeling I was meant to be grateful.

The next message was from Chesshyre and I was struck again by how drained and light his voice was; he had no news but in this case that was not good news.

I forced myself up off the couch and over to the dining table which served as my office. Time to tackle Peri's files. If what I needed wasn't there, I might as well give up now and turn the case over to the police, a day before my self-imposed deadline. As I scrolled through the documents I'd captured, I thought of myself at Cam's desk, turning the file pages quickly, eager to find the documents at the heart of Peri's story, already knowing the nature of files, fearing I would find little that was meaningful. It's never the complete official record many people assume a government file is or ought to be. Worse, there was not even a plain thread of narrative to follow; you had to construct your own incomplete version of the story from the debris.

As I searched through the load of inconsequential documents, I became increasingly frustrated. 'God,' I said, tugging at the short spikes of hair on top of my scalp, 'why do people file this crap? Because it proves they do stuff even though most of the stuff they do is useless.' Probably the most important things hadn't been written down at all, though there were at least brief references to why she was fostered in the first place—her father disappearing, then her mother abandoning her on top of a building, poor kid. Most of these documents were not even about Peri; she was just the presumed cause that set in motion all these meetings, phone calls and messages.

I'd nearly reached the end of the documents I'd swiped when I saw it. A letter from a Bronte Shaw at the Venice caravan park, Pandanus, to the department. The foster carer. Asking for money.

One address. One precious lead. I stood up, so elated that I had to move. Pacing the room, I thought about what I was going to do. I had an address in RaRA-land and I had to check it out. I brought up a map onto the large VaporView screen and zoomed in on the Pandanus region. Where else could Peri go? Shaw was the closest thing to family Peri had.

Shaw's letter, and the records of her calls, were all asking the department for more money. Looking after Peri had been a job, an income stream. I looked up, struck by the sense that this girl was at the centre of no-one's life. She was the means to an end: money for Shaw, milk and care for Hugo's parents, a job for me, a headache for Cam.

Baby Hugo was the exception. Peri might be the centre of his world. If I did my job properly they would both lose that.

I brought up my draft report for Chesshyre, tidied it up, added a paragraph, and sent it. It was short but at least I could reassure him I was on Peri's trail. I felt no need to outline the details of my leads, no need to mention the names *Venice* or *Shaw*.

I grabbed another beer and sat on the couch again, rubbing Frisk under the chin as I mulled over preparations for my trip to RaRA-land. Frisk dozed while I stroked his mane, his broad forepaws, his noble lion face. He smelled of oranges, the same scent as my aftershave. Must have patted him that morning with the stuff still on my hands. I pushed Frisk aside and sent a message to Henryk letting him know where I was going and when I intended to return. I did not expect, and would not get, any police back-up, but Henryk was my friend and if I vanished in the wilds of RaRA-land I wanted at least one competent person to know where to start looking for me.

I went out to Taj, concertinaed to his smallest silhouette in the access lane. As Ventura's only car, and for an extra fee on top of the annual block levies, Taj was allocated space and a place in the rounds of Bronson, Ventura's fat, lazy and easily frightened nightwatchman. Ray was only around to keep an eye on Taj during the day. Taj glowed blue briefly, acknowledging me.

'Early start tomorrow morning. Be ready by four-thirty.' I'd be on a tight schedule to drive up to Pandanus and get back in time to pick up Thomas but I wasn't going to miss out on an evening with my son. I'd just have to get back in time.

'Dude.'

On my way to bed, I paused at the dining table and flicked through the documents from my working file. I was no closer to understanding Peri's motive for abducting Hugo and what I'd seen on her file alarmed me. This girl had been neglected, that much was clear. Had her life made her hard, possibly even jealous of this kid? It struck me I was ignoring the best evidence I had: Peri's own words. I read through them again, more searchingly than the first time.

Dear Hugo,
I want to tell you about a day we had, nothing special but it was the most wonderful day. We sat under the green beech tree and you were lying on your special mat, the one you liked to pat with the animals on it. I picked you up and held you. You turned your head and kissed my cheek. Once. A baby kiss, soft as one of the new leaves on the beech tree.

That letter wasn't the kind of thing a nanny would write. What nanny wrote letters to a baby, for heaven's sake?

Dear Hugo,
It was tempting to do anything to make you laugh. Even rolling a ball in a silly way along the floor, so it zoomed into the wall or a window and you'd racing-crawl after it, giggling like mad. Or setting up a soft toy—the fat hippo—and knocking him over. Over and over. You laughing and laughing.

Dear Hugo,
I wrote these for you because I wanted you to know how it was when you were very little. Because you can't remember it yourself. And I was the one who was there with you. Who saw you and listened to you and knew how you were.

I ran the security footage on my slick again. Over and over this anxious girl stepped quickly, carefully, from the house, shut the door behind her, stroked Hugo's head. I searched her face. Peri cared for this baby. How had such an unloved girl kept any love in her own heart? This was the clue. Her feelings for this kid. And Chesshyre bloody knew it. What was he so desperate for me not to discover, what was in the story of this lonely girl that would explain her attachment to Hugo? Identification? Sense of loss? Hugo was probably safe. How I hoped I was right.

7

AMBUSH

We did not meet any traffic on our way to the Owls. The road petered from gravel to dirt that, judging by the ruts, hadn't made the acquaintance of a grader in a long time.

'What the fuck is *that*, Taj?'

'Eagle, dude.'

'Oh Christ,' I said as we passed the huge bird nailed upside down to a fence post, wings pegged out along the fenceline. 'Some evil bastards round here.' I drew my weapon out of my leg holster and laid it on the seat. I was vanishing from the real world, swallowed in a malign bog inhabited by invisible backwoods thugs.

The Venice was starting to look civilised in comparison.

I'd got up just after four this morning, checked my weapon, stashed a spare fuel cell in Taj's boot and scanned Taj once more to clear him of any tracking devices. Every stage in my journey into RaRA-land grew more sinister, more dangerous, than the one before. I'd passed over the sprawling pirate subdivisions of Edge City on the orbital road connecting to the Oceanic Highway, entered the Red Quarantine Zone that marked the City limits, and driven through once-beautiful country now revealed by the gold-red light of the rising sun lighting up the dark masses of vegetation along the highway to be utterly, drearily ugly.

The trees were stunted, suffocating under strangling webs of monotone green. The ocean side of the highway drowned in a sea of bushes thrusting up oval glossy leaves. Beyond the green shrouding the trees and roadside on the one hand and the shiny bushes on the other I could see only glimpses of beaches heaped with yellow-brown kelp. What had gone so disastrously wrong?

Superweeds. The land, lakes and rivers, even the surrounding seas, had been engulfed by a rising tide of weeds: morning glory, water hyacinth, bitou bush, Japanese kelp and many others. Weeds had infested the land for many years but some had cross-bred with genetically modified crops and acquired resistance to pests and herbicides, making them virtually indestructible. Land not kept clear by continual labour was rapidly smothered.

Welcome to the Northern Green Zone, announced a sign as we exited the roadside bay where I'd washed Taj, paying particular attention to his wheels, as I'd been directed to do before leaving the Red Zone. *An initiative of the Federal Government in partnership with regional and rural councils. By working together, we can keep the regions productive!*

'Disturbing,' said Taj as we pulled onto the Oceanic Highway. 'If that exclamation mark's meant to be reassuring they've screwed up bigtime. The Superweed situation must be far worse than we realised.'

'Taj, how is it that out of five hundred and one artificial personalities, I get the cynic?'

'I'm the PI model, remember? I got your back. Pollyanna's no use to you.'

As we drove further into the Northern Green Zone, into countryside that looked more like the rolling farmland I remembered from my childhood, my alertness shifted to a gnawing anxiety. Except for the raid on the Origins compound during the Charon case, it'd been a long time since I'd ventured into RaRA-land and I'd never hazarded the place alone. The raid, a tense operation I'd directed in pounding rain, had involved the over-armed and over-eager Tactical Reaction Unit. My best memory of that case was seeing the heavily bearded (and dripping), gorgeously gowned and bejewelled Trinity Jones forced to his knees in the mud in front of one of his own solar yachts by a TRU officer so heavily armoured he looked like a giant beetle in his shiny casing.

What was not so good was watching His Incandescence, now Serene indeed, walk free from the courtroom less than two years later, officially *not guilty*. The cult had very deep pockets; they'd fought the Charon case with the best legal minds money could buy. We never did find out the source of the endless flow of funds.

Trinity *not guilty*. That was the kind of thing that had made me drop out of law years earlier; couldn't believe in a justice system so naive it could switch between only two extremes: guilty, not guilty. Henryk liked the Scottish verdict: *not proven*. In other words, *you're guilty as hell but we haven't quite been able to prove it so don't go around skiting you're innocent*. A more realistic view of the world than the childish binaries: guilty/not guilty; good/evil; heaven/hell. Who can believe any of this unless they're stuck with the thought processes of a three-year-old?

A half-hour after seeing the dead eagle, with Taj steering around potholes, ruts and washouts, and me peering along stretches of fenceline for a number or a name, I worried we were reaching the end of the road. I thought of the storm clouds massing over Pandanus. As if reading my thoughts, Taj warned, 'We'll have problems if it rains before we get back onto the gravel. You should seriously consider turning back, dude.'

From the endless shanties rising out of the dust of Edge City to the land mummified in its shroud of alien green and the disconsolate towns we drove through, nothing had prepared me for the only address I had for Peri or her foster carer, Bronte Shaw—the Venice.

I tried to look more confident than I felt as I walked into the Venice, back into Peri's childhood. Past the sign at the entrance so pocked with bullet holes it was hard to make out what was on it, past dunes of rubbish towering far overhead, past the women washing clothes in the dirty canal, its banks compacted from solid garbage, past the wall of rickety shacks perched on flimsy stilts lining the canal, a sluggish tide of rubbish washing up under them, each shack a jumble of rusting corrugated tin, plastic packaging, star pickets strung with wire, fraying rope and broken plasterboard, each teetering shack looking as if it would topple into the canal with one shove.

In my first minutes in the Venice, I learned more about what made Peri tick than Chesshyre had ever known.

Edge City was a bastion of order compared to the Venice; I was beginning to grasp why so many people fled places like this to the promise of a new life.

And yet what awaited them, what had awaited Peri, in the City was so hard. Permanent residency was so difficult to get that even in the unlikely event that PapaZie, say, persuaded a resident to marry him, that marriage had to last longer than twenty years before he qualified for permanent residency himself. Without that, the City gave you nothing: no health care, no protection, no services at all. If they decided to evict you it didn't matter whether you lived under plastic along the highway or in a highrise, and it made no difference if you'd worked in the City for six days, six weeks or six decades.

Even that was not the worst of it. The real price was paid by your children, who possessed no birth certificates, existed in no records and were not citizens but drifted like phantoms, condemned to live in the shadows forever. And yet Peri had achieved the impossible. She'd made her escape from RaRA-land permanent. Must be something pretty important that made her risk losing that.

As I rounded the corner of a vast garbage mountain attacked by shrieking gulls, trying not to breathe in the stench of dirty water, excrement, rotting vegetation, salt and the haze of smoke from cooking fires, I tried to see this place through Peri's eyes. After growing up here Peri must've thought she'd died and gone to heaven, living in Chesshyre's house. Though when I thought of how disorienting even I found Chesshyre's place, stuck in its stone setting like a cut diamond, with its little lion, its captive stream and tree, its artificial sky and stars, its winged master and mistress, it seemed fair to ask not why Peri hadn't coped but rather how she'd coped so well. At least, up until the point of stealing their baby and fleeing.

My slick. Taj was alerting me.

Something heavy and sharp slammed into my cheek. I gasped as another rock hit me on the head. Blood trickled into my mouth. I looked around wildly but could see no-one except a woman at her cooking fire to my left. She kept her head down as rocks and pieces of hard, sharp rubbish flew at me from the garbage dunes ahead. I started to back away. No point brandishing my gun; I couldn't see my assailants and if they saw I had a gun it'd get me killed. A glass jar whizzed past my ear. I abandoned any pretence of dignified retreat and ran for it.

'Job's going as well as can be expected,' said Taj when I got in and slammed the door. 'You might notice I've sustained damage. Little thugs broke off my side mirror, scratched my side—*whoa*, dude, you okay? Drive you to hospital?'

It became clear, as I caught my breath over a cup of tea in the Naxos Cafe in Pandanus ten minutes later, why Chesshyre needed me as well as a Raptor to pursue Peri. No flier, and certainly not a heavily built military-trained flier like a Raptor, could do anything in RaRA-land without standing out like a beacon. He couldn't walk down the street, let alone question anyone, without every single person within a two-hundred-kilometre radius knowing about it. Such a creature was no use out here.

I showed Peri's photo to the elderly man behind the counter. He shrugged. She did look familiar, but no, he had no idea who she was, who she might turn to for help.

The waitress blanched when she brought me my order, her gaze snagging on my bloodied head and cheek, which were stinging badly and which I hadn't cleaned up too well, to judge by her expression. It wasn't just Raptors who were out of place around here. My idea of dressing down—jeans, clean T-shirt, light jacket—was hilariously wide of the mark and being roughed up hadn't improved this at all. The way I looked now would hardly inspire trust in Peri, if I found her.

Taj alerted me again. He was even more on edge than I was. I looked across the street to where I'd parked him and was not pleased to see three young men, local toughs to judge by their swagger, inspecting him.

I paid and headed for the car. One of the men—a boy, really, for all that he was wiry, rat-tough and packing some sort of weapon—came over and looked me up and down, balled-up fists deep in the pockets of his black jacket. I glanced at his shoes. Predictable. His type always sported shoes that cost about a week's average wage.

'He's the one,' Ratboy, clearly the leader, said to the other two. 'Heard you had a bit of trouble,' he said, turning back to me. He grinned, jerked his chin at the car. 'Nice. Dog's balls round here. Shame you let him get banged up like that.'

'Hey. I heard that.'

'Shut up, Taj.' This was good. This guy was a local enforcer or he wouldn't have been alerted to the incident in the Venice. Now he was checking out what was happening on his turf.

'I was hoping to speak to you,' I said.

Ratboy took half a step back. He had no way of knowing how much, or little, I knew about him.

'You're not a cop,' he said, testing the waters.

'No. No cop would wander around out here on his own. The thing is, I'm looking for someone. If I find her, it'll mean a lot to me. Plus prevent this whole place swarming with coppers.'

'Her?' Ratboy grew a fraction more interested. He'd picked up my hint that any information was valuable. Maybe he was calculating whether he could give me a lead without angering whoever he worked for.

'You'd be doing this whole place a real service,' I said. 'Local hero. Keeping away a whole taskforce of City cops. They can be a bit . . . what's the word? *Indiscriminate.* Hit or miss. Usually hit. Always so pissed off, aren't they, when they have to come out here? Take it out on everyone.'

'That right?' said Ratboy.

'Can we talk? Just for a minute?'

'We're talking.'

I looked up at the sky. Storm clouds were piling up over the sea. I ran my finger down Taj's polished side, felt the scratches. 'It's confidential.'

Ratboy jerked his head at the other two, who moved further off.

I showed him the Little Angels photo of Peri.

Ratboy's eyes widened. Jackpot. Quickly, I showed him the other photo of Peri, the one with her wings.

'Fucking hell,' Ratboy exclaimed. 'She actually did it. Always thought the bitch was crazy. She actually fucking did it.' He looked up, eyes dead as pebbles. 'Haven't seen her.'

'No,' I said. 'Wouldn't have thought so. Look, she's not in trouble. But if I don't find her, she will be. She's made a mistake and I can help her fix it so that the cops aren't all over her. And all over this place.'

Ratboy shrugged.

'She could even lose her wings.'

'Told you, haven't seen her.'

'Anyone else in this town she knew? Who would she go to for help?'

'Who were you looking for?'

'Her foster mother. Bronte Shaw.'

Ratboy snorted. '*Her*. ODed.'

Well, that was interesting. Wonder who in the Venice was now defrauding the department by claiming her payments?

Ratboy looked over his shoulder at the other two men. Suddenly he yelled, 'Look, I'm not telling you nothing!'

He pushed me hard against Taj. 'Now, fuck off!' But under his breath he muttered, 'Cody, Fig Tree Road.'

The streets on the way there were a wasteland of closed roller doors and dusty, broken windows but Cody's SeaChange Nursery was one of the few bright spots in Pandanus. It sported a broad lawn planted with new turfs to look like a patchwork quilt: squares of fluoro purple, blue neon, acid lemon. And there was a man who must be Cody himself, waiting for me on his electric lawn. A breeze sprang up. Ratboy must have called him in the five minutes it'd taken me to find the place.

A cloud passed overhead, dulling the colours, then moved on. 'Quite nice,' Cody said doubtfully, waving a sun-freckled hand over the now painfully bright grasses. 'Spectacular but you have to look after 'em. Can't make them too hardy, you know. Don't want to be making more Superweeds, heh, heh. These are called Accents. Contemporary Accents, some nonsense like that.'

Who around here would be buying from Cody? Couldn't see Ratboy investing in Contemporary Accents. The only real trade must be with the pharmers up in the hills. The bulk of his business would be under the counter, off the books, supplying locals with pirated crop strains.

Cody pulled his bucket hat, the colour of dirty sea-foam, down over colourless eyebrows and started along a sandy pathway between potted citrus trees. 'So, Ryan suggested I help you. If I know what's good for me I'll do just that. Still, how should I know where Peri would go? She just worked for me for a couple of years, that's all. Look around all you like, she's not here.'

'There must be someone else she knows, someone else who'd help her?'

I explained what she'd done, emphasising that if I couldn't find Peri, then the police would be after her. 'Hugo's parents are rich and they won't give up,' I said. 'They can make things uncomfortable for people out this way for a long time.' I gazed round the nursery, at the dark-leaved citrus dotted with bright fruit, the flowers, the herbs. 'Turn the place upside down.'

Cody scowled, scratched his head. 'Well, Peri's foster mother had a sister,' he said finally. 'Janeane Shaw. Up in the hills.'

'Bet she's bought a fair few things from you over the years.'

Cody looked at me.

'That's for you. And make sure Rat—Ryan gets this,' I said, handing Cody cash folded into a bag I'd scavenged from inside Taj.

'Don't worry. Ryan'll make sure he gets what's his.'

The road climbed steeply, winding around banana plantations. Weeds by the road tangled more densely. If Taj broke down or I was bitten by a snake, I'd be lucky to find help out here. The banana plantations were proof the locals had to be pharmers. Cody had given me Janeane Shaw's address: The Owls, Upper North Trunk Road. *Now, mate, you're not gonna mention me. Right?*

'You should know,' said Taj after time had passed with the only sound being the crisp of grit and dirt under his wheels, 'that we're now in a communications black hole.'

'Satellites?'

'No. Blocked, jammed or signal's not relayed. Intel suggests the locals access some old cable infrastructure but it's no use to you.'

How convenient. The lack of satellite services might be a nuisance to the locals but it also shielded them from surveillance. Even if relay facilities were set up, they'd soon be disabled. By now I was on edge. If I disappeared out here, I'd never be found.

'I must advise you to turn back.'

'Must you?' This day was exposing Taj to situations that were revealing behaviours I'd never seen before. Crucified eagle must be bothering him.

As I was thinking seriously about following Taj's advice, a fence-line started up along the roadside. After a few minutes the fence ran to a wire gate topped by a metal cutout of an owl with glass eyes. That was as good a clue as I was going to get. I stepped out and opened the gate as Taj drove through, then shut the gate. Once inside Taj again, I set my slick on my professional emergency frequency, though I knew it wouldn't do any good out here, and slid my gun back into its leg holster.

The track cut through thick bush. A few hundred metres along, it ran down into a creek. Further up the hill I glimpsed an old grey single-storey house through the trees. The track continued towards the house on the other side of the water.

'I'll stop here,' said Taj, slowing almost to a halt.

'I don't want to leave you this side of the creek, Taj, so close to the road.' Also, I hated approaching a house like this on foot—these people always had dogs. 'Aim for the centre—see those wheel ruts on the other side?'

'I must formally lodge a protest. My warranty will not cover this.'

'I'll take it on advisement, Taj. Now move. Whoever lives here drives through the creek all the time.'

Taj rolled forward, splashed, spun his wheels, found traction. My spirits lifted. Despite the fuss, Taj was having no trouble; we were nearly through.

A sickening *thunk*. Taj's nose banged down heavily. A hole in the creekbed and Taj had to find it. The engine died.

Fuck fuck fuck. Damn it to hell.

I tried to start the engine. Nothing. I opened the door and stepped out. Now the creek was flowing into Taj. Water was banking up inside so I opened the passenger door. *Un-fucking-believable.* Now the creek was running *through* Taj. He was silent. I felt sick. *Stay shiny, dude.*

Can't turn back now. I climbed onto the opposite bank and squelched towards the house.

Click. I froze.

'Hands up. Turn around slowly. Swear to god, you try anything, I'll blow your head off.'

The voice was dry, angry but controlled. I turned slowly, hands up. My worst fears about this job were being realised, one by one. *Remember, things can always get worse.*

She stood only just clear of the crowding trees, rifle at shoulder height, pointed at me.

'Janeane Shaw?'

She was lean, with short grey hair under a rabbit felt hat, her long legs encased in stained moleskin trousers over shabby walking boots. A reddish cattle dog, very small, looked up at her, back to me.

The woman moved a little closer, her rifle aimed dead centre on my chest. At least she looked like she knew how to use the thing. I felt sure this was where Peri would come for help.

'Your weapon,' she said. 'Very slowly. Show me.'

I pulled up my trouser leg.

'Undo the holster. Kick it over there.'

When I did, she retrieved the gun, opened it, tipped out the cartridge, stowed the empty weapon in one pocket, cartridge in another.

She craned to see past me, to where Taj was bogged in the creek, and shook her head. Trees creaked in the strong afternoon wind. The storm brewing over Pandanus must be heading this way.

She looked back at me, slitted her eyes. 'See you've been making friends round here already. Talk.'

'I'm looking for Hugo Katon-Chesshyre and Peri Almond.'

A startle. 'You the dad?'

'No. Hugo's father hired me to find him. Well, his mother and father.'

'*What?*' The woman, it must be Janeane, looked poleaxed.

'Hugo's parents,' I said, 'have hired me to find him. Peri's taken the baby and fled, we don't know why. Look, Janeane, you wouldn't just be helping Hugo's parents; you'd be helping a vulnerable baby *and* Peri. You don't want Peri in trouble for kidnapping. *You* don't want to be in trouble for that. You can see I'm not a cop but if *I* don't find Hugo . . .'

Janeane looked briefly at her dog, then back to me. Was the dog a puppy or a scaled-down version like Frisk? Or one of those new Perpetual Pups? My mind was racing. Why bother with the dull adult animal when you can have a cute, frolicsome kitten or puppy for the term of its natural life?

'So Peri Almond is here?'

'Didn't say that.'

'You've seen them.' I leaned over slowly, holding out my slick to her.

Janeane studied it for a moment, flicked past my details to the photos of Peri and Hugo and the Chesshyres, handed it back. '*Jesus*. Better come with me.'

Janeane stormed ahead of me towards the house. She was so angry it made me wonder what Peri had told her. She wouldn't've been too keen to tell Janeane she'd taken someone else's baby.

Janeane paused at the bottom of the steps to the house.

I pressed my advantage. 'There's a big difference,' I said as I came up to her, 'between helping a young woman on the run with her baby and helping a kidnapper.'

'Yeah, I fucking get it,' hissed Janeane. She walked up the steps, turned. 'Wait here. You can't go anywhere anyway.'

A moment later Janeane came flying out of the house and down the steps, more enraged than ever.

'What?'

She turned on me. 'She's taken all her stuff. Looks like she's gone already. You probably frightened her off.'

No. Please no. You can't be saying I've just missed her.

A moment. 'One place we could look. We'll have to be very careful, very quiet.'

I nodded.

'You can't force her into anything,' said Janeane. 'You know she can fly so all you can do, *if* we find her, is talk. Don't forget you need my help to get your scrap metal out of my creek.'

Oh god, Taj. How long was he going to be left with the creek running through him? What state was he going to be in by the time I got back to him? How the fuck was I going to get away from here, back to the City?

Janeane skulked along the bush track, rifle in hand, dog trotting to keep up. I followed, as quietly as I could.

We climbed down to a wild stretch of creek, well away from the house. After following it for a quarter of an hour, we came to where it joined a river pooling into bowls of deep green, water crackling like cellophane over low falls of rock. We crossed to the other side of the river over a trail of flat stones under shallow water. Janeane looked down at the sand, paced the riverflat, frowned.

'She *was* here.'

Printed on white sand: feathers, edge of a wing, a tiny foot.

Janeane scouted around in the brush and trees leading up from the riverbank, then waved me over.

'Bad news. She's headed up towards Moss's Bluff. Looks like she's flying away on us.'

Emerald-blue glinted in Janeane's hand. A feather.

Now Janeane was running up a track leading steeply away from the river. Despite my daily run I was in agony, chest heaving, stitch in my side. I stopped to catch my breath and my calves cramped. The pup shot past, gambolled back; it was having a fabulous time. Wind gusted, shaking trees.

Janeane slowed, held up her hand.

We moved forward, the wind covering our approach.

Janeane patted the air: *stop*. She darted ahead, out of sight around a curve in the track.

I heard a shout and then I was racing forward to see Janeane running ahead of me after a young woman. The track ended in front of them, and beyond and below rolled a green valley. The security footage of Peri had been brief but there was no mistaking her height or the rich red-brown wings.

Those huge wings were opening as she ran, the rising wind was catching them, Peri was already a metre or two off the ground without even flapping them, the cliff was about to fall away beneath her.

'Peri!' screamed Janeane, scrabbling to a halt. 'Peri, stop. Come back!'

Peri hovered above the cliff edge. She called out something I couldn't hear but Janeane, closer to her, reaching up almost to drag down on the chestnut wings, shook her head wildly.

'I didn't bring him here,' Janeane shouted. '*You* did!'

A gust of wind caught Peri, blew her sideways. She sheared round, slightly higher but still dangerously close to the cliff. Now I could see the startling flashings of light green-blue along the undersides of her wings. And I could see the baby in his sling, strapped to Peri's chest. Hugo, so close.

'Just *talk*,' Janeane shouted into the rising wind. 'I've disarmed him. You're safe. You can't fly in this weather. *Please*.'

Peri faced into the wind, wings wide, still just a few metres above the clifftop.

I'd come all this way and there she was, there Hugo was, and they might as well be on the moon. No way to reach them. No way up there at all.

8

BRINK

Peri half folded her wings and dropped till she balanced on the cliff edge. The wind caught her and she stumbled. No, no, no. Just what we needed, for the girl to plunge off the cliff in front of me. With the baby.

Janeane held out her hand. 'Just talk. No-one can make you do anything.'

Peri walked towards me, stopped, chin up. Defiant.

Better to drop my gaze. I took my sunglasses off to look at Hugo. Hard to believe he was right here. I'd studied his image so intensely that his dark hair, his calm eyes, were imprinted on my mind's eye. His legs were strikingly long and elegant for a baby, as if he already carried his grown man's shape in his baby body.

Janeane stepped back, keeping her eyes fixed on Peri's face.

I risked a look at Peri again, still only a few paces away from the sheer drop behind her. She settled her chestnut wings and I saw again the flash from their aquamarine undersides. Where the sun hit the feathers there were glints of purple. She was tall, straight-backed and tense, her bare arms powerfully muscled, but she held Hugo tenderly. Her dark hair, pulled into a ponytail, was as heavy and gleaming as polished wood.

'Janeane says you're alone.' Her voice was husky, as if she'd been crying.

I nodded. This close I was struck by her eyes, large and dark brown, shadowed. With grief? Exhaustion? She looked very young and yet older than she should.

Hugo faced me. Kicked his legs. Gurgled. *Baby Hugo appears healthy and well cared for*, I noted mentally in my report for Chesshyre.

'Hugo looks well,' I said.

Peri didn't answer. Twisted a silver ring on her right hand.

The red pup had worn himself out racing up the hill and now lay flaked out on the sun-warmed stones of the track, twitching a paw.

I tried again. 'How are you, Ms Almond? Are you alright?'

Peri said, 'So, if you're not a cop, what are you?'

'I'm a private investigator, Ms Almond, hired by Mr Chesshyre to find Hugo. You're incredibly lucky that the police have not been involved. Yet. I can see Hugo's safe and well and now the important thing is to return him to his parents.'

Peri said nothing, her face smooth and stubborn, wind ruffling her feathers. Not giving an inch. Precisely what fucking ace up her sleeve did this girl imagine she had? Maybe she really was nuts. Deep breath. Don't lose your temper. I stared at Peri's ring, a stylised gull, or maybe an albatross, too small to tell, moulded along the band. No surprise in that motif. Had she bought it when she got her wings, to symbolise her transition? Who else would give it to her? Not Chesshyre. Not his kind of thing at all. I thought of his insinuation. Did Peri believe she had a relationship with Chesshyre, some hold over him?

'Look, Peri,' I said, switching to her first name, 'Mr Chesshyre understands you've made a mistake. He's not looking to have you punished.'

Peri's mouth twisted. She didn't seem to think Chesshyre was being generous.

Annoyed, I pressed on. 'I've seen where you came from, Peri, I've been to the Venice. I know how much you have to lose.'

Peri flinched, as I'd hoped. So did Janeane. 'If you cooperate, you may even be able to keep your permanent City residency. The most precious thing you have.'

Peri glanced down at her wings. Well, fine then, her wings were more precious to her. 'Peri, you cannot risk being prosecuted for this. You may even lose your wings if you're convicted. *Why* did you run away out of the blue like this?'

Peri drew herself up, as if gathering her thoughts together with her posture. I sidled forward, half a step.

'I had—I *had to leave*. I had no choice. Something happened and—and I had to take Hugo with me.'

'What happened, Peri?'

Peri shook her head, backed away a half-step.

Then she was speaking again, very low. I leaned forward. 'I—I knew someone. Another nanny. I found her dead.'

Janeane and I looked at each other.

'Jesus, Peri! What?' I said. 'You found someone dead. Then you ran away?'

She nodded.

Janeane was white. Her rifle arm hung by her side, nerveless.

'What happened?'

'I don't know. She was upset; told me she'd seen another nanny she used to know when she was a kid but couldn't get the girl to talk to her. The girl pretended not to know her. So Luisa, that was my friend, Luisa Perros, said she was going to try and find out more about this girl. She asked me to meet her, said there were others. Then I—then I—'

'You found her?'

'Yes, washed up at Salt Grass Bay.'

'You think she was killed. How?'

'Implant. They can drop you out of the sky.'

'How do you know that's what happened?'

Peri sniffed, wiped her nose. 'I know.'

'What did she mean by others?'

'Don't know. Other nannies, I suppose.'

'What's so special about you?'

Peri looked away.

'Who do you think killed her? If she *was* killed.'

'I don't know,' Peri said, taking another half-step back. She stared at the ground. 'I couldn't leave him alone. In that house. I couldn't stay and I couldn't leave him.'

'I can see why you were scared, Peri,' I said. 'No-one could blame you. Good grounds for leniency. We can fix this, Peri. We can fix this. It can all be alright and you'll both be safe.'

'They didn't care for him,' Peri said. 'They were going to send him away.'

I stared at her. No, this was getting crazy. *Please*, Peri, don't complicate it all now. It's simple. You ran away because you were terrified, you took baby Hugo out of a sense of responsibility, didn't want to leave him alone, let's leave the story at that.

'You don't understand,' said Peri. 'You have to understand.' Voice rising to that kid whine: *it's not fair*. She took a deep breath, trying to shift back down. 'Peter and Avis had no time for Hugo. Big surprise, eh? Busy successful people. Kissed him goodnight sometimes when he was brought out all clean after his bath. I told myself that would change as Hugo got older and he didn't need me so much, you know, to feed him. But there was always some good reason why Peter and Avis were too busy for him.' She paused.

The wind dropped a curl of hair over Hugo's forehead. Peri brushed it away. Hugo grabbed her hand and laughed. Charming baby. A *happy* baby, by the look of him. Someone must love him. I swallowed, trying to get the dust from beating through the scrub out of my throat. Tom's babyhood was fading. Hard to remember exactly what he'd been like at this age.

A cloud moved over the sun. No protection up here; wind tore clear over the cliff, ripping at everything, trees, sand, leaves, flapping our clothes, gusting so hard it was impossible to think.

'Two weeks ago everything changed,' Peri said, flicking her gaze from me back to Hugo. She unfolded a wing and shook it irritably, scratching at a spot as if something was biting her. 'Some test results came back for Hugo. I wasn't allowed to see them of course but Avis just lost it. It seemed like he wasn't going to be a fledgling.

No wings.' The wind shook her, caught her unfolded wing, and she staggered, righted herself. 'It was like Avis knew all along he wasn't one of them.'

Peri started pacing, two steps to the side, then back to the middle of the track. Not good. She was winding herself up. 'Imagine poor Hugo, growing up, learning to walk and talk and none of it's exciting to them, none of it's good enough. All he sees is how sad and worried he makes them. Day in, day out. That little life.' Tears spilled down Peri's cheeks as she stared past me, as if seeing scenes she'd witnessed in the Chesshyre house. She smeared the tears away with the back of her hand.

'Then, three days ago, I heard Avis and Peter arguing. She said Hugo needed to be somewhere safe. They asked that cow from Little Angels to come over on the Monday. She was going to take Hugo away. Why else would she come over? She'd never come over before.'

Peri looked at me, challenging me, fresh tears running down her face. 'She was going to send him *away*.'

'I don't understand,' I said. 'If Hugo doesn't grow wings, so what? Can't they just add wings later, like they do with other people?'

'M-m-maybe,' said Peri. She was crying hard. Hugo was distressed, his mouth a wobbly O. 'She said it was temporary. Till they could *fix* him. But don't you see?'

A huge gust shook the trees. *Crack!* Janeane jumped. 'Fuck! That was too close.' A big branch had fallen across the track a few metres below us.

Peri was screaming now and not just so I could hear her over the wind. 'That makes it too late, don't you see? It's too late, it's too late, it's too late—'

Hugo was bawling and Peri was backing away from me, oblivious to the cliff; she wasn't seeing me or the track or anything present. The wind flurried, almost knocking her down. Those huge wings, her greatest power, were now putting her in real danger.

No choice but to risk it. I sprinted forward and grabbed Peri's arm. 'Come on, it's okay. It's okay, come on,' I soothed as I urged her away from the edge. What counted was my tone, could've recited *twinkle twinkle little star* for all the words mattered, like calming a trapped animal, like walking a kid through a burning house.

One step, two steps, keeping my pressure gentle, insistent, can't drag her, she'll rear back like a frightened horse, keep it steady, once she's walking it's easier for her to keep doing it, down here now, further down the track, now catch your breath . . . what I'd give to get out of this goddamn wind.

Janeane followed, keeping herself between us and the cliff edge.

'You don't feel safe in the City,' I said, keeping my hand on her arm, 'but you're definitely not safe out here. Look, I can offer you two options. You and Hugo come back to the City with me and we sort all this out, investigate what happened to Luisa. You'll be a witness, put away whoever did this to her. You'll be safe. Keep your permanent residency. Or, if it makes you feel safer, give Hugo to me and I take him back. You disappear.'

Peri's shoulders slumped, the image of a child shamed, defeated, but still she would not give in. 'No.'

Oh god. What was going on here? Chesshyre had told me nothing about what I was up against and there was obviously more I didn't know.

I dropped my hand from Peri's arm and paced down the track a few steps. Janeane braced her rifle against the ground, stock down like a walking stick. I spun round to face Peri. She'd calmed Hugo, who was now yawning. A spray of grit from under my heel hit the pup, who woke up and struggled to his feet.

'What are your options, Peri? You are not yet eighteen and you're on the run having committed an extremely serious crime. Where are you going to live?'

Sullen now. 'I have somewhere to go. I know what I'm doing.'

'Really?' I said. 'So you take Hugo from his family and you're going to live on the run. Is that the best you can offer him?'

That hit home. Peri glared at me but the defiance was draining out of her.

'You silly girl,' Janeane said. 'You're returning Hugo. You know that's what you have to do. PI's given you a good defence, go with it.'

The pup barked. I jerked my head up so fast I gave myself a crick in the neck. Now was the time for a Raptor to strike. Now I'd found Peri, out here in the open, I'd guided it straight to her.

A flock of big white parrots flew overhead, their squawks sounding like I always imagined the shriek of some prehistoric creature would. 'Awk!' exclaimed Hugo. He pointed to the sky. Peri stroked his arm, oblivious to my anxiety. Pursuit by Raptor must not have occurred to her. She thought I was all she had to worry about.

'You have to come back to the City with me,' I said.

'No,' said Janeane. 'Not with you.'

'What?' I said.

Peri, too, was surprised. 'But you just said I should go back to the City, Aunty Jan.'

'I did. You should. But not with him. Don't hand Hugo over till you're given reassurances about your own future. Once you hand the baby over, that's it. They can do anything they like to you. As you've seen with your friend. Luisa. You need help and independent advice when you get to the City. I'll give you a contact.'

Alright, well that just about fucking tears it. I'd thought I was close to victory and instead I was slammed into defeat. *I have had enough of this.* I was so angry I had to turn away, suppressing a strong urge to snatch Hugo and run like hell. If we weren't near the goddamn cliff, if Hugo hadn't actually been strapped to Peri in that baby sling, if Janeane hadn't been carrying that fucking ridiculous old rifle and if I wasn't scared she'd blast Hugo's head off with it while trying to hit me, I would've bloody well done it too. The disadvantages of my not being a cop anymore were glaringly obvious. I was alone, I had no back-up, and there would never *be* any back-up.

I breathed deeply and bit the inside of my cheek. 'Come back to the City with Hugo and get your advice then,' I said, 'but you have to give me a good result. I have to hand Hugo back to the Chesshyres soon or they'll turn this case over to the police.'

'No,' said Peri. 'They won't.' She unfolded her wings, drawing them right round her so they hid Hugo from view. She took a deep breath, as if she were about to dive into deep water. Janeane and I stared at her. 'I know the real reason they haven't gone to the cops.'

'Ah?' I said. 'Why *is* that?'

'What did Harper tell you about me?'

'She said you went to work for the Katon-Chesshyres because you agreed to wet-nurse their baby. That's how you got your wings.'

Peri's eyes widened. 'Huh?' she said, then she almost laughed. 'That's good. You believed her?'

I shrugged.

'Well, you don't know anything about the price of wings, that's for sure. The milk's just one instalment. Do you want to know what the real cost was?'

I held my breath.

'Might as well tell you now.' Peri picked up a branch, snapped it. She looked harder, older, as she said, 'I had to give them a child. I bore them a baby, *their* baby, and in return they gave me wings.'

Janeane gasped.

I gaped at her. '*What?*' I was going to fucking *kill* Chesshyre for this. And then I was going to kill him again.

'Yeah, big surprise, huh? Avis couldn't, or more likely wouldn't, so I had one for them. Their genes, my body. So Avis can have a baby with no mess, no stretch marks, no pain, no waddling around, no months of not flying. Women fliers don't like that, being grounded. Sometimes they never get back in the air, they say.' Peri drew her wings away from her sides and tucked them behind her; she put her arms around Hugo, who had fallen asleep in the dark nest provided by her wings.

Janeane put her hand to her head like she was trying to stop it splitting open.

'Bloody hell,' I said. This changed *everything*. Again. It was one thing to look for a kidnapper, something else to take a baby from his birth mother. No wonder Chesshyre hired me. The pieces fell into place in my mind, slapping down hard like mah-jong tiles at the end of an all-night game. *Bastards*. Chesshyre, planting his lies about Peri's 'crush' on him, worried she'd spill the beans, trying to get in first, discredit her. And strange little Avis in her skimpy costume with her taut belly that had bothered me so much and I hadn't figured out why. That unmarked belly had never been stretched by carrying a child. And Eliseev, no wonder *he'd* been so bloody nervous, he'd probably engineered the whole goddamn thing.

What's so special about you? I'd asked Peri. Now she'd told me. Had Luisa been special too?

The ruthlessness of it was breathtaking. Maybe they hadn't actually set out to destroy Peri, taking a foster child and using her body to get themselves a baby and then keeping her on for the milk; they just didn't fucking care what it did to her.

Janeane's advice was now dead right. There were good reasons for Peri to take Hugo back to the City herself and seek legal advice.

Janeane still looked shell-shocked. I turned back to Peri.

'So, let me get this straight,' I said. 'You used Hugo to get your wings.'

'No,' said Peri quietly, not wanting to wake Hugo, but with a hard snap as she bit off each word. 'It's not quite like that. Without my wings, *there would be no Hugo*.'

I was seeing a different person from the frightened young girl I'd first met half an hour earlier. This girl, talking about the deal, was the tough child who'd survived the Venice.

'Did you sign a contract for this deal?'

'Don't think so,' said Peri. 'There was so much going on—medical tests, waivers for the treatments and surgery—I'd be lucky to know *what* I signed.'

'Maybe,' I said. 'But you were underage and thus unable to consent to such a deal and I can tell you for sure that your legal guardian didn't consent to anything.'

'What do you mean? What legal guardian?'

'Stop,' said Janeane, holding up one hand, her rifle in the other. 'This has gone far enough. You can continue this conversation in the City. Right now, I need you off my property. Folks around here can be a little nosy. The good Samaritan thing, cup of tea and a biscuit, help you with your car, send you on your way, we've just about run out of that cover story.' She flicked her hand at Peri. 'Give me back my slick.'

'What?'

'The information, maps and contact details I've given you. Plans have changed, you're returning to the City with Hugo. Hand it over.'

'I don't have it,' Peri said. 'It's still at the house.'

'Alright then. Let's go,' Janeane said. She started herding us down the track, pretty much at gunpoint.

'Peri, you *are* coming back to the City with Hugo?' I fell into step beside her. 'If you are, we can sort something out and I can make sure you're safe, but if you keep running, no court in the world will be sympathetic towards you.'

'Yes,' Peri sighed. 'I'll bring him back. People like the Chesshyres always get their way, don't they?'

'I have to warn you there are serious problems with following the plan Janeane suggested. If you insist on bringing him back yourself, I can't say what Chesshyre's reaction will be, I can only try to persuade him to wait, and I have good reason to believe a Raptor is after you. If one is tracking you, your safety will not be his primary concern.'

Peri didn't say anything.

Exasperated, I ran a hand through my hair. 'Well, if there's to be any chance that this will work, I have to give Chesshyre—Peter—a timeframe for Hugo's return.'

'A week,' said Peri.

'*No*,' I said. 'They will not accept that. Two days. We'll meet at my flat on Friday morning.'

'I have to fly back,' said Peri, sullen again. 'I'll try to get there on time but it's not just up to me. There's weather and—'

'You have three days,' I said. 'That's it. Today's Tuesday. So, Wednesday, Thursday, Friday—that gives you till first thing Saturday. Get your advice but do it fast. Be there on time. I can't answer for what will happen after that. Listen,' I added impulsively, 'I'll try to help you.

Come to me on time and I'll do my best with the contacts I have. Okay?' *It's not that easy playing good cop/bad cop all by yourself.*

I glanced over my shoulder. Janeane didn't look impressed but Peri was looking at me. She believed me. Tough, innocent Peri. That young face. Could I even remember what it was like to be that young?

'You need me,' I said, 'to prove to Chesshyre that Hugo's safe and well.' I stopped and pulled out my slick. 'A picture.'

Janeane raised an eyebrow but Peri lifted Hugo a little into the crook of her arm. I moved closer. 'Let me just get his hair out of the way,' I said, pushing Hugo's lock of hair away from his eyes. By the time Peri flinched away from me, I'd already stepped back.

I took the picture. 'You're only postponing the inevitable. Understand I want what's best for Hugo.'

'So do I,' said Peri. 'Believe me, so do I.'

The pup skittered past us, then raced down another track branching to the left near the base of the hill.

'I've ruined everything,' said Peri so low I had to duck my head to hear her over the wind in the trees. 'I won't even be able to look after him. That's all I wanted, that he'd have *one* person who loved him and that he'd *know* that. That there was one person who didn't see him as a failure, one person who loved him as whole and perfect.'

'*Why*, Peri?' I said. 'Why is that so important to you?'

She looked away.

I put my sunglasses back on. Fine, don't tell me. Everyone has a sad story. Hers was not my business.

Janeane jerked her head at the track the pup had taken. 'Go back that way,' she said to Peri. 'I'll meet you at the house, help you prepare for starting back tomorrow.'

'I need to ask more questions about Luisa,' I said. Peri's revelation had sparked a whole new line of inquiry there but Janeane shook her head.

'Time for all that when Peri returns Hugo.'

'You need money.' I pulled out a credit slick.

'Don't take it,' said Janeane. 'It'll be used to track you.'

I tried not to smile at that.

'I've got money,' said Janeane.

I wrote my details on the only piece of paper I had, the receipt from the Naxos Cafe, and gave it to Peri.

'I'll tell my neighbour, Vittorio, to let you and Hugo into my flat if I'm not there.'

I smiled at Peri, seeing how worried she looked. 'Frisk will be there. That ought to cheer you two up. Peri, I'm not against you. Believe that.'

'Come on,' Janeane said.

My little grail, my quest, my pot of gold if you wanted to put it like that, was right here; hard to believe I had to turn around and leave Hugo behind. I hastened after Janeane.

Janeane's ancient car ground forward and winched my sorry Taj backwards out of the stream. She sprayed his engine with something and started it, and to my unutterable relief it coughed a few times and came back to life. She turned it off.

'Smart car,' Janeane said. 'Too bad it wasn't smart enough to avoid the hole in the creek.'

'Call me when Peri leaves tomorrow.'

'We don't have any services out here.'

'I'm sure you'd like me to believe that. Do what you have to do.'

Janeane didn't respond.

'Thanks for pulling me out of the creek. Watch out for other fliers. If you see one, it is *not* good news.'

Janeane surprised me by handing back my gun and cartridge. 'I pulled you out of the creek because I don't want you on my property one minute longer than you have to be. Looks like you'll have to get yourself a new car,' she added as I waded across the stream to Taj. 'They're never the same, somehow, once a creek's been through 'em.' I guess she enjoyed saying that but her tone was so dry it was hard to tell.

The first thing wrong, besides the wet and the smell inside Taj, was the fact I had to turn on the engine myself. And that was it. The engine was running, the car was moving but there was no Taj. It was just a car. Driving away from the Owls was a miserable experience.

After we left the Upper Trunk Road, my slick vibrated, signalling communication service coverage. I felt as if I'd travelled much further that day than the few hours' drive to Pandanus. Not only were the people of the Venice an underclass living outside the law, they seemed to be living in another country altogether, and by the time I'd reached the Owls, I'd journeyed back in time, as if Janeane, with her ancient car and ancient rifle and isolation, had contrived a way to live in the past.

These gulfs of time and place made Peri's leap to the City all the more remarkable. After seeing the Venice I could understand why Peri had sacrificed herself for a footing in Chesshyre's world. From what I'd seen of her file, with her father, at least, being a flier, it seemed she'd originally been one of the City elite, even before her treatments. Her height, her athletic frame, her smooth hair and flawless skin, all made her resemble Chesshyre much more than she resembled Janeane or the people in the Venice, even if I disregarded her wings.

When I was still hours away from the City, I rang Chesshyre, steeling myself for talking to him without losing my temper.

'Hugo's with you?' he said when he heard my voice.

'Not exactly,' I said. 'He's safe. She's returning him.'

'*What*? Where did you find them?'

Fair question but I didn't want to give his Raptor directions if I hadn't already led him directly to Peri.

'Before I answer that, I need to clarify something. I've done the best I can and now we need to trust the girl. You did the right thing, hiring me, but of course there's one thing I lack: wings. I couldn't grab her.' Arresting ordinary people was one thing; I'd done my share of running down alleys and hauling myself over fences. Arresting a flier, well, I could sure see why the force needed Raptors for that. 'You were wise not to send a flier after her, Mr Chesshyre. Two fliers grappling in mid-air over a baby would be incalculably dangerous.'

Chesshyre didn't say anything. *Shit*.

'You wouldn't have a back-up plan, by any chance?'

'I don't know what you mean.'

'Look, Mr Chesshyre, I saw the Raptor at your place.'

Of course I *hadn't* seen him, but Taj had.

'Private security,' said Chesshyre. 'That's all.'

'Okay, you don't have a Raptor. I'm just emphasising that if anything happens to Peri or Hugo because of this non-existent Raptor, it's on your head. Your best bet for getting Hugo back safely is not to frighten Peri. She's scared enough as it is.' Yes and I couldn't tell him why. If this friend of hers, Luisa, really was killed, then I had to tread carefully. I was starting to see how tight the flier world was and didn't want anyone tipped off, even by accident.

'I could see Hugo was well cared for,' I assured him. *You knew all along she wouldn't hurt him*. 'Things have gone well. Considering.' *Considering you haven't told me the truth about anything to do with this case*. 'We both know she has no choice but to come back, give up baby Hugo. But she's so young.' *Too young to have your baby for you, you callous bastard*. 'The very young don't always comprehend the forces against them in this world, how very bad the odds can be. That makes them dangerous. Our main leverage with her is that you aren't going to prosecute.'

'We just want Hugo back safely.'

'Good,' I said. *Why don't you ask me* why *Peri took Hugo on the run with her?* Anyone else would. Because you *know* the answer, that's why. You were going to send him away and she's the surrogate mother. She's over-attached. You hired me precisely to avoid having that conversation.

The storm that had hung over me all the way back from the Owls and Pandanus decided it was finally time to break. Wind rattled the car. Rain slammed into it like someone aiming a firehose. Water poured a solid silver sheet over the windscreen. I didn't think I could be any more sorry than I already was about not having Taj for the drive back but I slowed to a crawl and finally pulled over to finish my conversation with Chesshyre.

I still had one ace up my sleeve. It's always prudent to keep something in reserve but now it was more important to keep Chesshyre on the straight and narrow.

'The thing is,' I told him, 'I planted a tracking device on Hugo. We'll keep tabs on where he is at all times and make sure Peri keeps her part of the bargain.'

'Oh. Good,' Chesshyre said. I didn't tell him I couldn't pick up any signals until Peri reached airspace under networked coverage. I wanted Chesshyre to think I knew where Peri was as much for her protection as for Hugo's.

I was hopeful I could wrap this case up quickly. By late Saturday morning Hugo would be home and by Saturday evening I'd finish my final report and submit my final invoice. Chesshyre's life would resume its smooth, perfect course. I told myself that if I worked only on morally clear-cut cases I wouldn't eat very often.

By the time I was able to reach Henryk the storm had lessened a bit and I was well into the Red Zone. 'I've got something for you, mate,' I said, staring at the darkening road awash ahead of me.

'Ah,' said Henryk, 'so you're handing the case over?'

'No need,' I said. 'I found Peri. The baby's fine and she's returning him. But she's really scared; says she found the body of another nanny, Luisa Perros, at Salt Grass Bay the morning she ran away. Of course that's not proof of anything, she might just have fallen. Still, worth a look. I reckon we need to see the Little Angels records, there's definitely something not right there and—'

'*We?*' exclaimed Henryk. '*We* don't have to do anything of the kind.'

'But Peri's a witness—'

'Fantastic. Bring her in. She can make a statement. We'll take a look at Salt Grass Bay when we get a chance. Now don't waste my time asking me to do your work for you.'

A glow brightened ahead of us, a wash of light thrown up against the dark screen of sky. The car beeped. We'd left the darkness of RaRA-land behind. We'd re-entered the City.

I was late picking up Thomas, not helped by the fact I was stopped and questioned at the entrance to Silver Palms, the gated estate where Lily and Richard lived—not surprising given that both the car and I were wet, plastered in mud and dust, and looking thoroughly disreputable. When Lily, who had descended the steps at the front of her swank townhouse to buckle Thomas into his car seat, saw the state Taj was in, she tried to cancel the visit. Her eyebrows shot up when she saw the scratches on my cheek, the blood stiffening my hair and the filth staining my clothes and shoes from the Venice and my encounters with creeks and rivers at the Owls. I got round Lily by explaining I'd made an appointment with Dr Ruokonen and was considering her 'view'—as I put it—that Thomas should be a flier.

As soon as I said these words I knew they were true. My trip to RaRA-land had rattled me badly and I'd begun to think maybe Lily was right and we should put as much distance between Thomas and the underclass as we could. But I wouldn't allow myself to be crushed by her juggernaut; I'd find out from Ruokonen what the treatments involved and then decide what to do.

I was far more exhausted than I'd hoped to be for Thomas's visit. I'd had an early start but what had worn me out was the drive home. I hadn't realised how much wear and tear Taj usually saved me. Once I was back in the City I was almost beside myself with exasperation trying to work out a route on the still-passable roads.

At Ventura, I ran Tom's bath and gratefully peeled off my wet, smelly clothes and showered and changed while Thomas, captivated by Frisk as I'd hoped, stroked his fur the wrong way. Frisk removed himself to my closet.

Thomas settled into his bath, making circles through the water with his favourite toy, a purple jellyfish which lit up. When he let it go it pulsed slowly through the water over to the side of the bath and hung there, a violet moon shining on its domestic sea. I watched Tom in the bathroom mirror while I had another try at fixing up my cuts and grazes.

'I had enough,' Thomas announced. I leaned over to pull the plug.

'I can *do* it!' he shrieked, his three-and-a-half-year-old self-respect outraged. 'I do it! Myself!'

'Come on, Tom,' I said, hoping to cut short his howls of rage. 'You pull the plug then. Come on, mate.'

His mouth squared with indignation, his green eyes about to spill over, he reached down and condescended to pull the plug.

I stood up and grabbed Tom's special hooded towel from the towel rack.

One of the hardest things about not living with Thomas was keeping up with him, not only with the spurts of development in his abilities but with the ever-evolving ceremonial of each moment of his day. The rituals of daily life with a small child are as intricate, inflexible and ramified as those of a religious cult, and as with the law, ignorance is no excuse. I was always behind, on the seventh level of the ziggurat when daily life had in fact attained the eighth level.

'There's a lot of work for you, Dad, in this world,' Thomas observed sagely, as I lifted him out of the bath. He put his hand up to the cut on my head. I sat on the edge of my bed with Thomas between my knees as I towelled him dry. He giggled as I poked him gently here and there. I kissed him as I dried him, his cheek softer than cream against my skin. How much longer would I be able to hug and kiss my son this freely? How I would miss the sheer delight of holding him, the thrill his dry biscuity smell gave me. These were the pleasures parents never talked about, not because they're illicit but because they're so intense they're private. Other parents understand, you don't need to say anything, but non-parents never will; they still think passionate joy in the perfection of another body is simply about sex.

'You have a rough face, Dad,' chirped Thomas, patting my bristled chin.

When I sat down to eat with Thomas that night, Peri's situation appeared even crueller. I was used to feeling bad about Thomas, about shuttling him back and forth between me and Lily and Richard. But at least *he* was wanted; he was the centre of two households.

'Talk the trees, Dad,' insisted Thomas.

This was a drama I'd unwisely created to get Thomas to eat broccoli. I had to do the voices of the trees, worried the great giant Thomas was about to eat them. *Nah*, I'd say, as one tree to another, *he won't eat us, he's forgotten about us, he's eating his fish. See? He's looking over there—oh no, he's turning around, no, please don't eat us, aarrrghhh!*, as Thomas, giggling so hard I worried he'd choke, would grab a piece of broccoli and slowly, gloating over the tree's impassioned pleas to be spared, raise it to his mouth.

'Look, Dad! I ated the tree.'

Dinner took a while.

After I'd read Thomas his story—*Hansel and Gretel*, at least twice—and brushed his teeth, I put him into bed in his cloud pyjamas, kissed his hair and told him he was snug as a bug in a rug. Thomas wanted to know if the bug was a ladybug. I said I expected so. He then wanted to know, with the inexhaustible precision I associated with his mother, the colour and material of the rug. Red bamboo. Your favourite. Now *goodnight*.

He called me back. 'What if I get scared, Dad?'

I sat on Tom's bed and took his hand. 'Brave Thomas. We're not scared. Right?'

I grabbed a beer from the kitchen, then sat at the dining table, pushed aside a stack of papers in front of my desk slick and prepared to draft my report for Chesshyre. After setting the beer bottle on the table I wrapped my hands around it, not wanting to move or think for a moment.

There was deep pleasure in just sitting, in becoming aware of an unfamiliar feeling in the pit of my stomach, as of a knot untying itself. I let out a long slow breath. For the first time since leaving my flat on Sunday, the clock in my mind wasn't running through the hours since the abduction, the dread of time slipping away forming the backdrop of every thought. I breathed in and out again, thinking about Peri and Hugo.

Which of you by taking thought can add one cubit unto his stature? What had been an irrefutable argument for the power of God, fate, nature, was now as flimsy as a blade of grass bending in the wind. Now we could. We could take thought and add cubits. Or wings. Or anything we could imagine.

And was the consequence petulant rage when we didn't get our way? Was this the cost of our ever-increasing power? Ever-diminishing acceptance of what *is*? *Send the kid back, he's not what we ordered.* The Chesshyres wanted to get what they'd paid for. And they hadn't. That had driven Peri's fear for Hugo. Her crime a crime of passion, really. Not the usual deal; strange to think that's what it was, though. Understandable. She'd lived her life as a child who could be returned to sender at any time. And this mess that I was now sorting out, this was what resulted when life itself was a transaction.

I'd promised Peri I'd investigate what had happened to Luisa but when I searched the databases I had access to I didn't find any information on her. I couldn't blame Henryk for his unenthusiastic response. Cam, though, might want to know if Little Angels was up to no good; after all, her department gave the agency the accreditation that allowed it to operate.

'Sorry to ring you at home, Cam,' I began.

She was silent as I told her about finding Peri.

'Peri mentioned a friend, Luisa Perros, who was a nanny too. I have a strong suspicion she must have been supplied by Little Angels as well. We need to know if there are other girls besides Peri who've been in foster care and ended up with Little Angels.'

'No, Zeke, absolutely not,' said Cam. 'No fishing expeditions. If you get names from Little Angels then *maybe* I can work backwards, but I can't go checking files just in case. That would bring on way too much heat.'

Too much heat? I thought as Cam hung up. Good thing I didn't mention Perros was *dead*.

I turned back to the desk slick. I certainly was wearing out my welcome with my former colleagues. *Janeane Shaw, sister of subject's foster carer*, I dictated. *Slight build, one hundred and seventy centimetres.* Most people in my line of work failed, I knew, and they failed because they couldn't provide good reports to their clients. A talent for crafting reports was not why people got into this business. But it was crucial: you had to be in charge of the story. If you couldn't make sense of it or lost control of it then you were finished.

I stretched, threw away the empty beer bottle, and sat down again to redo the all-important summary paragraph. Something was nagging at the back of my mind, something I needed to look at again. I reread my interim report twice, a masterful blend of clarity, reassurance and lying by omission, even if I did say so myself. I said nothing of Peri's motives nor of her intention to seek legal advice. *Sufficient unto the day is the evil thereof.*

I flicked through my case file. There, the Little Angels catalogue. That's what I needed to look at. I paged through it. Luisa wasn't in it but that didn't mean anything. The catalogue only covered a six-month period. Still, it could be useful. I sent the information to Cam at home. She was already annoyed with me, might as well push things a bit further.

I downloaded the photo of Peri and Hugo, attached it to my report, sent it to Chesshyre, refilled Frisk's water bowl, and went to check on Thomas.

In the doorway of Tom's bedroom, I listened to his breathing in the semi-dark. *What does the future hold for you?* Thomas lay facing the wall. I stared at his thin back, marbles of his spine, shoulder blades so sharp they looked like they'd pierce his skin. There was where the wings would go, softening the boniness of his little boy body. My little boy, sweep of shining feathers down his back. What colour would they be? Lily would want something flashy. Anger rose in my throat at the thought of Thomas as a product, fashioned by us. Then I remembered the Venice. After my day in RaRA-land I'd do anything to raise him above a life like that.

I turned away, about to go to bed myself, when I heard a noise. I froze. Scuffling in the laneway beside Ventura, loud rustling, then a deep rumble. That was Frisk—I'd let him out after dinner—and I knew that growl. He was angry. His growl rose to a high-pitched snarl I'd never heard before. That sounded like fear.

'What the hell?!'

A loud smash.

I grabbed a light and my weapon and slipped outside, locking the door behind me. Frisk was roaring so loudly now my ears hurt.

A huge dark shape shot past, knocking me to the ground. Winded, I scrambled to my feet, the *churr* of air through giant pinion feathers beating in my ears. The biggest flier I'd ever seen was taking off in front of me. The wash of air from his wings almost knocked me over again. I shone the light up. A mask covered his face; over his nose, a metal beak glinted like a knife. He wheeled over us, blotting out the sky. Then he was gone.

Frisk crouched at my feet, snarling and hissing, showing all his teeth, eyes flashing gold discs reflecting my light. I was seeing a creature I did not know.

'Well done, Frisk,' I said. 'You just ambushed our Raptor.'

9

THE UNFORGIVING ELEMENT

The next morning, Wednesday, the morning of my appointment with Dr Ruokonen, Richard dropped by early to pick up Thomas. I'd slept badly, starting awake at every noise, now that I knew my fear of being stalked by a Raptor had hardened into alarming reality.

The first call that morning was from Chesshyre. I spoke to him as I pottered around my flat, setting out fresh water for Frisk and stacking the few dishes from Tom's breakfast in the sink. 'Did you get my report?' I said. What I meant was: *Call off your freak. You don't need him now.*

It didn't make sense; why would the Raptor be watching me instead of Peri? Was he fast enough to follow me and then go after Peri? Surely Chesshyre wouldn't have two on the case?

'Yes, I did get your report,' said Chesshyre. 'Thanks.'

'Only three days to go.' I opened the door to let Frisk out into the front garden where he peed on each mango tree in turn. What more was there to say? I had no more news for him than when I'd drafted the report a mere nine hours earlier but I realised, with horror, that that was the last thing I could admit. All Chesshyre knew was I'd planted a tracking device and therefore must know exactly where Peri and Hugo were. Their safety depended on him continuing to believe that.

'So you're tracking her all the way?' Chesshyre said.

'Yes,' I lied.

I told Chesshyre I knew from the tracking device that Peri and Hugo had begun their journey back to the City. I hoped like hell that was true. If it wasn't, and if Chesshyre's Raptor found that out, it was hard to say what would happen. For now, though, Chesshyre was elated. He asked me to meet him at his new tower project, Cloud City, that afternoon but would not say why.

Frisk sauntered back into the flat with me and I sent a message to Thien, my mechanic, to book Taj in for later that morning.

Then Sunil was onto me about the Church of the Seraphim job. Sunil asked me to meet him for coffee at one of our former hangouts, Kamchatka Joe's, at nine am. As I pulled out of the laneway I avoided Ray's eyes, pretending I didn't see his alarm over the mess that was Taj. By the time I escaped from the reek of it at Thien's garage, I was sneezing, my eyes streaming from the mould already sprouting in its humid interior. Poor Taj, he sure wasn't shiny now. Fine for Janeane to say I needed a new car—she could talk, hers predated the Flood—but I couldn't afford a new one, especially if I was going to help pay for Tom's treatments.

As I waited for the train to take me into the CBD near the government offices and Parliament House, and Kamchatka Joe's, I wondered about the job Sunil had for me. Coffee with Sunil was never just coffee. Sunil was never off-duty and he never did anything without multitasking; it was a point of honour. Every coffee with a friend was also a working meeting, every game of tennis also strengthened political ties and supplied him with valuable gossip.

As my train wound its way towards the CBD I prepared for my later meeting with Ruokonen, skimming recent articles on the treatments, searching particularly for adverse reactions and side effects. Most of the articles I found were relentlessly upbeat.

'Black ops,' were Sunil's first words as he rose from his seat in the gloom at the back of Kamchatka Joe's and clapped me on the shoulder. He grinned and shot his clean white cuffs out from his jacket, his handsome face alight with pleasure. 'Good to see you, *mate*,' he said as he turned away to finish the conversation he'd been having on his slick. As we sat down at the little round table and ordered, Sunil also sent a message to a crony, or, more likely, a group of them.

Black ops. That was how Sunil dignified digging dirt on a member of the Opposition. Ordinarily a job like this was routine, excavating old material, putting two and two together, making five. But this time Sunil wanted something more.

Sunil sipped his coffee, leaned towards me and said, 'My minister needs to know what this guy is really up to. We're going to get you a job interview with him, just so you can get into his office.'

'Sure, great,' I said. Work like this paid well and kept me busy, and as Sunil shook my hand and strode away, already speaking to someone else, I was glad I had something lined up even though payment for the Chesshyre job would have kept me for a good long time.

As I gathered my thoughts in Sunil's wake, a light flashed on my slick. The tracking device had begun signalling; Peri and Hugo must have reached flight space that relayed surveillance. When I looked up their location on the little screen-size map, I could see they were heading south, towards the City. I set the slick down on the table, then glanced at the screen again, just to make sure. After a moment I checked it a third time. Peri was keeping her word! My relief was overwhelming; my lie to Chesshyre had become the truth. But I couldn't exactly call and tell him the good news—as far as he was concerned, he'd heard this good news already. Now I just needed confirmation from Janeane. With luck, I'd hear from her before seeing Chesshyre this afternoon and I could reassure him once again how well the plan was working.

I ordered myself another coffee to celebrate. Things were going well. I was rolling in work and money. Sunil and I had already sketched out a plan of attack for the black ops job. One of the trickiest jobs I'd ever had was going better than I had a right to expect. And it looked as if my son would become a flier. Though I had mixed feelings about that, at least I knew now I was doing my best by him. I'd also get Lily off my back at last. And with a bit of luck Taj would be restored to me in a day or two.

But as I looked over my notes I realised something was odd about this new job. The dirt file I had to put together concerned a minor party MP, a member of the Seraphim. A *flier* as Sunil had mentioned on Sunday. Fliers were rapidly becoming my new area of expertise. In the space of a few days I'd gone from knowing little about fliers and caring less to having every waking moment consumed by them, professionally and personally.

First things first, though. I drained the bitter, delightfully strong dregs of my coffee, paid the grand larceny of my bill, and set out for my appointment. I was due at Dr Ruokonen's in half an hour.

I had climbed up to what must be the biggest treehouse ever built; it spread around the bole of an oak tree and across an enormous span of branches. The oak tree itself stood between two office blocks in a green slice of meadow named Diomedea Park. The material of this treehouse was like nothing I'd ever seen before; from the outside it reflected leaves and clouds and sky, which was why I hadn't seen it until I was standing directly under it, but sometimes it rippled like water, as if it were about to vanish. From the inside the walls were transparent. As I waited for Dr Ruokonen I peered out through the branches but then my eye was caught by a large VaporView on the inside wall cycling through images of birds and fliers in spectacular Flight, against banks of sunset cloud, plunging waterfalls, starry towers. Along the top of the screen ran the legend *Aquila non captat muscas*.

I had got as far as *aquila*—eagle—with my schoolboy Latin when Dr Ruokonen, a wiry woman in her forties with wings like polished tin, appeared and ushered me into her office. Her hair flopped over her forehead, the same brushed metal as her wings, and her cheekbones were high and prominent. She wore an expensive-looking silky grey singlet over darker grey pants. The clothes were tailored to her body, the singlet leaving her muscled arms bare.

We moved briskly through establishing our credentials and I was surprised when no flicker of recognition crossed her features as she glanced at my slick. Well, you learn something every day. Never did I think I'd be disappointed to meet someone who didn't know of the Charon case.

The outer walls of Ruokonen's office were transparent too and from where I sat I could see for a long way, even as far as Green Square Park and back to Parliament House in glimpses along the concrete canyons formed by the other buildings. Wind rustled in the leaves and tossed the oak's branches. No flier would feel shut in here. Looking out from inside the reach of a great tree, out over green leaves, I was floating, lofting through the air like a puff of cloud. A breaking wave of elation swelled through my body. Exaltation. God, I thought, this, *this* must be a pale shadow of what *they* feel when they fly.

Ruokonen sat behind her desk on a strange object, a slightly springy column with a flattened bend in it like a kinked strand of wire for a seat; a chair built especially for fliers. The column continued up to the middle of Ruokonen's upper back but there were no arms, no back, nothing to get in the way of the wings arching to the floor behind her.

'It's as if there's nothing between us and the sky,' I said, gesturing to the view.

'Yes. I feel that part of my job, Mr Fowler, is to show some of the possibilities.' Ruokonen leaned back slightly against the column of her chair. 'What does it mean to be a flier? It can mean a lot of things. What it shouldn't mean is doing things the way they've always been done, but with wings added on. So while this office expresses how I see the world, the way *I* want to work, I also use it to expand how people see they can use Flight in their lives.'

'I see,' I said. 'You were highly recommended.'

Ruokonen inclined her sleek head. 'How can I help you?'

'I need to know more about Flight,' I said. 'My wife, my ex-wife, wants our son to have the treatments. I shouldn't consent till I know what's involved.'

Ruokonen stretched her legs out in front of her, crossed at the ankle, and picked up a pen from her desk. The pen glowed sky blue as she tapped it against her palm, its light illuminating the logo *Diomedea* running along its length, the same logo I'd seen on Eliseev's building. Her wings rustled along the floor. 'That's wise,' she said. 'The difficulty is that I can give you all the relevant information but I'm not sure it'll help you make that decision. It is, finally, an emotional one. However, you are right to want to know. What's involved in the treatments?' She straightened up and fixed her gaze hard on me. 'You need to understand that a great deal is involved.'

Ruokonen placed the luminous pen back on her desk. 'There is an extensive amount of modification needed to enable a human being to fly. Far more than most people realise. Most of it you can't see. The wings are the obvious part of the transformation but without all the supporting alterations they're just fancy dress. To understand why so much has to be done, you have to understand a little about the physics of flight. Air is not a supportive medium, Mr Fowler. It is, shall we say, *unforgiving* of error.' A slightly grim smile bent her lips. I guessed she'd just uttered one of her favourite wry aphorisms.

'When wings were first added to human beings they were aesthetic only,' Ruokonen continued. 'People liked the look of them but they could not fly. Those wings were much smaller than the wings we have now. We didn't even try to make Flight modifications at first. That's because most people assumed an animal the size of a human being could not fly. The physics of it does not work for us. The amount of lift needed is just . . .' She raised her shoulders in a slow-motion shrug, her palms up, as if the forces at work were beyond words.

'Put it this way,' she resumed. 'The largest living bird species that fly have a maximum weight of no more than ten to fifteen kilos. Most birds aren't that big. The majority of living bird species fall in the range of ten to a hundred *grams*. So we are dealing with a weight factor in the order of five to ten times what Class Aves has generally been able to solve and Class Aves was, I think, the most successful in the history of life on earth.'

Ruokonen glanced at her slick, then refocused her gaze past my shoulder. 'If you look at the ancient class of pterosaurs, however, you find some *big* fliers. The biggest, Quetzalcoatlus, has been estimated at a maximum weight of two hundred and fifty kilos. Evidence suggests it was a good flier, though it would have spent most of its time soaring, so clearly it can be done.'

One of Ruokonen's own feathers, grey on top, shiny pink underneath, floated onto her desk. She ran her fingers over the vanes. I could see the feather shone with something beyond its own lustre. Traces of safety dust sparkled along the edges.

'But there is something else to consider, Mr Fowler. Birds, and other flying creatures, have only the materials supplied by evolution. Skin, muscle, bone, fat, feathers. With those they have achieved miracles. *Miracles*. It is incredible when you truly understand what they have done. Their adaptations for flight are extraordinary and extreme. Of course we've borrowed from them. But we have something they don't have.' She paused for emphasis.

I leaned forward. Her enthusiasm for this topic was compelling.

'What *we* have is the ability to develop new materials and experiment with modifications in much shorter timeframes. We're able to replace bone, for example, with a carbon-fibre–bone hybrid. This hybrid forms a light, flexible and extremely strong self-repairing lattice. It's allowed us to pare the weight load right down.'

'Hang on a sec.' I sat bolt upright. 'You replace their *bones*?'

'We don't take them out,' said Ruokonen, smiling slightly. 'Bone is constantly in the process of formation, Mr Fowler. We modify that process so that the hybrid is incorporated over a fairly short period of time. And it's so strong in fact that it saves us from having to modify the shape of the chest bones to attach the flight muscles. Think of a bird such as a pigeon: it has a reinforced breast bone like the prow of a ship, called a keeled sternum, to which the flight muscles attach. We've been able to avoid such a radical change in our form, not just by fabricating stronger bones but by growing muscles of greater explosive power, which means those muscles don't have to be as large as the equivalent flight muscles on a bird. The muscles for Flight are so powerful that they would shatter ordinary bone if it were subjected to that force.

'Now, the transformation to Flight is a complex sequence of procedures and starts with screening, of course, and I need hardly tell you that with children they must not know they're being tested. We observe them at play, at sporting events, examine a detailed medical and genetic history, that sort of thing. If they fail—that's not the right word but that's how they feel—imagine it. Being offered the opportunity to fly and then it's taken away. *Because you're not good enough*. That has to be avoided.'

I had tensed up and realised I was holding my breath. I didn't like the sound of what Ruokonen described. It sounded as if I'd have to be screened too. I'd hated the stressful series of tests I'd had to go through to qualify for health insurance before starting in the police force and now it sounded as if I might have to go through something similar again.

Ruokonen was still talking. I had to pay attention but my mind was reeling with the strangeness of what she was explaining. Ruokonen's words were making me feel a little foolish. Like most non-fliers, I'd assumed the transition to Flight was merely (merely!) a process of adding wings. But now I was realising how deeply ignorant I was about the complexity of Flight, more ignorant even than my own great-grandfather had been, who'd at least had the experience of flying in aeroplanes. I hadn't even done that. The true extent of the transformation appalled me. But I had to push aside my feelings and listen; this was my one real chance before the whole process began to try to understand what would happen to Thomas.

'Then, if the subject is suitable, there's infusion of the right DNA, both to the subject and to a culture of their cells from which we will grow their wings. For an older child or young adult, where we have to grow the wings separately, we culture them from the subject's own cells, and program them to develop as needed, as bone, feathers and so on, and we grow them, just as we grow skin for burn victims, for example. At this stage the person can choose what colour and pattern they want for their wings—'

'Why feathers?' I interrupted. 'We're not birds.'

Ruokonen frowned. 'No, we're not birds but feathers are the best adaptation imaginable for their function. I think you'd find universal agreement that no-one wants wings of naked skin, like bats. Besides being ugly, they're far less practical. Has it occurred to you why bats are nocturnal, Mr Fowler?'

I shook my head.

'Try leaving a bat out in the sun and see what happens to its wings. The sunburn and subsequent scarring will leave it unable to fly. Feathers have other advantages as an airfoil; besides their exceptional lightness and stiffness and variety of colour and pattern, they have the advantage of being able to separate.'

Ruokonen pressed a button and a picture of an eagle in soaring flight appeared on her slick. 'Look at the ends of her wings—see how the great primaries separate like fingers? Big birds do this and so do we. This cuts drag, increases lift and so reduces the energy requirements of Flight. You can't slot like that with skin wings, which is just one reason why bats tend to be small. I don't mean to imply that bats are poor fliers. They are superb fliers. It's just that they are limited in their options by the materials they've had to work with.'

Ruokonen stretched, rolling her shoulders, shaking and settling her own wings briefly. 'Before we grow the wings, decisions have to be made about wing size and shape. All creatures that fly are subject to the laws of aerodynamics. Flying ability and the types of Flight a flier is most suited for are determined by, among other things, the following four factors: wing area, aspect ratio, wing loading and wing shape.'

'Slow down,' I begged. 'Aspect ratio, wing loading?'

Ruokonen waved her hand. 'I'll explain those terms as we go. Let's start with take-off, the most demanding aspect of Flight. The ability to take off is, mostly, governed by the ratio of the flight muscles to total body weight. Ideally, if you are to take off from the ground, your flight muscles should make up about twenty-five percent of your body weight. We've been able to pare that back to around nineteen percent because of the greater explosive power of the Flight muscle fibres we've developed. We're very proud that we've engineered the modifications so that people are able to take off directly from the ground. The earliest fliers couldn't do that and had to dive off buildings and cliffs and so on. We are now into our second generation of fliers, Mr Fowler, and we are refining our techniques on each new cohort coming through. You still need to get a bit of a run-up though, to generate enough lift to get off the ground. You have to get at least just above your stalling speed.'

'I've noticed that fliers still tend to take off from buildings and cliffs when they can,' I said.

'Of course,' said Ruokonen. 'Taking off from the ground is the most physically demanding activity there is.'

'And the other factors?' I said. 'Wing shape and, what was it, aspect ratio?'

'Think of a hawk. Its wings are short and broad, perfect for manoeuvring in tricky situations and catching prey. It has a low aspect ratio. An albatross has long narrow wings, perfect for soaring and fast, low-energy-demand flight. It has a high aspect ratio.'

Ruokonen ran her fingers over the model of a flier skeleton on her desk. It was about half a metre tall. All the bones were precisely detailed and articulated. She stroked the outstretched wing bones. 'See, it's like having an extra pair of arms, but modified. Here's the humerus and this middle section is formed of the radius, ulna and wrist bones. This is the longest segment of the wing. This final part here is made up of the fused metacarpals—like the bones in the palm of your hand. The feathers anchor along the leading edge of the wing, here, and are free at the trailing edge, just like a bird, and that's where they can separate. As you can see, most of the wing is made up of feathers—this skeleton doesn't tell you much about the shape of the wings themselves.'

Looking at the model, this modified skeleton integrated with the wing bones, I felt a wave of nausea wash over me. I was seeing a hybrid creature, neither bird nor human, but something different. Other. A mammal shouldn't have arms and legs and then a whole other set of limbs. Three pairs. Like an insect. What was it? What were they? I stared at Ruokonen. What were we becoming?

'Now we come to the critical figures,' said Ruokonen. 'The numbers that really matter: *wing loading*. Wing loading is the ratio describing the mass that has to be borne up by the lift generated by each square centimetre of wing area. A low wing-loading ratio is around half a gram per centimetre squared of wing area. Birds with a low wing loading can take off easily and are good at soaring. Lammergeiers, for example. A high wing loading is around one point eight grams per centimetre squared and will give you a fast, powerful flier with great stamina, like a duck, which, however, will have some difficulty at take-off and be less manoeuvrable in the air. It's been suggested that a loading of two point five grams per centimetre may be the threshold at which flight is no longer possible.'

I nodded but the figures did not mean much to me. I could see they animated Ruokonen though; her cheeks had flushed slightly and her eyes glittered. This was the part of the talk that really excited her.

'Now listen to this,' she continued. 'With individual wing measurements of, say, two metres by one metre, a fifty-kilo human has a wing loading of one point two-five grams per square centimetre. Eminently suitable for Flight. Not that I'm saying you'd necessarily go with that shape. You need to tweak the shape depending on what type of flying you want to do. By paring down weight loads and augmenting muscle power, we've been able to reduce wing size and still have some room to move with regards to Flight specs—to alter dimensions for different kinds of Flight, without losing a favourable wing-loading ratio.'

'Oh,' I said. 'How on earth do you choose?'

'Well,' said Ruokonen, 'we tend to offer City fliers a compromise shape that gives them a fair amount of manoeuvrability but with the ability to do some soaring and endurance flying.' Here the slick showed an image of a flier with wings outstretched. 'They don't have the stamina of an albatross or the agility of a goshawk but then they don't have to migrate across the ocean or catch their food on the wing. For general purpose and pleasure flying it's a good shape. Bird wing shapes have evolved because their owners need them to survive. We have the luxury of adding wings on—we pay for the energy expense of Flight, if you like. Birds have to make it all count. We don't.'

I tried to picture what the Raptor might be capable of. 'If wing loading is so crucial,' I said, 'then how is it some fliers can carry another person?'

'You'll find there's at least one of several factors,' said Ruokonen. 'First, think of an eagle taking a lamb. The eagle is diving and already has enormous forward thrust and power. If a flier picks someone up they would usually be swooping down from on high. Second, you might have several fliers doing the carrying, such as in air rescue. Lastly, such a flight would always be very short, one way or the other. If you see what I mean.' She raised an eyebrow.

'Now, when the wings are grown, we attach them surgically and the sites they're attached to are already primed to knit together with the wings. There aren't any rejection problems because the cells are mostly your own DNA, even though they're modified, and your body recognises the additional genetic material as your own also. The treatments I've just described are somatic cell manipulation, of course. Somatic cells are all the cells of the body that do not pass on DNA to the next generation. With germline engineering—if we make changes in the germ cells, that is, the eggs and sperm of the parents—then the new children will just grow wings, and all the other necessary alterations, as they grow the rest of their bodies.'

'Wait a minute,' I said. 'Now you're talking alterations that will be passed on. Forever. Not just *adding* DNA to an individual human but altering the blueprint itself.'

'Yes,' Ruokonen said. 'For some of the new children. There aren't many. Yet. Flight modifications progress much more easily that way, though. And it's far more elegant to *grow* the wings than attach them.'

From what Peri had said, the Chesshyres were expecting Hugo to grow wings. As an architect Peter would desire the elegance Ruokonen was talking about. So, had one or both of them had germline engineering for Hugo's sake? I thought of Eliseev. Did he have the know-how for that? Well, Diomedea was one of the few outfits with the capacity, the sheer brute power of money, machines and expertise, for that kind of work, and Eliseev worked in their building, though that didn't necessarily imply a connection between them.

'Maybe growing wings is more elegant but how can you?' What I meant was how *dare* you? I struggled for an even tone as I said, 'It's one thing for an individual to choose all these things. It's something else to decide that their descendants forevermore will also be altered.'

'There are many who feel as you do. That hasn't stopped germline therapy to eliminate a number of medical conditions. I don't notice much agitation to stop that.'

'What about Origins?'

Ruokonen shrugged, as if it was beneath her even to acknowledge such fanatics.

'But those are not decisions we have the right to make. It's not just their descendants. It's the rest of us. You're splitting us off, into two species. Or more. God knows how many! Elegance is not a good enough reason.' I stopped, unable to express the strength of my feelings.

'You have the right to your opinion, of course,' Ruokonen said. I guessed she was used to dealing with the conflicting emotions Flight aroused in non-flier parents. She had to construct a convincing case for Flight to snare parents into agreeing to turn their offspring into fledglings.

Soberly, she continued, 'You have asked me to describe what happens, and I am telling you. Now if your son were to have the treatments there's no germline engineering involved, although later it could be done, if he wanted his children to fly more easily.'

'And if a baby of two fliers doesn't become a fledgling? Can the treatments still be carried out?' In other words, could a child like Hugo still become a flier like his parents?

Ruokonen thought. 'Well, as I've already indicated, fliers will not spontaneously have a fledgling unless they've had germline engineering themselves. It's a controversial area. There's not much information yet but available figures suggest that up to twenty percent of infants with flier parents who've been given germline therapy will still not fledge spontaneously. Standard practice has been not to attempt further treatments in those cases. That may be too cautious an approach but you should know that the treatments do fail in about fifteen to twenty percent of all other cases, and so it's been assumed that these babies are not good candidates. Personally I'm not convinced of that. There's not enough evidence one way or the other, there are still so few of them.'

Twenty percent of treatments failed. That was *after* the rigorous selection procedures. A high failure rate, especially considering the spectacular investment required just to give it a go.

Ruokonen was still speaking. 'The wings grow or are attached, the genetic material is added and there is also a medication regime. For a child the DNA therapy includes the timing of the development of Flight, which becomes as programmed as the drive to walk. It also includes avian navigational abilities.

'For older children and adults the medication regime is calibrated differentially, based on age, and part of its function is to give you the neural plasticity you need to incorporate such a vast retooling of your physical skills and even of your self-concept and your proprioception, which alters dramatically. You'd be surprised at the changes needed in brain-functioning, not just from the spatial demands of Flight, but from the expanded sensory input from the extra surface area of the body provided by the wings themselves.'

'Is Zefiryn part of the drug regime?' I said.

Ruokonen stood up from her desk and walked to a transparent wall to look out over the trees. She didn't seem surprised I'd heard of the drug. Well, it had featured prominently in the articles I'd skimmed, as it was one of the more lurid angles a journalist sending back dispatches from the wild frontier of Flight could tackle.

'Yes, Zefiryn is part of the medication regime. It's remarkably useful, particularly for finetuning sensory input needed in Flight, but like any medication, it should only be taken under medical supervision. In practice, all fliers take it. Zefiryn is not illegal, you know. Its status is in limbo; there are as yet no official guidelines for its use. I'm on one of the committees looking at those issues.' She came back to her desk and sat down.

'Some people say it's addictive,' I said.

Ruokonen rolled her eyes. 'It's possible to abuse any pharmacologically active substance,' she said. 'Any substance, really. Of course some become habituated.'

'Side effects?'

'You've looked it up, I take it.'

'Well, I read about the usual,' I said. 'Sweats. Weight loss. Tremors. Loss of affect. It's the rumours that interest me, that it's implicated in disappearances—'

'Rumours,' said Ruokonen, 'are just that, Mr Fowler. Rumours. Not data. Not evidence. I'm sure you can appreciate the importance of evidence. Now, other aspects of the regime involve ongoing assistance to the body in adjusting to the changing metabolism needed for the demands of Flight.'

'So their metabolism speeds up,' I said.

'In crude terms, yes, it does speed up. A flier extracts oxygen from the air with twice the efficiency that you do. They do it in some of the same ways as birds do, through air sacs inside their bones. The air sacs are connected to the lungs. These sacs also aid with thermoregulation, helping fliers dissipate excess heat generated in Flight. It's remarkably elegant because the wings themselves act as a bellows; as they move in flight they force huge amounts of air into these sacs and into the lungs.' She shook her head in admiration at the economy of the mechanism.

'So does the faster metabolism mean fliers don't live as long?'

'Certainly not,' said Ruokonen.

'Surely you don't know that yet,' I said. 'Are there any figures?'

'There are no data that I am aware of.'

'So you just don't know the long-term effects of all this yet?'

'I said we were into the second generation of real fliers though there have been odd prototypes around for some time. But first-generation fliers haven't reached old age yet.'

'Are there any side effects? There must be.'

'Well, I don't have recent figures but it's no secret that fertility is something of a casualty of the treatments.'

'Fertility,' I repeated. 'For how many?'

'Possibly up to twenty percent of fliers will have difficulty.'

'*What?* What does that mean?'

'The figures are based on both partners being fliers. Rates are better if the woman is not a flier. Individually fliers are still fertile—women have viable eggs, men have active sperm. But they don't result in babies at the rate we'd like.'

'That's a high price to pay,' I said. 'So what do you think is going wrong?'

'It's not my specialty but I think conception is not the problem. I would be investigating implantation if it were my area. Perhaps the woman is not sustaining the pregnancy. Body-fat levels may be too low; hormone levels may not be right. Also, to be honest, many fliers don't want to get pregnant.'

Women fliers don't like that, being grounded. Sometimes they never get back in the air, they say.

So the Chesshyres got Peri to have their baby for them before she was allowed to get her wings. That fitted what I knew about her membership of Flight Gym and Hugo's age.

'What else?' I said. 'There must be other effects.'

'Well, the whole thing is an effect,' said Ruokonen. 'It's hard to tease out what is the main event and what is what you'd call a *side effect*. Preening your feathers every day, eating seven times a day, practising flying for at least an hour every day, maintaining a drug regime indefinitely? These are not *side effects*. These are *what it is* to be a flier. I said that some treatments fail. They fail at the point where the person has to alter their sense of themselves, of who they are. Physically everything is going well but the person can't become a *flier*—they remain just someone with wings. You become a different person when you become a flier. Different things matter to you.'

'Do different things matter enough that some turn Wild?' I said.

'That's a myth,' said Ruokonen, a shade too quickly for the casual tone she was aiming for. 'Some fliers push the limits of their abilities. A few get lost or fall out of the sky and people claim they've turned Wild. It's rubbish. Ignorant scaremongering.'

'How can you know that for sure?' I said. Typical doctor, with her arrogant refusal to discuss something awkward. Only when it was so obvious it couldn't be denied any longer would the authorised version of reality catch up with what everyone knew.

Ruokonen stood up. 'I've put together a literature package for parents. Excuse me for a moment.'

I checked my slick as she left the room. A message. Henryk. *Checkd out SGB. NO bdy. No mre wld gse chse! MATE.*

Alright, Henryk, no need to shout. Great. No body. Trails on Luisa so far were ending in blanks. I could wait for Peri's return, grill her on everything she knew about her friend. But I didn't want to wait. Instead I sent a message to Wilson, the *hikikomori*, my old technician and my best hope of trying to crack Little Angels. I didn't know if Luisa had got work through the agency but it was worth checking, and I needed more information and names from the agency anyway. I thought for a moment then sent Wilson a PS. Could he have a go at Eliseev's systems while he was at it?

I got up and went over to the bookcase against the internal far wall. A series of thick texts took up the first shelf. *The Anatomy of Flight. Fliers: Some diseases and parasites. Inheriting the Wind: Papers from the 12th Annual Reykjavik Diomedea–MicroRNA/Corvid symposium on Flight. The Eye of the Hurricane: Ethics and values of Flight. DSM-XX-TR Casebook—Flier Supplement 2nd Edition: A learning companion to the diagnostic and statistical manual of mental disorders. Flight Specs: The journal of Flight specialities.*

I picked up the journal. 'Validity of DSM-XX Subtypes for Flier-associated Disorders: Specific diagnostic criteria—general physician/Flight specialist concordance' read the title of the main article. I put the journal back. The technical literature was as impenetrable as I'd expected. These books were for show, except maybe the essays.

Ruokonen would have anything remotely technical on slick and updated constantly. On the shelf below was a black book, silver letters along the spine. *Seven Ravens: Rhymes and tales for modern children*. I picked it up and flipped through the pages idly, until my attention was snagged by something familiar. Called 'Bonaparte', it was the rhyme Avis had started to sing. I read over the whole thing.

Baby, baby, naughty baby,
hush you squalling chick, I say.
Peace this moment, peace, or maybe
rough wild wings will pass this way.

Baby, baby, he's a giant,
huge and ragged, heartless, wild.
And he breakfasts, dines, rely on't
every day on naughty child.

Baby, baby, if he hears you
as he's winging past this house,
swooping down at once he'll seize you
just as hawk on little mouse.

He will take you, higher, higher,
o'er the icy clouds so tall.
There he'll drop you, little baby,
you will fly before you fall.

Well, that was brutal enough to be authentic. It must be based on something very old. I put the book back and wandered over to the transparent outside wall. I was becoming aware of the physical split between fliers and non-fliers. Our medical and scientific reality was different, our experience of the physical world radically different, but it had not occurred to me that they would have their own culture, their own stories, even their own ways of raising children. What sort of father could I be to Thomas when I couldn't even share the most important element of his life? What protection and advice could I offer about a realm I would never experience?

Ruokonen returned and handed me a small slick. 'You will want to look at this if you're serious about your little boy having the treatments.'

'Thank you for your time.' As if I hadn't paid for it. *But ye are forgers of lies, ye are all physicians of no value.* Thanks for that, Job.

Ruokonen was already speaking to someone else on her slick. 'Yes, yes,' she said. 'I told you, I've already scheduled time for that. Yes, I'll be giving evidence to the authority. I'm unlikely to forget a meeting with the minister. Well, reassure Dr Summerscale I'll *be* there.'

I paused on my way out. 'Dr Ruokonen, do you have children?'

Ruokonen's face was impassive. 'No.'

'What is *Aquila non captat muscas*?'

'An eagle does not try to catch flies, Mr Fowler. It means—'

'Yes,' I broke in. 'I understand what it means. Don't sweat the small stuff. It all looks big from where I'm standing.'

'Look,' Ruokonen said, softening, 'I don't envy you having to decide. I do understand—well, not understand, but I do sympathise. It must be hard.'

'Was it worth it? For you?'

'I think the answer to that is obvious.' She shook her wings. A gleam of rose flickered.

'I guess,' I said. It didn't help. I could ask every flier in the world and it wouldn't help.

I clambered down the tree, my head spinning. Ruokonen had been right. The information had not made things clearer. As I walked through the meadow, I looked up at the sky, a sky now brassy with late-morning summer light. The sun had beaten the smaller meadow-dwellers into submission and the grass lay silent. A magpie zoomed overhead, out of the oak branches and off across the City.

Hast thou with him spread out the sky, which is strong and as a molten looking-glass . . . Doth the hawk fly by thy wisdom? . . . Doth the eagle mount up at thy command? Not exactly. But we gave ourselves wings, we mounted up at our own command. By our wisdom? Well, that's the question, isn't it? The how-many-dollars-does-it-take question that Flight is these days. One topic we hadn't discussed and yet it was the most critical: how much does it cost?

How much does it cost?

Does anyone know the answer?

And yet, I could *see* Thomas, flying above the clouds. Soaring in the warm air above the desert. Skimming over the sea. My little boy, lost to me forever. As he would be anyway. But how could I bear for him to become another creature altogether, with another creature's genes inserted between him and me? Not just another creature, a whole different order, class, of life. My real question now was not what could Thomas *do*, it was what would he *be*? Finally, though, the only difference was which choice would make him happier. No way to know that. No way ever to know.

As I walked towards the nearest station Thien called me.

'Yes?' I said, dodging a bike zooming past me with two live banana trees tied on the back.

'Do you want the good news or the bad news?' she said.

'Hit me with it.'

'I'm very sorry but we can't resurrect Taj. We can refit the AI so the car can navigate but we can't retrieve Taj's history and personality profile.'

'*What?*' I was shocked. It hadn't crossed my mind they wouldn't be able to resuscitate Taj. Taj, gone forever. Taj, who, I now realised, was the closest thing to a partner I'd had since setting up on my own.

'We've run diagnostics on your car,' Thien continued. 'I'm guessing you didn't know about the redback hitching a ride.'

'Jesus wept, Thien.' A redback was one of the newest tracking devices on the market. 'I checked it out before I left the City.'

'I know, it's a bitch, eh? Don't blame yourself. These bastards read inert, like dirt or a dead insect to the kind of tests you can run. We spend a fortune keeping up with this kind of shit. We only bother 'cause of the government and security service contracts we get. The beauty of it is, when you plunged Taj into the creek you buggered it up. This has cost someone a pretty penny.' Thien's voice brightened. 'Someone must think you're important.'

'Yeah,' I said. 'Great. Was there good news in there? Must have missed it.'

10

CLOUD CITY

It hadn't occurred to me Chesshyre would take me *up*, to the top of his tower, but he'd insisted. My stomach plummeted as the lift zoomed skywards. *End Mixed Zone*, flashed the display panel as we rose, still accelerating. *What the hell does that mean?* I was about to demand, when I gasped. The floor beneath my feet had winked into transparency. Now I could see nothing but a soaring panorama over the City through the walls and below my feet. Cold sweat trickled from my armpits and my breathing came shallow and rapid.

I checked Hugo's position again, as I had every few minutes since the signal began transmitting; Peri and Hugo were still heading south. This reassured me against the uneasiness triggered by the Raptor last night and now the knowledge I'd been followed. Still hadn't heard from Janeane, though.

'Ah,' said the investor, a flier who had joined Chesshyre and me uninvited at the base of Cloud City, 'I'm looking forward to going up on that prow.'

A message. Wilson, saying he should have some results for me later that night. He wouldn't try to enter Little Angels' or Eliseev's systems until after hours.

Aspire to Cloud City, the display panel prompted. *The life you evolved to enjoy*. It streamed images of the stratospheric swirl of the central tower with a prow jutting from the top, cleaving fluffy white clouds the way a ship breasts heavy seas. When finished, this prow would boast a forest with waterfalls in freefall over the edge, down the buttress reinforcing the prow for hundreds of metres. About a third of the way down the central spire what looked like the top of a cloud forest broadened out from the spire into a filigreed canopy over the City.

'We've entered the section of the tower that will rotate,' Chesshyre remarked to the investor.

'Rotate?' I said. The lift began to slow.

'The tower is like a shattered, mechanical whorl of an opening flower, a practical shape because the structure's mass diminishes as it rises. This distribution of mass makes the structure more stable, as does the prow with its buttress. From above the cloud canopy two-thirds up, however, the top section will rotate three-sixty degrees every ninety minutes.'

The lift stopped. The doors opened onto blue air. The investor bounded out first and Chesshyre followed into that nothingness. As if that weren't bad enough, the display in the lift announced: *250th floor. Restricted Zone. Fliers only*.

Chesshyre turned and raised his eyebrows as I hung back. 'Come on,' he said, smiling slightly. He shivered his wings right down to the tips, a deep shudder of what seemed like irritation that made all his feathers shift in a papery rustle. The shiver released a wave of the peppery sandalwood smell I associated with Chesshyre. The more time I spent with fliers, the more I saw they had a whole other language, an array of winged gestures, from the massive stretch of unfolded wings to the subtlest quiver. This language was one of the many things that made fliers so alien to us normal humans. 'It's perfectly safe.'

Safe! What was safe about being dragged to the top of Chesshyre's little dovecote, a kilometre above the earth?

Gingerly, I crept out of the lift. To my horror I found myself in the open, no roof above me, no parapet between me and the edge of the building.

Ahead of us stretched the field of the prow, broad at its base, near where we stood, and narrowing to a sharp point in the distance. Its surface, unornamented as yet with the forest and waterfalls promised by the lift display, waved green and silver in the breeze.

'This way,' said Chesshyre and, unbelievably, he climbed down a shallow flight of steps onto the prow and began crossing its broad surface, the investor ahead of him beating a glossy path through the shining grasses as if through water. The weirdness of walking over an alpine meadow in the sky was heady. Grasses interleaved with meadow flowers rustled at my knee and released a musky-sweet scent as I crushed them underfoot. The grasses flowed up to the edge of the prow, which fell away on every side, undercut as steeply as the curved hull of a ship.

Directly ahead of me, rising up beyond the sharp end of the prow, a thunderhead exploded silently, white and grey billows puffing outwards and upwards so fast I felt I was being swept upwards myself and the rush poured through me, a stream of exhilaration and motion sickness.

'I'm going to test out your house thermal generator,' the investor called to Chesshyre.

As the prow narrowed I slowed. That shining thunderhead was about to unleash extreme weather onto this unprotected field. 'Mr Chesshyre,' I called. As he turned, the investor leapt off the prow and was blown back over our heads.

'This is not the weather to be testing a thermal generator,' Chesshyre muttered.

The prow pointed eastwards and I could see past the thunderhead all the way over the City to the sea. I twisted my neck to watch the wind streaming the anvil of the thunderhead high above us into the west, where, through the incomplete top floor behind me, I could see a broken view of the low rampart of mountains rising up from the plain. To the north and south stretched more City suburbs and the gleaming coastline. Shafts of sunlight broke here and there through the swift-moving cloud and the wind set up a low harmonic moan over the plain and through the tower. The investor was now a dot arrowing westwards and down. Was he coming back or simply vanishing in that abrupt way unique to fliers?

'Strange,' Chesshyre said as he came up to me. 'I can't even imagine what it's like out there.' He indicated the horizon, his hand describing a precise, graceful arc, an architect's gesture delineating space, that sketched the coastline receding from us.

He was talking about RaRA-land, which was more unimaginable to him than outer space. Perhaps it was just as well. He didn't understand the danger Peri and Hugo faced in such hostile country. Still, I could hardly blame him for that; I hadn't seen it myself until I was sitting in the Naxos Cafe.

'You'll see why we're here in a minute,' said Chesshyre and stalked alongside me through his sky-high savannah like the winged predator he was.

I edged towards the prow's end, taking comfort from Chesshyre's solid presence beside me. The bulk of his wings shielded me from the wind.

Finally we reached the point of the prow, its edges barely half a metre away from me on either side. Ahead of us jutted a sliver, like the bowsprit projecting from a ship, and at the end of this glimmered a clear shape that seemed no more than an interruption of the light. I squinted, trying to make out the borders of this structure. It shifted slightly in the wind. Without hesitation Chesshyre stepped onto the bowsprit. He turned to face me, waiting. If he expected me to use *that* as a bridge he could think again.

Chesshyre could not be serious, bringing me here. It was not safe, and even when it was finished it would never be safe for the likes of me.

The bridge laid down its narrow course over the dizzying drop, lacking sides or handrails. 'No,' I said. 'I can't go up there.'

A brief smile illuminated Chesshyre's face. 'Yes, you can. There's something you must see.' He stood, his wings partly unfurled for balance, and held out his hand to me.

Now I was in a quandary. I did not want to take his hand, to be led like a small child. Every time I entered the world of fliers, whether riding the flying fox, climbing Ruokonen's tree or, now, panicking at the beginning of this pathway, I was swept, for good or ill, back into childhood, with its wondrous possibilities, its abrupt terrors.

Chesshyre waited, his hand outstretched, his blue feathers ruffling in the wind. I couldn't back away now; for one thing, I couldn't make it down to the ground by myself as I'd noticed the lift was security-keyed to Chesshyre by his voice. The moment I'd entered that bloody lift I'd unwittingly put myself in Chesshyre's power.

'Don't worry,' Chesshyre said. His voice was calm, even slightly mocking, but now there was a forced, steely quality to his composure. He was becoming impatient with me. I was sweating, my skin cold and waxy. 'In the unlikely event you were to fall, I'm strong enough to catch you.'

Jesus wept, what was this—a thinly veiled threat? Did he do this kind of thing for fun? Oh, yes, I could imagine Chesshyre out on the town for the night, finding some poor girl, bringing her up here, forcing her to yield. She'd be like jelly in his arms, and she'd see the same cold amusement in his eyes I was seeing now.

All at once I was certain it was something he was perfectly capable of doing. Horribly, for a moment, I could understand exactly why it would be such an intense pleasure for him; a demonstration of his command, not only over his own powerful body and Flight skills but over the life of one of us lower creatures, non-fliers. And in his own space, a space that he'd created.

I swallowed hard, stepped onto the bridge, and took Chesshyre's hand. His palm was dry and as his hand closed around mine the heat of his flesh sent a shock through me. That overclocked metabolism. Would Thomas be that warm? The bridge reared up at weird angles as my knees melted. Wisps of cloud blew under our feet, over our heads. Without Chesshyre's grasp I would fall.

Now I was sure he'd done exactly this to Peri: brought her here, taken her in this terrifying place, Peri long-limbed, fragile, Chesshyre's blue wings covering her, high on this spar in the gathering twilight.

Chesshyre pulled me to the middle of the bridge. The cloud swirled down, wrapping us in cold grey. 'I have to know if I can trust you,' he growled, his voice deeper and angrier than I'd heard it before. He transferred his grasp to my shoulder and I winced as his fingers gripped me. 'You've already taken this case to the police, haven't you? Don't lie to me!'

I stared up at him. I knew he'd had me followed and now, too late, I understood why he'd brought me here onto this bridge, where he could interrogate me, use my vertigo to torture me until he was satisfied I was telling the truth. I'm no innocent when it comes to interrogation techniques myself and I should've seen this coming. As a cop I'd experienced how quickly an encounter could turn from a businesslike meeting to an ambush that threatened my life but now, as a private operator, situations like this were more ill-defined. When did I challenge Chesshyre as the contract between client and investigator switched to the stalking of hunter and hunted? We slipped back and forth across that line without acknowledgement, like the night before when I'd surprised the Raptor spying on me.

'Of course you can trust me,' I gasped, *he-knows-I-lied-he-knows-I-lied-he-knows-I-lied* racing through my mind. Structures hundreds of metres below swam up to greet me through gaps in the mist. There was nothing I wouldn't have said. 'I didn't go to the police. I got help from an old friend. That's all. Don't you think they'd have knocked on your door by now if I was lying?'

Chesshyre stared deep into my eyes. His breath was hot on my cheek. His fingers gripped my shoulder tighter, causing me real pain, but to shake him off would be suicide.

My slick vibrated in my pocket. *Thank goodness.* Here might be solid proof I was telling the truth, enough to get me off this bridge alive. 'Can't talk here,' I panted. 'Something I have to tell you, very urgent. About Hugo.'

'*What?*' said Chesshyre.

'Off the bridge first.'

Chesshyre stared at me a moment longer, then grabbed my wrist and led me off the walkway which at its end opened directly into a transparent room hung over the abyss like a flower bowing over its stem.

Once safely away from the doorway, I fumbled for my slick and saw that it was, finally, a message from Janeane.

'That was confirmation,' I said, still trembling with fear and pain, 'that Peri is on her way to the City, with Hugo, as per our agreement. You can stop spying on me. Maybe now,' I added, 'you'll believe what I tell you.' Chesshyre snatched the slick from me. He was lucky I didn't punch him for what he did up on that bridge. I felt like laying him out cold.

So I had mixed feelings when Chesshyre handed the slick back, with an expression I'd never seen before, his face glowing with pure, unalloyed joy. It surged over him so strongly I felt the backwash of it too. If I'd not been so light-headed with reeling from terror to anger to relief myself, I might almost have been embarrassed to see such naked feeling on the face of someone so reticent. He looked expansive, a man who was unexpectedly friends with all the world.

'That,' said Chesshyre, 'is wonderful news. Thank you.' He was almost giddy. 'Wonderful,' he repeated. 'You've done a great job.'

I stood for a moment, catching my breath and looking around me. *Room* was too ordinary a word for this place. *Pod* might be a better description for this undulating transparency where there was no abrupt angle between floor and walls and roof, its material as clear as water, like the walls of Ruokonen's treehouse. The view was now mostly the texture and drift of cloud.

'This is my office,' Chesshyre said.

Of course. It was worthy of him. He'd created this, the premier spot in his own building, and why shouldn't he claim it for himself?

So this was how it was to be. We were to pretend nothing had happened on the bridge. Now I had to put aside my anger and fear and accept Chesshyre's sudden sunniness. What choice did I have?

A drift of grey cloud cleared below and I found myself staring down at what looked like a giant chessboard, its black and white squares bounded by a dark embankment.

'There's something I've wanted to say to you,' I said, turning back from the outer wall to face Chesshyre. He'd picked up a slick from his desk and now glanced at me, his eyes widening in alarm.

'*Sanctus Ivo erat Brito, / Advocatus, et non latro / Res miranda populo.*'

He stared at me. 'You've got to be kidding me. *You* went to St Ivo's?'

I smiled.

'Jesus, your dad must be disappointed. A St Ivo's boy going into the police.'

I laughed aloud at that. 'No. Well, yes.'

He recited, '*Saint Yvo was a Breton and a lawyer, But not dishonest —An astonishing thing in people's eyes.* I used to look at that painting of him every morning in assembly: lawyer, book in hand, enthroned between rich and poor litigants, an angel at his head, a lion at his feet. Remember what they called him?'

'Yes,' I said. 'Every day of my police training. Saint Ivo: advocate of the poor. Patron saint of judges, lawyers, jurists. And orphans. An interesting list.'

'And abandoned people,' said Chesshyre. 'Don't forget them.'

'No,' I said. 'I spend my professional life trying not to forget about them.' *But you designed the Church of the Seraphim. Do you go there now, instead of the church of your childhood?* Not only will fliers have their own city in the clouds but there's a religion just for them too, though angels were now out of a job, what with all these winged types turning up at the gates of their very own heaven.

Chesshyre motioned at the shadowed wall opposite and the entire surface lit up, glowing with a complex, many-layered design; he circled his hand in mid-air and the design rotated. The design was a section of Cloud City.

'Look at this,' Chesshyre said, using hand gestures to flick through cross-sections of Cloud City. For the first time I could grasp fully the size and intricacy of the proposed city, which was much larger than the complex we were now standing in; far-flung sections of it extended over the entire central area of the City. Cloud City would frame a complete existence for fliers. They could live, work, play, study, shop, swim and fly without ever leaving it. When this city-in-the-sky was finished, we non-fliers would be living in the shadow, literally, of their new world.

My head was spinning. I pictured Thomas living in Cloud City, working in these vertiginous offices, flying to a perch at the top of a waterfall, playing with his children in that park hung on the edge of a chasm, living his entire life without touching the ground. I saw myself visiting him there, an old man who'd have to meet him down on the lower levels while Thomas's real life would be inaccessible to me, beyond my imagination.

I pointed to parts of the design that looked as if they were ruined, melting into air, reminding me of the roofless feel of Chesshyre's house. 'Those areas aren't really unfinished, are they?'

'No. Flier spaces let in the sky as much as possible. We hunger for space, even in the form of drops, chasms. It's one reason fliers and non-fliers aren't good at sharing spaces. *We* get claustrophobia; *they* get vertigo.'

So I belonged to a *they* now.

I sat down on a bench against the wall, staring at the new city, overcome with awe. Was *this* what Chesshyre had wanted to show me? Chesshyre moved in a different world to any I'd known before and, like Peri, I could not see any space for Hugo to share in it. This irony seemed to escape Chesshyre, who'd created this separate world for fliers—*fliers and non-fliers aren't good at sharing spaces*—before coming to terms with Hugo's failure to fledge. Chesshyre and I were mirror images of each other, struggling with the same dilemma. He'd be a flier father with a non-flier son; I was a non-flier father with a flier, maybe, for a son. Each of us contending with a child completely unlike the one we'd expected, hoped for or could understand.

Chesshyre moved closer to me. 'Truly, Hugo was well?' he asked, the lines between his eyes deepening. He put his hand on my arm for a second, as if he could feel whether I was telling the truth.

I nodded.

'The arrogance,' Chesshyre said. 'The presumption of that little—who the hell does she think she is? How could she think she'd do better for Hugo? And she's subjected him to who knows what dangers! We've given Hugo everything. *Everything*.'

No doubt you have. But how can Hugo, without wings, inherit your world?

Chesshyre was pacing. Now he stopped. 'Fowler, *what did Peri tell you*?'

Finally, the question I'd been expecting all along. It wasn't in Peri's interest for me to answer it.

'It doesn't matter, Mr Chesshyre. I was hired to do a job. I've done it. I want what you want: Hugo home, safe and sound.'

'Of course.' Chesshyre straightened up, rubbing his neck. 'I can't bear the waiting. Every minute drags like an hour.' Then as suddenly as a cat scratching at a flea bite he grabbed an odd-looking comb from the top of the desk and raked at a spot on one of his wings.

He flung the comb down and pressed his hands into his eyes. 'You want to know the truth, Fowler? I love my son. Whatever that girl has said or done, that's the truth.'

I could see the pain on his face. He looked tired. I did feel for him, then.

'You're asking a lot of me, Fowler. I have to trust you, I have to wait for Hugo.'

There it was, that was as close as Chesshyre would get to apologising for threatening my life on the bridge.

'It won't be long now,' I said, more gently than I felt. 'But, Peter,' I added, using his first name unexpectedly and watching him startle, as I'd intended, 'you really do have to trust me. Peri is returning, as you've seen. Don't do anything to put her or your son in danger. You *must* call off your Raptor.'

'I don't know what you're talking about.'

'Peter, come on! That bloody thing was at my flat last night. It was terrifying—'

I broke off. I'd been about to add that he'd put my own son at risk but the look on Peter's face of stunned confusion, followed by fear, was so real that I fell silent. He truly did not know what I was talking about. And that was the worst news I'd had in a long time.

I frantically ran through a list of people who knew about this case. Avis. Harper. Eliseev. Who else could have put a Raptor on my trail? Why?

'I must go,' I said. I really wanted to get back down to the ground. Through the dimmed walls I could see flashes of lightning and hear the deep collision of thunder.

Chesshyre blinked, came back to life. 'Come this way.' He stepped out of the room and to my great relief did not aim for the bridge but climbed downwards along a walkway I hadn't even seen from above as we'd first entered his office. This walkway led to a door that opened into the curving buttress underneath the prow itself. As we approached the door, thunder and lightning brawling around us, it slid back and I hurried inside to safety.

As we paced along a corridor with rooms opening off from it to our left, I could see to our right thick rain falling past round windows that looked like portholes.

After a moment the rain hardened into a barrage of white and I heard a heavy banging, as if a mob were throwing stones at Cloud City.

A flier was walking, no, striding towards us down the corridor and Chesshyre called out, 'Halley!'

'Peter. I've been trying to get hold of you. I know you've been working twenty-hour days but you just cannot go to ground in the weeks before SkyNation. Especially as you're the star this year.'

SkyNation. I'd heard of the annual SkyNation parties but hadn't taken any notice. A three-day debauch for wealthy fliers hadn't held any interest for me.

A tall woman in youngish middle-age swept up to us, bringing a breath of lustrous cold with her, as if she carried the wild weather in from outside on her feathers. Ice crystals slicked down her hair and feathers as if she'd been dusted with sugar. Her coat and dark trousers were spattered with mud. There was that light in her eyes and on her pink cheeks that you see on children when they've been running and playing.

She shook out her feathers, then looked at Chesshyre and me, inquiring. It was clear she expected him to explain my presence; she was the first person I'd seen who assumed an air of authority around Chesshyre.

I was taken aback. The woman was striking, sturdy for a flier and all dark and light, pale skin and dark gaze, her wings patterned and barred, grey and black and cream, like a hawk's, her dark hair piled up on her head.

'This is Zeke Fowler,' said Chesshyre. 'Zeke, Halcyon Kohn.' Well, that explained her self-possession. This was Halcyon Kohn, the *celebrated* Halcyon Kohn. I'd just been introduced to the senior partner of the firm. I thought of Peri on her lonely flight back to the City with Hugo. That an abandoned girl from RaRA-land had joined this elite even as a servant seemed more remarkable to me the more time I spent in their world.

Kohn inclined her head, then surprised me by shaking my hand. She turned to Chesshyre, saying, 'Peter, Arto Flores has been asking for you again. He's getting so desperate he's taken to pestering *me*.'

Chesshyre's mood had fractured; moments ago he'd been delighted by the news that Hugo was returning but now he looked almost as uneasy as I felt. Fliers were so mercurial; was it the treatments, all the drugs they took? Chesshyre raised his eyebrows slightly at Kohn as if to say *And?*

Kohn smiled, puzzled. She said, 'I don't understand why you don't just take him on. He's rich and he wants to build a dance training centre for fliers. Are you just showing him who's boss or what?'

'I'm *busy*,' said Chesshyre. 'Look, Halley, I like Flores but he's living proof you can be the smartest guy in the room and still have no more visual sense than a fruit fly.'

Halley. So that was her nickname. These two were close then. I'd never seen Chesshyre speak with such energy to anyone else.

'I don't have time to educate him and I'm not in the mood to have someone fight me every step of the way.' Chesshyre looked so austere I almost laughed. What tests did clients have to pass for Chesshyre to condescend to work for them?

Kohn caught my expression and allowed the slightest creasing around her eyes to suggest her thoughts might be similar to mine on that subject.

'Alright, alright,' Chesshyre said. 'I'll speak to him myself.'

'Do it now,' said Halcyon Kohn. 'Or you never will. I can show Mr Fowler out. I want to look in on level thirty myself.'

'I'll keep you informed,' I said to Chesshyre as Kohn led me away.

Kohn matched my stride as we walked; she was at least my height, though of course her wings made her more massive. She tilted her head like a great falcon, and said in a low voice, 'So you're looking for little Hugo? It's going well?'

'Yes.'

'So Hugo is safe? He'll be back soon?'

'Yes,' I repeated. 'He is safe.'

She let out a sigh. 'That is such a relief. We've all been beside ourselves and I hardly dare ask Peter anything. I don't know how he's kept working through all this. I suppose it's just as well that he has.'

'Yes.'

So Kohn wanted to question me. Well, that was fine because I wanted to question her too. An opportunity to speak to her alone about the case was too good to pass up, especially now that things were happening, like a Raptor checking out my flat for reasons I couldn't yet grasp. I didn't know everything that was going on and, worse, it seemed Chesshyre didn't either.

'So, you know Hugo then?' I began.

'I wouldn't go that far. I've seen him a few times.'

The porthole windows we were passing showed bright sun striking down through a stream of falling water, water the building was shedding after the rainstorm.

'And Peri Almond?'

Kohn frowned.

'The nanny.'

'Yes, yes of course. She used to wait for Peter here sometimes, at the office, when she'd been in the city with Hugo.'

'Did you find it odd that a country girl like Peri had wings?'

'I wouldn't know, Mr Fowler.'

'Ms Kohn, it's very important that you tell me anything you know about how Peri got her wings.'

Kohn was silent for a moment. 'How is this relevant?'

'Peri took Hugo,' I said. 'Hugo will be returned safely but he's not back yet and I have to know what factors will influence Peri's behaviour.'

Kohn stopped and turned to look at me. I returned her stare. She ruffled her feathers and the movement shook a heady powdery floral odour from her wings. She narrowed her eyes, then stood up straighter. I felt the stab of elation I always got when I could see someone had made up their mind to speak.

'I knew that Peri looked after Hugo.'

'Did you think she was good with him?'

'Yes,' Kohn said. 'She had an ease with Hugo and maybe that irritated Avis. That was the feeling I had. It's a cliché, I guess, because there's truth in it. The mother's jealous that the nanny who spends all the time with her baby is more at ease with him than she is.'

'You don't think Peri could have been a bit . . . unstable?' I ventured.

Kohn shook her head. 'I wouldn't know. Obviously something was wrong. Avis—' She hesitated.

'Please,' I said, very quietly. 'You're not being disloyal. Anything you can tell me might help . . . Peter. And Hugo.'

Kohn sighed. 'You've met Avis?'

'Yes. She was under a lot of stress.'

Kohn grimaced. 'She's *always* like that.'

'Oh. You mean—there was a vacuum? Peri filled it?'

'Something like that.'

What did she mean? What really went on in that house? The risk you take, I guess—if you outsource your whole goddamn life, you can't be too surprised when you find someone else living it for you, can you? Still, Peter was Kohn's colleague, her friend, and I'd assumed she would see Peri as monstrous, entirely to blame, for what had happened. That she did not think so was surprising. I wanted to ask if she knew about the bargain between Peri and the Chesshyres, but if I spilled the beans on that deal Chesshyre really would kill me. I edged as close to discussing it as I dared.

'Do you know their doctor, Dr Eliseev? Didn't you ever wonder why Peri was able to nurse Hugo?'

Kohn fixed a piercing stare on me, then turned away. That she would not answer this seemed unfathomably sinister to me just then, as if she must know much more than she would tell me. We were at the end of the corridor and I blinked in the sudden sunlight as I came out of the exit and found myself at the broad end of the prow again. Storm clouds had been torn into grey shreds far overhead and were streaming away and the meadow was heaped with white so dazzling it hurt my eyes.

'Oh, this is great,' said Kohn. 'I've been so looking forward to this.' Her low voice was now pitched higher with excitement as she stared out over the field of ice, the meltwater rushing over the edges of the prow exactly as promised by the billboard.

'What is it?' I said.

'Indescribable. You have to see it.'

Kohn splashed her way across the wet field and for the second time I walked through that meadow, now slushy with ice and rain. Kohn headed for the northern side of the prow and as I neared where she was standing, leaning almost over the edge, I could hear the rushing as the water streamed over and fell into the sky. Water seeped into my shoes. I edged as close as I dared, not wanting to slip. What could be so wonderful that Kohn was beckoning me so urgently?

A gust of wind blew a pane of droplets back up into the air above us, thinning it to vapour. This shawl of water billowed right over us, dropping in sheer veils of crimson and gold and sea-green and blue and purple, the water unravelled into pure blazes of colour by the shafts of the afternoon sun. I'd never seen anything like it. A net of indigo unrolled at our feet then sheared itself into azure ribbons. We stood still, wrapped in this whirl of colour spinning over us and falling away down the flank of Cloud City, the dye washes running iridescent over the paper-white tower.

We said nothing, we made no move, we just stood together so close I could feel Kohn's breath on my cheek, waiting for the earth to turn, to alter the angle of the sun's rays and switch off this shimmering rainbow scurry.

Through the transparent falling sheets of colour I could see the enormous chessboard on the ground below us again. 'What is that?'

'That? That's a house thermal generator. Did you know, Peter is considered the best house thermal designer in the world?'

'I have to ask—'

'Sorry,' said Kohn. 'A house thermal is a thermal that appears consistently in the same place. So, if you're clever, you can design a spot that will have properties, such as that alternating light and dark with the dark boundary, which will generate consistent thermals. Naturally Peter's designed for a few house thermals to take up residence around this site.'

The light vanished from the water. My feet were numb. I backed away from the edge.

Kohn caught up with me. 'Peter is brilliant, you know. I hope you can see that.' At last, we were heading for the lifts. So, was this her answer to my questions about the Chesshyres? Not to judge Peter by ordinary standards? Was she afraid my investigations would harm him?

As we waited for the lift, Kohn looked at me in the way Chesshyre had when I went to his house; she wanted to see this space through my eyes. 'You're the first non-flier to set foot up here,' she said. 'I'm surprised Peter brought you here.'

So was I, believe me, so was I.

'It's overwhelming,' I said.

'You managed. You even enjoyed it, a bit.'

I smiled at that. *Lady, you don't know the half of it.*

She smiled back. Was this woman, this flier, this senior partner of the firm, *flirting* with me? It had been so long since that happened I told myself I couldn't read women anymore. I was misinterpreting simple friendliness.

The lift opened its doors and I stepped in, though not with as much relief as I'd anticipated. Much of my fear had drained away after the confrontation with Chesshyre on the bridge.

'Actually, I need someone like you,' Kohn said. 'How would you like to attend SkyNation? As a guest of Kohn Chesshyre Li?'

I stared at Kohn. So she did want something from me. But what? And why? Such an invitation was a once-in-a-lifetime chance. Even fliers had trouble getting into SkyNation, I knew. You had to have contacts. Now I had contacts.

'I thought SkyNation was only for fliers.'

Kohn shook her head. As the lift flashed into the mixed zone its floor turned opaque. 'SkyNation is *mostly* for fliers. It's not just a party; it's a laboratory, where we test out different ways of how fliers can live. What does being a flier mean? Does it mean merely being able to fly? It's not that simple.' Now Kohn sounded like Ruokonen. 'But my difficulty is that this year I've had to seek planning permission for SkyNation because for the first time it's being held above the CBD. One permit condition imposes a quota of non-fliers in attendance which I'm not even close to filling. Peter couldn't care less; he's above worrying about that sort of thing. I'm the one that has to deal with the department. Most non-fliers turn to water just at the idea of SkyNation, though I've found a few climbers and even a construction worker or two with no fear of heights. You've coped up here today so I think you'd do well.'

'Really? Maybe. Depends when it is,' I said.

'Starts two weeks from Friday.' Kohn handed me an irregular palm-sized slick, depthless and blue, a piece torn from the sky. 'You'll need that to get in. It's keyed to me. Without it even I won't be able to help you. People out there would do a lot to get their hands on one of these. Keep it safe.'

The lift slowed. We'd reached level thirty.

'Thank you, Ms Kohn,' I said as she left the lift.

Before the doors closed she said, 'Please, call me Halley.'

More proof of that mercurial flier nature. Did I really want to spend time up in the sky with such impulsive, crazy people?

Perhaps I did. When it reached the ground I bounded out of the lift. I wanted to run and jump the way a child does for joy, wonder, relief. Instead I walked quickly towards the light rail, head up, looking into the sky, out into the rain which was whirling around in great blowy gusts again, even more pleased with myself than when I'd entered Cloud City. This was an extraordinary chance to learn more about fliers, close-up. I owed that much to Thomas.

As I stared up at the sky I noticed a dark figure circling above Cloud City. It was so high, it must be enormous to look that big from the ground.

Of course I shouldn't have felt so pleased. Hugo wasn't back yet, a Raptor was shadowing me, and I was disregarding my cardinal rule: things can always get worse.

At the entrance to the light rail I checked the sky again. Not many fliers up there, weather wasn't good enough, but that one large flier seemed to have followed me. Unless he was circling so high it just seemed that way. I was at a serious disadvantage; he was just a big spot to me but at that height, if he was on Zefiryn, he'd be able to see me and everyone else on the street with the clarity of an eagle. Was I being followed? I felt like a rabbit cowering under the threat of a hawk.

During the trip home to 80 Metre Road Station, I made notes on the work I'd done that day, keeping a small window open on my slick which showed me the signal from Hugo's tracking device.

After ten minutes or so during which I'd been engrossed in my notes, I glanced at the signal window again. Then I banged the slick and shook it. *Shit*. Something wrong with the screen. It showed the signal going haywire, zigzagging, darting. I enlarged the window but that was no help. The dot representing the tracking device zoomed nonsensically about the screen. I opened other windows but they were working fine.

No, no, no, no, no fucking way, I muttered to myself. I shook the slick again but the signal did not settle.

I wiped my palms on my knees and pounded the heel of my hand against my forehead as if that would clear my thoughts. If the slick wasn't playing up then what the hell was happening to the tracking device? No way could Peri have discovered it. As I watched the signal's mad dash the horrifying thought forced its way to the forefront of my mind: what I was seeing represented reality. Something terrible was happening to Peri and Hugo.

By the time I reached my flat the signal had blinked on and off several times, then disappeared completely.

PART

2

Havoc's basic rules of flying:

1. Try to stay in the middle of the air.

2. Do not go near the edges of it.

3. The edges of the air can be recognised by the appearance of ground, buildings, sea, trees and interstellar space. It is much more difficult to fly there.

[Raptors] . . . are much less numerous than ravenous quadrupeds; and it seems wisely provided by nature, that their powers should be equally confined and limited as their numbers; for if, to the rapid flight and penetrating eye of the Eagle, were joined the strength and voracious appetite of the Lion . . . no artifice would evade the one, and no speed could escape the other.

—Thomas Bewick, *The History of English Birds*

11

FALL

Peri had never felt so purely exhilarated as she did when leaving Janeane's. Leaving the Venice, she'd been full of nervous anticipation. Escaping from the City had meant running on adrenaline, in fear for her life, certain she could hear the wingbeats of her pursuers at every turn.

Now Peri was heading into the unknown. Today her new life began. I have my wings, she told herself, with deepening excitement, and I have you, Hugo, and I have my freedom, even though it meant lying to Zeke and Janeane about returning to the City. That should give us a few days' head start, though.

It was discouraging, then, on the very first morning of this new life to be shocked awake from her old nightmare: left high and alone in the City night, frozen until the sun baked her skin to the heating metal below her. *Don't move. Wait. You'll fall.* I'd so hoped I'd left all that behind. No such luck.

Peri's steady wingbeats rowed her through the sky, the strong strokes bringing her wings right up to meet tip to tip above her and right down to touch below her. She kept her arms by her side. Sheer giddy pleasure to skim through air, transparent blue and gold. *Look, little man, at the sky sailing those puffy ships of cloud above us.*

Hugo was wrapped in his cloudsuit against the cool air, protected with hat, mittens, soft jacket, such a warm bundle secure against her. He faced away from her, looking out into the sky. Can you see how beautiful it is, little man? He *was* enjoying himself, babbling and cooing with pleasure in his baby way. As they headed towards the coast, a large flock of red-tailed black parrots flew up, squawking, in front of them, then sheared off to left and right around them, converging again ahead. Hugo gasped and laughed. 'Awk! Awk!' he crowed after them.

When Zeke Fowler found us, Hugo, I was so frightened because I thought I was going to end up like Luisa. He must understand why I couldn't come back.

Zeke asked me what kind of life I was condemning you to but the point is I know what I'm saving you *from*. He doesn't know anything about fliers and you don't either, poor little man, but I do. *I'm one of them*. I think I always was right from the start, long before I got my wings. I know what the treatments do, the ruthlessness and determination you need to make them work. Nothing but perfection works for fliers. But you *are* perfect! If your parents can't see that then they're not really parents, are they? You can't think I've taken you from your mother and father—they were already leaving you behind, Hugo.

A shadow fell on them, making Peri shiver as a heavy cloud moved between her and the sun. She looked over her shoulder but saw no-one behind her. Was Zeke telling the truth about a Raptor coming after them? If someone *was* following her right now, it would still appear as if she were heading for the City. Even if a Raptor shadowed them from afar, they should be safe. As long as they kept heading south.

The final threshold was the large river delta a few hours away. If she kept flying south, she kept her promise to Zeke. But if she turned at the delta and flew upriver, into the hazardous dry heart of the continent, heading for Ash's like she'd planned, then she sealed her fate and Hugo's. At that moment she'd know if she really was being followed. At that moment the Raptor would strike. If she could only outfly him for a little while, she'd have one critical advantage: she knew where she was going, thanks to Janeane's information and contacts. She'd prepared, stocking up on energy strips and water. A Raptor would be reckless to follow her, unprepared, on such a dangerous flight over hot, barren country.

Ash's city, her final refuge, its buildings strung like white shells along an ocean she'd never seen, had always been remote. People had always escaped there, hoping to start their lives over, and with each passing year, as fewer and fewer planes had flown there and as the roads were allowed to crumble into ruin, it had receded more and more into inaccessibility. The ideal place to disappear.

Had any other lone flier dared the journey Peri was about to attempt? She could have jumped out of her own skin, she was so young and strong and happy. Ready for the challenge ahead.

The moment of truth will be when I turn inland.

Peri gave Hugo a gentle squeeze. He gurgled and kicked his legs against her thighs. 'I hope you'll forgive me, Hugo. One day you'll understand.'

Peri had started out early that morning, before the sun was up, when all the world was cool and grey. Safest to get away from these hills before anyone could see her clearly against the burning sky. She would fly south of Pandanus and then out over the sea for as long as she could. Over the sea was safest, where there were fewer people.

It was the land that entranced Peri as she flew south that morning. She exulted in its formal, industrial beauty, all senses heightened in her nervous excitement. She reckoned she was flying at about two hundred metres and from this height she could see the patterning of colour and texture: fields strict as tiles, squares of raw red earth ripped into furrows and laid next to rectangles of emerald pasture, the joins shocking as cuts.

Peri knew the old farmhouse she flew over, with the ruts and tracks scratched over the earth around it like crossed-out scribblings on old paper, was the old Lane farm and the brown stream winding between hills was Fish Creek where she swam with turtles when she was a little girl. Low-lying patches of morning mist clung to the saddle of the low peak Janeane and her friends always called Gin Shop Hill, blurring the gap under dense white cobweb.

Weak morning thermals rising from the darker fields and from the tin roofs of farm buildings surprised and delighted her. *Blue thermals*, Havoc called these, as they were not puffing out any clouds above them. 'For every column of rising air, there's an equal amount of sinking air,' Havoc said. 'Don't worry about it; when you hit the sinking air you won't drop 'cause it's spread out over a larger area.'

Some thermals detached themselves from the hot spot that generated them and floated downwind; Peri only knew she'd hit one when she was bounced upwards by one of these invisible bubbles of rising air. The push thrilled her, the extra energy a gift.

Acid-green pasture crumpled like silk next to rows of lavender bushes carved thick as stone. Clear sounds rose singly through warming air: the falling note of one crow, the cough of an old farm truck, the swoop into full volume chanting of cicadas.

A dot moving over fields of burning gold startled her before she realised the black speck was her own shadow. She was so small against these vast fields; she and Hugo hung over this molten gold, seeming not to move at all, though she was flying swiftly.

Finally, the fields gave way to roads and uneven scrubland covered in drab green. When she crested the last hills between her and the sea the sight took her breath away. Below her, turquoise ocean serpentined between white sandbanks and rolled blue and deeper blue to the horizon. The shallower water near the shore washed clear green, liquid glass, over parallel ridges of sand. The wind stirred the water and the shining green moved in the light, shimmering like an immense abalone shell with its fine silver and purple lines.

Peri realised she was now too close to Pandanus. It wasn't safe to fly low over the town but she dropped anyway. Here she was, a *flier*, just as she'd dreamed it, all those years ago. She had her wings. She was free. There was the curve of the main beach, looking from above like a wedge of yellow melon bordered with a green rind of trees and behind them the row of shops, even the Naxos Cafe, just as it was the day she'd left. It was a risk but she was so close, flying a little south of Pandanus, and she banked, coming around and lower over the Venice, which was scattered like a jumble of smashed crockery and torn paper heaped in ridges at the ocean's edge. Hard to believe a world of suffering could be so small, so contained, from up here. All seemed quiet. She should be much higher and heading over the sea but she had to fly, just once, over the Venice. Black dots crawled over the paper dunes; people picking through the rubbish. What would they think if they saw her soaring above them? She wished Mama'lena was still down there, that she could imagine Mama'lena looking up at her. *See, I did it.* She dipped low over her old prison; she could imagine her younger self running along the sand beneath her, cheering. *You can do it.* She'd become the very thing that had sprung her free from the trap, the image of escape.

Peri swooped up sharply, beating her wings hard. Her brain, her wings, had reacted before she even knew what it was she'd heard. That familiar whine, hurtling past her. She knew that sound too well; she'd heard it often enough in the Venice as Ryan and his gang had got older. Another one, two, closer this time. Someone below was taking potshots at her.

She had her answer then. Far from her fantasy of the other kids crowding round her in awe, this was what she inspired. Meanness. Hatred. *Bring the bitch down.*

Time to flee, again.

Breathing hard, Peri pushed up towards a simmering cumulus cloud over the sea and used the strengthening thermal beneath it to spiral her up to around a thousand metres. Up here, she'd be no more than a spot to anyone below: a small target. What had she been thinking? She *knew* the danger. She had no right to expose Hugo to this. She needed to think more clearly about the risks she was running.

Once Peri let the momentum of one spiral turn push her out of the thermal, headed in the right direction, she allowed herself a smile. She was still inexpert at using thermals and was proud of the manoeuvre.

Peri put kilometres of ocean between herself and the town. This far out over the sea a chain of islets—teardrops, tadpoles of land with tails of white fringing sand—lit up the ultramarine sea with their pattern of lime paisley. After an hour's flying south, she came back to the coast; she needed the energy from the thermals over land.

A lopsided mountain, bare of trees on its sheared-off side, rose up from the hinterland. *Damn.* Grims Peak, *Cloudmaker* to the locals; it means I'm not as far south as I should be. This flight was taking longer than she'd planned, poring over the maps at Janeane's. Before the treatments she couldn't have understood how she could memorise in one glance all the information she needed, all the rivers and ranges and directions and landmarks distinct and fixed in her mind. Now, though, a shiver of doubt crawled down her spine. My navigation's fine but my timing's out. I'm so much smaller than I realised. How could I think I can cross this continent?

The ocean and sands were deserted and Peri dropped down to around two hundred metres. Lower again, about one hundred metres, the sea flooded her vision and her breath with salt blue and green. All she could see were sheets of wet glazing expanses of sand with a floating layer of watercolour; pale blues and whites reflected from the sky. Easy to fall into a trance, flying above these mirror-sands; Hugo had been lulled by her long-distance rhythm into sleep but she must not drift away into dreaming on the wing because she was navigating by landmarks, like Cloudmaker now falling away behind her, aided by basic celestial navigation abilities, such as orienting to sun and stars, that Havoc had helped awaken in her.

Then they were leaving the salt-white sands behind and Peri marvelled at the precision of the sheared edge of the land below. Red cliffs met water with the exactness of lines drawn on a map. There was no blurring, no gentle shelving of sands; the continent came to an end here and *stopped.* The cliff was sliced straight down, showing its bands of rust and cream and grey. Seabirds dotted ledges and fractures, white plumage gleaming, their bodies speckling the rock with shadow.

'Looks like layer cake, eh Hugo? Wish we could take a bite.'

Peri dropped below the brow of the cliffs. That edge, where the wind zoomed over the top, picking up speed as it was released from the compression of being forced against the cliff wall, was the most dangerous area. If she flew in the compression zone, there was a very real risk she'd be blown back over the cliffs and into the violent vortices of wind called rotors. She needed to stay either above and away from the cliffs or well below the ridgeline.

'*Remember*,' Havoc had said to her, 'remember that air is a *fluid*. Air flows like a river. Look for what gets in its way, like a sharp rock sticking up, or even a large tree. Rotors spring up downwind of those things. Wind eddies around obstructions exactly like water swirls around a rock in a river.'

It was worth dropping to the right height for the ridgelift, though; she needed to rest her wings and she needed the extra energy it gave her. Oh bliss, here it was, strong steady lift below the ridgeline, air rising as it hit the cliffs and was forced upwards, warmed by the rock faces heated by the morning sun.

As long as the cliffs lasted Peri soared along the ridgelift; when they petered out just after the triangular point of Shark's Tooth, she allowed herself to drop a little and hunted this way and that, now seeking the boundary of the convergence zone, where cold air from the sea hit warmer air from the land. The sun was high; one must have sprung up by now. Ah, there it was, she'd found it, and with rising joy and relief she tracked right along that invisible line that was like a shallow cold front, using its energy to help power her flight over the long arcs of beach below.

She was not experienced in this kind of flying; Havoc had taught her the theory of using ridgelift, thermals and convergence zones but most of it was still just words to her. Her flights in the City had been too short for her to become expert in using lift in all its forms. She was learning on the run.

Hugo woke up. Peri gave him water and an energy strip chewed to a sweet pulp.

Something glittered so brightly it hurt Peri's eyes. A few hundred metres back from the beach, tangled in green weeds, huge creatures hunkered down, their massive heads tipped forward. 'It's a graveyard for trucks, Hugo,' said Peri. 'They look like giant sad grasshoppers, don't they, with their big heads down like that. Dead trucks.'

'Tah-tah-tuh,' said Hugo. 'Tuh. Tuck.'

Peri dropped her gaze back down to the waves; they were running faster and more ragged than she would have expected under such a sky. A soda-water sky, Havoc would have said. *You know how it feels:* clear and sparkling, trickling over the wings, bubbly, heady.

Peri looked inland, searching for the Woolpack, a blocky squared-off ridge rising up behind mangrove swamps. The Woolpack would orient her again, let her know how much further to the river delta. She couldn't have missed it. Where was it? She must be flying slower than she thought. Was she really going to risk turning inland, making the long run up that river? If she was being followed, did she have the strength to push herself hard, after her hours of non-stop flying?

Peri looked behind her. She couldn't see anything in the sky with her, not even any birds. From below rose up the hissing of the surf; the swell was getting bigger, the breakers rolling in larger as the afternoon coastal wind sprang up. Foam laced its white membrane over the backs of the waves and churned sand drifted pale brown through the water.

No place for you here, Janeane had said to Peri. That was true—and what if there was no place for her now in the City? How could that be? It had been so exciting, arriving there, knowing it was her true home, especially once she got her residency. She patted the permit under her skin. The City had been her place, and she'd lived in the best part of it, in Peter's house. Waking up in her room every morning, on that narrow white bed smelling of lavender, in the clean quiet room washed with light reflected from the sea, was like waking up into a dream.

She'd spent her entire pregnancy there; Peter and Avis insisted on hiding her away but they'd fussed over her too, especially her health. 'Now eat this,' Avis would insist, mixing up one of her green vegetable sludges in the blender every morning and urging her to swim in their pool and nap every afternoon. It was a good life. She gorged herself on the riches of that house, staring at the real Al-Rahim paintings and the Andy Silver photos on the walls, running her fingers over the falling glitter of the rainbird sculpture in the courtyard, trying foods she'd never even heard of before.

Peri lived in a gilded cage, barely setting foot outside the house and courtyard for many months except for medical examinations and the occasional visit to the nearest beach, or her illicit excursions at Peter's command. But her secret liaison with Peter had existed in a dark world of dreamlike intensity that had nothing to do with the rest of this life.

It seemed to Peri that she was weirdly intimate with both of them, Peter and Avis. She was their employee, she lived in this glorious place at their whim, she had no idea what rights, if any, she had, and yet she was tied to both of them by the most intimate bond of all, her own flesh. She was carrying their baby. Except for her own parents, still unknown to her, who else was linked to her in this way? Not Janeane. Certainly not Bronte. She would probably never see Mama'lena again.

Gorgeous, expensive objects appeared in the nursery and Peri, shyly handling the toys, twirling the exquisite little earth, was happy to know how much the baby would be loved. She was doing the right thing; the baby would be healthy thanks to her and he'd be treasured by his parents. And she would get her wings.

Peri knew it was the baby who was being so well cared for. Even so, she was unprepared for the instant change in her status once Hugo was born. Still torn and raw from the birth, she was now a worker, with not a minute to call her own. No more reading, no more naps. She still had to drink the green sludge but now she had to make it herself every morning. 'You've got to keep up your milk supply,' Avis said. Her months of exquisite leisure were now to be repaid, with interest. Her dream life had ended with the first contraction.

The other change, the one Peri had to work so hard to hide, was in her feelings towards Hugo. It was one thing to imagine Hugo's happy life when he sailed, invulnerable, inside her. Now all was different: now his tiny form was exposed to the sharpness of the world, now she had to protect his body in the imperfect safety of her arms, now he suckled from her breasts, now she could breathe in his breath as scentless as air, now she awoke even before he could cry for her from his nursery, now she watched him sleeping on her bed, fascinated by the crumpled rose of his mouth that even in sleep pursed in tiny sucking motions, now his heady smell acted on her like a drug; now it was much harder.

Now the empty quiet she'd loved so much about Peter's house disturbed her; that quiet meant Peter and Avis were away. Their excitement about their newborn child did not mean that they spent less time working or partying. Clearly Avis blamed her, Peri, for coming between her and Hugo. Hugo was always sleeping or nursing. Peri remembered very well the first time Avis tried to cuddle Hugo and he'd arched his back away from her. He wriggled and grizzled until Avis, flushed with anger and humiliation, handed him back to Peri. *Please, Hugo*, pleaded Peri silently, *please don't make it worse.* He had, of course, by settling peacefully into her arms the moment Peri took him. Must have known it wasn't going to work from that moment. The *look* on Avis's face. She did try again a few times but she got more and more tense every time and so Hugo struggled and struggled. The more I knew what to do with Hugo, the more Avis hated me. Oh god, what would she do if she suspected her husband preferred me too?

Hiding the growing intensity of her love and fear for Hugo was so hard. She needed her daily escape to the babies' park.

The babies' park—there was never anyone else there, the parents were all busy—was a square of fenced lush green, an extravagance in the City and one the nannies would never have seen before working for their rich families. Green fertile land, watered and tended purely so that the children of the wealthy might enjoy it. In the deep shadow of the trees the girls sheltered, rocking their charges in their prams.

Peri was one of only two girls breastfeeding. The other nannies didn't speak much to them but Luisa and Peri didn't care. They propped themselves up against a tree and talked together about how they kept up their supply, how often they fed, the pressure they felt when the baby was weighed. It wasn't enough to keep the child safe and loved; it hadn't occurred to them before they started that they'd be directly responsible for their baby's growth too.

Peri was delighted when Luisa confided that she too had escaped to the City. 'I think my home was worse than yours,' Luisa said quietly.

'At least you were left alone, mostly. The creeps who ran our compound believed any disobedience was a sign of a child's evil nature. They beat it out of us with lengths of heavy cable; can you believe they all wore bits of it around their necks on a string, just so we'd never forget? I mean, who's proud of being a torturer in their own home?'

'God, Luisa.' Peri laid her hand on Luisa's arm.

'God doesn't come into it. Or if he does, I *hate* him,' Luisa said.

Next day at the park, Luisa gave Peri a little silver ring, showed her the matching one on her own finger. 'You're my sister,' she said. 'Forever.'

Forever. Forever hadn't lasted long. Peri looked down to the waves, the same ocean that had closed over Luisa, that rolled her body back and forth, that would strip the feathers from her wings. Somehow, Luisa's wings had been the death of her. They were the cause of Peri's troubles, too.

Something strange loomed ahead. Peri squinted, trying to make out the dark things under the surface glitter of the sea. The water had taken a big bite out of the land here. Behind her a headland had crumbled into the sea and the sand from the beach had been dragged away, exposing grey rocks. Waves sprayed up against the cracked end of a road. 'Hugo, what *is* that?'

Tall curves were sticking up out of water. Dead palm trees. How could they still be standing in these waves? Even taller metal poles were scattered between the dead trees; light poles, glass long since smashed. Brown rectangles shivered under the water and huge irregular outlines, like splashes of water or ink, contoured around these shapes. Long ramps striped with black lines plunged into deeper water. Peri dropped down for a closer look. This place was enormous. The dead palms lined what had been seafront. 'Hugo, this used to be a resort! Oh, it's so eerie. The sea's swamped it. Those brown tiles are the roofs of the villas and look there, that was a swimming lagoon, only now it's full of sand and seawater and things growing all over it. There's even a couple of cars sunk at the bottom of the pool. Those black lines are lane markings on the waterslides. Why are those palms still standing? One's tipped over there, most of it's been washed away. Oh, I see—look, Hugo, they were cemented in place but now the cement's cracking.'

The resort must have been luxurious, once. Now the multi-million-dollar development was under water. Could Peter's house suffer the same fate, the cliff cracking and sliding into the hungry waves below? Trouble had come, hell and high water had come, and there'd been nothing they could do to stop it.

Peri's awareness diffused as she stared at the white smudges edging the waves as she coasted, adjusting her position to the shifting of the long, invisible convergence zone. At last there was the Woolpack rising up behind dense mangrove forest bordering the sea in scallops of deep nubbled green fringed by silvery blue-grey water. She was still at least an hour, maybe more, from the delta. The sky around her—she twisted her head to look—was still empty. So much for Zeke's threat about her being followed.

Still, real trouble always comes when you least expect it, Mama'lena used to say, and Peri now knew that was true. It had. The very thing she had most wanted, the goal that had driven her every thought and action, was her undoing. Trouble came with her wings. They'd lost her her job and her lover.

It began the moment she woke up from her surgery. She was more disoriented, more shocked, than she'd been even after giving birth. She'd made her own way home and huddled on her bed, the new, strange wings folded down her back. Stunned as a bird that had smashed into a window, she lay still, barely able to breathe, vomiting from the drugs, wondering in horror, *What have I done?* No turning back now.

Poor Hugo had been looked after by another girl and fed with milk Peri had expressed before her surgery. Peri was terrified she'd be sacked as for days she'd lain crushed by the burden of her wings; the tortured, paralysed muscles of her back were unable to lift them, and she did not dare get up to look in the mirror. She'd been so sure of how beautiful she'd be with wings but now she was too frightened to see how monstrous she must be with these dead things stuck to her.

When Peri finally was able to drag herself out of bed and start caring for Hugo again, she was alarmed by how Avis looked at her. How could she have been so stupid, not to realise how much more Avis would hate her now? Now that she was presuming to be like her.

When Peri hauled herself and Hugo in his pram to the babies' park, the other nannies refused to talk to her at all. They walked away. Luisa didn't. 'You're still my sister,' she said, but she came to the park less and less often.

Now Peri and Hugo were on their own. She hadn't had much to say to the others but it had been something. There'd always been the babies to talk about and they'd exchanged stories, survival tips. Her wings meant Hugo was snubbed too.

Who does Hugo play with? Avis quizzed Peri whenever she saw her. Peri could see she was worried that Hugo spent too much time alone. It wouldn't take her long to put two and two together, to blame Peri—or, rather, her wings. It didn't help that Peter made it clear he disagreed with Avis. Far from humiliating them, Peter had decided Peri's wings gave them status.

That little problem came to a head at the party they threw to give Hugo his fledgling name. 'It's going to be Gyr, after Gyr falcon,' Peri overheard Avis saying excitedly to a friend. Peri helped with the preparations, putting up decorations, assisting the caterers with the food. She was banished when the party started. Peter and Avis's colleagues and friends, a whole rustling flock of them in gorgeous clothes (some designed by Avis, Peri was sure), turned up with presents. She lay in the dark in her room, listening with pleasure to the music, to the sound of adults laughing and talking, realising that somewhere deep within her this sound felt deeply familiar, reassuring. She sat up. Had *her* parents held parties? Certainly she'd never heard these sounds at the farm or in the Venice.

Footsteps came towards her room, the tread heavier than Avis's. Peri smoothed her hair, her heart racing so hard her chest hurt. Why would Peter risk coming here, with Avis in the house?

Peter entered her room, carrying Hugo, who was fussing, sucking at his hands. 'You need to feed him,' Peter said, sitting on her bed, his weight sinking him into the mattress. Peri took Hugo, feeling unaccountably shy, and began to nurse him. Peter watched her, his expression unreadable in the dim light. This was the closest Peri had been to him since she'd got her wings. His presence, the scent from his wings, the weight of him on her bed made her dizzy. She missed him so badly that just being near him was like being drugged. Peter stood up.

'Wait, please,' said Peri. 'I've got something for you.'

She leaned over, one arm holding Hugo in place, and reached into her bedside drawer.

She held out the glass ball with the rose in its centre and he took it. 'Thank you.'

Oh, god, I am such an *idiot*. He's going to hate me for this. What's he supposed to do with it?

'Bring Hugo out when he's finished,' Peter said as he left.

She had edged into the living room with Hugo twenty minutes later, blinking as she came into the bright lights. She looked around for Peter but he was out with most of the guests on the broad rock ledge overlooking the sea. The ledge was outlined with lights, and pink, lime and turquoise spotlights illuminated the rocks and waves so far below.

'Ah, there you are,' said Peter, who'd obviously had something to drink and seemed to be feeling reckless. Rather than sending her straight back to her room he handed Peri a glass of champagne. Shocked, Peri took it, her other arm still balancing Hugo. *What are you doing?* Peri wanted to ask but instead she had to smile politely while Peter introduced her to the guests who'd crowded around her, fascinated by Hugo and by her too, the nanny with wings. 'Oh, no,' Peter was saying to a tall, very thin woman, 'of course it's not dangerous that she has wings. It'd be dangerous if she didn't. Don't you see? She'll be able to look after Hugo properly, keep up with him when he fledges.'

Avis swept onto the terrace, a shower of gold wrapped around her from neck to thigh; it glittered as it ran but stayed in the same place. When Avis moved the streaming gold flickered to emerald, to ruby, to opal. It scattered a scented cloud around her. Was there any sort of real fabric there, Peri wondered, or was it some kind of illusion? Peri had never seen anything like it before.

Avis took Hugo from Peri to show him off to the guests. Peri twisted her silver ring. Hugo should be drowsy and content after his feed but the lights and the music, the noise and crowding from all the strange people when normally he'd be sleeping was unsettling him. *Be good, Hugo, be happy, please*, Peri prayed under her breath, but of course Hugo would not cooperate. Avis jiggled Hugo, put him over her shoulder, walked with him; she did everything right, Peri thought, but she couldn't do anything right. Hugo's grizzling intensified into red-faced wailing.

Avis virtually threw Hugo at Peri who hurriedly took him to the nursery, where she had him settled and snoring in ten minutes.

Peri's memories of the night blurred after that. She remembered shivering in horror in her room as she heard Avis scream at Peter after the guests had left, something about Peri humiliating her in front of their friends. She couldn't hear what Peter said but Avis didn't let up. It wasn't the first argument they'd had about her but it was the worst.

If only Avis knew. Peter hadn't touched her since her surgery. Just as her wings were inflaming Avis, they seemed to repulse Peter.

One day a few weeks after the party, Luisa had shown up at the Chesshyre-Katon house, asking for Peri and Hugo. And lo and behold: she had wings! So that was why she hadn't been to the park. *They wanted a sister for Violet*, Luisa explained. *Baby Amy*. Nothing more needed to be said.

Except that Luisa had told Peri her horrible secret: a device had been implanted that tracked her and limited her flying range. *It's an electronic leash. They can bring you right down out of the sky with one of these. Just a precaution, they said, now that you have wings. So there it is*, she'd said, shrugging. *Real bastards, aren't they, with all their fake religion? Just like the self-righteous creeps I grew up with. Your bosses haven't told you? I'd check anyway.*

At last she had a friend to fly with in the little free time they shared. They'd talked a bit about their earlier lives and mostly they talked about flying but they did not discuss the price of their wings. Not until Luisa came to her one day, upset, saying, *I've seen someone I used to know. Never, ever thought I'd see her again. And she was pregnant. Working for a flier family, like you. Like me. I tried to talk to her but she wouldn't speak to me. Pretended not to know me. She was jumpy. Oh, Peri, I was so shocked. I never thought I'd see anyone from that hellhole ever again.* Two weeks later, Luisa had contacted Peri, extremely agitated, wanting to meet her at Salt Grass Bay. She had something to tell Peri, she'd said. Something important . . .

Cold air hit Peri's cheek, snapping her out of herself. The wind was picking up. Turbulence was increasing along the convergence zone and Peri decided it was wiser to fly above it for now. She shook her head, feeling tears prick at her eyelids. There'd been no time to mourn Luisa and now, at the beginning of her long journey, was not the time to start. Thinking about her life in the City, though, she was wondering. She was almost at the river delta. If she made that turn, kept going to the other side, she'd be just another illegal immigrant. She didn't want that life, how could she force it on Hugo? Maybe, just maybe, the extremity of her flight would give both Peter and Avis pause. He was their child. Maybe they'd come to realise that they'd miss him, that all along they'd really wanted him, just the way he was. Surely they'd be full of remorse by now? Perhaps she'd done a good thing after all.

Time to return Hugo to his family.

Warm relief flowed through her muscles at the thought of not making that turn up the river delta, of not, perhaps, having to outfly a Raptor. How much easier to keep going, back to the City, back to the only place in this world both she and Hugo belonged.

And now there was Zeke, who'd said he'd help her. If he could find out what happened to Luisa he might be able to protect her. After all, Peter didn't kill Luisa and if I give Hugo back he won't kill me. At least I don't think so.

Peri saw herself, all those times with Peter, each one more dangerous than the last. She saw herself pinned to the edge of a building, higher than she'd ever been before. She'd gone of her own free will, sort of, though she remembered feeling Peter's firm grip on the back of her neck as they ascended in the lift, wondering what Peter was going to do with her; not presuming to ask, not sure what she hoped or feared or wanted from him.

He'd taken her right to the edge that night, walking her along the bare girders of his unfinished tower, then laying her down so that her head hung back into the abyss, lights winking and moving so far below her, the other bright towers of the City suspended upside down in the sky, the rush of air over her face and neck, Peter's usually bland voice rough with desire, saying, *Don't be afraid, I won't let you fall*, but of course she had been afraid, that was the point, and her terror subsided only a little as he held her in his arms and covered her with his wings, sleek and warm, the sandalwood scent of his skin and peppery spice of his feathers enveloping her as he entered her again and again, fiercely, no depth or closeness ever enough.

She'd wept with fright and pleasure that night, the two so mingled that she could not separate them for she had never felt anything so intense, her whole body quivering like a plucked wire. As trust in his strength flowered in her, she relaxed a fraction, just enough to enjoy the sensation of warm wind breathing over them both and the blurred lights and sounds of the City rising up from so far below.

Oh I love you, she'd breathed softly into his shoulder, so low he couldn't hear her.

They never spoke about what happened between them that first night. But they had an understanding.

Every few weeks, without warning, Peter would take her somewhere new: one of his constructions, a cliff high above the sea, the arch of a bridge. Each time she allowed it, letting him hold her life in his hands. The rush of each encounter left her floating for days, euphoric.

Even scarier were the times he'd taken her in the house, in his own bed, every encounter riskier than the last.

That's not love, my dear, said Luisa, when Peri confessed her secret, dying to tell someone. *That's adrenaline.*

Peri didn't care. She was drunk on her new-found power. She could never have dreamed that this worldly, powerful and reserved man, this high-flier that half the City looked up to, was obsessed with her, let her see his feelings at their most unguarded and raw. She, Peri Almond, saw a Peter Chesshyre no-one else knew.

Peri had never known such passion could exist; she knew she would have given him her life. She hoped it wouldn't come to that.

Breathe in the rhythm of Flight. She must settle into a tempo that would carry her all the way back to the City, the work of it emptying her mind. Instead it was always while she was flying, her mind streaming with impressions from the sea and sky, the feel of the wind and sun on her wings, that her thoughts crowded in on her. This was the only time and space in which she could think, up here, in Flight.

The air over the ocean was fracturing into cold sharp winds slicing at Peri, the sky was hardening. The water below her was changed too, the transparent green of that morning, the deep blue of the afternoon swell, was now sullied by brown clouds drifting through the water. This wasn't sand. There were bits of wood and tangles of floating rubbish; outflow from the river delta. She soared higher but still she couldn't see the river itself, just the spreading murk from its load of dirt emptying into the sea. This was it; she'd fly on. No turning back. She twisted the silver ring on her finger, round and round. She'd keep her word and return Hugo.

A strong wind sprang up, blowing from the south-west, buffeting Peri's face and her right side, pushing her away from land, further out over the sea. If the wind grew any fresher she would not be able to make headway against it.

Peri searched the cloud ahead and to the right of her, trying to make out what the weather had in store for her and Hugo. There was something wrong with this cloud. It was hundreds of metres high and darkening fast, blocking the slanting rays of the mid-afternoon sun. It was too tall. That was it. Fair-weather cumulus did not grow that high. Worse, it was not alone. The cloud ahead was one among a series of towers merging into a wall along the south-western horizon. Her beautiful fair-weather cumulus had grown into towering cumulonimbus and now formed a dark bank. A squall line.

Why hadn't Peri noticed what was happening to the cumulus? She'd ignored the most basic lesson of Flight. *Pay attention*. Don't fly with a head full of distractions, Havoc said. *Pay attention*. She'd done the opposite, flying along absorbed in her own memories, worries and plans. Well, now she had something to worry about.

The sky was roiling, coming to a massive rolling leaden boil. Dark, crackling with fire.

Peri turned her head towards the land. She must get down, out of this wind, and find somewhere to wait out the storm, but as she looked behind her she saw *it*.

Her wings faltered for a moment and she had to force herself back into her flying rhythm. Flying far behind her and to the right, on her landward side but coming fast towards her over the sea, was a black dot. A raven. That must be it. It *must* be. But what raven would follow her out over the sea into a storm?

Peri looked back at the clouds, at the blackening squall line ahead, now visibly closer. Whatever happened she must not fly into that. Her stomach plummeted with dread. *Every take-off is optional. Every landing is mandatory.*

A squall line was one of the most dangerous weather formations. A squall line ran extreme winds at its leading edge. A squall line at best meant severe weather but the clouds directly ahead were burgeoning up and spreading out at their top into the anvil shape of a supercell storm, the most dangerous storm of all, with its rotating cyclonic updraft.

When Peri glanced behind her again, the black dot was larger and gaining on her. It was bigger than any bird. It could be only one thing. This was the Raptor Zeke had warned her about, the one she'd looked for all day. Now here it was, Peter's Raptor, so intent on tracking her that he too was flying into the storm. Oh god. There was no way of letting him know that she really was returning Hugo. Maybe they didn't care about that, maybe they just wanted to be rid of her, once and for all. Over the water, away from prying eyes on land, the Raptor would kill her and grab Hugo.

Peri had been cruising, using as much low-energy soaring as she could. Now the wind was pushing back at her and her breathing grew laboured as she drove harder with each wingbeat, trying to stay on course to the south. Her flight muscles burned, depleted from the hours she'd flown already. The increased power she now demanded of them was too much. Soon, all her muscles would give out. If only the storm had been coming at her from the sea she would have been able to turn inland, try to outrun the storm that way or find shelter and hide. Now, with the Raptor gaining on her, that course was too dangerous even if it had been physically possible.

Peri concentrated on forcing herself forward as fast as she could.

What should I do? Let the Raptor catch me, give him Hugo? Better than risking both of us being killed in the gathering storm. But the Raptor won't just wait for me to hand Hugo over. If he catches me, he'll kill me, drive me down into the sea. No-one will ever find me. So easy, much easier than letting me live. I'm a nuisance to them alive; I've proved that over the last few days, haven't I? Luisa's body rolling in the water. It was a good plan. Except for those clouds looming. Neither of us planned on them.

Visibility dropped by the second as the sky darkened and the wind whipped drops of water into Peri's face. She couldn't tell if the wetness was rain or water whisked up from the sea raging below. Peri shook her head and clawed her damp hair away from her face. So hard to think in the mounting roar of the winds and waves.

Hugo was crying and Peri put her arms around him. 'It's okay, little man, don't worry.' The rising shriek of the wind tore her voice away.

The Raptor would have real trouble tracking her now. He had no more control in this weather than Peri did. Even if she were to risk her own life to hand Hugo over to the Raptor, there was now no safe way to do it. Both she and the Raptor had to concentrate on survival. Above all, she must keep away from those clouds. If she had to fly in cloud she would not be able to keep her wings level and then she could spin into a death spiral and not even know it until she stalled, far too late to save herself.

Peri burned more of her failing energy by forcing herself higher, though she had no way of telling, in this wild dark air, if she'd fought her way up another twenty metres or another fifty. The higher she was, the further away from the downbursts, the less likely she was to smash into the ground. *You'll fall.* But there's no way to fly over the top of this storm. No escape that way. Cumulonimbus blows up into the tallest clouds of all, twelve thousand metres or more.

Peri glanced over her shoulder and was appalled to see the large black shape, illuminated by light hitting the sea through tears in the cloud, about a kilometre behind her. *My god, he's sticking to me, even in this chaos. Is he mad?*

Peri drove herself forward grimly. No chance of outrunning the squall line now. I'm crossing over the threshold into my worst nightmare. Every flier's worst nightmare.

I am flying into a big storm.

Flying blind.

She hadn't been paying attention to her surroundings and now she would be punished. If only she could land, get Hugo to safety, it wouldn't matter what happened to her. But landing was impossible. Dropping meant losing lift, losing the little power to manoeuvre she had. She'd be heaved sideways, as if she were no more than a wisp of straw. She'd seen birds blown about by strong winds in Pandanus. How did they get to safety? Maybe they didn't. Birds died in storms; she'd seen their broken bodies washed up along the tideline.

The air grew more turbulent. It was more frightening than being smashed by a big wave. This was surf too, the wildest she'd ever felt: one minute she and Hugo were tossed up fifty metres into the air, the next they were slammed sideways a hundred metres. The updrafts building this stormfront, whipping this dark froth so high, were blowing fifty knots, maybe more.

Hugo had been screaming, his tears torn from his face by the storm, but now he was quiet, silenced by terror or the wind snatching his breath away.

The cloud looming in front of them could be the height of a skyscraper. Or a mountain. No way to tell, nothing in the sky to give it scale. Lightning above stabbed closer. Thunder terrifying beyond thought: a wall of sound breaking, denser than dumping surf, *air is a fluid* and this crashing fluid was deafening, crushing. The very atmosphere cracked and rolled away in pieces.

Lightning too close now, sky splitting like a rip in space opening onto the sun, eyes shutting against her will and still the light searing through lids and when they opened again she was falling through a black world, her sight burned away. When it returned, strange lights and sparkles crawled over the darkness. *Another strike any closer than that and we'll die.*

The lightning was playing tricks on her eyes. She could have sworn she saw something in the light of the last flash. Two things. Big and black. Wing shapes. There couldn't be two Raptors following her. *No.* Eyes must be deceiving. After-effects from the brilliance. Now they were everywhere. Dark shapes swarming. Another flash. No, there was nothing.

A wind shear tossed them across the sky, its force smashing into her chest, knocking her breath from her, crushing her wings against her. She fluttered, frail as a moth. No guarantee she was flying straight, that all her desperate effort was hauling them out of this by so much as a metre. She could just be thrown around and around endlessly by the storm, a broken twig smacked around the rim of this whirlpool in the sky.

The sky, once dark, ripped with yellow light, was now utterly black, its only illumination coming from lightning flashing over wastes of rain-lashed sea. The rain hadn't reached her yet but it was coming; it would finish her off. She hadn't preened her wings with the oil used for long sea trips. Most of the water would roll off her wings but some would stay, dampening feathers, weighing her down.

Rain poured in torrents, waterfalls in the sky. They were tossed higher than ever, then pitched into a roaring abyss. Peri had no idea how high above the waves they were. The rain struck hard and icy. Some of it *was* ice, rattling into them, pinching, biting. As they were flung higher, into colder air, they were thrown into the middle of a hailstorm, balls of ice the size of oranges slamming into them, bruising them. A warm spot opened on her forearm. Blood where ice split skin.

Terrified, Peri threw her arms around Hugo. His hat had long since been clawed away. He was dangerously cold.

Peri's strength was failing. How long had they been struggling in the maelstrom? Pointless to fight the storm: some gusts pushed her up and sideways, helping to keep them aloft. But she couldn't leave it to the storm to keep her up. No time to worry about keeping her wings level; she had to concentrate only on generating lift, forward motion and thrust, whenever the wind allowed. Her wings ached from the hail and deep pain from exhaustion cramped her muscles.

She rubbed Hugo hard, trying to warm him. She lifted her own skims, fitting them over Hugo's head so his body was next to her skin. The temperature was still dropping.

A bank of thunder cracked, falling all around. The sound threw them through the dark, reverberations shivering their bones. Peri felt like her flesh, her organs had been vibrated to jelly. How was she still conscious?

Her wings numb, Peri pushed forward with one last burst of strength. No reserves left. If she couldn't force her way out of the storm now they were gone.

Havoc's hoary old joke: *What do you call a flier who doesn't check the weather? A flier who doesn't make a flight plan?* Who didn't do any of a dozen things he claimed were necessary? The answer always the same: *A little late. Ha ha ha.*

A blast knocked them sideways, spinning. Time slowed. *Don't move. You'll fall.* The wind surfing them along, higher and higher.

Now they were dropping.

No more strength. Drained away in the cold, burned up against the wind. *You'll fall.* It didn't matter what she did now. *You'll fall.*

Her will to save Hugo was all that had been keeping them up. For how long? An ice age. Not enough. Not good enough.

Something on her cheek. Water that was not icy rain.

I'm sorry, Hugo.

No way of knowing whether she was whispering it or screaming it or thinking it as they fell into the dark.

A thundering wall of night rises ahead, howling upwards with more power than an express train. The noise of it is beyond horror. To touch that funnel of whirling dark is certain death but now they are seized and flung up, helpless and light as leaves.

Higher and higher they surf, zooming upwards so fast through blackness and wind that Peri can't breathe, she can't hear, they've breached the wall of rotating cyclone at the storm's heart.

Oxygen levels are dropping, temperature plummeting.

Spiralling into blackness. Dots of starlight prickling her eyes.

Ice coats her body. She's losing consciousness as they rocket higher, faster and faster. As she blacks out, a thought glances across her mind: How strange. I'm going to die from falling *up*.

I'm sorry, Hugo.

Night roaring upwards, sky zooming up, stars falling past them into the abyss, tossed for a second above the cloud so very high that for one flaring instant she sees the rim of the earth shining.

Falling into blackness again.

Terminal velocity.

Over three hundred kilometres per hour. Ninety metres per second.

When you have wings, you *can* fall.

Wind and rain and thunder are all the world.

12

MISSING

Bright light, so bright I squint and blink. Fresh green comes into focus. Sun falls on a meadow in a forest, starred with white flowers. Lily hands me a glass of wine and we walk hand in hand along a path into the darker trees. I'm happy but something isn't right. There's something I've forgotten. Lily points and I look up. A pair of eagles circles over our heads. I've never seen an eagle before and I'm excited. They tilt and balance on the wind, the ends of their huge wings fringed, separated like fingers. We walk along the path into the gloom under the trees but the path is blocked by a barbed-wire fence. Lily's ahead of me, she's reached the fence but she's run away and I'm about to run after her when I look back because something big and dark is tangled in the wire. It's one of the eagles, upside down, wings pegged out along the fence-line. The ground is falling away beneath my feet; there's a white moon where the eagle's head should be. Its wings are still moving. I don't want to turn my head to look at the moon because I know what it is. My neck locks, muscles rigid. I wrench my head around. The white moon is Tom's face.

Thursday, but only just. Two in the morning. A rotten night's sleep, even by my standards. I checked my slick and the result was the same as the last two hundred times—no signal. I told myself Peri might still turn up but couldn't get rid of the sick dread writhing like a trapped octopus in the pit of my stomach. The device could've fallen off but the worst-case scenario was most likely: it stopped signalling because something bad had happened to Hugo and Peri. And it was my fault. I was followed into RaRA-land; I led the Raptor straight to her. After my encounter with Chesshyre on the bridge I was seriously worried about what he'd do when he found out Peri and Hugo were missing.

Now I couldn't even doze. I lay there, eyes staring hard and dry into the dark, willing myself not to check the slick again. Nothing from Wilson, either. Should've got back to me by now. *What's happening,* hikikomori *boy?*

The only feeling bleaker than two in the morning is three in the morning and that was on its way, shadow looming over the horizon. By four in the morning you can kid yourself you're starting the day early. But you can't put a good face on three am. It's a desert, the hour when you're stranded, high and dry, tormented by how terrifying life is, aware you survive by refusing to see the truth of this.

I blinked my eyes, trying to relieve their painful dryness, my back aching, trying not to think of all the other pains age has in store for me. Thomas's physical absence nagged like an old injury and I fretted about the failures I'd already chalked up as a father: the ordinary grief and shame of parenting, the everyday betrayals of even the most loving home, one sharp word as bad as a blow to Thomas's cheek. Worst of all was my impatience in the face of Tom's relentless love, my inability to just sit with him and look into his perfect face, into the green curve of his eye, rounded like the rim of the earth. This failing hurt more than any other: I was always distracted, always busy, always adult, working, cooking, reading, *doing*. I couldn't just *be* with Tom. He wanted me *now*, I was his best friend, but for how long? When he's older, he won't have time for me. I know this already, I know this before it's too late and *still* I can't just soak him up till I'm so full it will last me the rest of my life.

I turned on my reading light and fished out Peri's letters from where I'd stored them in the bedside drawer. I had already read them over obsessively, looking for clues.

Dear Hugo,

Your first, favourite toy was a blue and red parrot with stretchy legs. You could just fit its triangle feet in your mouth. The parrot crackled like paper and tinkled like a bell, depending on if you crumpled it or shook it. I wanted to tell you before we forget. Before I forget.

I put the letters away and turned off the light. Hunting the fugitive coolness stored on its underside, I shoved my head under my pillow. Its freshness vanished in seconds. Groaning, I punched the pillow and turned onto my side.

When I woke again it was four-thirty. I lay there, thinking about a section of law I'd read over and over recently. A statute meant to protect flier and non-flier alike. That law said no buildings were to be built that non-fliers couldn't use, as if we were disabled and needed special provisions for access. I could see this law was dissolving in a sea of change so deep and wide we were already in well over our heads.

We get claustrophobia, *they* get vertigo.

I could hear Henryk's dry voice, saying, as he did about virtually every case he'd worked on: *If all you've got on your side is the law, then you know your arse is well and truly in a sling.*

Finally, defeated, I got up at five and took Frisk for his walk. We didn't run together after the first time; lions don't really like running. My right knee, I had to admit, was grateful for that.

We wandered the quiet streets near my flat for nearly two hours. I thought hard as we walked, passing women who were up early to take their offerings to the temples. Should I go to Henryk right away? I agonised with each step. If I turned the case over to the police now and Peri then turned up as we'd agreed, I'd ruin everything, not just for myself but for Peri too. Chesshyre would be incandescent with rage and it was just possible he was still trying to protect Peri as well as himself. On the other hand, if the missing signal meant Peri and Hugo had come to grief, I'd never forgive myself for delaying.

I kept glancing up at the sky. No large spots circling. Didn't see too many fliers hovering over my part of town.

As I walked I didn't really see the small offerings of fruit and flowers wrapped in banana leaves that had already been set out in the intersections of streets and on the steps of shops but I absent-mindedly stepped over them all the same. By the time the sun rose, people on bicycles and scooters were passing us, calling out greetings to Frisk, who padded along the street, lowering his big head to sniff at the offerings, pricking his ears to listen to a bird talking in a cage hanging on a verandah, picking up his paws delicately to avoid the grimy water sluicing down the gutters. *Hello*, the bird called after us. *I've got no money. That's alright. Hello. Hello!*

Frisk pulled at his lead, dragging me towards one of the food stalls near the 80 Metre Road intersection. Something large and glossy black flew past my line of sight and I cringed. The black creature landed next to a food stall and started tearing at a garbage bag with its thick, arched beak. *Cau cau cau*. Bloody jungle crow. Frisk gave him a wide berth; the thing looked like it could have our eyes out in seconds.

The smell of pork and mango fritters deep-frying floated through the still-cool morning air. I bought a bag and shared them with Frisk as we walked back to the flat.

My slick vibrated and I was so anxious to answer I almost dropped it into the gutter, my fingers still greasy from the fritters.

Lily.

Hello, I said, my head spinning with adrenaline and the heat of the morning sun and my lack of sleep.

Standing in the garden at the front of Ventura, I fished in my pocket for my key. I looked up. This was becoming obsessive; couldn't seem to stop doing it.

My whole body went cold.

Cold like I'd stood under a cold tap.

A dark figure was circling. Very high. Not a jungle crow.

Oh, *come on*.

No way.

Jesus wept, Zeke, would you get an everlovin' grip? Probably been lots of fliers circling here, there, wherever, you just never noticed, never looked for them before. Said yourself you hardly looked at the sky anymore.

Shaking my head, I let Frisk in, fed him properly, made tea. Lily had informed me she'd scheduled the initial screening and assessment tests for Thomas; if he passed those, he could start the treatments as early as next week. Lily always did work fast. When she made up her mind to act then yesterday was already too late for Lily. Once the results of the screenings were known, I would be expected to give my consent to the procedures. I told her I'd spoken to Ruokonen and that I'd left her office with grave misgivings but Lily didn't pause for breath and I doubted she'd even heard me. If I was going to fight her over this, I'd have to make up my mind to do it soon.

I took a deep breath and scratched my head. Thunder reverberated and seconds later the rains came pouring down, as they had virtually every day so far that summer. Water cascaded down my window, distorting my view of the mango trees in the front yard and the street beyond. Vittorio and I had nagged Ventura's body corporate to get the damn gutters fixed but here they were, overflowing again as they did in every rainstorm.

It never rains but it pours, as my mother had been fond of saying. Peri and Hugo were missing. I had until Saturday morning to come up with something credible for Chesshyre but today I had to work on my black ops job. On Saturday, Chesshyre would be demanding to know where Hugo was. I'd better have some answers.

And now I had less than a week to decide if I wanted my son to be a flier.

I glared at the black mould creeping up the ceiling, thanks to the rains and Ventura's disintegrating gutters. This dump was crumbling in front of my eyes. And Taj was dead. My only partner, disappeared as if he'd never been. 'The forces of entropy are well and truly arrayed against us, Frisk.' He looked up at me from the dusty floor, where he lay grooming himself with his tongue.

Henryk called. 'I've done one more thing. I've put in a request to CaFS to see if they've got a file on Perros—wouldn't have thought to do that without knowing the department's a factor in your case. So far, Almond's the only lead we've got on Perros.'

'LAC Jasinski,' I said, 'that's above. And beyond.'

'Always,' said Henryk. 'When there's a dead body involved, I always go that extra distance. One day they're going to find that out and stop promoting me. I sure am looking forward to that witness statement from Almond, Zeke.'

Oh *shit*. One more reason Peri not coming back was a disaster. 'What makes you think a dead body is involved, Henryk? Seeing as your people didn't find one?'

'Had a bad feeling. So, you know, we often go back for another look, right?'

'Yes?'

'The unit I sent did find something.'

'Wasn't a ring by any chance?'

'How the hell did you know?'

'Silver ring, gull motif?'

'Always knew you were psychic.'

'Peri had one and I wondered who in her life would give her something like that. It was the sort of cheap ring young girls exchange sometimes. I thought, well, who'd care about her becoming a flier? Not the kind of thing the Chesshyres would ever do.'

'Sounds like it could belong to Perros. We can compare it to your girl's, show it to her when she comes in.'

I took a deep breath. 'About that. Henryk, I'm really worried about Peri and Hugo. They were on their way back to the City yesterday but the signal tracking them cut out.'

'So you want me to look out for them? Great, Zeke. Wait till your little plan goes haywire, then call for help. But my problem is that *they* haven't been reported missing either. I have no evidence of any crime or misadventure in their case and I can't continue to allocate police resources on the whim of an ex-colleague.'

I was silent while he got this off his chest. Then I said, 'But this thing with Perros does suggest there's something bigger going on than just a missing persons case.'

Henryk sighed. 'I'll do what I can. We'll do all the usual checks—hospitals, clinics and so on—see if anyone turns up fitting their description. I can use the Perros investigation to cover any work we do looking for Peri and Hugo.'

I thanked Henryk and drained the rest of my now-cold tea. I needed to get cracking on my black ops job—investigating the Seraphim MP—especially as this might be my only paying job soon enough. But focusing on that job was going to be difficult. Henryk's news hardened the dread I felt into fear; it proved that not only could Peri and Hugo be dead, it was probable. I had to do all I could to find out what had happened. Well, Chesshyre had wanted a good investigator, and he'd got one. No need for him to know just how much investigating I was doing on his time or that my investigations were broadening far beyond what he wanted.

I had to have that data from Little Angels, which I hoped would provide the information I needed to unleash Cam onto the departmental files. Eliseev's records were critical too. He was the only other piece of the puzzle I had. Time to send another urgent message to *hikikomori* boy, but knowing his hours, he was most likely asleep for the day.

I showered and dressed in my best suit for my job interview at the Church of the Seraphim, arranged for me by Sunil—though the Seraphim MP, David Brilliant, didn't know that. Sunil had arranged for my name to be among those chosen for interview by the recruitment company.

Craning my neck, I stared up at the ice fall of the Church of the Seraphim, with its rope of mist unbraiding itself. Peter's design took my breath away. Simple, even severe, it had the irregular harmony of a natural form—landslide, glacier edge. But I resented its inaccessibility to non-fliers. Chesshyre's doing too. *Peter couldn't care less; he's above worrying about that sort of thing*, Halley had said. I had to wait for a flunky to escort me up into the inner sanctum because I needed *special arrangements* to enter this church. Arrogant bastards. The flunky, a young man, appeared and I followed him into the office block next door, the one still sporting gold letters that said: IF GOD WANTED YOU TO FLY, HE'D HAVE MADE YOU RICH.

As we rose up to the twenty-fifth storey of the office block I began to feel dizzy and it wasn't just from the overpowering perfume from the flunky's black and silver wings. Yesterday I'd had to cope with the vertigo of Chesshyre's building site. What horrors awaited me in his church? I had my doubts whether I really would be able to cope with SkyNation.

The flunky led me to the eastern wall of the office block, out a door, and onto a transparent bridge from the office block to the church, which we entered through a side door. Here we stopped.

We were standing on a small platform inside a cave of cobalt ice. The flunky stepped back and locked the door behind us.

Shafts of light fell from above into the darker depths below. Running out from our little platform was a walkway suspended over the void. Near the back of the church, upon a square white pillar, flickered a fire. Behind this a large VaporView silently poured a fall of fog into shadows below; a serene face framed by six wings of fire glowed in the fog. A seraph. Was this their altar? If so, it seemed that this church set out to show that its members revered the elements of fire and air, or perhaps that they had mastered them.

Through the clear facet of the roof above, I could see sky. The front and back of the church were also transparent. A walkway ran from our platform and joined the central aisle of the church—what I'd normally call the nave though there was no transept—and the flunky now led me this way towards the fire altar. The suspended walkways were just wide enough to spare me the worst of my vertigo but they lacked railings.

Chesshyre's building was even more beautiful inside, with the sky falling into it, but someone had muddled the blue space. We passed winged figures in alcoves lining the walls: angels; a green glass Garuda; Hermes, the messenger god with his winged feet and winged helmet; a Nike; a boy who must be Eros. A gold disc of sun near the fire altar sported wings, making the sun look like nothing so much as a flying coin, which seemed only too fitting. Sad though; the church would have been ravishing if it had been left empty.

As we neared the fire altar, the flunky veered to the left and we entered a doorway leading to a series of offices behind the main body of the church. We stopped in front of a door bearing a gold-lettered sign: *Office of the Archangel*. Archangel? I curled my lip. Hadn't these guys had a decent education? They must know archangels ranked low in the medieval hierarchy of angels, with the seraphim themselves making up the highest rank.

When I entered his office, David Brilliant, Archangel and MP, was standing at his window, looking towards Parliament House, his back to me, his wings sweeping to the floor. He was talking loudly to a group of advisers, as if making a speech. The flunky hesitated in the doorway, then beckoned me into the room where we went to stand with the advisers, all winged. I could already guess my job application would not be looked on favourably as I was not one of the elect. There was one other non-flier in the room, a tall, pale man with a high shiny forehead who'd folded his long limbs into the armchair at one side of Brilliant's desk. Must be eccentric; who let himself go bald anymore?

Brilliant kept talking without turning around and I was grateful for the chance to take in the strange scene. Brilliant's wings were the gaudiest I'd yet seen, horizontally striped in bars of red, green, blue and gold. His office was decorated in a similarly garish style, every wall covered with paintings of men and women with wings. Reproductions of Giotto and Fra Angelico paintings of annunciating angels crowded uncomfortably next to a gloomy Romantic painting of a dying Icarus. This man must be the culprit, responsible for cluttering Peter's pure design with a jumble of kitsch. Did Peter hate him for it? Now he was refusing to work for Flores, whoever he was. Maybe Peter was growing wary of clients he couldn't control.

Brilliant's flow of speech did not lessen and I focused on what he was saying.

'Mankind has images of angels over six thousand years old. We have images of angels, winged gods and goddesses and winged bird-humans from every culture and time. Ancient Egypt, ancient Africa, South America, wherever you look. These beings are always links between heaven and earth. The Church of the Seraphim believes that humans are meant to attain our true, winged form to embody, like the rainbow, this bridge between heaven and earth, between God and Man.' Here Brilliant paused and drew in a deep breath, resuming in a more hectoring tone.

'What we believe is that angels *will* exist, that our race has always known its destiny, that it is our sacred and solemn task to *become* angels, that this is why we have never been satisfied, why we've always striven to go beyond, to surpass every achievement, one after another, until we stand on the brink, *this* brink, of oneness with the heavens, to unite heaven and earth. Yes, unite! We are so close!'

Brilliant dropped his voice. 'The veil between the worlds shimmers,' he whispered. In spite of myself I leaned forward, as did his advisers. Even the pale man sat up, fanning out his remarkably long fingers, then twisting them into a whitish knot, and stared at Brilliant.

I suppressed an impish urge to interrupt, to ask whether Zefiryn was the church's version of the holy sacrament.

'We have only to put out our hand,' continued Brilliant, almost breathless, drunk on his own rhetoric. 'When we truly achieve this, we will discover a new world, a new dispensation. New revelations will be granted us. We will walk, nay, we will *fly*, into a realm of gold.'

Brilliant paused. Scattered applause from the advisers. Was he rehearsing a sermon for the church or a speech for the parliament?

An adviser piped up, 'But won't people—I mean non-fliers—won't they say we're leaving them behind?'

'Ah,' said Brilliant. 'Glad you mentioned that.' He turned around and I saw that he was a beefy red-faced man with slicked-back dark hair, his vivid wings contrasting with his sober white shirt and dark suit trousers. Brilliant looked like a corpulent middle-aged executive who'd been plucked from a board meeting, briefcase and all, and been given these gaily striped wings. I saw I had to revise my belief that all fliers must be lithe.

Brilliant continued in his high-flown style, as if thousands were listening. 'In religions based on the revealed word of God, God and humans are separated, with angels bridging the divide. Angels reveal the divine word and carry out God's will. This can include showering people with grace, marks of special favour and even salvation. Who's to say we can't help non-fliers?' The pale man winced and hunched over, his shoulders stooped. Something in Brilliant's words had offended him.

Brilliant paused and his face hardened. His voice rumbled. 'But we can only do this if we are allowed to pursue our true path. We cannot be dragged down by those who are not chosen. Religions have argued about the true nature of angels; were they purely spiritual entities, did they have material bodies or were they spiritual bodies who could assume physical form? We will answer that question. We will assume the perfection of angel form and *then* we will achieve the spiritual perfection. We must tread the path of glory laid out for us.'

Brilliant had walked over to his heavy wooden desk but he did not sit down. The advisers moved across the office towards the door in a rustle of feathers and papers, some already speaking into their slicks as they moved.

'There's more,' said Brilliant to the woman who had questioned him. 'I haven't finished writing it yet. I need to say something about how, far from leaving non-fliers behind, we need their help to do our work. It is not enough that the rest of humanity does not hold us back from our mission, in fact it must help us or we cannot succeed.' Brilliant looked over to the pale man sitting in the armchair, who nodded slowly. 'Which is why we are blessed to work with good friends such as yourself.'

'Yes,' said the pale man. 'We'll talk more about the right way to *explain* that. To the literal-minded it seems strange we could have common interests.' He broke off, wheezing, exhausted by his few words.

Brilliant stared at him, his look of concern shading into disapproval. The pale man unfolded himself from the chair and at his full height was one of the oddest-looking men I'd ever seen, elongated like a stork in human form but with his chest puffed out like a pigeon.

The advisers, except for the woman who'd questioned Brilliant, left the office, followed by Storkman.

Brilliant was still talking to his adviser. 'The human project is *over*,' he said. He must have liked that phrase, for he repeated it: 'The human project is over. The post-human project, the supra-human project, is now underway.' I could see why he'd waited for Storkman to leave the room before he tried out *that* little slogan.

Brilliant sat down heavily behind his desk, waving me to the chair in front of him, and took the slick proffered by the flunky, who then left with the adviser. Brilliant and I were now alone. He made a show of examining the slick. I looked to my right out the window. The park between the church and Parliament House was lush, shaded by figs and banyan trees.

Brilliant looked up. 'An impressive résumé.' I'd only glanced at what Sunil had concocted but apparently I had policy experience in bioengineering. If Brilliant probed me I'd sound like a fool but I suspected Brilliant was the sort of man who did the talking. I was not proved wrong.

'We need someone who can truly understand the issues facing the Seraphim,' Brilliant began. I'd expected him to say something like this. This was code for preferring to hire someone with wings. 'However, someone . . . like you could also be useful, in liaising with other independent parties, for example.' Brilliant waved a hand at the closed door to the corridor. 'You saw our friend there. He'd be more comfortable working with someone like you.' *The human project is over.* Yes, I should bloody well think he *would* be more comfortable working with *someone like me*.

Brilliant propped his elbows on the desk, steepling his fingers. 'The more I think about it, the more we probably need two people for this position. Someone such as yourself and, ah, someone naturally more in tune with the aims of the church. Just why would you be interested in working for us, Mr Fowler?'

This question I had prepared for. I waffled on about wanting to work on the cutting edge of policy, a natural extension of my work in bioengineering. Inspiration struck and I confessed an interest in family policy: how did non-flier parents minister to the spiritual needs of flier children, as they were going where their parents could not follow, and so on and so forth. I laid it on a bit thick but Brilliant's eyes widened. Oh Christ, he was actually impressed. How could Peter bear working with such a confused and, at least on current evidence, not very bright bunch?

Brilliant's slick rang with a clarion call of trumpets, a shimmer of harp strings. Could the man really be such a cliché? I looked at the paintings of baby angels around the room. He could. Or maybe Brilliant really was brilliant and this sentimental kitsch was part of his cover. Maybe he was a steely, calculating genius, manipulating his flock. Most likely he was both, sentiment and steeliness meshing perfectly.

'What?' Brilliant was saying. 'You can't be serious. Can't you handle it?' He looked up at me. 'I'm sorry. Bear with me.'

Ah, well done, Sunil, staging a diversion, just as we'd planned.

Brilliant rose to his feet. Now he was agitated, walking around the room. 'Well, if you're sure it will only take a few minutes.'

Brilliant put his slick away. 'Hope you'll forgive me,' he said. 'Something urgent has just come up. Perhaps we can reschedule?'

'That's okay,' I said. 'I'd rather wait.'

Brilliant looked flustered. 'Oh, fine. Right. Look, I'll be back in a few minutes. I'll send Uri in to look after you.'

'Please don't bother on my account,' I said. 'I've got some catching up to do.' I raised my slick. 'I'll be fine.'

Brilliant was putting on his jacket, which fastened around his wings. 'Sorry. I'll be as quick as I can.' He trotted out the door.

Don't hurry back now. When he'd gone, I waited a minute, listening. I went to the door and looked out but saw no-one. It was clearer to me, after listening to Brilliant rehearse his sermon, why Brilliant had given himself the title of Archangel. He aimed to become a Seraph, his speech had implied, but would not yet claim to be so exalted.

Now I needed to move quickly. I'd done this kind of thing many times but today I was strangely clumsy and slow. My hands were damp and I fumbled my slick, dropping it, swearing.

Phew. What the hell was *wrong* with me? Getting into and out of situations like this was my job. Usually I was stone-cold steady but Luisa's apparent murder, my lack of sleep, my fears for Peri and Hugo, my anxiety over Tom, were unnerving me.

Finally, I recorded a few seconds of myself innocently reading. Then I plugged in and uploaded the images so that the view of me reading would be played on a loop to surveillance devices covering this room. I searched the room, wondering whether the church had security I didn't know about. If I was caught, Sunil would cut me loose—*Zeke who? Sorry, don't know what you're talking about*. That's the deal with black ops.

My surveillance technology was good but Sunil's was better and he'd given me a slick with more access codes than even I had. I slipped it into the larger screen on Brilliant's desk and let it get on with downloading the files while I prowled around the room, picking up papers, briefs, speeches, copying as much stuff as I could.

One of Brilliant's minions put his head around the door as I was putting a speech back on Brilliant's desk but he was speaking to someone else and by the time he glanced at me I was next to the window. The minion nodded at me and withdrew.

My slick. *Finally*. *Hikikomori* boy surfacing. Good news/bad news. Story of my life these days. Encrypted file. Accompanying notes from Wilson: *Little Angels file—accessed several layers, not all the way in. Enough 4U? More will cost. Typical small business, bit more secure than norm, not hardened target. BUT!!! What's deal with Dr E???? Cracked government agencies with less security.* Cerberus *fortifications. Not dealing with that; hope whoever's protecting him doesn't track* me *down. Human intel only way.*

Thanks, *hikikomori*. Human intel. Yes, but how was I going to get into Flierville? No way in there without being tracked and recorded.

I could break into almost anywhere in the City and leave no traces but Flierville would test my ingenuity.

Brilliant reappeared, shaking his head. I was sitting in my chair, guilelessly reading a news update, having retrieved my image-loop a minute or so previously, upon Sunil's signal that Brilliant was heading back to his office. I'd also been checking for the signal from Hugo's tracking device but it hadn't shown up. Not that I'd expected it to. Every time I thought of Peri and Hugo I felt a sick fall in my belly, the same feeling I'd had standing on the point of the prow in Cloud City and walking down the central aisle of the church over the cavern.

We wrapped up the interview, with Brilliant promising to contact me in a few days. I left the church through a back exit onto the park facing the rear of Parliament House and walked away with the uncomfortable feeling that Brilliant might actually offer me work, which was not a scenario I'd planned for. I'd assumed I'd be unacceptable to the church and had quite looked forward to waxing indignant over my rejection and perhaps even threatening them with action in the anti-discrimination tribunal.

On the train back to 80 Metre Road Station, I glanced at the Little Angels file and skimmed some of the stuff from Brilliant's office but I was distracted. Peri and Hugo, and Luisa, hovered in my thoughts and were the cause of the churning in my guts. Thomas was on my mind just as constantly. If he became a flier I didn't want him getting mixed up with that church; I didn't want him to become convinced of his own superiority and destiny as a flier. Yet wasn't I contradicting my own aims by feeling that way? Didn't I want to raise Thomas above the crowd, literally, by transforming him into a flier? Like my own parents sending me to St Ivo's, I wanted to give him a better chance in life but didn't want him to take on the attitudes of the class to which I was trying to give him life membership. Didn't make sense. Change but remain the same. Be better than I am but don't show it. One of those impossible injunctions parents force on their children.

I was distracted too because I was pondering how much double-dealing I would risk with Sunil. Ordinarily on a job like this I'd be paid to work through the material I'd gathered and present it predigested in useful form. This time, though, Sunil had directed I was to hand everything over without looking at it. Usually I'd have been only too delighted to oblige. Not this time. This information would touch closely on many things I needed to know, in relation to not only Peri's case but also my anxieties for Thomas. I was not used to betraying clients this way. Still, what Sunil didn't know wouldn't hurt him. I'd send him the material that night, sure he had no way of finding out I'd kept a copy of it for myself.

At Ventura, I fed Frisk and settled down to read the material Wilson had sent me from Little Angels. Much of it was different versions of the catalogue I'd already seen. Inquiries from families. Were there other girls like Peri, girls who'd done more than just look after baby? If so, there were no obvious requests for wet nurses. Everything seemed above board. No mention of girls wanting wings. There was the information on Peri that I already had from Chesshyre plus a few other messages, including one from the Church of the Seraphim recommending her to Harper. How had she known anyone there? No mention of wet-nursing or surrogate motherhood for her, though. Not surprising; stuff like that wouldn't be written down.

I sat up. Finally, a reference to a Luisa. Nothing in a catalogue; there was a request for a girl and then mention of just one name, Luisa, sent to someone called Abbey Lee Wright. This Luisa, if it was the same one, had been sent to Wright's family four years ago. I checked the address listing, called the location up on my desk screen. Images of the house gave nothing away, though the place looked expensive, enough to suggest hiring a nanny would be no big deal for these people.

I went back to the Little Angels material. I'd have to check out the Wright house when I got Taj back. There was a whole file of forms I hadn't looked at; I began paging through them. Each form was a Little Angels application for a temporary work permit with the girl's name and the sponsoring family. There were several permits and extensions for Peri but no reference to permanent residency. There were no permanent residency applications at all in the files Wilson had sent me.

With the lists of girls' names, their ages, a bit of background on where they were from and their work experience, I had enough information to call Cam at home.

'I've got names and dates for you.'

'Send the list to me here,' Cam said. 'There is some serious shit going down at the department. A request came in from the police and I've never seen anything like it. They're trying to keep it quiet but a hornets' nest has been stirred up. I'm going in on Sunday—hope no-one else will be there and that it's not too late.'

'Not too late for what, Cam?'

'Just—just wait, Zeke. I'll talk to you soon.'

The next morning, Friday, as I shaved I thought of Henryk in his dark suit at the minister's office. Then I smiled. My best ideas often came to me as I shaved and I'd thought of a way to get at Eliseev's records. I wasn't going to enter Flierville at all.

Instead, I looked up the prospectuses for every private school in the City. It took time but finally there it was, the distinctive maroon and gold uniform. *Per Ardua ad Astra.* Of course the school's databases were not public but even I knew enough to get through such basic defences. There was Ellie Kahdr, her personal details—lactose intolerant—and contact information for her mother, Mira Kahdr. Best of all, there didn't seem to be any other caregivers. Mira and her daughter were alone in the world. Their address was interesting: Junction Road No. 5 at the end of Winston Road, better known as just 'Off Winston Road'. That was a Central Lines address and about as specific as addresses ever got in the great hive of the City's oldest slum. Mira's number was on the school records of course but it would not be wise to ring her now, at work. I'd frighten the wits out of her. No, personal contact was the way to go and I knew just the man, one of Central Lines' brightest stars, to open negotiations. Better to wait till after midday at least to contact PapaZie though; he rarely went to bed before four in the morning.

I started work on the Brilliant material with Frisk asleep on my feet, a living golden rug. Would lions be such a universal symbol of power if people understood just how goddamn *lazy* they were? Unlike Frisk, I had to work all day. There was so much stuff from Brilliant's office that it was hard to know where to start.

I set the AI on the slick to make a rough first pass, sorting names and categorising subjects the way Sunil usually asked me to do it, particularly pulling out financial transactions and names of prominent associates. When Sunil got the material he'd also look for references to other Seraphim and well-known fliers and so I looked for them too. Right away I found many exchanges with Chesshyre but they were old, to do with the design and construction of the church. My guess that Brilliant had been a difficult client was confirmed; he was unpredictable, expansive and excited in one message, querulous and stingy in the next.

I didn't know exactly what I was looking for yet but the flier world was tight; there might be something that would give me a lead on Peri or Luisa. I knew how fallible the AI was though. I settled down again with a cup of tea; there was no substitute for doing most of the reading myself. Hours later I looked up, bleary-eyed. Time to contact PapaZie. One more time I paged through the matrix the AI had set up of the various projects the church was developing. At a glance I could see each project, who was associated with it and the funds attached to it. Or some of the funds. It seemed there was some obscurity around the church's financial dealings. The projects had names like Chalcedony, Serein, Hermes and Pinion that gave no clue to what they actually were.

I got up, stretched, rang PapaZie.

'I know that place,' PapaZie said when I gave him Mira's details. 'Off Winston Road. Good cafes, restaurants, all along there. And a soap factory in behind. She will know me, so many nights singing and playing around those cafes. Everyone know me there.'

'Be discreet,' I said. 'Make it a good thing to do, not just for money, you know? She'd be helping a vulnerable girl, not much older than her daughter.'

'Yeah, I know, I know,' PapaZie said. 'I know these people. They work hard, care for their children. She might do it but it's risky for her. You sure you go ahead with this?'

'I'm sure.'

Towards the end of the day, I picked up my car; I hated not being able to think of it as Taj any longer. We navigated across the City through the long golden afternoon. The car needed my help; the AI was naive and still learning how to use the combination of GPS data and information (or more likely misinformation) provided by the City itself. It needed the cunning Taj had built up over years. Much of the pleasure I'd taken in the car was now gone.

I drove to the Abbey Lee Wright address. It was late enough to hope that someone might be home but no-one came to the door. I scouted around a little but there was nothing, just the green lawns and quiet streets of the rich.

Oh well. I got back in the car and looked up Abbey Lee Wright but of course there were a few of them, and how could I be sure Harper had got the spelling right? There were Abby Wrights and an Abbey Lea. I looked up the fliers, then filed the links to pore over later. I'd rather find someone at the house; after all, I knew Harper had sent a Luisa there.

On the way home, we skirted the rim of the harbour, where a dark bank of cloud was blowing up from the sea. As it drew closer to the City, the wind freshening, turning the sea choppy grey and white, buffeting the palms on the headlands, I watched its progress, fascinated and a little alarmed. This was one of the wildest, stormiest summers I could remember. A seagull blew past me, shrieking, as the wind picked up. Fliers would have to be careful in this weather too or they'd be blown sideways just like that gull.

Then it hit me. Oh no. *Oh no.*

The weather. City-dweller and non-flier that I was, I hadn't even thought of it. The rain was hitting now in great blowy gusts. I checked the slick, looking up Wednesday's weather. It had been clear in Pandanus. I checked further south. There it was, a big storm off the coast. The same storm, probably, whose trailing edges had lashed Cloud City when I was there with Chesshyre. I stared at the animated map, its innocuous contour lines and its cute spinning circles showing the front and the supercell storm moving through. Poor Peri. Poor little Hugo. I was used to thinking of Peri as a runaway girl, not as half-bird. That the weather posed a real threat to her hadn't even occurred to me. That frantic zigzagging on my slick as I watched the last signals from Hugo's tracking device: had I been watching Hugo and Peri's final moments struggling with this storm?

Knowing about the storm pitched a new element of chaos into the picture and though Henryk had already promised to do this, I spent any moment I could spare from helping the AI navigate in trying to contact every hospital, clinic, police station and doctor's surgery within a plausible radius of the storm's centre, trying to find out if any persons matching Peri's or Hugo's description had been brought in. None had. Consumed by these tasks, I nonetheless snapped to instant alertness as I reached the door of my flat and found it wide open.

My first thought, a wild flaring of hope, was Peri. Had she somehow returned early? Had she got in and left the door open? No, that darkness, that silence was sinister.

I slid my weapon out of its holster and edged towards the door, listening. I had a good idea of what had broken into my flat and I did not want to meet him. There was no sound. I crept inside and paused, the rising pressure of my blood thudding in my ears like footfalls. I was wary but exhausted and didn't want to be taken by surprise. I crept further into the hallway, listening. No sound. Could I be mistaken? Could I have somehow neglected to close the door properly?

After my eyes had adjusted to the darkness, I saw jumbled outlines that told me there was no benign explanation awaiting me. I'd seen scenes like this too often before. I moved into the living room and the flat brought the lights on. *Bloody hell.* The place had been trashed. My stuff lay tumbled everywhere; books, papers, cushions, blankets, even clothes and kitchen utensils had been brought in here and dumped. There was something vengeful in this, as if in failing to find whatever he was looking for, my house-breaker had punished me with this wanton desecration. At least, I fervently *hoped* he hadn't found what he was looking for.

I went straight to my dining table, my heart painful in my chest, as if someone was squeezing it hard, but to my intense relief my desk slick was still sitting there. Presumably it was still there only because the intruder had been able to download its contents or, conversely, because he knew that he would *not* be able to break through its security devices and into the encrypted files. After all, no-one should be able to even switch the thing on except me, or at least someone in possession of my irises, but who knew better than I did that no security device was infallible? Later I could try to check whether its security had been breached but if the intruder was a real expert I might never know for sure.

Oh Christ on a bike: if my data had been stolen, heaven help me if Sunil found out. I groped for my personal slick in my inside jacket pocket. It was there; I always kept it on me, no matter what. Even if the intruder had erased my desk slick, all the most important information was copied onto my little personal one.

The flat felt empty. Quickly, quietly, I cased the other rooms. They were empty, in disarray, the chaos complete. *You bastard.* And where the hell was Frisk? Had he been abducted? I methodically searched each room, examining objects, snapping pictures of the mess for the insurance report I'd have to file. No point treating this as a crime scene; I'd never be able to prosecute the perpetrator for this.

As I sifted through the mess in my bedroom, a dark spot on the pillow caught my eye. Dried blood. On my pillow. Frisk's. I could see the scene play out like a film: Frisk, asleep on my pillow—of all the comfy spots, the one most forbidden, most tempting. *Bad, bad Frisk.* Why couldn't you have been in the closet, shedding fur on my jumpers? But my closet had been ransacked too. No safety there. Frisk asleep, surprised by an intruder. He would have growled, his territory threatened, all that big-cat courage roused, that great lion nature animating his diminished body. He would've sprung and been smashed back down. Then what?

I stepped outside the flat, pulling on a jacket even though it was warm, and locked the door behind me. Oddly, the lock still worked. I peered at the door. Now that I inspected it, the door appeared unmarked. Whoever had broken in had done it smoothly. A professional then, which made me even more uneasy. Breaking in would not have been hard. I'd generally relied on Ventura's down-at-heel look and unfashionable location to protect me. I was an advocate of the theory that too much obvious protection tended to attract the wrong sort of attention. Besides, Ventura had had surveillance fitted a few times and every time the cameras had been stolen or smashed within days.

I searched around the building, calling for Frisk. Up and down the driveway I went and around the small, lush garden filled with durable blooms engineered in lasting colours: semi-permanent spider lilies, hibiscus, frangipani. I peered up into the branches of the mango trees. Scouted the street. Nothing. As I came back to my front door I examined the frame again and this time something caught my eye. I picked it up. A dark red feather. A *red* feather.

No, no, no. Not possible. Two Raptors after me? Who would send a second one? Had to be a flier; Henryk had said they only worked for fliers. Rich fliers—well, that was a tautology, to be a flier was to be rich. Except Peri. And Luisa. Others like them? I could be pretty sure no nannies were sending Raptors after me. Not a cop, like the Archangel Michael. Chesshyre could conceivably have a second Raptor if something had happened to the first one. Brilliant, checking me out? Surely not, breaking in was over the top. Or maybe it wasn't. He'd want to know who the hell I was if he'd discovered what I'd done. That would strongly indicate he had something to hide.

I thought back to the incident in the Ventura laneway when Frisk had surprised a Raptor for the first time. No way of knowing if it had been the black one Taj had seen or this one with the red feathers. Dark red looks black at night. Chesshyre had pretty much admitted the black-winged one was his but I had no proof he'd come near me since bugging Taj. And he'd seemed genuinely shocked when I'd asked him to call off his Raptor during my visit to Cloud City.

Inside, I tied back the mosquito net draped over Thomas's bed. My nervous exhaustion and lack of sleep were catching up with me. I had to get hold of Henryk but my eyes were gritty and dry and I needed to close them for a moment . . . I lay down and put my head on Tom's pillow, breathing in his sweet dry smell from the sheets, images and sounds all mixed up: Frisk crouched to spring; Peri and Hugo at Janeane's; Chesshyre gripping me on the bridge; fur matted with blood; Thomas flying.

I woke suddenly. Oh god, how long had I slept? I jerked upright into pitch blackness, my thoughts scattered, and fumbled for my slick. 'Henryk?' I said but there was no answering voice; I'd been awoken by a message from Lily. I scanned it rapidly. Thomas had passed his initial assessments.

I staggered into the bathroom, stripped off my crumpled, sweaty clothes and had a shower, hoping to clear my mind. Still drugged with sleep, I checked the time; much too late to call Henryk. *Goddamn it.* I sent Henryk another message, asking him to contact me first thing in the morning.

Tom's room was the least chaotic in the flat and I sat on his bed to read over Lily's message. It was disconcerting. The way Ruokonen had described it, I'd assumed the assessments would be part of a long, exhaustive protocol. Apparently not. Knowing Lily, maybe she'd found a way of fast-tracking the procedures. Now she demanded my consent. Put up or shut up time. Look what Peri had endured to get her wings. I could make it so easy for Thomas. Like every child, it was his dream to fly but I didn't think Tom had ever seen a flier. Did he even know his dream was possible?

Brilliant's phrase was haunting me: *The human project is over.*

Two in the morning again, as it seemed to be all the time these days. Sleep was impossible so I began the demoralising task of cleaning up. I moved through the flat, absently picking up objects, half-heartedly trying to restore order. My thoughts kept turning to Peri and Hugo. I sat down and ran the security footage of them again: Peri closing the door, stepping to the cliff, disappearing, over and over. She'd fled in terror and it looked like she'd been right to be afraid. Over and over, pale and frightened but determined, she turned away from me, stepped into thin air. Were these to be the last images of her and Hugo?

A weight settled on my chest as I pondered the severity of the storm, the ruthlessness of the Raptor. What had happened to Peri and Hugo? The heaviness spread to all my muscles and even to my brain. It was hard to remember what I was supposed to be doing. I must be coming down with something. That would fit. Right about now *would* be the time to get sick and I could only hope it was a cold or flu and not some exotic parasite from RaRA-land.

I woke up on the couch early Saturday morning with a stiff neck and a dragging weakness all through my muscles but I began searching for Frisk again right away. I started with Vittorio, who was appalled to hear that Frisk was missing and frightened that a creature as large and dangerous as a Raptor had been able to break into and trash my flat without his knowledge. His thin anxious face creased into a hundred worry lines as he explained that he'd gone out for a drink with a friend and that he'd noticed nothing amiss when he returned. I then spoke to neighbours I knew a little, the ones who'd stopped to pat Frisk, or talked to me in the corner store, then to those I knew only by sight. Some were shocked, others indifferent. *Sorry, can't help you.*

There was no sign of Peri before I left and none when I returned. Back at the flat I showered, dressed, made myself tea. I couldn't eat. Instead I jumped up and looked out the window every five minutes, thinking I heard something. I didn't expect Peri to show but I could not stop myself from waiting.

At nine am Chesshyre rang.

'We need to wait a little longer,' I said. I was going to have it out with Chesshyre for endangering Peri and Hugo with his Raptor, but not yet, not till I was sure Peri would not turn up.

Chesshyre called again at ten and again at eleven and again at midday. Not a good sign. It didn't seem Chesshyre was getting information from anyone else. So, that made it unlikely the red Raptor was his. That would fit with his denial at Cloud City, when I'd accused him of staking out my place. But if that meant that the Raptor at Ventura the first time was the red one, and not Chesshyre's, then it couldn't be Brilliant's either because the first time the Raptor checked me out I hadn't met Brilliant yet.

My head hurt. I took a painkiller and worked on the stuff from Brilliant's office in between Chesshyre's phone calls, trying to figure out what the church's projects were. I opened the matrix. I could assign many of the messages and documents I'd stolen to one of these four projects, though of course there was a torrent of everyday trivia I had to dump under other headings, everything from complaints about air-conditioning to tracking investments.

Chalcedony and Serein I could file and ignore; one was a recruitment drive, trawling for more fliers to attend the church, the other was a set of policies and strategies centred on Brilliant's career as an MP.

Hermes and Pinion, though, these two raised my hackles. The more I looked, the more it seemed Pinion was the most sinister; it was a strategy focused on the church's enemies, how to discredit them, shut them up—even, if I read between the lines, threaten them. So, the church had a dirt file of its own; it'd been running its own black ops.

Hermes was the most obscure but what set alarm bells ringing for me was how tightly held under wraps this project was: Brilliant was only communicating with one or two people about it. Understandable if it was small. I started sorting through the financial transactions to be allocated to Hermes on the matrix. After an hour I looked up, got the matrix to run some calculations.

I ran my hands through my hair and pulled at it.

Hermes was not a small project. Money was being funnelled through it in regular, large amounts that were always roughly the same and through one person only. Brilliant's communications to this person, someone calling themselves Sparrow, were cryptic. And the money only went one way; it was all *from* the church, *to* . . . whoever. Some trust or account. There was no way I'd be able to work out who really got the money.

I got up, stretched. Didn't matter that I couldn't find out that detail. Others could.

I looked at the red feather lying on my desk. I was no closer to figuring out who sent the Raptor who'd left that feather; I didn't *know* any other fliers. Unless it was Avis, for some weird jealous reason of her own that Peter knew nothing about. That made no sense. Unless she wanted the girl killed.

Oh shit.

Unless it was whoever had killed *Luisa*. After all, the thing had first turned up after I got back from RaRA-land, after I'd been told about Luisa. I couldn't see how anyone could know about Luisa but I had initiated database searches, I had spoken her name to Henryk. Anyone with enough power and enough paranoia could possibly have hacked those calls and searches.

I went outside, looked up at the sky. No large dark spots circling. Why would there be? They must have everything on me they could get by now. Unless they were waiting for Peri.

Henryk did not call or answer my message. Must be busy today, doing something unreasonable like taking the twins to soccer clinic. No reaching him now till Monday morning.

A message. *MK Central Lines Sun am Off Winston. Best Quality Cafe Isn't It.* Thank you, PapaZie. Mira was going to meet me with the information I'd asked for. At least one thing was going right.

I drank more tea and fell asleep in the wet heat. I awoke to the insistent cricket-chirp of the slick by my head on the kitchen table. I stared at it balefully, not sure where I was or even who I was. Consciousness came more fully as the slick chirped on and on. I was paralysed.

I could not reach out to answer it. I left the kitchen to take another shower, trying to wake up fully. Things were going no better than could be expected.

As I turned the shower off I heard the slick again. I dried myself and dressed. The light outside my bedroom window showed the heaviness of late afternoon. The slick was still shrilling. I picked it up.

'We need to talk.'

By the time I drove to Chesshyre's house, dusk was falling. I didn't enjoy the ride in the flying fox but after Cloud City and the church it held no terrors for me.

Chesshyre silently received me in the living room and led the way to where he had clearly been sitting for some time, looking over the water, a half-empty bottle of wine on the table next to him. Where was Avis?

Chesshyre indicated a chair, also facing out over the ocean, then poured me a glass of wine. I hadn't tasted real wine since my wedding but I had no intention of drinking Chesshyre's. A breeze was blowing up from the sea, lifting the hot, damp hair off the back of my neck, and the sound of the waves was loud in the room. I realised Chesshyre had retracted the roof and the transparent wall so that we were sitting in the open air. We were silent. Perhaps Chesshyre was waiting for me to speak, to explain what was going on or propose a course of action, but I was so tired that I just sat there for a moment and looked up at the first few stars.

I listened to the water breaking against the rocks far below. I imagined flying out over the ocean on a still night like this. The temptation would be to fly forever, to join the albatross and stay out of sight of land, skimming fast over the waves. I snapped out of my reverie. Time to ask serious questions.

'Peter,' I said, 'it's time you were straight with me. Peri may still be on her way but I have no idea where she is now. She can vanish, literally, into thin air. And my car was fitted with a tracking device.

Someone, your Raptor I presume, was keeping tabs on where I went in RaRA-land. I'm concerned he might've caught up with Peri. Is that why she isn't back?'

Chesshyre turned on me. 'So, should I go to the police? What do you propose I *do*?'

'Yes, of course you should go to the police,' I snapped. 'But you never had any intention of doing that. How could they succeed where your bloody Raptor has failed? Worse than failed—*killed* Peri. Maybe even Hugo. Not much point going to the police if you're as unforthcoming with them as you have been with me. We need to know what's really been going on.'

I heard Chesshyre shift in his seat, the stiff rattle of his feathers.

'Come on, Peter. I've been doing my homework. Would you like to know a few of the things I've found out?' I turned to face him and, though his expression was unreadable in the night, I could sense the tense posture of his body.

'So,' I began. 'Number one, I know that girls from the country don't get wings for wet-nursing. Two, I know who gave birth to Hugo and it wasn't Avis. What I *don't* know is why Peri also got permanent residency.'

Chesshyre was silent.

'Well,' I continued, keeping my tone more reasonable than I felt, '*if* Hugo is still alive and you expect he'll just be returned to you, no questions asked, you are mistaken. Things have gone too far for that. There are going to be questions about what you did to get him.'

'No,' said Chesshyre. 'That's why I hired you. Hugo is *our* baby and Peri has been paid well for her part.' *Paid well.* Emphasising that Peri was also to blame.

'It's not a deal that would stand up,' I retorted, my fury at Chesshyre returning. 'Peri was underage, don't forget. She could not consent to a legally binding contract.'

'You think there's a court that would award Hugo to *her*?'

'That's not my concern,' I said, 'but you should think hard about what arrangements you're willing to negotiate. You don't hold all the cards anymore. And another thing: a second Raptor, a red one, broke into my flat and trashed it and Frisk has disappeared.' I wanted him to hear that Frisk was injured, vanished, dead.

'I've told you,' Chesshyre said, 'that Raptor has nothing to do with me.'

'Whose is it then?'

He shook his head.

'Really? You have no idea?' I stood up. 'Right. I'm not working for you anymore. Just so we're clear about that. It's too dangerous. Plus you've lied to me from the start. I've already taken this to the police. If you give a damn about Hugo, you will too. *And* I've told them I fear Peri and Hugo are dead.'

I left Chesshyre sitting in darkness.

It was only on the drive home that I reflected that Chesshyre had not yet paid my last, big invoice. My rash, self-righteous action had just cost me a lot of money.

13

INTO THE WILD

Her fingers were clenched tight, so tight that the pain had passed from agony to numbness. Peri was crouched on the burning circle of metal, pinned by the light, but something was tugging at her; her fingers were prised away from the hot metal and at first Peri was so relieved to be rescued that it took a few seconds to realise something was wrong. Something important had been left behind.

Wait, she cried. *We have to go back*. No-one heard her. *Wait!* screamed Peri. *Why can't you wait?*

With each second, as the column of light whirled into a spinning vortex, the winds accelerating, the air shining horribly, the light blinding her eyes as surely as darkness, Peri's desperation grew as she was torn upwards, higher and higher. She could never find her way back. The loss was irreparable.

When Peri awoke she didn't know who she was. Or where she was.

Her mind was blank. She could see colour and shape but it meant nothing. That expanse of grey there could be a wall or a rock face or a cloud. She felt a heaviness at her back and heard a rustle of feathers as if some giant bird were in the cave with her. So she was in a cave. She wasn't sure why she had decided this. A surge of alarm washed over her as her most recent memories flooded in, as if this other part of her mind had just opened a door and been overwhelmed. Storm. Black sky. Falling. She remembered who she was and whose wings those were that she felt.

They were hers.

Were they still so strange? Would they ever be part of her?

Something worse was coming into consciousness and she cringed as if one of the thin stabbing suns of lightning were about to strike and she knew what it was but had no image and no words to put to it but it was coming and it was about to crack. The silent sharp edge of light cut her. She was illuminated and would have given anything to remain in darkness a moment longer.

Hugo was not there.

Peri sat up, throwing off a light, warm blanket, and looked around wildly. Was Hugo asleep in the cave with her? There was nobody else in this small space, more overhang than cave. What had happened in the storm? She'd lost consciousness in the dark. No memory of being brought here surfaced. Whoever had helped her might say to her, *Baby? We didn't see any baby.*

Sobbing with fear, Peri searched around her, though she knew Hugo wasn't there. 'Hugo! Hugo!'

Her terror increased when she realised that her skims were torn and dirty and her hands and feet and ears were bandaged. A thin grey bracelet circled her wrist. Peri jumped up and ran out of the cave, its entrance half obscured by a green curtain. It was not even a thought, only a recognition, as she ran, that the green curtain was a hanging, dripping swamp, starred with flowers, like the vertical swamp behind Peter's house.

She was falling through the air. The swamp had obscured the drop at the very lip of the cave.

I'm going to die.

The air was cold, with a pre-dawn chill, and silent. The cliff sped upwards past her in a blur.

I can fly and I shouldn't be falling like this but it's happening too fast and I'm stiff and cold and . . . there. *Now.* Peri's wings were pushing her upwards even as she was thinking this. They had come to life themselves and were saving her, just as if they really were part of her body and took seriously their job of preserving that body's life.

Each wingbeat thrust her higher and she was rising into grey still air. A slash of orange burned along the edge of the world. Peri soared over the clifftop. Blue mist pooled between bronze trees. A cloud rolled over one cliff face like a waterfall, pouring white and thick into the valley. On a landslide down one cliff to the west, facets of jumbled rock, giant dull cabochons, started to catch the morning light. A pair—no, a trio—of eagles revolved against a cliff face rising from the other side of the valley.

'There you are,' said a voice above her in the still air. The voice was deep but its tones were soft and clipped so that Peri hardly heard the words.

Startled, she looked up. Above her soared the biggest flier she had ever seen, his wings glossy dark chocolate with undersides shaded copper with hints of purple.

Peri angled her wings to spiral upwards so that she was flying alongside him. 'Hugo?' she gasped, the urgency of her question so great she could not find other words. The man looked puzzled but the dread on Peri's face must have struck him for he said, 'Oh, you mean the baby! He's fine. So that's his name, eh? We've been calling him Storm.'

Peri's wingbeats faltered. The man said, 'Stay close and just a little behind me. Our people need to see that you're with me.'

Peri followed the man as he folded his wings a little, falling in a controlled dive towards the trees on top of the cliff where she had fallen from the cave. As he dived below her she was intrigued by a patterning on his wings that she'd never seen on any flier: a lightning bolt flashed diagonally in golden feathers down the deep brown of his wings, one half of the jagged bolt on each wing. The flash was echoed by another golden bolt shining in the glossy black of the man's short hair.

The man pulled out of the dive while he was still well above the trees. Now Peri could see a white thread unspooling down the cliff wall. They aimed for the thread, dropping until it grew into a ribbon.

Above and behind the waterfall, Peri could see a small beach bordered by a semicircle of green river flat dotted with fliers. The man arrowed down towards a pool in the river, splashing into it in a flurry of wings and water. It was a splendid sound, surrounding her in the grandeur of Flight. Peri was conscious her landing in the pool was more albatross than swan—she tumbled over herself, swallowing a mouthful of river, then righted herself and waded onto the shore, water sliding from her wings.

A woman with deep blue wings came up to Peri and handed Hugo to her. Peri couldn't speak. Tears started from her eyes as she took Hugo to a patch of cleared ground on the river flat and sat down with him, her back against a log. Hugo wriggled with delight as she felt him all over, was this really him, was he really okay? She was alarmed to see that Hugo's hands and feet were also bandaged and his arms and legs were mottled with bruises, but at least nothing seemed broken. How long had she been unconscious? What day was it?

Peri sniffled and wiped her tears away and kissed the top of Hugo's head, breathing in his heady scent, that smell she would know anywhere. She kissed his hands and nuzzled his neck, and felt her heart subside into a slower, peaceful rhythm. Hugo cooed and patted her cheek, each soft touch thrilling through her like the flutter of wings. She straightened up and held him so that he could suckle.

With Hugo settled, nursing, Peri watched the fliers gathered around a small, smokeless fire in the centre of the clearing. As far as she could tell, there were no non-fliers here. What was this place, *who* were these people? She slid the grey bracelet around her wrist but there was no getting it off.

Seeing that Peri had finished the first part of her reunion with Hugo, the woman with blue wings came over to her. 'I'm Finch,' she said, setting Peri's waistband at her feet and handing her some energy strips to eat. 'At least I am *here*. My nom de guerre, you could say.'

'I'm Peri. This is Hugo.' Peri rummaged in her waistband with one hand, the other supporting Hugo, and pulled out a tablet of Opteryxin to swallow and a dose of Aileronac to inject. She hesitated, unsure whether to take a second dose to make up for the time she'd missed, then decided against it.

'Can you tell me what these are for?' Peri said to Finch, pointing at Hugo's bandages.

'You need to speak to Jay,' said the woman. 'He's the one who gave you first aid.'

The man—*Jay*—had disappeared but soon returned with a falcon perched on his gloved fist. He knelt near the shallows of a pool and the falcon fluttered off, splashing and ruffling in the water. There was a clear tinkling sound as the bird moved.

'What's he doing?' said Peri.

'He's giving Shaheen, our peregrine, her bath.'

Finch sat by her while the others went about their business. They ignored Peri; whether out of tact or genuine lack of interest she didn't know. The fliers nearer the fire looked young, barely out of their teens, but they were older than Peri and looked confident and self-possessed. Jay was older again, perhaps in his late twenties, and Finch must have been at least forty-five. She was short and wiry, with deep-set blue eyes in tanned, lined skin and long dark hair that was the same indigo as her wings.

Four of the young fliers, having finished breakfast, conferred briefly, then waded into the river and took off from the cliff edge. They shrank into black dots against the sky and Peri realised the three eagles she'd seen against the valley wall must have been human.

Peri watched the peregrine finish her bath; the bird shook the water off her breast and preened her feathers. She bobbed up and down as she drank the river water.

'Come on, sister,' said Jay. 'Stop bowsing.' The falcon hopped onto his fist. She was a large, beautiful bird with slate-blue wings, a dark cap, pale face and throat, regular barring on her belly and strong feathered legs. The tinkling sound was made by little bells attached to bands around her yellow ankles.

Jay brought the falcon over. 'You're admiring our Shaheen,' he said. 'A fine girl, eh? We did have her mate, a lovely little tiercel, but we lost him, unfortunately.'

Peri stared at the falcon until Finch turned to her and said, 'So, what are we going to do with you? Dealing with you alone wouldn't be too hard, but a baby as well . . . that makes things difficult.'

Jay squatted on his haunches with the falcon still on his fist. Peri felt a strange sensation watching the mirroring of man and bird, as if a carved Garuda, like a statue she'd seen once in the Church of the Seraphim, had come to life and was looking at the smaller winged creature on his hand, the great sweep of his wings paralleled in the graceful arcs of the falcon.

Jay said to Finch, 'Pale Male had a few words to say to me. He said I'd made the decision for the unit by saving her and the baby. He said I'd acted unilaterally and outside the chain of command and *I* said I had no choice. In a storm like that—it was a split-second decision—I'd like to think he'd have done exactly as I did.'

'What did Pale—I mean, what did Niko say to that? Jeez, Jay, you're going to have me calling him that.'

'Well, *you're* not allowed. Anyway, he said I was right.'

Jay glanced at Peri sidelong, the tilt of his head reflecting the way the falcon cocked her rounded head. He was taller than Peter and heavily muscled with skin that gleamed like polished wood. Short black hair stood up from his broad forehead. His thick brows arched slightly over long, dark eyes. His mouth was wide, with the elegant curve of his upper lip longer than his lower lip. Elaborate abstract blue tattoos ringed his massive upper arms. Peri assumed that, like Mama'lena, he must be from the Islands. 'I've taken a risk for you two. Make sure I don't regret it.'

'Thank you,' said Peri.

'So what did you and Niko decide?' said Finch.

'She stays. We need to know more about her.'

'What is this for?' Peri held up her wrist with its grey bracelet.

Jay frowned. '*That* is your monitor. It kept you secure while you were recovering in the safest place we had for you. It also tells me where you are at all times. Don't try to remove it. You cannot.'

'Oh.' Peri felt as if the breath had been knocked out of her. So that was why Jay had appeared the moment she left the cave. These people were really serious about something, but what was it? Why did they see her as a threat? 'What about these?' Peri said, pointing to Hugo's bandages.

Jay considered her. 'How are you feeling?'

'Tired.'

'And your hands and feet?'

'Tingling.'

Jay nodded. 'Frostbite,' he said. 'Or frostnip, probably. You were coated with ice when we caught you and both of you are covered in bruises. You took a pounding from the hail.'

Jay squatted next to Peri, the falcon still on his wrist. He drew a small kit out of a pocket in his trousers and from it took out an injecting pen. 'Hold still.'

He pressed the pen to Hugo's arm, then took out a second pen and pressed it to the skin of Peri's shoulder. 'Analgesic,' he said. 'You've both had narcotics against the pain during the initial rewarming. You've also had shots against tetanus, antibiotics against infection and anti-inflammatories against further damage from inflammatory mediators. Your bandages are covering aloe vera dressing to aid the skin in healing. His dressings should come off later today. He was subject to minor frostnip only. Babies can be such tough little buggers.' Jay ruffled Hugo's hair.

'Fortunately you had him right next to your skin,' Jay continued. 'That's a good way to prevent frostbite. Though a better one would be to avoid being sucked up into a supercell storm to a height of over nine thousand metres.'

'Nine thousand metres!'

'Yes. Higher than Mount Everest. Jet aeroplanes used to cruise at around that altitude but it's not recommended for most fliers. We call it the death zone. You endured temperatures of minus fifty degrees Celsius, perhaps even lower. A handful of fliers have survived similar experiences but it is not the norm.'

'Why did we live?'

Jay shrugged. 'I'd say it's because you're both very young and resilient and you lost consciousness. Your heart and metabolism slowed down in the blackout, which enabled you to survive the hypothermia and lack of oxygen at that altitude.'

Peri shuddered. 'It happened so fast—faster than you can imagine.'

'Not faster than *I* could imagine,' said Jay.

Peri almost smiled at the magnificent condescension in his tone. Who could he be, to say such a thing so grandly?

'But your ascent *was* almost inconceivably rapid. You two rocketed from about four hundred metres to over nine thousand metres in less than fifteen minutes. That's quite a ride.'

'How do *you* know how high the storm took me?' said Peri.

Jay shot Peri a glance as sharp as the falcon's. 'You really don't know?' he said.

Peri shook her head.

'That's interesting,' said Jay. 'We'll leave it at that for now.'

The falcon moved restlessly on his fist. 'May I?' Peri said, extending her hand.

Jay shook his head. 'No. You don't touch a hunting bird.' He turned to Finch. 'I've been flying her at hack for a month now and she's still trained. That's good for a haggard hawk. Sweetest-natured haggard I've ever had.'

Peri dropped her hand.

'Jay is our strongest flier by far,' said Finch. 'You're lucky he's one of the ones who found you in the storm.'

E-chup-e-chup-e-chup, said the falcon, looking at Jay, the notes so ringing Peri felt them in her bones. Shaheen swivelled her gaze back to Peri and Hugo.

'Which does make us wonder,' said Finch, 'why you and Hugo were out there in those conditions.'

'Yes. Of course. I—it was a mistake. Of course. You saw how fast the storm blew up. I had no idea . . .' Well, that was true enough. 'I was visiting my—my aunt and I was taking Hugo back to the City. I thought it would be safe to fly. I was wrong.'

'I see,' said Finch. Peri could see they didn't believe her. She looked away. It was better to keep on with questions of her own.

'How long was I, was I . . .?'

'You were unconscious all day yesterday. We brought you and the baby in late the day before.'

'Oh.' That meant it was Friday morning. Zeke Fowler would not know yet that she would fail to keep her word. Where was she? Was she close enough to the City that she might still make it back in time for Zeke to help her give Hugo back?

'Yes,' said Finch. 'The little fellow cried for you but you had to sleep.'

Peri looked up at the swath of dull green and brown bush, streaked vertically white and satiny grey, rolling up like smoke from the river bank opposite.

'Where are we?'

Jay ignored the question and, turning to Finch, said, 'Shaheen will need to gorge sometime in the next few days. If we take her to the bramble farm there should be plenty of rabbits and maybe a few small birds for her.'

Peri guessed they would not tell her where they were until they knew more about her. Hugo pulled away and sat up. Peri tucked her breast back into her shirt, which was tattered, like all her skims, from the storm, and studied Jay, who wore only a pair of military-style trousers with the cuffs rolled to mid-calf and faded to the no-colour of bleached grass, a large knife in a sheath belted around his narrow waist, and the thick glove upon which perched the falcon. Finch was clothed in drab grey shirt and shorts.

Peri risked another question. 'What are you doing here?'

'We're learning to fly,' said Finch, so flatly that Peri could hear there was a whole world hidden within the words.

'Oh,' said Peri. Anyone who could survive the storm that had nearly killed her and Hugo must know how to fly in ways she'd hardly dared to dream were possible.

'I wish I could stay with you for a few days,' said Peri. 'Learn more about how you fly.'

'You'll get your wish,' said Jay.

'But I can't stay,' said Peri, her heart thudding in her chest at the steeliness in Jay's voice.

'It's not your decision,' said Jay, his voice deep and harsh. 'You'll stay until I've decided it's safe for us that you leave. *If* you leave. We saw you weren't alone in that storm. Not everyone has a Raptor after them. That's too much heat for us.'

'That's why I have to go,' said Peri, hearing her voice tighten, rise in pitch. 'I have to take Hugo to safety.'

Jay laughed. 'Whoever is after you has no chance of finding you here, believe me. You aren't going anywhere till we're sure of you. Don't try to leave without my permission.' He waved his hand at the bracelet on Peri's wrist. 'Understand me? That monitor can do more than just track you.'

'I understand,' Peri said. No point arguing with Jay now; she had to make him see he could trust her and she'd have to do it quickly.

'Do you realise the Raptor didn't survive the storm?' said Finch.

'Did you kill him?' said Peri.

'No,' said Jay. 'We just didn't save him. Our only option was to save you and Hugo.'

'Thank you,' said Peri, feeling her words to be inadequate, though her gratitude was tinged with anxiety. She was now a prisoner. How far would they go to protect themselves? They'd let the Raptor die, after all.

'You will thank me,' said Jay, staring hard at her, 'by doing as you're told.'

Hugo rubbed his eyes violently. 'He's tired,' said Peri, dropping her eyes from Jay's gaze. 'Is there somewhere safe I can put him down for a nap?'

Finch led Peri past the river flat and then turned along a stream spilling into the river. Peri squatted down and wet the edge of her shirt, using it to scrub at the dirtiest patches on Hugo's skin, but that only thinned the dirt and spread it over more of him. She gave up and pulled one of his shirts from the waistband. Later there would be time to wash him properly.

'We had him playing in the sand by the river early this morning,' Finch said. 'I'm not surprised he's tired.' She stopped on a miniature white-sand beach. 'In there,' she said, pointing to a track leading into thick brush against an overhanging rock wall. Peri followed the track until it opened out into a sand-floored shelter under the overhang. A young man lay on his side, cushioned on his wings, dozing on a wafer-thin mat. A khaki mosquito net was fastened so that it covered most of the area of the shelter. Peri settled Hugo onto another mat, which was surprisingly comfortable, though it was hardly thicker than the sheet covering it.

'Put this on baby,' said Finch, handing her a grey bottle, 'and yourself, every morning and evening. Cover all of you, especially ankles and wrists.'

'What is it?'

'Military-grade mosquito repellent. We have some nasties out here and what they carry you do not want.'

Peri knelt next to Hugo to spread the astringent gel over him. Then she covered herself with it. Its fumes made her eyes water.

'I have to stay with Hugo,' Peri said.

Finch shrugged. 'Remember what Jay said. He's not kidding. You owe him your life. And Hugo's. Don't forget that.'

Peri nodded. Later she would make Finch see why it was so important for Peri to take Hugo away to safety.

After lunch, some of which Hugo vomited back up over Peri, and after she'd cleaned him and changed his padding and washed them both and he'd settled into his afternoon nap, Peri found her eyes closing again. She was still exhausted in mind and body.

Late that afternoon she was awoken by the thud of running feet. Calls of 'Glass-off! Glass-off! Come on!' rang through the trees. She and Hugo were alone in the shelter.

Peri picked up Hugo and carried him towards the river flat. A young woman with green and scarlet wings and long dark hair pulled into a ponytail pushed past her.

'What is it?' said Peri. 'What's glass-off?'

The woman called back over her shoulder, 'Jeez, you really are some kind of wuffo, aren't you?' and hurried on.

Peri found Finch on the river flat pulling on grey leggings and a long-sleeved grey top.

'What's going on? Is everything alright?'

Finch stared at her. 'Are you serious?' she said. '*Glass-off!* Couldn't be better. Why don't you come with us? Hey, Phoebe!' The young woman who had pushed past Peri looked up from where she was hurriedly grooming her wings.

'Take the little boy for a while, okay?'

'No *way*,' said Phoebe, returning to her rapid grooming. 'I am not missing glass-off for anyone, not even you, Finch.'

'Okay, okay. You'd think we didn't get glass-off here every few nights at this time of year, the way everyone's so precious about it.'

Phoebe paused, her expression serious. 'The way I see it is this: I'm only going to get to fly so many glass-offs in my whole life, right? And glass-off's only about, oh, *ten times* better than sex. Even Raf admits that.'

'Alright, but you're helping later on, you understand?'

'Yeah, yeah,' muttered Phoebe, slipping away from them towards the cliff edge.

'Just bring baby with you,' said Finch, slapping on mosquito repellent. 'Glass-off's about as safe as it gets when you're flying anyway.' Straightening up, she handed Peri the repellent, then looked her up and down. 'No possible way can you fly in *those* skims anymore,' she said. 'Tell you what. Grab the sling for baby and meet me back here. I'll have something more, ah, suitable for you to change into.'

When Peri returned to the river flat, Finch handed her a set of soft bluish-grey leggings and top. As Peri pulled them on she kept examining them, puzzled. Finch laughed at her. 'Don't try to decide what colour they are,' she said. 'The whole point is that they're about the best camouflage you can wear. Against clouds they're grey-white and against sky they're whatever shade of blue the sky is.'

'They feel like silk,' said Peri as she put Hugo into his sling.

Finch grunted. 'Well, they're not. They're many times more precious than that. Take care of them. You won't be getting another set, that's for damn sure.'

Peri followed Finch along the sandy path to the cliff edge and took off a few seconds after her. It seemed that all the fliers here, fifteen or so in all, were now strung out in a line above the cliff. As she took off she felt the most powerful smooth lift, strong as water, sliding her up a sunlit mountain of air, and now she was floating high over the ridge and everywhere evenly streamed upwards this buoyant transparent ocean.

This was no mere thermal: this was massive release of all the day's heat from the valley and now she and Hugo, silent and breathless, were sliding along the plateau of risen glass, with the other fliers suspended all around them as if in honey, some also silent, others whooping and laughing. Below the eastern cliffs the valley was sunk in an indistinct indigo sea, washed with purple along the ridgelines, and down in the dusk of the valley floor floated slivers and bubbles of liquid steel—water catching the last light—but up on the ridgeline it was still golden afternoon with the trees shining green and white-trunked in the simmering sinking sun and the sky was still blue and the clouds were catching a rim of steel fire along their undersides as luminous as the fragmented water in the valley and it was singing with such clarity that Peri knew she had never truly seen mountains or valleys or water or clouds before.

'Watch out for the cooling bumps,' sang Finch as she sailed past, her wings still and poised as she slid down one side of the glassy mountain. 'They'll catch you round about sunset as the air starts to cool off. But till then—hey, it's like flying in champagne! Champagne with all the bubbles rising and it's taking you right to the top of the glass. Just swirl around in it as long as you can.'

Once the sun had fully set and the glassy air developed ripples and slumps and fractures, Hugo started from his dreaming trance and began to grizzle. For the first time while flying with Peri he struggled against the sling, whining and kicking.

Peri dropped towards the cliff face. She did not want Hugo to shatter the air with his crying while the other fliers were still enjoying the final drifts of glass-off.

When Peri landed, she found Finch already on the river flat, eating a cold supper, which she shared with Peri and Hugo. 'Just tell me *how good* was that?'

'I don't believe in heaven,' said Peri. 'But I just experienced it anyway.'

Finch laughed. 'Funny you should say that. This is actually called, on some old maps, Heavener Ridge. So you just experienced the Heavener glass-off.'

Once they'd finished eating, Finch told Peri to put Hugo to bed. 'Phoebe will stay with him,' she said.

Peri was not happy about leaving Hugo in the shelter with the brusque young woman but he was already drifting into sleep as Finch shepherded Peri back to the cliff.

'Where are we going?' said Peri as she pushed her way through the brush along the track, which gleamed faintly in the gathering starlight. A heady night scent rose around her, a dry tang of bark and shrub, a wild perfume of leaf and flower and faint yet distinct river odour.

'You'll see. This is our work,' Finch said in a low voice. 'Finding out. We work on this ten to twelve hours a day. Not only in the air but on the ground, thinking, talking, comparing. Working out the technicalities, the specs. Pushing the envelope. Do you believe the doctors who gave us the treatments know the possibilities? Of course they don't. Most have never flown themselves. And Flight Gym instructors are used to controlled conditions and they're used to working with beginners. Flight Gym's a bloody aviary. It can only give you the barest beginnings of the skills you need. We've got to figure out what the real possibilities of Flight are. There are people who know about the mechanics of flying from aircraft and birds, and believe me, we study what they say, but we are dealing with *Flight*, with how it feels and works in your own body, and nobody knows much about that yet.'

'That's why you have Shaheen,' said Peri.

'Of course.'

'Are you the only ones doing this?' said Peri.

Finch balanced on the cliff edge as she stared into the dark, up at the brightest stars Peri had ever seen. Brighter than they'd been over the sea and even brighter than at Janeane's.

'No, we're in touch with other groups,' said Finch. 'I'd hate to think it was just up to us. You can't do this in the City; there's too much else to do and too many other pressures and distractions, especially if you're rich enough to have wings. And there's not the variety of conditions to practise in. *And* you need a group. If you try to do it on your own you might end up turning Wild. So, do you feel rested? You should. You've slept and glass-off is just happy hour, eh? It's not exactly hard work.'

'What—why—' began Peri.

'One of our most important areas of exploration is night flying,' said Finch as she unfurled her wings. 'Jay is taking a group but I think you and I should start off alone.'

Together they soared into the warm night. Peri kept silent, concentrating on mirroring Finch, as much as she could mirror the dark outline flying against the night sky. Peri was acutely aware of how much larger and clumsier all her movements were. So hard to concentrate only on her flying. It felt wrong. There was always that rushing panic, beneath thought, when she left Hugo. She was certain disaster would overtake them both when she was not with him, especially if she concentrated on something else and let go her constant, diffuse awareness, as if she held him in the world with the net of her thoughts and bore him up safely only with the force of her continuous attention. He might wink out, a falling star, if she lapsed.

Flying at night felt more three-dimensional than during the day. All Peri's senses reached out as the night engulfed her. The dark wrapped tight around her and extended in every direction. She floated upwards. There was still warm air rising but no proper thermals to do the work for her. She was strong. She could power herself up.

Peri watched Finch, imitating the angling of her wings and body. Finch slowed a little and Peri caught up, staying behind her right shoulder. Finch was *teaching* her. This was a flying lesson, with Finch exaggerating her movements a shade more than was natural. There was a flow to Finch's flying as easy as walking. She didn't think how to do it. She just did it. Peri began to hope this might be possible for her.

Finch moved in closer until she was flying wingtip to wingtip with Peri. 'Ordinarily, I wouldn't take an outsider like you on a flight like this but Jay thinks that the sooner you feel part of the group, the better. Jay already made that decision, now we have to follow through. We took responsibility for you by saving your life, we took you over, really, but for this to work you owe us much more information. For a start, you can tell me what the hell you were really doing out there in a storm with a baby.'

Peri drew her breath in sharply.

'You have to tell me,' said Finch.

'I know.' Peri looked across at Finch's dark shape against the stars. 'The weather was fine when I started. It was stupid to fly without better tracking of the weather but I had no instruments. I had a flight plan but it wasn't nearly detailed enough.'

'We do that all the time,' said Finch. 'Flying without instruments. But not for long journeys. *Something* was driving you. What was it? We need to know if what you're running from is going to come looking for us.'

Peri sighed. 'I was working in the City. For a family. Well, they weren't a family. Yet. The agency that sent me to them had worked out what I wanted. What they wanted. How both of those things could come together.'

Peri could feel Finch staring at her.

Peri bowed her head. 'I would give them a baby. They would give me wings.' It was painful to speak these words, hard to believe she'd spoken these terrible words twice in a few days when she'd never said them before, not even to herself. To admit the starkness of the bargain she had made. She sank down in the air, her very muscles weakened by sadness. She was the bad mother in the fairytale, giving away her first-born for salad greens.

But the child was not mine. I did not think he would be mine. That's no excuse. I know that now.

'My god!' exclaimed Finch. 'Peri, you poor thing. That's dreadful. So you took him and flew away?'

Peri shook her head. 'It's complicated. My friend was killed. She'd made the same deal as me. And they were going to send Hugo away. You've no idea how they . . . Anyway, I had no idea what I was agreeing to,' she said. 'I was so *stupid*. I had no clue; I'd never been pregnant. I didn't know . . . how could I? . . . what it does to you.'

Finch blew out her breath noisily in a sigh that could have been disbelief, pity, outrage. 'So, no-one knows you're here?'

'How could they? *I* don't even know I'm here. I don't know where *here* is.'

'But they'll be looking for Hugo. What do you plan to do?'

'I was going to take him to—well, a long way away. But I changed my mind. I'd decided I had to return Hugo, that ultimately he was better off with his family, but then the Raptor was after me. Finch, you *have* to let me go. I have to take Hugo back. Soon. Or god knows what will happen to me, what they'll do to me.'

'I see,' said Finch. This time, Peri could hear Finch believed her.

The stars were tantalisingly near. Peri drove herself higher. She wanted to get closer to them, further from the ground. She'd never flown at night before without Hugo in her arms, without navigating carefully, concentrating hard. This was different. Lighter. How high could she fly? The air chilled along her arms but she was warm from the work, the soft feathers of her wings skimming her back. It would be glorious just to see; after all, they had talked about pushing the envelope . . . and the night was so calm.

Higher and higher.

The stars were so bright. Surely it was possible to get closer to them? They were glassy and sliding, like melting ice. They were singing. What were they singing, in those high shivery voices? She had to swallow, make her ears pop so she could hear them.

Up here the air was freezing, stinging the frostnipped skin under Peri's bandages and each breath, each wingstroke, was hard work in the thin air.

She was dizzy.

Where was Finch?

She looked down.

Nothing.

How high was she?

Below, all was dark. No landmarks: no campfire, no pale thread of waterfall, no darker and lighter shades of cliff face. A layer of cloud had gathered, far, far below, too distant to make out any shapes. Cloud formations were still described as if from the ground, looking up. Peri was not yet used to seeing them from above.

In her rapture under the stars she had no idea where she was or even whether she'd kept her wings level; was she dizzy because she was spiralling down and didn't even know it?

Peri tried to power upwards. The only safety lay in gaining more height but she was gasping for breath. The singing of the stars was higher too, piercing. They were too high. *She* was too high, but it was dangerous to drop; she might dive out of control. *No visible horizon and the stars are no help, shrilling in my ears like that, can't tell if my wings are level. Don't panic, breathe, can't breathe up here—*

A wingtip brushed briefly across her back.

Finch was flying next to her. Where had she been? 'Concentrate. We need to fly lower so you can breathe better. Don't worry so much about keeping your wings level. We've found there's an internal gyroscope of sorts. It'll work; you have to learn to feel it. Most fliers are too frightened to practise this or trust it. You need others to help you through the first few times.'

Finch coaxed Peri down into warmer, heavier air and they flew eastwards over dark country. As the wheel of stars revolved over them, Peri relaxed into the cadence of long-distance flying, her wingbeats and heartbeats slowing into the rhythm. They had been flying this way for about an hour when she said, 'So, what was that?'

'You were flying high,' said Finch. 'That was good, just under five klicks.'

'You're joking!' said Peri. 'Why did you let me?'

'Come on, Peri. I'm not your Flight Gym instructor. We're not here to hold your hand every minute. We'll help keep you safe but you have to push yourself. You have to feel these things for yourself. Feel the joy of it, too. Find your own reasons to fly.'

'Doesn't seem possible to fly that high.'

'You'd be amazed. Cranes can fly at six thousand metres. Some geese fly higher—they even surf along the jet stream. You need to find your own ceiling, work out what's safe for you. Raptors experiment with that.'

'And the gyroscope? The internal horizon?'

'There's a lot of controversy about that. I am certain there is one, that it has also come through in the modifications, whether in bird DNA or in some added spec, which would make sense to me, but no-one's discussed it in the official literature; they just recommend you don't fly in cloud without an altitude watch. Some experts argue that some have the gyroscope and others don't. That it's only present in some treatments. Impossible for us to check because we don't know where in the sequence it's coming in.'

'That would explain why no-one speaks of it,' said Peri. 'If only some have it, and they don't know who, it's too dangerous to mention.'

'Maybe,' said Finch. 'But I think they don't understand it yet.'

'You mean it's part of some other modification and they haven't realised it?'

'Perhaps. So far, everyone we've worked with has had it. That's the interesting part. The difficulty is that there's no easy, surefire way of getting you to feel it and trust it. We just have to work on it as best we can.'

'You don't wear an altimeter or any other instrument,' said Peri, as they turned to head back. During the turn she tried to experiment with how she might feel an internal horizon but it was frightening and didn't make sense when she could use the stars to help her as she banked. They righted themselves and checked their heading.

'Ooooh, cranking and banking a bit there, weren't you?' laughed Finch. 'That was a sharp turn.'

When Peri didn't answer, Finch continued, 'Birds have navigational abilities so remarkable that we're still struggling to understand them. Echoes, ghosts of these, have come through in the modifications. If we work at it, we believe we can become more perceptive and skilful in using them, but you can't do that if you're relying on an altitude watch. You know that birds have a barometric sense in their ears but did you know that if you were as sensitive as a duck, you'd be able to tell which floor of a building you were on just by sensing changes in barometric pressure? That's useful for avoiding storms too, of course, as well as for telling whether the air you're in is rising at a constant rate or sinking at a constant rate. I mean, you can tell when you *enter* a thermal, you can *hear* it, specially if you get a boomer, but without a variometer most fliers don't know whether the air they're in is rising or sinking. We're not as sensitive as ducks yet, that's for sure, but I've flown enough to know my height under most conditions.'

Finch began to fly faster and, despite her fatigue, Peri forced her wings to match the new rhythm.

'Even more remarkable is compass sense and map sense. Compass sense, knowing where north is, requires an internal timer to work if you're cueing from the sun. Some birds, like homing pigeons, can navigate as if they knew their latitude and longitude at all times. That's map sense and we can't explain it. It doesn't rely on orienting to sun or stars, though birds can do that too, but homing pigeons can home just as accurately when it's overcast and when they're released somewhere they've never been before. Don't you think it's worth investigating abilities that astonishing?'

They flew on over dark country, the only sound the wind through their feathers. Peri wanted to keep flying but she needed to rest her wings. The analgesic Jay had given her had worn off and she felt every one of her bruises, as well as aching from her overworked muscles.

Finch said, 'The flight watches have everything: altimeter, artificial horizon, satellite navigation, time, wind, airspeed, pressure, variometer, weather forecasting and more. It's all there and you don't have to do any of it yourself—and why would you? It's dangerous and it's hard. The problem is, you will never feel what it's like to *fly* if you use those all the time.'

'And I will never feel what it's like to hit the ground at two hundred k an hour either,' said Peri.

'Well, you will if you don't learn to deal with the dragons for yourself.'

'Dragons?' said Peri. 'I don't understand the way you people talk at all.'

'That's because you've barely flown outside of Flight Gym, and you haven't flown with other fliers, have you?'

'No,' said Peri.

'Dragons are all the unseen dangers fliers face. Turbulence, rotors, wind shear, even gravity waves. For example, when you fly you've got to look for rotor triggers and avoid them. No instrument can help you do that. And if you're not willing to do that work, why bother flying at all?' added Finch. 'It's a lot easier not to.'

They were flying in a black sphere, its top half pricked with light. Peri felt as if she extended beyond her body, as if she reached out through her head, through each feather in her wings, into the darkness. She felt extended through her great primary feathers especially, as if they were sensitive antennae, picking up messages vibrated through the air. There wasn't a clear boundary. How far out could she feel her way?

Finch said, 'If anything happens to your watch, if it slips off your wrist or the satellite link is down or you bash it against a rock or land badly or it just stops working, what then? You're disabled. Flying blind, without any of your own abilities. You're not really a flier. Just a tourist. That's all most fliers are. Just tourists dependent on expensive gadgets and an even more expensive drip feed of drugs.'

Peri thought. She could see that for many fliers what Finch was saying would never matter. They'd use their watches and fly barely conscious of all the forces at work in their new world. They would not give themselves to this new life. Who knew what it might mean? For many of them, wings had not come at such great cost as they had to her. But she, who'd sacrificed so much, could she bear to feel that barrier between her and Flight for the rest of her life? If she didn't make the element her own, how could what she had gone through be worthwhile? There was no way forward other than the one Finch was showing her.

'Does your group have a name?' said Peri.

'We're called Audax.'

'It's more than you were used to at Flight Gym, isn't it?' said Finch as they splash-landed in the black water pooling above the waterfall at the edge of Heavener Ridge. Peri hadn't seen any sign of the Audax camp from the air. Even though she could now see the small fire in the clearing, shielded from above and on three sides by a kind of metal oven, there'd been no telltale spark of light through the trees. She only recognised where they were from the twisting strands of water down the cliff face.

'You know, they don't have a clue in the City,' Finch said as they walked out of the water, passing a group of three black-clad fliers on their way to the cliff edge. Peri assumed they were a patrol. 'There wouldn't be ten people in the City who really know how to fly. Wings are a fashion accessory or at best an extreme sport to them. It's too scary to become a real flier. Because you know what? Wings are *heavy* unless you give something up. Otherwise no freedom. No true Flight. Becoming a flier is not just about gaining wings; it's about letting other things drop away.'

Before Peri could say, *What things? What do I have to drop?*, Jay appeared and spoke to Finch. They left on some mysterious errand, telling Peri to help herself to the food hidden in the cool larder among the stones under the water.

Peri found Phoebe sitting outside the circle of firelight with Hugo wrapped tight, sleeping, next to her. After bolting fruit and energy strips standing up, Peri settled herself next to Hugo. Phoebe, who had acknowledged Peri's return with the slightest tilt of her head, was grooming her wings by a lightstick, which was hung under cover in a tree. No-one flying above, or approaching the camp from any direction other than from the river, would be able to see it. After a few moments Peri began grooming her wings too.

Something relaxed in Peri as she worked over each feather until it gleamed in the blue light. Finch's words had loosened the tightly pulled knot of self-loathing and fear around Flight that she'd felt ever since gaining her wings.

If no-one in the City knows how to truly fly, then maybe I'm not hopeless after all. With these people, maybe it's possible to learn to fly. How could I have known this was what I needed? Flight Gym was supposed to be enough.

Before the transition, you never think beyond getting your wings and your first flight. Like giving birth—you couldn't imagine what happened afterwards, until you did it. Then you understood, though no-one could tell you, that birth was just the beginning of your transformation, not its end. No-one warned you that you could feel just as lost after the transition to Flight. Well, who was going to confess their own doubts and weaknesses? Luisa, maybe, but we had so little time together. I need to learn from these people. There's no time now; they have to let me take Hugo back to the City, but maybe I could come back here?

Exhausted, Peri picked up the bottle of repellent from where it sat next to Phoebe and covered herself and Hugo with the gel again, laid one wing over Hugo, covering his little body from neck to toes, pillowed her head on her other wing and slept.

When Peri woke it was deep night. She and Hugo were alone but then she heard fliers splashing down into the river. Hugo snuffled and snorted and started to wake up. She cradled him against her breast and he suckled briefly. As Peri watched fliers wading out of the river and up to the lightstick she thought about how much food they must need, and the waste pit they all had to use, across the other side of the river and well away from the water. A new pit would have to be dug soon. Even this small flock put pressure on the wilderness.

Finch materialised from the trees behind the river flat and sat next to Peri. Two young male fliers walked by and as they passed the tall one with blond hair looked over to where she was nursing. He turned back to his friend and said, laughing, 'Man, there's some serious groundsuck potential there.'

Peri turned on Finch. 'What does that mean?'

'Ah,' said Finch. 'You *really* haven't spent much time around fliers. Don't worry, that's just Rafael—Raf; he doesn't mean any harm. He's one of your rescuers, you know. Anyway, it's a compliment. Ground suck is anything that pulls your attention away from flying.'

A circle formed around the fire as fliers arrived and gathered to talk while they ate. Peri's stomach fluttered with the tension of her uncertain status as both prisoner and member of the group. She was on probation. It was up to her to prove herself to them. They had to trust her enough to let her return Hugo, as she'd promised. Hugo cooed at her in her lap. She answered him under her breath, mimicking each sound. *Aboowah. Baabow.* He patted her cheeks and looked into her eyes. She stared back, falling into that open gaze.

Finally, nine fliers had joined them. Peri could not see Jay. They were armed with knives, Peri noticed, though several also had holsters on arms or legs for compact weapons she'd never seen before. She would have liked to take a closer look at those but knew better than to try. Peri searched their faces. Which one was Niko, the famous Pale Male who wasn't sure if Jay should have rescued her? That man there, wading out of the river, who looked about forty and was now besieged by other, very young fliers, who were surrounding him, almost mobbing him, talking to him, questioning him, competing for his attention, that *must* be him. Niko must be the name he used with this group in which everyone had an assumed name. He cast a sidelong, curious glance at Peri. Before she looked away in confusion she had a glimpse of a tall, rangy man with steel-coloured wings and a thin, elegant face. His hair stood up in silver bristles, as if he were an enormous, short-crested parrot.

The fliers were talking about the extremes to which they pushed themselves, the tightness of their spirals, the speed of their descents. While Peri was struggling to follow what they were saying, Hugo snoring softly against her, someone came and stood over her, blocking out the stars. Jay.

'How did you go?' Jay said to Finch.

Peri waited for Finch to answer, to hear her verdict. 'Good,' she said. 'She specked out.'

Jay laughed at the expression on Peri's face. 'Specked out is good. Means you went so high you became just a speck in the sky.' He crouched next to Peri, opening the small bag he'd set down on the ground. 'Give Hugo to me.'

Peri lifted the sleeping baby into Jay's arms. Gently, Jay removed the bandages from his hands and feet. 'Hey, little brother,' he said as Hugo woke briefly, then drifted back into sleep once his bandages were off. Jay inspected Hugo's skin, then wiped it over with a cloth he'd removed from a package. As he bent his head over Hugo, the lightning bolt striking across his hair gleamed in the firelight.

'More antiseptic and new skin,' Jay said, sealing the old bandages up and putting them into the bag. 'Look, skin good as new, eh? Kids heal so quickly. He won't need any more dressings. Even his bruises are changing colour faster than yours.'

A bellow went up from the other fliers as they realised Jay was among them.

'Safety meeting!' one yelled. 'Safety meeting, safety meeting, safety meeting,' the others chanted until Jay stood up and walked over to the centre of the group. He patted the air with his hands to quiet them.

'Looks to me like you've already started your safety meeting,' he said, gesturing to the bottle of something, Peri presumed it was beer, in Raf's hand.

'Yeah, safety meeting started at least a half-hour ago,' Niko said from where he lolled against a log, his wings draped over it. The younger fliers formed a semicircle opposite Niko at a respectful distance.

'Please, sir,' said Raf, 'I wanna know how to pay the rent.' The others laughed. 'C'mon, safety meeting. Give us your energy lecture, man.'

'Bullshit,' said Jay. 'You can't be serious. You are such a bunch of fucking wuffos, you really are.'

'Steady on,' said Niko.

'Safety meeting, my arse,' said Jay. 'You all need to get some sleep.'

'We have to wind down,' said one of the young women. 'We had some big air today.'

'What's a wuffo?' whispered Peri.

'Newbie,' said Finch. 'They're always saying, *What for you do this? What for you do that?* So, wuffos.'

'Big air, eh?' Jay was snarling as he paced the circle, clearly enjoying himself. 'Big air, *Jesus*, you call *that*, what you had today, big fucking air? It never ceases to amaze me what a pathetic bunch of wuffos you all are. Certain members of Audax,' he spun gracefully on one heel, acknowledging Finch and Niko, 'excepted. You poor little rich kids get your treatments all paid for by Daddy as your graduation present, your wings are slapped on by some ignorant doctor who's not even a flier, you're booted out the door with a gazillion pills and a year's membership of the Dead-as-a-Fucking-Dodo Flight Gym and you think you can fly!'

As Jay turned again in his pacing, Peri admired the way the lightning bolt zigzagging across the back of his wings seemed to glow with its own light.

'Well,' Niko said, 'we don't, actually. That's why we're here. We're not all as lucky as you, with your six years of rigorous training with the best of the best. All at taxpayers' expense too.'

'Luck,' grunted Jay. 'You call what I've done and what I've been through luck? Anyway, I know all that, I'm *here*, aren't I? I'm not off somewhere making my goddamn fortune.'

'You're a good man,' said Niko. His voice was quiet and Peri was fascinated by the way each flier strained to hear his every word. If Jay was their commanding officer then Niko was their political leader.

'Okay,' said Jay, holding up his hands. The light from the fire illuminated his brown face from below and struck sparks of red from the iridescent undersides of his wings. 'You want me to talk about energy, eh? So, someone recite the first rule of flying.'

'*Maintain thine airspeed, lest the ground arise and smite thee*,' yelled Raf.

'Yes,' said Jay. 'That's it. Airspeed is one form of energy in the bank while you're flying. It's your scarcest resource, by far. First thing is: every millisecond you're in the air, you're paying rent, eh?'

'Right!' roared the young fliers.

'And why are you paying rent?'

'First law of motion!' said Raf. 'The first law of motion states: *A body at rest tends to remain at rest, while a body in motion tends to remain in motion in a straight line unless it is subjected to an outside force*.'

'And that outside force is?'

'Gravity!'

'So every second you're in the air you're paying rent. In energy. To overcome the force of gravity. You're paying tax, too, and what is that tax?'

'Drag!' said the young fliers.

'Alright. Drag and dissipation of energy through heat loss in accordance with the second law of thermodynamics. Now, what do you have in your energy budget? What's in the bank, people?'

There was a rattling of feathers among the fliers. One of the young women said, 'Well, muscle power?'

'What gives you muscle power?'

The young woman looked around her uncertainly.

'Fuel. Respiration. So, food and oxygen, yes?' said Jay.

The fliers nodded.

'I'm glad we can agree on *that*,' said Jay, raising his eyebrows. 'So, that's chemical energy and it goes one way only; it's not reversible. Once we use it, it's gone, transformed into work and dissipated as heat and drag. Also, it takes *time* to convert fuel into chemical energy for flight. But we have several other forms we can use. Such as?'

'Lift,' said Niko.

'Lift as in the force generated by a body moving through a fluid? That's mechanical energy and without it we couldn't fly at all. When a flow of fluid is deflected by a solid, such as your wings, the flow turns one way and creates lift in the opposite direction, according to the third law of motion.'

'I was thinking more about thermals, things like that.'

'Good. That kind of lift includes thermals, compression, convergence, ridgelift, wave lift, glass-off and wind. All those forms of lift are ultimately solar energy; you use it to supplement your own chemical energy. Of course solar energy is not just your glorious ally, it's also your most terrifying adversary, as anyone who has flown into wind shear or rotors or thunderstorms knows only too well.' Jay glanced over at Peri and winked. Peri was grateful she was seated away from the fire; she hoped no-one could see her blushing.

'In the real world we can't be said to be using up solar energy when we use the lift in a thermal. But there's another very important form of energy we use all the time. I've mentioned it already.' Jay stared around the circle. 'No? Didn't *any* of you study physics? Pale Male?'

'Yes,' said Niko. 'A long time ago. Remind me. Remind *us*.'

'*Mechanical* energy,' said Jay.

'Uh, you mentioned airspeed,' said Raf.

'That's one form of it. Airspeed is kinetic energy. The amount of kinetic energy is proportional to the square of your airspeed. And?'

'Ah, actually I do know this,' said Niko. 'Potential energy.'

'Yes. In other words, your *altitude*. Most of the time that's the biggest deposit in the energy bank you've got. Remember what they drill into you in Flight Gym: *When in doubt, hold on to your altitude. No one has ever collided with the sky.*' Jay paused.

Peri lifted her head and looked up at the stars. *I* managed to collide with the sky. If breaching the wall of the updraft wasn't colliding with the sky, then what was it?

'We use this potential energy constantly,' Jay continued. 'Every time we take off from a cliff we're converting potential energy to kinetic energy. Every time you glide or dive or bank you're converting potential energy to kinetic energy. Every time you use your speed to push you higher, you're going the other way, converting kinetic energy to potential energy. Your kinetic energy and your potential energy together make up the mechanical energy at your disposal. Now, there are some very beautiful things about mechanical energy: one, it's *fast.* You can convert it into the form you need instantly. Two, it's *reversible*. You can convert altitude to speed and back again, in just the way that a rollercoaster does, as many times as you like, though you'll dissipate some energy as you do it.'

'What about what you said earlier about airspeed being a scarce resource?' said Raf.

'You can see now that of all the forms of energy you're using, airspeed's your most limited. Therefore, it's your most critical variable. Pay attention to it. You run out of airspeed faster than anything else. Keep it for when you need it; when all else fails it'll buy you a few crucial seconds but that's all.' Jay paused to take a mouthful from the bottle that Raf opened for him.

'If you run into trouble remember this: you will always have *exactly* enough airspeed to get you to your crash site.' Jay looked around the circle as they laughed. Peri waited for his attention. When he finally glanced at her, she felt a rush of giddiness, like falling.

'Now, how does all this affect your flying? Well, for ordinary City fliers, not so much. Most of their flights are short. Some of this stuff they'll do instinctively, like using house thermals for soaring or ramps for take-off: they're topping up their energy account with altitude, see? But we're different. *You're* different. You're learning how to fly long distance and under all sorts of conditions. And to do that, what I've said will really start to change the way that you fly. You'll prepare your flight plan strategically, sketching out your projected route, altitude, response to anticipated weather and other conditions, with everything that I've said in mind.' Jay handed the bottle back to Raf and resumed pacing, his hands outlining each of his points in the air.

'Your strategy will affect your behaviour during flight too; that is, your tactics. You need discipline when you think about your energy budget. For example, on a long flight you'd never just soar up to a higher altitude whenever you damn well felt like it, as you'd be cashing in airspeed and a whole lot of chemical energy too.'

Peri's cheeks burned. Jay was describing how she'd flown that last day with Hugo, before the storm; raggedly, impulsively, climbing and diving with hardly a second thought. She'd tried to find and use lift but she'd flown without discipline or understanding. And she'd actually thought she could make it across an entire continent. The birth of a supercell storm had escaped her notice until it was too late. She should dig a hole in the ground and cover herself with dirt for shame. She hardly deserved to be alive after the stupid things she'd done.

'Instead,' said Jay, 'you'd wait until you found a thermal or ridge-lift and you'd use that to take you up to cloudbase. You'd also be very aware of *blue holes*; you wouldn't just launch yourself into the space between clouds thoughtlessly. You'd think about whether you should skirt it and use the lift under the clouds around its rim to get you around the hole and on your way. You might even attempt dynamic soaring, gaining kinetic energy by repeatedly crossing the frontier between air masses of differing velocity. Birds of prey are good at this: they climb into the wind gradient, swapping ground speed for altitude, while preserving airspeed. They can even gain energy by turning downwind and dropping through the wind gradient. But that's getting real technical now, eh? You'll have the chance to practise some of this tomorrow. Now get some sleep. You're going to need it.'

Peri didn't like the sound of that but she was too tired to ask questions. She said goodnight to Finch and crept away with Hugo to the sand-floored sleeping shelter. For the moment decisions were out of her hands. Tomorrow she would appeal to Jay. Perhaps Finch would vouch for her, tell him her story. They were so strong, these fliers, so much more powerful and confident. How could they think she could pose any danger to them?

Sleep came so deeply that it was as if her consciousness winked out, light swallowed by a black hole.

14

JUNCTION ROAD NO. 5

Sunday morning I woke up sunk in dread. I didn't want to face the chaos of my flat. The disarray was a good reflection of the mess the case—and my life—had become.

Assuming Peri and Hugo were still alive, my flat was now the most dangerous spot for her to show up—the Raptor was bound to be watching it—but there was no way to warn her.

I hauled myself out of bed. Being already exhausted and demoralised made it the perfect time to do something useless, like drive back out to Abbey Lee Wright's place.

This time, a man answered the door, looked me up and down. 'What are you selling?'

I showed him my licence, asked after Abbey Lee Wright. The man shook his head. 'Bought this place from them a year ago. Don't know where they moved to. Some fancy place they'd had built for them.'

'They?'

'Abbey Lee was the wife.'

'They were fliers, weren't they?'

'Yes, they were.'

'Kids?'

'Look, what's this about anyway?'

'Everything's fine,' I said. 'They're not in any trouble. Just trying to find someone who used to work for them, that's all.'

The man nodded. 'They did have kids. A toddler, I think. And a baby. Very little. I do remember that.'

'Did you meet the husband?'

The man laughed out loud. 'Oh, yeah. Once.' He shook his head as if he couldn't believe what he'd seen.

'Something odd about him?'

'Oh, it's just . . . you wouldn't forget *this* guy. Not if you'd seen him.'

I was really interested now. I had this feeling right at the back of my head, a feeling I got sometimes when I knew something was about to join up, two different strands of information weaving together.

I smiled. 'What was so unforgettable about him?'

The man laughed again. 'The *wings*. Never seen anything like it. I mean, stripes, right? Red and green and blue and gold. Guy was a freakin' licorice allsort.'

I sat at a table outside the Best Quality Cafe Isn't It in Central Lines. Mind you, the concept of *outside* was a little theoretical here; this winding lane was more like a tunnel because the houses and shops and warehouses met overhead, plunging the street into perpetual twilight. This most crowded part of Central Lines would be great to live in if you were a vampire; no risk of exposure to sunlight. No risk of a Raptor spying from on high either; he'd see nothing but a baking savannah of patched, rusted, peeling roofs.

I shifted my chair; hot air from the bakery across the street was blasting me and my other side was being cooled by a fan from within Best Quality Cafe Isn't It. It was still early but sweat trickled down my back and my shirt was wet under the arms. Frying eggs and spicy smells from the cafe competed with synthetic perfumey roses and limes from the soap factory, and a stench of dirty water, blocked drains and grease traps.

A waiter came out, set down the house specialty of fresh buttery roti and hot malted.

'Thank you,' I said, wondering whether to ask after Mira, deciding against it. PapaZie hadn't specified a time, just said to meet her in the morning.

I studied my slick. My exhaustion was shading into that euphoria which can overtake you after a night or two of bad sleep, my mood elevated by my visit to the house that used to belong to Abbey Lee Wright. The new owner's information was just what I'd needed to point my searches in the right direction and I'd found her, the right Abbey Lee Wright.

Wife of David Brilliant, MP.

Christ on a bike.

So Luisa, or at least *a* Luisa, had worked for David Brilliant. Of course, as rich fliers Wright and Brilliant would have all kinds of help, including a nanny for their—I checked—yes, two kids. How had they got those children? I studied images of Abbey Lee—she was thin, like most fliers, but that didn't prove anything. The thing now was to find out if a Luisa was still working for Brilliant. If not, why not? If she was missing, why hadn't they reported it?

I looked up from my slick at the dim street thronging with people. I knew this kampung well. It'd been one of my hunting grounds in my former life as an officer of the law but it'd been a long time since I'd visited. No telling how many informers, petty crims and errand runners for the crime bosses I'd tracked down here.

I sipped the hot malted. On my way in, as I'd picked my way through the mud between the shacks, I'd come to a large sign I hadn't seen before: *Main Street*. Main Street was not a street at all but a rounded hump that formed the kampung's central spine. Walking down the middle of the concrete semicircle which was at least three metres across, I suddenly remembered what it was: a large, leaking water main. Ah, Main Street. Now I got it. Very good.

Cam and her colleagues considered Central Lines a 'mature' slum. That meant some shacks had concrete walls, and the residents had organised basic services, such as pirated electricity. Some shacks had their own water tap—an inconceivable luxury in the Venice or most parts of Edge City—and they all had televisions or other screens of one sort or another.

Even in the funereal shadow of Junction Road No. 5, the tin and concrete walls around me glowed, just as I'd remembered, in every shade of aqua, turquoise, saffron and hot pink paint and were plastered with archaeological layers of stickers, graffiti, murals and posters advertising films, toothpaste, oil, politicians. Strings of orange and pink lights outlining doorframes here and there shone weirdly through the morning gloom, advertising gambling dens and cramped bars (Zipper Hurricane, $pooky Baby Gang and BAR BAR BAR BAR! looked like places to avoid).

A group of teenage girls sauntered past Best Quality Cafe Isn't It. A woman hurried up to one girl, whose hair fell down her back, thickly braided with jasmine and a jewelled snake I assumed was not real, or at least not alive. Her hair was longer than her skirt. They had a brief argument. The girls lounged away. The woman, dressed in a purple shirt and trousers and shiny purple beads at her wrists and throat, turned towards the cafe. Mira.

I raised my hand. She came over, shaking her head, and sat down, putting her bag and sunglasses on the table.

'Everything alright?'

Mira rolled her eyes. 'Well, you know.'

Was Snakegirl the demure Ellie I'd seen in the school databases? Well, it was the weekend in Central Lines after all.

The waiter appeared. Mira ordered tea.

'Thank you for meeting me,' I began but Mira held up her hand.

'I haven't brought anything for you,' she said.

'Oh. I see.'

'I don't think you do, if you could ask me to risk my job.' Mira looked around her. A rhythmic pounding started up, a few blocks further back along Junction Road No. 5.

'I'm sorry,' I said. 'I know it's a lot to ask—'

'No,' said Mira. 'It's *impossible*.'

'Okay,' I said. 'So, why are you here?'

Mira looked down at her tea.

'You'd like to talk,' I said.

She looked up, eyes shiny.

'I want you to know that you're on to something.' She hissed the words.

'Yes. Good,' I said.

'Don't give up. Especially for Peri. She's different.'

'Yes, I am seeing that,' I said.

'No, no, you *don't*,' said Mira. 'She is really different. They—' Mira began to weep. After a couple of minutes she rubbed her eyes, blew her nose. 'You know, about the babies?'

'Ah, Peri said she had one. As a surrogate.'

Mira nodded. 'Yes. There's more of those.'

'Women fliers don't like being pregnant?'

Mira shrugged. 'Some do, some don't. Some can, some can't.'

'I see. And Eliseev helps them?'

Mira nodded, drank her tea.

I looked around. There could hardly be a better place in the entire City to have a conversation like this; no flier could see us, no-one could overhear us in all this noise and no human drama, no weeping or screaming or laughing, was unusual or worth noticing here.

'And Peri? Why is she different?'

'She—she didn't know. They didn't *tell* her.' Mira was crying again.

I reached across the table, took her hand. 'Please.'

Mira looked up. 'Peri was already pregnant.'

'*What?*' I dropped her hand.

'The day of the embryo transfer. They tested her. She was already pregnant. Very early. She didn't know.'

'*Jesus*,' I gasped. 'To Peter?'

'Yes. And . . . and . . . she was already out cold, so they left her there while they decided what to do. And they decided to do *nothing*. They brought her out but of course she thought she'd had the transfer.'

'Who decided? Eliseev? Eliseev and Peter?'

Mira stared away over my shoulder. She nodded slowly. 'Dr Eliseev talked to some people. He was very excited. And he talked to Peter—to Mr Chesshyre. I was there, monitoring Peri. And Dr Eliseev said this was good, they wanted *this* pregnancy to continue, that it was better, better for him, better for the company, better for the baby, better for Mr Chesshyre.'

'And Peter agreed?'

'Yes.'

I sat back. 'Wow.'

A moment.

Mira took a deep breath, looked around for the waiter. Ordered more tea.

I'd come to a stop, a machine switched off. My exhaustion caught up with me and I wanted to just put my head down on the table. I could sleep right here, amid the competing racket of televisions blaring from first-floor windows, the squawking of chickens, the fire-eater attracting a crowd a few doors up.

'So, let me get this straight. Peri agreed to have a child for Peter and Avis. But they found out she was pregnant and Eliseev persuaded Peter to go ahead with the child she had already conceived? She gave birth to her own child—genetically, physically, in every way? And she didn't know?'

Mira put her head in her hands. 'Yes. No. I mean, yes, she didn't know.'

'What about Avis? Did she know?'

Mira pursed her mouth, as if sucking a lemon.

She's always like that, Halley had said.

'Mira, does Avis have some sort of problem? Like, oh, I don't know . . . takes too much Zefiryn, something like that?'

Mira shook her head. 'Wouldn't know.' She thought. 'It's possible. Zefiryn's not addictive, though.'

'People can take too much of it.'

Mira looked annoyed. 'It's not addictive the way nicotine is. Of course you can take too much. It's a bit like alcohol—well, it's *nothing* like alcohol in its effects but you know, you can take a little every day without too much damage. But you shouldn't take too much. Lots of people are fine with it. Some aren't.'

'*Why* did Eliseev and Peter do this?'

Mira rubbed her hands over her hair.

Hikikomori boy's message: *What's deal with Dr E???? Cracked government agencies with less security.*

The building. The *building.* Eliseev's whole building was wired up with what *hikikomori* boy called Cerberus fortifications.

'Mira, who did Eliseev talk to? Someone in Diomedea?'

Mira nodded.

'So Diomedea was interested in Peri's pregnancy?'

'They were interested in her from the beginning. As soon as Mr Chesshyre brought her in. Dr Eliseev did the full work-up—well, they always do that.'

'And Dr Eliseev usually consults with Diomedea.'

Mira's expression was flat. 'There's nothing bad about that,' she said. 'The opposite. Dr Eliseev's work with Diomedea is precisely why he's so sought after. He has access to all the latest research and treatments. Don't you see? Diomedea is the *leader*—well, along with MicroRNA/Corvid and a few others—but Diomedea is really the leader in the field. They keep an eye on just about every flier, every series of treatments, every transition to Flight and as much follow-up information as they can. I mean it's not as if there's so many fliers that that's difficult.'

'And in Peri's case, Eliseev actually performed some of the latest research,' I said. 'He'd already done the germline engineering on Peter, before Peri got pregnant?'

'Of course. He could hardly have been ready to do the embryo transfer if he hadn't already done that. It was—it was also to do with her history.'

I'd read some of Peri's file. *Think*. What would interest Diomedea? Something I'd read without paying too much attention, because I had been so focused on finding Peri, now stood out. The very incident that led to her being taken into foster care. Her father had disappeared and she'd been abandoned by her mother on a rooftop. She was three. Burned by the sun, clinging to a railing, it had taken them an hour to uncurl her fingers.

'Her father went missing. Does that have something to do with Diomedea's interest in Peri?'

Mira was checking something on her slick. She nodded without looking up. She wanted to bring this to a close; she'd had her big emotional release, cried over poor Peri robbed of her baby, what mother wouldn't feel bad for her? But she wasn't going to do anything about it.

'Why did Diomedea want Peri's pregnancy to go ahead? And why did Peter?'

'I don't know everything,' Mira said, starting to gather her things. She put her sunglasses and slick away in her bag. 'But there was something about Peri being second generation. One of the first. The Chesshyres—they weren't—they aren't. Second-generation fliers, I mean.'

'Second generation? You're telling me Peri's father was a *flier*?' I shook my head in disbelief. Mira's silence was confirmation: Peri's father was a flier. 'So Diomedea was keen for Hugo—for Peri's child to be born. Because *her* father was a flier. Guess that really does make her exceptional. Oh, oh, now I get it.' I hit my palm to my forehead.

'What?'

'Her permanent residency. Of course. Diomedea would be able to make that happen. And they wanted to make sure she—and Hugo—stayed where they could find them. So they could keep studying them. But why did Peter—Mr Chesshyre—'

Mira stood up. 'Like I said, I don't know everything. But Dr Eliseev promised Mr Chesshyre that Diomedea would pay for *everything*—Peri, the pregnancy, her wings, anything Hugo needed. That—that adds up to a lot.'

'Peter's rich,' I said. 'That can't be the only reason.'

Mira looked down at me. 'Really?' she said. 'I think I must know more rich people than you do, Mr Fowler. Dr Eliseev did say to him one thing though—something like, you know the saying, *a bird in the hand . . .*'

'You mean Peter's chance to have his own child might not come again?'

'Yes. If we aborted her child, went through another procedure with the embryo transfer, more drugs, all that, it's not pleasant—and what if she changed her mind? Maybe it wouldn't work with Avis's genetic material, Dr Eliseev said that too.'

'And Peter had what he wanted: his own child.'

'I never said any of this,' Mira said, pulling out her wallet. 'Find your own evidence if you can but I won't back you up. We never met.'

'I see,' I said. 'You want me to help Peri, somehow, but you don't want to upset your boss even though what he's done is criminal. Or at the very least unethical to the highest degree. And you don't want Diomedea exposed either.' I waved my hand to indicate Mira should put her wallet away. Least I could do was pay for her tea.

'Diomedea hasn't done anything wrong,' said Mira, shaking her head and giving money to the waiter. 'Not that I can see. *They* didn't tell Dr Eliseev not to tell Peri about her baby.' She looked at me, challenging. 'If it wasn't for Diomedea, Peri's baby wouldn't even exist.'

One way of looking at it. I noticed she wasn't bothering to defend Eliseev.

'Good luck,' Mira said as she walked away. Within seconds she was swallowed up by the crowds. I'd wanted to ask her about Luisa but I'd done well enough to get the information on Peri. And Peri was the special case, the one that had upset Mira, made her question what she was doing working for Eliseev. Even if Luisa had been sent to Eliseev to have Brilliant's babies for him, Mira probably had no motivation to tell me about her. Except. Except that she was dead.

I walked away up Junction Road No. 5, thinking about everything Mira had told me. I should be furious with Chesshyre but I was too tired for any more rage; I'd already wanted to kill him a few times on this case, what was one more outrage, even if it was the worst of all? Poor Peri.

The pounding that had started up earlier was getting louder. I crossed an intersection with a drainage canal and saw, along its cement banks, men and women slamming the mottled ground with mallets. Bright dust flew into the air. I drew out an old tissue and held it to my nose as I walked past. They were pulverising old paint chips into dust so that it could be reconstituted as paint. The scene was gorgeous—cement stained in streaks of crimson and azure, green and gold, air hazed by flying rainbow spray, but the dust would be poisonous to breathe. The people pounding wore no protection, their singlets and shorts fiery red and lush green with paint dust.

But Mira was more representative of Central Lines than these men and women pounding paint. Many people in Central Lines were educated, worked in good jobs and could have afforded middle-income housing. Except that there wasn't any. So here they were, in the kampung, which did have a few more luxurious sections further up the embankment, where houses and apartment blocks sported stone facades and satellite dishes.

I was almost out of Central Lines, heading towards where I'd parked the car, when a loud 'Ah!' went up from the crowd milling around one of the light-rail stanchions. They were looking up at the embankment where dots of green and blue and crimson tumbled down the face of the apartment blocks, swinging sideways from the stalks of satellite dishes and swooping low into the slum. Now they were careening madly through the gaps of the light-rail stanchions, looping over the rail line itself, just skimming it, and then dropping towards the pavement, only to run up the sides of the light towers and zoom into the air again. A cheer went up from the crowd; shouts, clapping. It was those wild flier-athletes again, the ones who used the whole City as their playground, and the crowd loved the entertainment. They gasped and whooped and the fliers whooped back, waving down to the crowd and disappearing into the blaze of noonday sun.

I stood staring into the sector of sky where the fliers had vanished. The red Raptor. He had to be Diomedea's. Had to be. Who else could afford—and had a motive—to hire one? Eliseev would have alerted

Diomedea but they didn't get onto tracking me until I'd got back from RaRA-land. Now they were keeping an eye on me because they didn't know where Peri and Hugo were; no-one seemed to. The Raptor broke into my flat trying to find any information that I might have on Peri and Hugo. What would he do if he found them though? From what Mira had said, Peri and Hugo represented an important investment for them so it was doubtful that he'd harm them. Did Diomedea know about Luisa? If they knew, and if it was nothing to do with them, they might be concerned for Peri and Hugo's safety. Maybe the Raptor planned to spirit them away somewhere.

I did more work at home on the material from Brilliant's office and found a subsidiary project attached to Hermes; at least, the money spent on it had been allocated the same cost centre. This project didn't seem so obscure. Titled 'Nest Egg', it was a series of small programs in towns across the regions. The point of the project seemed to be to spread a little money, and goodwill, among non-fliers: drop-in clinic here, community art venture there. They referred to these programs constantly in public statements as proof that they were not elitist, not solely City-based and not concerned only with fliers. Nest Egg was a necessary—though rather pathetic, if you looked at the actual amounts of money involved—element of Brilliant's strategy as an MP, rather than as a church leader, it seemed to me.

I got up from the dining table. I was getting nowhere with the church projects and could find no mention of Luisa.

My head was fuzzy and I struggled to pull my flat into a sort of order but late that afternoon I ended up on the couch wondering why the place didn't look much better.

I lay on the couch and watched the news, feeling as if the couch was engulfing me in vile grey glue sticking to my arms, my legs and, worst of all, invading my brain, sticky threads snagging each thought. Was whatever sickness I'd picked up going to kill me? Should I be taking myself to hospital? I couldn't move. Finally I slept, news channel still on, still repeating its images of landslides, monsoons, sporting events.

I woke much later and lay there motionless, staring at the news, recalling why I'd got out of the habit of watching it. With each passing minute I was becoming more certain that Peri and Hugo were dead. Would it have made any difference if I'd taken the case straight to Henryk? If they'd died at the hands of the Raptor, or in the storm, it had already been too late, less than twenty-four hours after my return from RaRA-land. My mistake had been to take this case on in the first place. I'd had misgivings from the start and now I was being shown just how greedy and culpable I was for ever going along with Chesshyre. *He* was responsible, finally, for putting his son and Peri at risk but I wasn't much better, was I? He'd used Peri for his own gain and perhaps I too had made decisions more for my benefit than hers and Hugo's.

I flipped over and studied the pattern of cracks and flaking paint on my ceiling. It wasn't much easier to breathe even on my back; my chest was tight, as if my ribs were wrapped in the coils of a boa constrictor. I felt my forehead but it wasn't hot. I considered taking painkillers; certainly I was in some sort of pain but I couldn't move to look for them.

Hard to believe it was just a week since I'd begun working on this case. So much had happened, it felt like months since I'd first walked into Chesshyre's house. Time to take stock. Most entries in the ledger were losses, severe ones: acquired Frisk, lost him; Taj irretrievable; flat trashed with unknown consequences for my professional future and reputation; found Peri and Hugo, lost them; probably about to lose Thomas.

Impelled by the small charge of energy thinking about Tom gave me, I sat up. Time to answer Lily's message from Friday night. So what if it was three in the morning? She was so keen for an answer about Thomas, I'd bloody well give her one.

I woke a few hours later on Monday morning, still on the couch. The news was still on. The first bleary thought in my mind was to contact Henryk but as I pulled out my slick from where it dug into my ribs, I saw Henryk had already sent me a message from the first session of an all-day national meeting. It was no use trying to speak to him that day.

The rest of the morning I continued working through the information from Brilliant. I left the TV on. Chesshyre tried to contact me but I ignored him. At two pm the TV started broadcasting proceedings in Parliament House. I looked up. Would I see Brilliant in action? Should've thought to look at events in the House before. A question was asked about a high-speed rail project. The camera panned the chamber. Only a few MPs with wings. There was Brilliant. The man looked half asleep. Big lunch? I put my head down, went back to work.

Someone was making a speech. He had the most irritating voice, wheezing and pausing for breath every sentence or two. I looked up, about to switch the screen off, and stopped, thunderstruck. It was Storkman, the elongated balding man I'd seen in Brilliant's office. Storkman was an MP along with Brilliant. Well, Brilliant had mentioned working with other independent parties. Who was he? I waited for the program to identify him. As I waited, I tuned into what he was saying.

What he was saying was incendiary. He was attacking fliers, including Brilliant, as unholy abominations, hybrids whose hubris, arrogance and unnatural mix of human and animal would bring down the wrath of God on all humankind. The camera showed Brilliant looking away, bored.

This was Storkman. Whom Brilliant had referred to as a good friend.

The program scrolled an ident. Storkman was Harris Waterhouse.

And Waterhouse was an MP with the Origins Party.

Holy shit. Now there was a nasty surprise. A prickling of anxiety spread over the skin of my face and neck and arms. I rubbed my forehead. I had so devoutly wished never to be connected to anything involved with Origins ever again.

Are you sure you know what you're dealing with here? I wanted to say to Brilliant.

Seeing Waterhouse was an Origins MP was worse than a shock; it was more like ripping open an old, badly healed scar. The Origins Party was the 'respectable' face of the Origins cult and the fact it had any success at all was deeply disturbing. Trinity Jones would never subject himself to the discipline of parliament, but he'd been cunning enough to manoeuvre a few of his more rational-seeming followers into the political arena. If Trinity was crazy, and many people thought he was, then he was crazy like a fox.

Origins also argued—and they were shrewd enough to stress this as their contribution to public policy—that it was essential to maintain a population of unaltered humans against innumerable, unspecified catastrophes. This position earned them some popular sympathy and support. Some people were happy to vote for Origins MPs, despite the more dubious or even criminal activities of the cult. They did so because they liked the idea of a conservative sect preserving an unaltered group of humans as long as it was *other* people, cult members, who took their chances with disease and disability. Waterhouse's refusal to fix his baldness and other afflictions, like the unnaturally long limbs and the wheezing, were not the result of individual eccentricity then, but the badge, the sure and certain proof, of his allegiance to Origins.

But what did the Church of the Seraphim and the Origins Party have to offer one another? These two groups loathed each other, each hating everything the other stood for. Presumably they gave each other minor party support on the Opposition benches: you scratch my back, I'll scratch yours. That *my enemy's enemy is my friend* crap.

I turned off the screen and checked my desk slick again. No evidence of tampering or damage to it but I wasn't reassured, and as I worked a shadow grew in my mind. I tried to shrug it off but it nagged at me until finally I had to stand up from the dining table and scoop up my sunglasses and slick and cap. I couldn't sit still any longer; might as well search for Frisk.

But that wasn't what was bothering me most right now.

My unease was growing because I'd sent my consent to Lily earlier that morning. Christ, didn't I know better than to make a decision at that time of night? Especially as I had plenty of evidence that my mental state was not at its best right now.

As I searched, looking into every front yard and back alley and under every hedge for blocks around, I tried to sort through the implications of the information I was organising. It was linked, of course, to my anxiety over Thomas. The puzzle I was piecing together was not coherent yet; it was all coded, all hints, insiders speaking to each other, but the outlines were becoming clearer to me despite the many missing pieces. The picture surfacing was not a pretty one.

And yet, though I was still in the middle of finding out about the treatments and the machinations they inspired, I'd told myself there was no point in putting off deciding about Thomas any longer. I'd probably never feel certain about what the right decision was and at least I could honestly say to Thomas that I'd done my very best for him. Hard to imagine he could ever be angry with me for helping him to fly; so easy to imagine his fury if I stood in his way.

As I looked for poor Frisk—modified, it seemed to me now, greatly to his own disadvantage—I shook my head at myself. I'd been frightened and exhausted last night. It was hard to think of a worse time to make such an important decision yet I'd gone ahead and done it. I'd done it partly because I couldn't bear the uncertainty of it hanging over my head any longer.

Now it was too late. I'd consented. Even if there was still time to reverse my consent, I knew Lily too well. She'd have told Thomas already that he was going to fly. How could I step in and stop that now?

By the time I returned home from my fruitless searching, it was an hour or so before dusk and I was relieved to see PapaZie and his band setting up in my front yard. The more people around me right now the safer I felt. I went up to PapaZie and asked after his health and his family. Where was his little girl, Kossiwa? Mostly I wanted to bring the conversation politely around to whether PapaZie or anyone in his network of family and friends had heard about the break-and-enter or seen Frisk. Something else was bothering me as a result of my thorough exploration of the neighbourhood and PapaZie was the most likely person to be able to set my mind at rest. But PapaZie's dark face clouded when I asked after Kossiwa.

'She is very sick,' PapaZie replied. 'I need to take her to hospital.'

I need to take her to hospital. Meaning only one thing. He hadn't taken her to hospital. He could not afford it.

'PapaZie,' I said, 'what is it?'

'I do not know. Some goddamn mosquito disease I've never even heard of.'

I was shocked. Never in the years I'd known him had I heard PapaZie swear.

I fumbled for a credit slick. 'I didn't pay you properly for what you did for me. Let me give you this.'

'Thank you, my friend,' PapaZie said. 'Something else you should know.'

'More bad news?'

'Yes. It's Ray.'

That was it. That was what had been bothering me as I'd hunted through the streets: no sign of Ray.

'He's been taken away,' said PapaZie. 'Don't know where. City don't want him anymore.'

'*What?*'

'TB,' said PapaZie. 'City find out you got TB, they throw you out.'

'Oh, *Jesus*,' I said. PapaZie clasped my hand. Selfishly, I wondered about Ray's samosas, hoping he hadn't passed anything nasty on to me.

At the front door of my flat I was alarmed to find Cam waiting for me. In all the years I'd known her, she'd never visited me at home. 'Come in,' I said.

'Could I have a cup of tea?' Cam looked around my kitchen, slipping her bag off her shoulder. 'Actually, have you got anything stronger?'

'Beer.'

'Thanks.' She wandered through to the living room. 'Bloody hell, Zeke!'

'My flat doesn't usually look like this, you know. I had an unexpected visitor. Case is bringing on some heat.'

Cam's face paled at that and I saw how drained she looked as she settled herself on my couch and said, 'Yeah, think I'm beginning to see why.'

I sat next to her. 'So?'

'So,' said Cam. She took a swig and held on to the bottle, rubbing its coolness along the side of her neck. 'I feel sick. I went to work yesterday, as you know, and today as well, but I won't be going in tomorrow.' She looked at me, then away as she said, 'I couldn't check all the names you gave me but of the ones I was able to check, yeah, something stinks very badly. The number of names of girls *known to the department*, as they say, is high—about forty percent of the girls Little Angels has on its books, if I extrapolate from the names I was able to check.'

I raised my eyebrows as Cam said, 'I was curious about Mrs Harper. I had a snoop around and found that Mrs Harper used to be a Ms Kernaghan. Quite senior in CaFS by the time she left.'

'Shit,' I said. 'Left to set up Little Angels?'

'Yes.' Cam set the half-empty bottle on the table and closed her eyes. She looked shattered, older, her face lined and drawn, her hair escaping from its clip looking more grey than blonde. 'Who better to know all the ins and outs of that market, seeing as we're the ones who regulate it?'

'Gamekeeper turned poacher.'

'Wouldn't be the first. Every former minister does that.'

'She's getting current information from the department?'

'Yes.'

'So someone inside is helping her.' I recalled our interview and felt a clenching of shame at the memory of how I'd tried to intimidate Harper with talk of the department and the minister. I'd threatened her on her home turf without a clue that it was terrain she knew far better than I did. She'd been smart enough to let me think I'd alarmed her.

'She's a cunning old trout,' I said.

'God,' said Cam, yawning and stretching, 'I could just curl up here and go to sleep, I'm so tired.'

'What are you going to do, Cam?'

'Zeke, I'm finished. What I've done has finished me. I'm not going in tomorrow. I'll probably never go in again.'

'What? What are you talking about?'

Cam sat up and rifled through her handbag, drawing out a small slick and handing it to me. 'That's it,' she said. 'Give it to Henryk. Only information he's going to get out of CaFS on this case. Zeke, when I went in on Sunday, I couldn't get *any* of the relevant files. System's been locked down. I realised as I tried to access one after the other that I had to give up or I was going to trigger security to come after me. I probably already have. They've probably followed me here. I can't hide that I went in on Sunday. Just as well I went in Saturday night too, with some of the names you sent me, as that's the only reason I could get any files at all. I took the precaution of not recording their movement—remember I told you someone had done that with Almond's file? Took a leaf from their book. Covered my tracks, though it probably won't help me.'

'Jesus, Cam, I don't get it. What are they doing?'

'Well, they're certainly withholding information from the police. They're probably *destroying* it. After all, the police will crack their delaying tactics eventually. That's why you must give this information to Henryk in person; don't risk sending it to him.'

'Why do you think they're doing this?'

'You know as well as I do, Zeke. Someone senior, maybe several senior managers, are in this for profit with Harper. Don't you see? These girls are *perfect* to be used as surrogates or wet nurses or anything else fliers want. They're damaged, they're poor, they're alone. No families to cause a fuss if anything goes wrong, no families to interfere, withhold consent. Young, fertile girls, with eggs as young as they are. Even better, as wards of the state, their story is *known*. There's a file on them. Harper and her people will know *everything*; their medical history, their vulnerabilities, how to target them, use them, even break them if they have to.

All that information built up over years of work, *my* work, Zeke, the hard work of people like me, trying to *help* these girls. Those files are a fucking *goldmine*, Zeke.' Cam burst into tears.

I put my arm around her.

After a few moments Cam drew away from me. She looked around at the living room. 'Zeke, this isn't good. Seems like someone's after you, too. Hope I haven't brought more heat your way by coming here. Are *you* okay?'

That was my Cam. Her calling to look after others always resurfaced, no matter how tough things were for her.

I said, 'No, I don't think I am. I think I'm getting sick.'

Cam widened her eyes. 'Really? Why?'

I described the weakness in my muscles, my exhaustion and difficulty sleeping. Cam leaned over and placed her hand on my forehead. Her palm was cool and dry.

'You're not feverish. You should see a doctor if you think you've picked up something in RaRA-land.'

'You don't think I have, do you?'

'No.'

'Well?'

'Zeke, if depression is an abyss then you're walking along the edge, looking down into it. You're overtired and anxious and becoming quite disorganised if your attempts to clean up your flat are anything to go by. You need to step back from the brink. When did you last sleep properly? When was your last decent meal?'

I shrugged.

'Thought so. Listen to me, I know about this stuff—enough to know things are going to be bad for me for the foreseeable future. You think because you haven't walked into your old station and put your gun to your head and pulled the trigger, like some of your old buddies have done over the years, that you can't be in that bad a state. Well, I've got news for you. You're carrying trauma from your years on the force. I've known this about you for a long time and now the weight of it is sinking you. Something about this case is going very deep with you.'

I said nothing but I was trembling with that shock you feel when someone tells you what they really think and they reveal a version of yourself that you don't recognise and yet know is at least partly true. It's a rare, disturbing experience.

Cam sighed. 'I'm sorry to leave you like this but I'm on the verge of collapse myself. Promise me you'll get this information to Henryk.'

I nodded, hardly daring to look at her. I just wanted to close my eyes and sleep but I forced myself to walk her to the door, saying as she left, 'Be careful, Cam.'

Later that night my sleeplessness returned and I lay awake, thinking. Though the flat was small, it felt echoingly empty without Frisk, without Thomas. Who knew when I could have him to stay again? Explaining to Lily why I couldn't have him over would not be an easy conversation. Cam's information went round and round in my head. Even though I knew this case was blowing up into something big, that it involved the Church of the Seraphim and Diomedea, and even the Origins Party, I was still shocked that the department, or at least part of it, could be as corrupt as Cam had discovered.

Early the next morning, Tuesday, I appeared in Henryk's office, greeting him by saying, '*The last enemy that shall be destroyed is death*—Corinthians.'

'*Preoccupied with the world, who thinks of death, until it arrives like thunder?*—Milarepa,' Henryk answered without missing a beat. 'Thanks for the cheery start. Man, you look like *shit*. How's it going?'

'Terrible,' I said. 'Taj is gone forever, I was tracked, my home staked out then broken into, and my little lion's disappeared, presumed dead. Also Cam came and saw me last night, saying her career's over because of the information request you put in on Luisa Perros.'

'*What?*'

'I know. The department is stalling you, destroying files. She gave me this to give to you. Says it's all you're going to get out of CaFS right now.'

Henryk turned the slick over in his hands. 'Jesus. Thanks for this.'

I waved my hand. 'Nice to help you out for once.'

Henryk said, 'I'll get someone onto it right away. We'll have to interview Perros's employer's family and associates; looks like that might be my only avenue just now, since I take it your girl hasn't shown up? I guess I won't be getting a statement out of her anytime soon.'

I grimaced. 'I'm still hoping she'll turn up. Eventually. Do you know who Luisa's employer was?'

He shook his head. 'Not yet.'

'Well, that information won't be on the CaFS file; I imagine her file will have been closed at around the time she was picked up by Little Angels. She won't have been the department's responsibility for some time now.'

'So, do *you* have any idea?'

'I'm not absolutely certain but I have good reason to believe it was Brilliant, the Seraphim MP, and his wife.'

'Oh great,' said Henryk. 'They'll be worse than the Chesshyres to crack. I'll have to move quickly. The commissioner hasn't told me to back off yet but it's probably just a matter of time.'

'Something else,' I said. 'I've got information on Brilliant you might want to look at. I've been going over some of the church's dealings and there's one project with a lot of money changing hands but it's completely obscure. Can't make out what the money's for or who's receiving it at all.'

'Hmm,' said Henryk. 'Have to be careful how we'd investigate that. The project's air of mystery doesn't prove it's shady though you and I both know there probably *is* something going on. Still, I'd need some sort of excuse to go after him.'

'Luisa,' I said. 'Send a flier—guess it'd have to be Mick—to interview Brilliant about Luisa. Innocently. She's missing, why haven't they reported it and so on. It might pressure him into doing something stupid; from what I've seen of him, he's not that cool a customer. I'll give you the information I've put together from Brilliant's office; between that and whatever you pick up from Mick's visit, you may have enough to follow up on Luisa and maybe even the Hermes project.'

'Hermes, eh? How very classical of them. The messenger god.'

I fanned myself with a paper from Henryk's desk as I described the break-in and told him about my talk with Chesshyre and with Mira.

'This is some serious shit,' said Henryk.

'I know it. I don't dare have Thomas to stay overnight till this business is finished and I can be sure no more rogue Raptors are going to trash my flat and kill members of my household.'

'The problem is,' said Henryk, 'the parents still haven't reported their baby missing. They could just tell me the nanny's taken baby on holiday if they don't want us nosing around. If I persist, Chesshyre could easily make trouble.'

'The point about what Mira said, though, is that Peri's not just the nanny anymore and they're not just the parents. We need to have a serious conversation, mate. This is getting into deep waters.'

'Yes,' said Henryk. 'But I can't do it till Thursday night. As if this shit with the department and Perros isn't enough, we're a bit bloody busy right now with a raid on a facility up north. You know how it is with RaRA-land cops—no resources at all. We've been ordered to help them. Never rains but it fucking pours. So, come for dinner with me and Vivienne on Thursday night. Should've got somewhere with Brilliant by then.'

'That would be great,' I said. 'What do you mean raid? What facility?'

'Belongs to a company called Diomedea—' Henryk broke off, seeing the expression on my face. 'Heard of them, have you? Oh, of course you have, your talk with Kahdr. Anyway, they've been broken into and they are going seriously batshit about it, so we have to look interested, you know? They haven't got any Raptors in RaRA-land of course, so Durack's off up there. I'll have to send him round to Brilliant's before he leaves. And luckily for you, he'll be in about the right part of RaRA-land to keep an eye out for Almond and the baby. I've briefed him on your case, he'll do what he can while he's up there.'

On Tuesday afternoon I took my desk slick out to a nearby cafe and worked there for several hours. I turned my personal slick off because Chesshyre kept trying to contact me every hour or so. The flat remained in chaos; I still couldn't face straightening it out and felt apprehensive there on my own. Of course I'd been carrying my weapon ever since the break-in but was still considering what extra security precautions I might take.

After the cafe I moved on to the Malacca, a cheap restaurant where I knew PapaZie's friends and family hung out. PapaZie's brother, Emem, was there and, on the pretext of asking after Kossiwa—who, I was relieved to hear, was now in hospital—I sat with him until his natural politeness forced him to ask me to have dinner with him and his cousin. It was late and I'd drunk a fair bit of palm wine before I made my way home.

On Wednesday morning, after another bad night made much worse by the palm wine, as I passed my car in the access lane on my way to buy breakfast I heard a *whoof*, a sort of sneeze. I peered underneath. Frisk lay battered and bloody in the shelter of the car. Must have dragged himself there painfully during the night. Who knew where he'd hidden or how far he'd had to haul himself to get back to his territory?

Tangled in Frisk's mane was a red feather, one of the great primaries. Loss of that primary would have cost the Raptor when he took to the air. I went down on one knee and gently disengaged the feather from the lion's mane. Thanks for that, Frisk. It might come in handy. He whimpered as I touched him, sneezed again, half opened his eyes.

I took him to a vet. She looked up at me from dressing his wounds and bandaging an ear. 'Nasty injuries,' she said. 'Walk him every day; that's his rehabilitation.'

Outside the vet's a message came from Henryk: *Mick 2 Brill. Tense little xchange, can u imagine? LP did work 4 him. M let B know* we *knew she had 2 kids 4 him. Didn't know 4 sure but fell 4 oldest trck in bk, didn't dare deny it. Did what u'd expect; claim L left, argument over wages, didn't report L missing said assume working 4 someone else. M sceptical—B faked concern over L but nervous as hell. Big ears in place.*

Mostly I felt relief that I hadn't wasted Henryk's time on Brilliant. Finally, finally, as slowly as an ocean liner starting from a standstill, the case was moving ahead. *Dead slow*. But ahead.

That afternoon began well enough. I'd explained to Lily that I couldn't have Tom to stay overnight but she must have felt generous since I'd consented to the treatments and we had the afternoon together instead. My delight at having Frisk back, even in so sorry a state, and my anticipation at seeing Thomas, finally gave me the impetus to clean the flat. By the time I'd finished, poor Frisk dozing on the couch as I worked, the place looked and smelled as crisp as a new bedsheet. I left Frisk asleep and picked Thomas up from Lily's townhouse at Silver Palms.

Tom burbled so excitedly as I buckled him into his car seat that I could barely understand a word he was saying. 'Look, Daddy,' he finally managed to squeak. 'It's 'portant, Daddy. Look!' He brandished a drawing for me, a drawing of himself flying over the City with wings as bright as a butterfly's.

'Wow, Tom,' I said enthusiastically, trying to hide the sinking feeling the drawing inspired in me. 'It's so beautiful.'

'Oh yes indeed,' said Tom, nodding at me with the solemn certainty of the near four-year-old. *Oh yes indeed* was a new phrase for him, something I could imagine Richard uttering pompously numerous times a day, and I could tell Tom was proud of it.

I studied the drawing for a moment before starting the car and tried to suppress my anxiety as Thomas described meeting his specialist, Ruokonen. 'That's great, sweetie,' I said, folding his drawing carefully and stowing it in a side pocket. 'I'll really enjoy having this to look at.'

I took Tom to the movies. As I endured the only film Tom wanted to see, *The Persimmon Thieves*, about four flier kids and their many adventures, I marvelled at how quickly becoming a flier was already cemented into his identity. At the gelateria I took him to after the movie, as Thomas chattered away about all the things he'd be able to do, something clenched in me relaxed. Parents were frightened of the future because they always feared that moment when they could no longer protect their child. That moment was arriving sooner than I wished but how many parents could give their child entry into such an exhilarating world?

Thomas pointed at the pigeons flocking up above the light-rail line running past the gelateria. 'I'll fly right up to the sky, Dad. I'll fly through rainbows and into the clouds!' He bounced on his chair as he spoke.

My slick. I assumed it was Chesshyre again but checked anyway. Lily, letting me know I had to make sure that Thomas, who'd already started preparatory drug therapy, took his afternoon doses.

Later, while I was driving Thomas back to Lily's, he fell asleep in the car. As I stopped the car outside Lily's house I turned round to look at him, at my son, who I still thought of as a baby, who was now entering a realm where I could not follow. He seemed more deeply asleep than was usual for him when he took a nap in the car.

I got out, opened his door, leaned in. Tom's skin was pale and waxy, his breathing low. I shook him. He was floppy, his head lolling forward.

My legs turned to rubber. I rang Lily while still trying to rouse Thomas. She rushed out of the house, followed by Richard, who was already ringing an ambulance.

'What the hell is *this*?' I yelled at Lily. 'A reaction to the drugs?'

'I don't fucking *know*!' Lily shrieked.

The ambulance arrived ten minutes later, a miracle possible only because of the relatively good repair of the streets around Silver Palms. In most parts of the City you'd be better off taking a rickshaw or the light rail.

I followed in the wake of the ambulance as best I could but lost it long before it reached the hospital.

15

RAID

Peri was woken while it was still dark by a solid-muscled young woman with short fair hair. 'I'm Leto,' she said. 'Come with me.'

Peri picked up Hugo and almost ran to keep up with Leto, whose grey-blue clad body and blue wings were always on the instant of fading into the deep dark morning in among the trees ahead of her. She'd seen Leto the night before, her face lit up by the firelight and by her look of rapt concentration during Jay's lecture.

Peri followed Leto into the main clearing. Jay, Finch and Rafael were squatting on the sand, peering at a slick in Niko's hands. Their faces loomed out of the darkness, illuminated from below by the screen.

Niko nodded at Peri as she sat down but otherwise she was included in the group without comment and it struck Peri this was an unfamiliar but agreeable sensation. Hugo began to suckle as Peri listened apprehensively to Niko. What was going on? All of the others, except for Niko, were chewing on energy strips as they listened.

'Now,' Niko was saying, 'you'll each have one of these slicks. You'll fly most of the day and then you'll stop and rest. You won't move on L1 until after one-thirty am. No-one's hit L1 yet. It's guarded but mostly against non-fliers. I've got the codes we need on the slicks I'll give you. Don't ask how I got them. Obviously you won't risk drawing attention to yourselves by flying in a group, so each slick has the route loaded so that you can navigate separately.'

Jay stared in turn at each flier in the circle, his handsome features stern, as if to assure himself that they all understood. Peri dropped her gaze to Hugo. Seemingly satisfied, Jay turned back to Niko.

'I'll program our plan of attack onto the slicks in real time,' Niko continued. 'You know, the usual routine. That way we can keep in touch and respond to anything unforeseen as the mission unfolds; it's also insurance in case any one of you is . . . ah . . . unexpectedly detained.' He stood up and gave a slick to each of them. 'Rest a bit and eat up. You'll get underway just before civil dawn.'

Jay stood up and as he came towards her Peri saw he was carrying four small bags and a lightstick. He was wearing the same blue-grey camouflage skims as Leto and Peri and Finch.

'You're not taking me with you on this?' Peri whispered to Finch.

Finch nodded, reaching up to take one of the bags from Jay.

'*Why?*'

'Audax doesn't carry passengers. You're part of the group. You do what we do.'

'No, no, no, Finch, *please*, I have to take Hugo back safely. I have to go. If I keep my word I just might be able to work something out.'

Jay shook his head. 'I saw what came after you. You have no chance of working anything out with whoever sent *that* after you. You are part of this operation and you'll do as you're told. This is your only chance to move forward with us.'

The grey bracelet on Peri's wrist felt tighter, heavier. Tears started to her eyes; she blinked them back. Tears would not change Jay's mind; if anything, crying might make him decide she was too much of a risk to this mission. The idea of taking part in whatever Audax were going to do terrified her but she could see Jay's point; they might trust her if she performed well. It was the only chance they would give her. Sighing, she put Hugo over her shoulder and heaved herself to her feet.

Jay handed one bag each to Leto and Rafael and kept one for himself.

'What's that?' said Peri.

'Weapons,' said Leto, drawing out a sleek object from her bag. As she checked its parts, Peri could see it was a small crossbow.

'Aren't you going to give me one?'

Jay shook his head. 'Not this time, sister.'

A shock thrilled through Peri at his words. *Sister*. She'd heard him say that to other Audax members. Could he feel anything for her? He'd saved her life; that must have forged a bond between them.

'I know how to use one,' said Peri. The old longbows she'd practised with in Pandanus were hardly in the class of this weapon but she knew she was a good shot, though that had more to do with the exercise of her skill and strength in aiming stones, tins, glass or any other rubbish to hand at the mongrels of the Venice.

'All the more reason,' laughed Jay. 'I will give you these, though.' He handed her a pair of thin soft shoes. Peri turned them over in one hand, her other arm still around Hugo as he goggled over her shoulder into the lightening grey between the trees.

'Landing slips,' said Jay. 'To protect your feet, especially if your landing is uncontrolled or at speed.'

Peri nodded. So, she was supposed to be part of Audax. She was trusted enough to take part in a dangerous mission but not trusted enough to carry a weapon. *And they're making sure that I suffer the same fate as they do if they're caught.*

Jay beckoned Peri closer. She sucked in her breath as he unwrapped the bandages from her hands and feet and ears. No pain but the new skin was more sensitive; she shrank a little from the cold morning air. Jay held the lightstick up and checked her skin.

'Good.'

Jay inspected Hugo, tore open a package, peeled a brown square from its backing. He smoothed the patch onto the skin of Peri's upper arm and though he did it skilfully, his roughened fingers left marks. Warm, all down her arm where he touched her, warm like lying in the sun. The rest of her was cold; if he put his arms, his wings, around her, she'd be so warm, all over, finally she'd thaw from the storm, heal from the frost.

'What's that?' said Peri.

'Transdermal nutrition patch.'

'Activated by body heat. Jay knows all the right supplies to steal,' said Finch, looking up from where she had been checking her own weapon, finally securing it in her backpack. She mustn't be expecting trouble on the flight itself then, Peri surmised, or she would have strapped the crossbow to her body.

'Especially the more up-to-date military goodies,' Finch added. She was wearing a patch too. 'Saves us time on long flights where speed is critical. We won't stop so often to eat. Flying burns energy at such a ferocious rate that we need a continuous source of kilojoules for so long a flight, over and above the energy strips we'll consume.'

Peri's skin still tingled where Jay had touched her. She could almost hear Luisa's voice. *That's not love, Peri. That's frostbite.*

Finch stood up, brushing sand off her skims, and moved next to Peri as she put the slips on her feet. 'You're coming with me,' she said, handing Peri an empty backpack. Peri peered at her in the morning gloom as she adjusted the pack's straps over her shoulders and settled the pack between her wings. What was she going to put in it? Energy strips, water, slick; everything she needed for the flight out was in her waistband. There was so much she wanted to know. 'Who will look after Hugo?'

'Phoebe,' said Finch. Seeing the look on Peri's face, she said, 'He'll be fine, Peri. He's done without you for a day already.' Finch pointed to where Phoebe had materialised from the trees surrounding the clearing and Peri was surprised to see a bandage on her ankle. So, Phoebe was carrying an injury. Peri hoped she wouldn't resent being left behind. *God, I wish it was me staying behind. No point thinking like that. Just get through today. Do this thing.* Surprisingly gently, considering her usually brusque manner, Phoebe took Hugo into her arms.

'Goodbye, little man,' said Peri.

Finch ruffled the baby's hair, then turned to Peri. 'We need to get a head start. Civil dawn is almost upon us.'

Peri hurried after Finch. 'What's that?' Did Finch mean that she, Peri, was slower than the others, thus the head start?

'Eh?' said Finch. 'Oh, civil dawn? That's when the sun has risen to six degrees below the horizon. There's just enough light for objects to be distinguishable.'

'Oh. Finch, what if something happens to us?' Peri said as Finch headed towards the cliff edge. 'I have to come back to Hugo; I can't just disappear on him.'

'Niko understands that,' said Finch. 'Believe me, this mission is the quickest way to ensure your future with us. Now, watch me. I'll be wind dummy.'

'What?'

Finch tightened her waistband and groomed her primary feathers as she said, 'Whenever there's more than one flier, it pays for the most experienced flier to be the wind dummy at the beginning of each flight. So, I take off first. You watch me and gauge wind speed and strength and other flight conditions by studying how I'm flying. Now, have you peed?' Peri nodded. 'Good,' said Finch. 'Take small sips of water frequently; that way less of it ends up in your bladder. If you smash into the ground or a mountain or a tree, your bladder's much less likely to burst if it's empty.'

Finch took off down the steep grassy run that was their favourite launch point and Peri watched how she rose high and fast above the cliff to avoid blow-back and rotors over the ridgeline. After a few moments Peri followed, copying Finch's manoeuvres precisely.

'Finch, tell me about this mission,' Peri said once they were high above Heavener Ridge and flying wingtip to wingtip. 'It sounds dangerous. And illegal. Niko said L1 hadn't been hit yet. What's he talking about?'

'Easier to understand once we get there,' said Finch, turning east into the faint grey pre-dawn. 'It is dangerous and illegal, which doesn't sound too different to some things you've been up to lately. You're lucky this was planned by Niko; he's cautious and he's never lost anyone. Niko's interested in change, the big picture. Have you noticed there are more women than men in Audax?'

Peri shook her head.

'Niko's policy,' said Finch. 'Women get the job done, no grandstanding, he says. Doesn't like too many men in any one group; says they're show-offs. Jay isn't like that though. Raf's our daredevil but we need at least one.'

Below Finch and Peri puffy cloud rolled to the horizon, crimped with blue shadow and pink light, regular and sinuous as braided hair. After the sun rose, Finch took them beneath the cloud.

'Just so you understand our strategy on this day's flying,' said Finch after thirty minutes, when they were warmed up and in the rhythm, 'there's a saying: *you fly the sky or you fly the ground*. If you're on a short joyflight you fly the ground: you look for ridgelift, you watch out for rotors and low wind zones, you look for thermal generators and avoid lakes because they don't generate thermals, and you scout for LZs.' In the strengthening light Finch pulled a pair of tinted goggles from her waistband. She slung them across to Peri, who had to dip a little to catch them, and then pulled out another pair for herself, adjusting them as she spoke.

'But on a long flight like this we're going to fly the *sky*. We're flying near to cloudbase or top of lift. We'll harvest the thermals powering the clouds and be virtually invisible to anyone on the ground. That means we're looking for cloud streets—cumulus forming parallel rows along the direction of wind flow with all their cloudbases at the same level. We might even luck into a blue street. Blue streets form when you get the same long line of lift but it's too dry for cloud formation—so they're much harder to find because you can't see them.'

'I've never flown a cloud street,' said Peri.

'Really?' said Finch. 'They're quite common over the ocean. They can stretch for hundreds of kilometres.' She sighed. 'It's glorious, sailing along on the might of all those thermals under the rows of cumulus, and if you're clever enough at jinking from one cloud street to another you can keep it going, oh, for ages.'

'I haven't had that pleasure,' said Peri. 'I couldn't go looking for cloud streets. I was lucky to make it to my Flight Gym classes. Even if I'd had the time . . .'

'What?' said Finch. 'What is it, Peri?'

'Have you heard of Flight Checks?'

'Yes,' said Finch. 'I've heard of them.'

Peri looked at her grey bracelet. Jay hadn't told her exactly what it could do. Ruthless of him, really, and shrewd, building up that anxiety in her; it tracked her but was it also a leash, able to pull her up short whenever he wanted?

'Bet you never had one put in against your will. Anyway, you know they limit your flying range. Parents fit them to their fledglings but the ones they put in adults, *those* ones can pull you down like you've been shot.'

'So no ranging over the ocean searching for cloud streets for you then,' said Finch. 'That's too bad. I hope we'll swan along the white road at least once today.'

Peri concentrated on looking forward to that—her first cloud street—rather than her fears about where it might lead her.

The land below was wilderness. The lack of sharp edges was the clearest sign of this from the air; the pure and plain demarcation between field and field, the precision of fences, the slicing geometry of roads, were all missing. Instead they flew over expanses of mottled brown and grey, the earth scored with irregular oval lines, shapes that reminded Peri of the lagoons and fringing reefs she'd seen as she'd flown down the coast. With its worn, softened contours, it looked as if they were flying over the flat, dry bed of an ancient sea.

'A blue day,' said Finch. 'Good lift but no cloud streets because the lift is too high; there's no real lid to it.'

The brown land ran out into salmon-coloured earth or sand, folded with swirls of vegetation so dark that its green colours edged into purple. Then they were soaring over jumbles of rock the same rich orange-red as the earth, the rock fissured into gorges of unfathomable shadow.

Peri and Finch flew all day, stopping briefly only three times where there was good cover of trees for rest and food. As they drew further away from Heavener Ridge, they occasionally dropped lower for Finch to check their progress against landmarks. Then they used a thermal to take them back up to near cloudbase.

'Watch the cloud shapes, particularly height relative to base,' said Finch, as they headed for some towering cumulus. 'Stay away from clouds that are much taller than they are wide because they may overdevelop, as you found out with your storm. Also watch out for clouds with a wide base; those ones can overpower you. When you're pulled up irresistibly into the cloud, when you can't get away, that's cloud suck. That's *too much* lift.'

It was the shadows that Peri noticed first. They were flying over a wide green and brown plain and to their right was a long ridgeline. East of the ridgeline she saw a broken line of shadows dropped over the land. Peri looked up. Above the shadows sat a row of flat-bottomed puffy clouds.

'Finch!'

Finch turned her head. 'Yes,' she said and headed straight for the clouds. 'You need to dolphin. Dolphining means you slow down for the lift under the clouds and you speed up for the sinking air between them. The point of that is to stay at the same altitude. Takes practice.'

Then they were in it, lofting like dandelion seed. To the west humped the dragon's spine of the ridgeline and below them stretched the long, irregular line of shadow. But it was a line just the same, all ahead of Peri, running for kilometres and kilometres of towering multi-thermalled lift. This was almost as intoxicating as glass-off, this was flying as she'd always dreamed it would be, this effortless rush, this dash across country that felt as if it would never end.

The gap between the ridgeline and the white cloud ahead showed up as intense blue in the distance.

'Blue hole ahead,' said Finch. 'Look, we're in luck, we can jink over to the next one.'

Peri felt as if she were flying down the side of a mountain as she hit the sinking air, accelerating like a rollercoaster, then came the swoop up and slight slowing under the next cloud street.

'Oh my god,' said Finch. 'Look at that. I have *never* seen that before.'

Peri was wafted up by strong warm air. Above them unspooled a long curving roll of cloud with none of the puffed edges of the squat clouds they'd seen earlier. On either side of them at the same height ran more long tubes of cloud, white and as precisely cut as fat noodles side by side on a blue plate.

'The sky is striped!' said Peri.

'Like a tube of freakin' toothpaste. *Unbelievable*. Look how defined the edges of the cloud streets are.'

After an hour of rapture they ran out of cloud streets. 'Looks like the sky gods really turned it on for you today,' said Finch. 'For your first time. Happy?'

Peri nodded.

'You should be. You could fly for years and never experience that.'

The country began to look less wild, to show more recent scars of neglect and abandonment. One of these, a dead hydroelectric dam, made Peri shiver. The great hole in the earth lay empty. Below the crumbled rim of the dam, massive chunks of concrete bristling with its steel reinforcing bars torn from the ruined curtain wall were scattered and broken down the dry wash of the extinct river like the discarded toy blocks of a giant. Concrete leaked rust stains the colour of old blood.

They followed the scar of the dead river until it petered out into exhausted land left to rising salt, its deadly white scribbles stitching scars of raw earth, eroded hills and crumbling levees. The bones of splintered farmhouses weathered under the white sun. They saw few birds, except, here and there, a crow.

Ahead of them, glinting on the horizon, was something exquisite and unsettling. Vast belts of deep jade, kilometres long and wide, alternated with shocking crimson and magenta. There was no variation within the bands; there was not one grain of colour Peri could see that was paler or darker than any other. Where the bands ended began an even more remarkable phenomenon: a broad square of blue extending as far as the eye could see. This blue was broken up into a mosaic of giant squares, graded exactly from one to the next by increasing depth of colour of every shade of aquamarine, from almost white to the pure blue of a warm shallow sea.

The squares gleamed in the sun as if they'd been lacquered.

'Well,' said Finch, 'I've seen the green and pink bands before. Blue squares are new, though.'

'I know what it is,' said Peri.

'Yeah?'

'Andy Silver. Must be.'

'What?'

'Andy Silver, the artist. You know her?'

'No, why should I?'

'Oh. I just thought . . . well, Peter and Avis had pictures of her artwork.

Finch snorted. 'Artwork? Those are salt extraction ponds.'

'Yes, it is salt but it's art too. She says she makes art that becomes an environment fliers fly through, like feathers of colour that contour the wind, fly up into the clouds and dye their edges. Colours from algae swirling in ocean currents. She must be *living* out here, making these blue squares with salt, out in the wilderness for months, maybe years.'

'Let's hope she doesn't turn Wild in the process,' grunted Finch.

Peri couldn't understand Finch's indifference. Peri had been tiring but now she was flying in a trance of blue. In the heat the blues vaporised, powdering her; she tasted hot blue salt. She was like one of those giant manta rays she'd seen in nature films, flapping its wings through a transparent tropical sea. On and on she soared over enamelled shifting blue as if driven onwards by it, forgetting fatigue, pain, fear. They were lifted by the blue as if by a thermal and perhaps it did have special thermal properties; perhaps, Peri thought, this was their *blue street* except it lay below them instead of invisibly above.

'Careful,' said Finch. 'You're sinking into it.'

Peri shook her head and urged herself higher, alongside Finch, aware she was sacrificing airspeed to do so.

'You have to watch out for that,' said Finch. They were now

flying over heavily treed hills. 'You fly straight to whatever you concentrate on. Someone I knew ended up crashing into a lone tree in the middle of a field with hectares of open space all around him. He was focusing on what he wanted to avoid, but instead you have to focus on where you want to be.'

They flew for several more hours until twilight. The sun fell into the west behind them, washing the trees and plains below in gold while the land and rising hills ahead sank into blue, deeper blue and lavender. Peri pulled off her flying goggles and stowed them in her waistband. Below her, the tops of the trees flickered with rose fire as they tossed their crowns in the level rays of the sinking sun.

A road unrolled beneath them, pale strip against darker unlit country. No lights, no cars.

'Did you know,' Finch said, 'that birds navigate by roads too? Easier for them. Often they follow roads even when that makes their journey longer. They'll even zoom around roundabouts.'

'So much for distance as the crow flies,' said Peri.

'Don't know about crows,' said Finch. 'But birds do follow the routes we make. One more way we've left nothing unchanged in this world. Suppose they've done it ever since Romans built roads, or since tribes made paths through the grasslands.'

After a while Finch said, 'L1 is isolated. You'll see why when we get there but it also makes it easier for us.'

'Niko said something earlier about the usual routine. Does that mean you've done this kind of thing before?'

'This is the biggest strike so far,' replied Finch. 'At least in my time with Audax. Till now we've kept a low profile, didn't want anyone to come looking for us. But Niko's growing more ambitious. He *wants* to attract attention this time.'

After another hour they landed in a field and got into cover, a belt of bushes and trees forming a thick windbreak along the edge of the field. 'The others will be nearby soon,' said Finch.

They ate a little, dozed and waited for another two hours. It was nearly midnight. Peri could see from her slick that L1 was slightly to the east although she couldn't tell how far away it was. After another half-hour their slicks vibrated with a message from Niko.

'Now,' said Finch. 'Follow me.'

They moved among the trees, then ran along the fenceline until they came to a thicker patch of trees. Finch led Peri to a clearing down on the far side of the hill. From the edge of the clearing, hidden by a rim of trees, Peri could look across and up to a rounded hill, its sides smooth as glass. That must be L1. Nothing called attention to it except the too-perfect shape of the hill.

Peri saw a dark figure and shrank back.

'It's only Raf,' whispered Finch.

Rafael came over to them, followed by Jay and Leto.

Finch gathered the fliers around her and they crouched in a circle. Peri could see they all carried crossbows except her. 'We're going in in two parties,' said Finch. 'Leto and Peri, come with me; Jay and Raf, you two know where you're going and what you need to get. We'll be picked up by remote tracking so put these on.'

Finch handed them each a slip of material that unfolded into a dull, dry film which clung to their faces. Peri could see and breathe through it but it was disconcerting to see the faces of the others as obscured as if they were wearing veils.

'We've got forty minutes if we assume surveillance picks us up right away,' Finch continued. 'We'll get in without setting off any alarms—Niko's seen to that—but they'll still have visual scanning. We could have up to seventy minutes if they're a bit slow but we can't count on that. Diomedea believes L1 is safe because it's isolated; non-fliers can't get near the place and City fliers wouldn't bother coming this far out. Hardly anyone knows it's here. So this is our best chance. It'll be much harder after tonight. That's why we've waited, till we know what we take will be significant. They shouldn't catch us so the main thing is not to be tracked back. We'll fly back in our two groups and we'll leave no later than two-twenty am.'

Finch stood up. 'There's a few things I want to make clear before we go in. First, no wilful destruction. We're after information, that's all, and a few supplies. We're not here to destroy anything or to stop Diomedea's work. You know what Niko thinks: Diomedea's breaking the law and we're the avenging angels. You'll see things you don't like. Tough. Deal with it. You'll have a better idea of what goes into giving you wings. Think anyone in the City wants to know? We're not here to condemn the ethics of Diomedea's research; we're here to make the true results of that research available. If you don't agree with that, you'll have to do something about it on your own time. We all have wings, we've all benefited from their research, and from MicroRNA/Corvid and the others. So get as much as you can, as fast as you can, don't do any damage, and get out.

'One more thing. *Do not even think* about releasing anything you see in there. That would be cruel, possibly catastrophic. You don't know what's been done to them or if any of them has a snowball's chance in hell of surviving five minutes outside of L1, let alone the danger of spreading modifications into remnant wild populations. Understand?' They nodded back at her, faceless ghosts in their masks.

'Good,' Finch said.

The apprehension that had been building in Peri all day, so like the anxiety she used to wake up with on the mornings before her medical procedures, now curdled in her belly and in her blood, setting hard into fear. What did Finch mean? What were they going to see in there? Peri thought with envy of her future self: in less than two hours, she hoped, she'd be back outside this place, would never have to see it again. She drew in a deep, deep breath. In a sense, she *was* that future self, right now. She must hang onto that idea: she just had to get through the intervening time, minute by agonising minute.

Jay took Finch aside and they had a brief, low discussion apart from the others. Finch paced a step away, came back, movements springy, tense. Jay shook his head. 'Just a contingency. Look, it's okay, if she's really—' Jay looked over at Peri, dropped his voice further.

'I *know* what to do,' Finch said, walking away.

God. *What* were they going to do? Finch and Jay were talking about her. They must be; everything else had been worked out, she was the variable, the wild card. The problem. Were they going to abandon her here? They couldn't be that cruel. No running away from whatever they'd planned; they were her only way back to Hugo.

Rafael and Jay took off, invisible against the dark sky. No moon; no doubt a factor in the timing of this raid. Peri, Leto and Finch flew in tight formation over the ramparts at the crown of the hill and down, landing on a paved courtyard near a set of doors. They were in front of a complex of low buildings topped with one high dome.

Peri was gasping for breath. She'd never flown that close to buildings before. If not for her flying lesson yesterday and for all the concentrated flying she'd done over the last few days she wouldn't have been able to keep up. How long since she'd fled Peter's? Just over a week. She'd fled on Saturday afternoon and it was Saturday again, or rather very early Sunday morning. Now she was officially late returning Hugo. No time to think about that now.

Finch and Leto led Peri to a doorway, where Finch swiped her slick past a reader. The door slid open. *Hello, Dr Summerscale*, flashed the reader. A long hall stretched in front of them. Luminous film on the walls gave them just enough light to see by. Finch and Leto carried lightsticks and had clipped their crossbows to their waistbands.

'What is it?' whispered Peri to Finch, pointing at the walls.

'Combjelly. Seamouse cells. Saves Diomedea a packet on energy costs. We'll see if we can pick up data on that stuff too.'

Finch stopped outside a door. 'Leto, you go in here, get everything you can in the third-level racks. Start with the blue boxes. Your slick has codes to unlock the cabinets. Peri, this way.' She pushed through a door on the opposite wall and led Peri into a large, dark room. Peri gagged on the warm stench of feathers and droppings and heard rustling and shuffling as they came in. Finch slid a red gel over her lightstick. Eyes gleamed at them from the darkness. 'Don't stop, don't look, don't disturb them,' said Finch, hurrying her into another room. 'Now, Niko said the reader was in here. You're lucky we were about to do this raid. I'm not sure you'd have been allowed near our camp otherwise.'

'What do you mean?'

'I mean we need to know who the hell you are. We've already initiated database searches but the information wasn't detailed enough, though so far your story checks out. Wouldn't be the first time someone's tried to infiltrate us, though involving a baby seems to be going a bit far. After tonight things are going to get a lot hotter for us. Over here.'

Peri moved over to a tall cabinet. 'You don't believe me,' she said.

'I do,' said Finch. 'But that's not important.'

No, what was important was what *Jay* thought. Obviously. Cold rage burned in Peri. He was the one whose tests she had to pass or she'd be left behind, child in the woods with no trail of stones to follow home, no trail to follow anywhere, he didn't care, she'd just have to wait here till Diomedea decided what to do with her. Her whole life, other people decided what to do with her. The one time she'd taken her life into her own hands wasn't working out so well either.

'Well, you can't tell who I am unless this reader has access to all the DNA databases.'

'CHR,' replied Finch as she inserted her slick into a slot on its surface. A rectangular panel lit up. 'Comprehensive health records. Comprehensive's a nice word, isn't it? Refers to inclusion of DNA information. Give me a hair.'

Peri plucked out a hair and handed it over. 'How can Diomedea have everyone's private CHR?'

Finch drew out a clear cel from her waistband and held it up to the panel light. In the cel was another hair. She laid Peri's hair next to it on the cel and slid the cel into the panel. 'They don't. Big controversy about this a few years ago. Diomedea bought access to the DNA section of the CHRs only, but that's incredibly important, sensitive data. The government *sold* them access in the name of research and improving health. Great if you can afford it. Diomedea said it couldn't do its work without access to population records, which is probably true, and it promised flow-on benefits to national health, medical and research organisations, which it hasn't quite delivered yet. That brings us to why *we're* here.'

Finch grabbed the cel from the reader, looked at it briefly, smiled to herself, then sealed it into her waistband. 'Good,' she said. 'Let's hope all the data's there.'

Good? Did that mean Finch was satisfied with the results from the reader? Would she, Peri, be flying back to Heavener tonight?

Finch led Peri across the corridor to a ramp. They darted up the ramp and at the top entered an observation deck, a transparent-walled room overlooking a well of dark space. Lights flickered on. '*Shit*,' muttered Finch. 'We've triggered them.'

Peri stopped, entranced. Down in the well a patch of rainforest, trees at least twenty metres high, grew up towards the clear ceiling. Tags of all colours covered the trees. Peri started. As the lights continued to flicker on, the tags shifted, detaching from their trees: millions of butterflies, dragonflies, mayflies, moths, beetles, flashing gold, green, copper, aquamarine fire.

'So,' said Finch. 'They've turned their attention to insects too.'

The whirl of colour spiralled up towards the light, creatures beating against the windows of the observation deck.

'Damn,' said Finch. 'Need to get away from here.' She dragged Peri along a walkway into another wing. With relief they saw the lights flick off behind them. Finch switched her lightstick on again. 'A few things have changed since Niko's informant left. Wait here a minute.' She slipped Peri's backpack off her shoulders and disappeared into the dark.

Peri stood alone in the passage. In the low light thrown off by the walls she could see surveillance cameras trained on her. She peered into the gloom. Where had Finch gone? Couldn't hear her, couldn't see her. This was it then. She was being dumped. Finch had said *good* but that could've been to put Peri off her guard. Security would pick her up soon. Even if Finch didn't mean to abandon her, she'd be caught. Jay was here but wouldn't or couldn't help her. No way back to Heavener.

She crept to the edge of the passage, away from the field of view of the camera. A door. Pushed it open, black depth yawning in front of her. She'd wait here, till she could hear Finch. If she returned.

A long dim gallery stretched away, hung with swathes of shining silk.

Awestruck, silent, she walked the length of the room staring up at vast fragile sheets as gauzy as dragonfly wings, glowing azure like a Ulysses butterfly, ruby like hummingbird throats.

No creature, no giant butterfly or bird grew this tissue, yet it twitched, reacting to something, perhaps her presence stirring the air, heat from her body, squeak of footsteps on the glassy floor.

She paused.

The shuddering sheer expanses of colour were alive.

Why was she here? If they'd just wanted to find out who she was, they could have taken a hair of hers to the reader, no need for her to go with them. That proved they intended to leave her here. What a simple way to get rid of her. And they still had their little hostage, Hugo, more than enough incentive to keep her from informing on Audax.

Minutes ticked: time itself pooled emerald, blue.

The air she breathed was infused with shimmer. Forward, back. No reason to move either way.

Peri stood in the centre, the very heart of Diomedea's most important research facility. She was alone and the building hummed all around her.

16

RAPTOR

By early afternoon the raiders reached Heavener Ridge. Phoebe brought Hugo to Peri and she nursed him and fed him fruit and biscuits while Niko debriefed them.

Jay stood silently at the edge of the group as Niko talked, inspecting each of his primary feathers. Peri's eyes were drawn irresistibly to the bruises flowering, darker patches on dark skin, along his arms and neck. Jay scowled, contorting himself to make sure each flight feather was intact. Patches of new skin were sprayed on his chest and face. A few smaller wing feathers had been broken and were now taped up. Jay had borne the brunt of Diomedea's security. Raf was hurt too. His arms showed bruises where his skims were torn and a patch of hair had been cut away to dress a wound on his scalp.

'I've made a preliminary pass through the data you sent me as you returned,' said Niko. 'Looks exciting, though it's going to take a while to unpick it all. There's a truckload of unpublished scientific papers, including work we've suspected they were doing on how to get off these damn drugs. The real story is we can now prove they've falsified research, even published articles using falsified data. I for one am looking forward to disseminating the real stuff. What do you think, should I start my own scientific journal?'

Jay laughed.

Peri's head nodded. Beyond exhaustion, she could barely remember anything from the time she heard Finch whispering her name in the passage at L1. *Peri, Peri, where the hell are you?* The running, the brutal flight home, exhilaration the only thing moving her wings, joy that she was returning to Heavener. To Hugo.

When she woke up it was early evening and Hugo was sleeping, curled up on one of her wings. She was under the overhang but could not remember how she'd got there. Finch was shaking her awake. 'God,' said Peri, stretching. 'I could've slept a lot longer.'

'Come with me.'

Peri picked up Hugo and followed Finch back to the river. No-one else was there. Where were they all? Training flights? Maybe reconnaissance. They didn't cook, they hardly ate fresh food; they didn't care about anything except flying. Energy strips were enough for them most of the time.

Peri tried to shake off the last shreds of dream clinging to her. She had been walking down that gallery in L1, hypnotised by the sheets of lustrous colour, and then she was running, the sheets peeling off the wall, flying at her, chasing her. They were alive, pieces of life, and they were going to wrap themselves around her, suffocating her in all that filmy sheen; they would have their revenge for their fastened, cancerous growing. *Kill us*, they shrilled above the range of her hearing, just hissing and shirring in the wind. *Kill us!*

Finch sat Peri down on the sand. Peri put Hugo onto her lap, leaning him into the crook of her elbow. He twisted round to pull out one of the small green feathers from the underside of her wing and started playing with it.

'Peri, I've had a look at the results from the L1 reader.'

'And it tells you I am who I say I am.'

'Yes, but—'

'What would you have done if it hadn't?' Peri interrupted.

'Never mind about that. I never thought that was likely anyway.

I need to tell you something more important. It'll affect what you do, and what we do with you. Jay is dead against letting you go yet but Niko says we can't guarantee Hugo's safety and I think that's right. These results change everything anyway.'

'How?'

'I compared a hair of yours to a hair of Hugo's in the reader. The reader analysed the DNA of both samples and the result is unequivocal. You didn't just give birth to Hugo: you're his genetic mother also.'

Peri looked up at the shifting silhouettes of the leaves in the canopy above them. The sky was still blue but the clouds had caught fire from the sunset she could not see, down here among the trees. She heard the words Finch had said to her but they made no sense. Analysing the meaning of each word one by one didn't help. A dull ache in her throat spread down into her chest and belly and back and wings and sent shooting frills of pain down into her legs. Her muscles were punishing her for her overtaxing of them. Why, *why* did she have to be put through this, made to feel even more pain over Hugo? She glared angrily at Finch.

'No,' said Peri, shaking her head. 'That's not possible. You're mistaken.'

'There's no mistake,' said Finch. 'These results are clear. You're his mother.'

'*Contamination*,' said Peri through gritted teeth.

'We both know that's not true, Peri,' said Finch with a gentleness that was infuriating. 'Diomedea has the best readers that exist. Why are you so upset by it?'

'Because it's crazy,' said Peri, tears now starting from her eyes. Her hands had balled into fists at her sides. Hugo started at the rage in her voice and began to whimper. 'It doesn't make any sense. They paid me to have *their* child! Peter and Avis's child! How could I give birth to my own child and *not know*? What am I supposed to do *now*?' Peri scratched at her head viciously, as if something was biting her. She thought of her and Peter, together. Of course he could have made her pregnant, that was possible, but . . . but they'd paid her to have *their* child. No-one had ever suggested Hugo could be anything else. Why, if Hugo really was hers, had he been allowed to live?

The day of the embryo transfer. She'd been laid out on the operating table prepped for surgery, and she knew Eliseev and Peter were there but she remembered only masked and gowned figures looming over her. Her terror as her consciousness slipped away, how against her own will she'd fought the anaesthesia, the descent into timeless non-existence. Someone held her down, forcing the mask to her face. It must have been then that they discovered she was already pregnant. They must have decided, *Peter* must have decided, to continue with the pregnancy. And not to tell her. To betray her. To let her think the baby belonged to him and Avis.

'Has it occurred to you that maybe you *did* know?' said Finch, breaking into her thoughts. 'Your actions are a clue. The fact you were willing to give up almost everything for Hugo. The body has its own wisdom. They say mothers can pick the smell of their newborns from that of a hundred other babies in a darkened room. Anyway,' she added, 'you should be pleased. Now you know you're Hugo's mother in every way, you have rights. You just have to work out how to claim them.'

Peri could see herself months after the procedure back in the dimmed labour rooms behind Eliseev's office, where he had broken her waters. The cold metal of a cabinet pressed into her at waist height as she leaned her palms flat on its top, bracing against a contraction as it peaked. The relief as it ebbed away was overwhelming.

Hours later there was no peak, no trough. Pain stretched into an endless plateau and the grinding within her was grinding her whole being into dust and she paced, the warm room now stuffy, constricting; she wanted out, she wanted to walk and walk, feel air flow over her skin, only constant movement could help her bear this but Eliseev would not allow her outside. Peri's self, her soul, her every nerve-ending was forced up against raw scouring bedrock. She could not distance herself from this by a hair's-breadth. There was nothing else in life, except death itself, where the only way out was through. On her knees, she begged for help. She was frightened and utterly alone.

Eliseev and Peter watched her but they were far away, on the other side of the pain. They were masked and gowned as before. Would Eliseev cut the baby from her? The men barely seemed human; she could see the glitter of their eyes but they would not look into her face. Eliseev allowed her gas and as she inhaled the air buzzed and sparked; she could not see or hear, there was only the grinding, boulders crushed by a glacier. Peter had not wanted her to have any pain relief but Eliseev had been all for it, in fact it seemed to her now that he would have preferred her to have no memory of the baby sliding from her in the rush of blood and water. Weakened by blood loss, she lay on the bed in the labour room while Eliseev and Peter took the baby; she'd not held him or even seen him. She heard him crying, the sound weakening as he was carried away.

Hugo's cry had cut her heart like a broken piece of glass. For the first time she feared this deal was not going to work.

Now, Finch left Peri and Hugo, not saying where she was going or what she was doing. Peri had noticed that Audax members rarely told her anything not directly involving her.

'Wait,' Peri called. Finch turned. 'What have Jay and Niko decided about me?'

'We haven't decided. But then, neither have you.' Finch plunged into the trees.

Peri turned to the baby, *her* baby, as if he were now, for the first time, a stranger. The child gazed back at her, his eyes deep as the sky. *You knew*, said Peri. *You always knew, didn't you?* Hugo broke into one of his dazzling grins. I should have known too. Sometimes I did but I thought I was crazy. She picked him up and snuggled him into her skin. He patted her shoulder with his tiny, perfect hand.

After she settled Hugo to sleep, Peri found Jay near the grassy launch site. He was alone, about to take off. She could see only his outline, darker than the deep blue dusk.

'Jay,' she said, the anger in her voice almost fracturing it; she didn't know who she was anymore. Like planets and moons knocked out of their paths into disarray, realigning, she was now the centre; Hugo orbited her. She was not a satellite, an accessory to other lives, infinitely replaceable.

Jay watched Peri as she marched up, landed one punch, two, hard, on his chest. He gripped her wrists.

'Stop it,' he said. 'That hurts.'

'Not as much as you hurt me. You were going to *leave* me. I hate you. I *hate* you.'

Jay was still holding her wrists.

'Let me go.'

He dropped them. 'I wasn't going to leave you.'

'You were.'

'We had to make sure.'

'What were you going to do?'

'I saw what came after you. And your timing, turning up just before the raid: you can't blame me for being wary. As far as we all knew, including you, Hugo wasn't even yours. You were asking us to accept a strange situation.'

Peri sank onto the grass.

'Seems to me I might not be the only one you're angry with.'

'Really?' said Peri. 'Perceptive, aren't you? If you want to know, I'm not going to just hit Peter. I'm going to kill him. I'll kill him.' She clenched her fists. 'That he could do that.' Her voice rose. 'I swear, I will kill him. I will!'

Jay laid his hand on her shoulder. Peri shook him off.

'You don't believe me, do you? Do you think killing Peter would be hard for me, after everything I've been through?'

'Promise me something.'

'What?' Peri stared at Jay.

'If you decide to hit me or attack me again, make sure I see you coming, like I did tonight. Don't ever sneak up on me.'

'Why?'

'So I don't lash out without thinking. I don't want to hurt you.'

'Of all the patronising—'

'I'm not patronising you, you silly little—' He paused, took a breath. 'Alright, now I'm patronising you. Peri, I'm twice your size and I'm trained to—' He broke off and sat next to her on the grass, pushed wet strands of hair back from her cheeks. 'Peri, I saved you in that storm. You'll always have a claim on me, something more than one adult usually owes another. That's just the way it is. Funny how when you do something for someone, you owe them, not the other way round.'

'Like me and Hugo.'

'Yes. Someone told me once the surest way to get someone to care for you is, somehow, make them do something for you. People fall into the trap of doing the opposite all the time; they serve another, hoping they'll be loved for it, but all they do is fall deeper themselves with everything they do.'

'That sounds cynical.'

'Not at all. It's the way love actually works. It's not about freedom or equality or self-interest, two independent individuals coming together, balancing, give and take the same amount; that's a transaction, a balance sheet, not love. Love is service or it is not love. And I've spent a lot of time thinking about service. That is what my life has been. The more that is demanded of you, the more you give. The more you love. As a mother, you know this. The one you love most is the one who has taken you over, put your very life at risk.'

Peri listened to the grass shift in the warm breeze. In the dark east, summer lightning split, white water falling down distant purple cliffs of sky.

So that's why Peter and Avis never cared for Hugo and I did. Do. I never understood. They never gave up anything, they never risked anything, and the less they did for him, the less they loved him. I thought it was the other way round, that they did nothing for him because they didn't love him. Maybe that's what they thought too. Probably wondered what was wrong with them. If they'd just acted like they loved him, day in, day out, wiped his bottom, bathed him, fed him, got up every night, love would have come. No escaping the work if you want love.

Peri squeezed Jay's hand and got to her feet. 'I'm going to sleep.'

The next morning, Peri set Hugo down on the sandy river flat and stared at him, looking at each feature more closely, with more attention than she had ever dared. She had played with his fingers and toes and rubbed his tummy and kissed his nose, mostly when Avis and Peter had not been around, but she had never dared take that inventory of the newborn that parents do, looking at each feature to see that it's perfect, to see who it resembles in the family. She had been afraid to do that, afraid perhaps of loving him too much, or in the wrong way, and what would have been the point of trying to see who he looked like anyway? It had been none of her business.

Now Peri looked with new eyes. She was his mother. Hugo linked her to the family, the parents and grandparents, she'd never known: a living message from the past she could not read. The slight tilt at the corner of his eyes; the mouth with its full upper lip crumpled, a newly opened poppy; fragile eyelids lit at the edges with violet shade, like paper-thin shells: whose features were these? His brow, so wide across the temples, that was Peter, her link to him and generations of his family forged, unbreakable.

The deep anger kindled last night still burned in her. Peter had known and never told her. He'd made love to her while she was pregnant and never told her. And Avis, was she in on it too? That would explain her coldness. But why would she have gone along with it? Peter had made her, Peri, pregnant and he'd let her bear the baby, thinking Hugo was not hers. He'd known and kept this from her. *He'd* stolen Hugo. *He* was the kidnapper.

Peri ran her hands down Hugo's long legs. That could be her or Peter. His toes, rounded out at the end, like frog toes, and his shiny dark hair, the slightly square face, the rounded chin, that was her. How had she missed it? She hadn't looked for resemblance, would not have believed it if she'd seen it. Some babies look like the men and women they will become but Hugo had the blank perfection of childhood. His adult face was still hidden.

Peri picked him up again, breathing in his hair and the skin at the back of his neck. He smelled of his own shortbread smell, river water, earth. So hard to grasp, to truly believe, that not only was it permitted for her to love Hugo, now it was her duty, it was required. That would take getting used to.

What was the difference between choosing to love Hugo and having to love him? What did that feel like? She wasn't sure she'd ever had a choice. But she was bound to him now, there truly was no choice. What a relief—not just that she would not give him up but that she could not.

Her own parents must have thought they were doing the right thing, giving her up, and she knew that they'd been wrong. She could not do the same to Hugo.

Early afternoon Finch came to find Peri, who had stayed by the river with Hugo all morning, playing with him, feeding him, dozing next to him while he napped. She'd washed his hair, rinsing the suds into a bowl Finch gave her and, carrying Hugo on her hip, lugged the water away to dump it near their waste pit, well away from the river, as Finch had instructed.

All the while Peri wondered: how do I feel? How *should* I feel? Should I try to be with Hugo even more intensely than I thought I had the right to before? Or should I be calmer, more relaxed, the way a *real* parent should be, trusting in a bond that wasn't, or shouldn't be, under such pressure? That would be more sane, wouldn't it? Thinking about it, it's obvious I have no bloody idea what normal love between parent and child looks like. Did I see *any* in my childhood? The way Peter and Avis were with Hugo, *that* couldn't have been normal, could it? Maybe for them it was. But not what you'd want. No. I don't think so.

So when Finch urged Peri to come on a flight with her and Jay, she was reluctant to leave Hugo but also relieved for a brief respite from the uncertainty of renegotiating her relationship with her baby. Her baby! If in fact that was what she was doing. Really, that was not right. She was realigning her thoughts but the way she looked after Hugo would not change. What changed was her approach to their future and she'd not had time to think about that yet.

'We're going on a short flight for Shaheen's sake,' Finch said. 'Come with us. You need to use your muscles today so they don't seize up altogether.'

Peri left Hugo with Raf and Griffon, who'd come down to the river flat and were now playing with him roughly in the way that young men will. Hugo splashed and giggled with them as if he would burst with joy.

'See?' said Finch, as Peri paused before turning onto the path leading to the launch run at the cliff edge. 'He's happy!'

Shows how much you know, thought Peri as she followed Finch. Hugo was not really old enough yet to spend long periods without her. Especially since he was not used to anyone else looking after him.

Jay met Finch and Peri on the cliff edge. He had his falconer's glove tucked into his waistband and a whistle on a thong around his neck.

'Wind dummy?' said Finch.

Jay nodded, looking up and away from them.

He took off into the afternoon light. The sun was high, the sky lit with white puffs of cloud above them evenly spread, handfuls of crumpled paper scattered across a floor.

'Mid-level cloud,' Jay was saying to Finch as Peri rose to meet them. 'Between two and six thousand metres. *Ac flo*.'

Peri closed the gap with Finch and Jay, who didn't look like they were working at all. They floated up like puffs of smoke and were almost as hard to see. There was nothing shiny on them, no telltale glints from watches or jewellery, no flash of glitter from the wings like she was used to seeing in the City. These two were virtually invisible, not something any City flier wanted to be.

'Altocumulus floccus,' said Finch to Peri. 'Higher up. But we've got some cumulus over there to head towards, long as it doesn't start to o'd.'

'Air rising ahead of a cold front,' continued Jay. 'Could've transformed from altostratus or cumulus or arisen from turbulence or convection at middle cloud level. Means there could be a thunderstorm later. Finch, you two acted as lemmings just then. What's the point of me playing wind dummy if you don't pay attention?'

'I did,' protested Finch. 'I just did it very fast.'

'No, you *didn't*,' said Jay.

Finch said, 'Okay. I didn't. Sorry.' She added, 'So, did you check all the indicators before you came out? Not just wind but height of cloudbase? Lapse rate?'

'Fuck off,' said Jay. 'Can't you calculate lapse rate yourself by now?'

'You know I can't.'

'Well,' said Jay, 'you can try remembering that in the afternoon of a warm day like this, environmental lapse rate is likely to be greater than the dry adiabatic lapse rate, which gives you a superadiabatic lapse rate. Yes?'

'Hey,' said Finch. 'I know I just set a bad example to Peri but you indulging your frustration with spoonfeeding all of us wuffos, and to you *everyone's* a wuffo, is a poor example too. You could explain to Peri what the hell you're talking about.'

Peri concentrated on the way each beat of her wings forced huge draughts of air into her, and glided into the gyre Finch and Jay had set up, mounting higher with them in wide, easy curves. Higher and higher until the land flattened out into a mantle of colours. This high there was less fear, her breath came back. Here she could really fly. They had slipped the surly bonds of earth. They rose higher, until the air began to chill and the clouds were nearer, grey along their undersides.

'Lapse rate,' said Jay. 'The simple version is that lapse rate describes the decrease in air temperature with increasing elevation—' He broke off as a piercing *witchiw-witchiw* fell through the air towards them.

'Shaheen,' said Finch. 'She's waiting-on. That means she'll stay above us until we get to where we're going.'

'There is something useful you can practise. Cloud snapshots,' Jay said as they rode the lift towards cloudbase. 'A habit you should get into. Clearly, you need to keep a better eye on the weather.'

It was true. She did not understand the sky or its clouds nearly well enough.

'So,' Jay said, 'you need to watch out that clouds are not overdeveloping. Cumulus have the potential, always, to o'd, and if they do, you're going to get strong wind, rain, possibly hail or thunderstorms. Get into the habit of taking mental snapshots of clouds on your flight path. Take them regularly, say once a minute. Find a point of comparison to work out their speed or development—their position relative to a mountain or a tree, or height relative to another cloud. Clouds can change surprisingly fast and with nothing in the sky to give them scale except other clouds it's easy to lose track of how fast they're growing—or decaying. If a cloud is growing taller rapidly, well then, you know what to do.'

'Get the fuck out of there,' said Peri.

Jay laughed.

They flew westward, heading towards a bank of cumulus clouds piling up on the horizon. Peri tried to practise taking mental snapshots of the cumulus far ahead but it was a struggle. There was nothing near them that was stable as a point of comparison and it was difficult even to try to fix all the shapes and heights and positions of the clouds in relation to each other in her mind and then compare those things again a minute or two later.

Jay's the best flier I've ever seen. But some of this stuff I'm learning is taking all the joy out of flying. How I can feel the rush of it when I'm worrying about blue holes and my energy bank and taking cloud snapshots every sixty seconds? Is this really what I wanted when I got my wings?

Finch seemed to pick up Peri's mood. 'How're you going?'

'Not so good.'

'It might help if you understand you're looking at a few different types of cumulus there. For example, those scattered puffy bits of cumulus nearest us are classified as cumulus mediocris or *cu med*. Not an appealing name but it's a pretty type of cloud, the kind you want to see on a nice day for a picnic. Mediocris just means they don't get that high. Shifting to the plane behind those, you've got a striking example of cumulus pileus—'

'Let me guess,' said Peri. '*Cu pil*?'

'Exactly. And those gorgeous deadly big fellas behind the cu pil, the ones that look like giant cauliflowers exploding upwards in slow motion?'

Peri laughed.

'Cumulus congestus.'

'*Cu con*?'

'Yeah. Cumulus *always* indicate instability which is one concrete result of Jay's precious superadiabatic lapse rate.'

'My head hurts,' Peri said.

'Practise, my dear. That is all. I'm sure learning to fly isn't as hard as learning to play the piano, you know. It's just that the consequences are different. No-one ever died from hitting a wrong note.'

Jay stooped into a dive, Finch and Peri following. They pulled out of the dive and began a wide spiral downwards.

They dropped towards forest rolling down into a shallow valley. Peri could see forest all around to the horizon. They dropped further and the country began to resolve into individual trees, rock faces. Now they were down in the shallow valley, flying not far above the treetops. Peri's skill at this kind of flying had increased dramatically in the last day or two. As they sped over the treetops Peri saw a patch of soft green too lush for this wilderness. The old, empty farm stood out like a green beacon. Jay slowed, diving steeply, then beat his wings hard to soften his impact.

'Ugh, *boink*,' shuddered Finch as Jay hit the ground. 'Too hard and too fast for me. Guess he's used to it.'

Finch spiralled up, waving Peri to follow her.

'Watch,' said Finch.

Jay raised his whistle and blew three short blasts. Shaheen circled below them.

'She's hunting now,' said Finch.

'What did Jay call her? A haggard hawk?'

'Most falconers fly hawks they've raised themselves, who're almost afraid to go out of sight of the man or woman who's fed them since they hatched. But a haggard hawk is a queen; she's wild-caught, full-grown into her breeding plumage. She may even have raised young. She's a survivor who's been able to feed herself for years. Naturally they're much riskier to fly, easier to lose back to the wild. But Jay flies her at hack—that is, free—and she returns, especially since her tiercel was killed. I wonder if she doesn't see Jay as her mate, maybe a kind of super-male, though of course with birds of prey the females are larger, so greater size is not a masculine quality.'

'What is a masculine quality, then, for birds of prey?' said Peri.

'Lightness,' said Finch. 'Size and power is for the females. To hunt with a female peregrine is the ultimate for falconers and *only* the female is given the title of falcon.'

Jay raised his arm to the falcon.

Peri heard the whistle of wind and saw the bird plummeting, a dark thunderbolt. The falcon caught something in mid-air and brought it to Jay. He fed her a morsel and with a chinking of bells she was away again.

Peri circled higher. Her vision grew stronger the higher she balanced, just here, under the clouds. Down there were the old round yards, railings sagging and broken. The spot was peaceful, melancholy, reminding Peri of the abandoned farms in the hills behind Janeane's property. She dropped, imitating the falcon's dive, and pulled herself up, beating her wings strongly to gain height again.

All the way out here, we're safe. But for how long? In the City, we're both in danger, unless I return Hugo to Peter, all on his terms. Give him back what he bought. Can't do that now. Finch was right. Now I have to find a way to claim Hugo.

The falcon stooped again and brought something to Jay, her every movement heralded by the small music of the bells.

Peri balanced herself on a warm updraft; how long could she soar without a beat of her wings? Her control was growing so fine that she could concentrate on the minute angle of each primary feather.

She needed time to think. What would it be like if she stayed here? She could see herself, long green years ahead, years of flying and foraging, of growing tough like the Audax fliers. Could she make that choice? To hide in the woods? She'd never be able to come out into the world again. These people would be her whole world.

Audax fliers won't stay here forever though. And what about Hugo? This life's impossible for him. No other kids here and what would he learn, except to be an outlaw? All they care about is flying; to them he's incomplete, just like he is to Peter and Avis. How long can I keep carrying him when I fly? No way for an unwinged person to live with Audax.

Jay fed Shaheen the small birds she'd caught and bagged the rabbits for carrying back. The two of them took to the air. In a heartbeat Shaheen was flying above all of them, her long, slender wings beating in shallow, powerful strokes. Soon she was out of sight.

'She'll be resting on one of her perches on the cliff face by the time we reach Heavener,' said Jay. 'She does about fifty klicks per hour in level flight. Of course, when she dives you're talking well over three hundred klicks per hour—that's ninety metres per second—fastest creature on the planet.' He sounded as proud as if Shaheen were his own daughter. He tossed the bag of rabbits to Finch. 'Take that back for us?'

'Sure. What are you doing?'

'See you back at Heavener. Peri, come with me.'

'Don't be long,' said Finch. 'Sky's becoming more unstable.'

Soon she was a black spot diminishing against darkening clouds.

'What is it?' said Peri, following Jay as he circled above the old farm.

'It'll be here somewhere. Should be, on a summer afternoon like this.' Jay turned sharply, the fringe of his primary feathers brushing her wing.

He rose higher, scanning, then dropped.

Jay centred his gyre above an overgrown garden that must have been near the now-vanished farmhouse. Directly below them sprawled a tangled mass of deep green shiny leaves and pink flowers. Peri circled above Jay.

Distant bees or nameless grass-dwellers hummed, tuning themselves up in the afternoon sun. Her fears crowded in on her. She had to leave Audax and Heavener Ridge. The sun melted the tightness in her limbs, warming her sore muscles, burnishing her feathers. She sighed, wishing her thoughts, her fears, would dissolve in the heat.

The heat. Sun had awakened something. Peri spiralled over the dense leaves, the pink flowers. Just *here*, luscious scent streaming upwards in the golden furnace of afternoon, concentrated essence of a thousand roses. Sky steaming in roses. Clouds simmering vapour of roses. She breathing roses, sweltering in roses, sweating roses, rose tear warm on her cheek.

'I see you've got it,' said Jay, sweeping closer, the *whoosh* of his wings a steady beat in the still air.

'It's bliss.'

'It's a thermal. Sometimes you can find a thermal by scent. You can fly along and suddenly be startled by a smell, putrid or gorgeous, rising along with the thermal. I found this one above the rosebushes a while ago. Knew it'd appear again on a warm afternoon like this. That's not all. Other things rise too. Look.'

Peri looked down, focused. Scraps of colour freighted the rising air: butterflies lavender, blue, yellow, white; watergreen dragonflies; pink petals. Peri turned as tightly as she could so that she was almost hovering, allowing the warm air infused with perfume, blossom and insects to engulf her.

'Thank you,' said Peri.

'We need to go,' said Jay.

A stiff breeze sprang up, blowing an ominous cloudscape towards Peri and Jay; they had to work hard to make headway against it.

There was no mistaking the rapid growth of these clouds. Peri was flying into the most complex sky she'd ever seen, other than the supercell storm. She was flying into a series of shifting vertical planes, like the layers of flat scenery, one behind the other, creating a sense of great depth.

The nearest layer, the one they were now flying through, was darkening sky with wisps of black cloud. Behind that towered a cumulus congestus cloud that bulged deep eggplant purple and must be thousands of metres high. Directly behind and swelling out from the side of that cloud, the afternoon sun lit up another mass of cumulus congestus so that each billow glowed white, crisp as frost, intoxicatingly bright next to the dark cloud massed against it. Behind the white cloud shone sky as blue as heaven, as if all the darkness in front belonged to another day altogether.

'Wow,' said Peri.

'CC over there,' said Jay. 'Need to get moving.'

He accelerated and Peri pushed herself to match his pace.

'Look,' he said, pointing to the purple cloud. Horizontal flickers of lightning. 'Cloud-to-cloud lightning.'

They swooped as low as they dared. It was scary, thrilling, racing these clouds, speeding over the trees and rolling plain, and now she was putting it all together, glancing at the land formations below, comparing them to the clouds, glancing down again. When her concentration was this single-minded, when she was flying for her life, then she could do this, put it all together the way Jay was teaching her. Simple. All she had to do was think of absolutely nothing else. *Wings are heavy unless you give something up*. All she had to give up was everything. Everything but flying.

She hardly wanted to admit it to herself but there was a release in concentrating on her flying. A relief. Her Flight training in the City had been taken out of her own sleeping time. Even then she'd always been anxious. What if Hugo wakes, what if he needs me, what if the milk I've left for him isn't enough?

Now there was a freedom in wearing herself out with such single-minded purpose. She felt guilty, indulging in an illicit pleasure. She had to push thoughts of Hugo—*her* son, her *son*—aside to concentrate on each detail of finetuning her skills. She was racing those overhanging clouds, knowing this time was precious and running out so fast, even though her new understanding, surprising her every few minutes like a cold wave submerging her, was both delicious and anxiety-provoking. Creeping up on her, Peri felt, was a lust for Flight.

Now, gloriously, they burst out from under the purple cloud. Its rumbling faded behind them and they sped bathed in full sunshine over the valley leading up to Heavener Ridge and now they were sweeping up on the ridgelift and she and Jay were laughing, silly from relief and joy and the rush of it, she wasn't losing that at all, it could only grow higher and faster and stronger, just like that erupting purple cumulus.

By the time they splashed into the river, Peri was exhausted and elated in mind and body.

Late afternoon stretched ahead of her. Again she played with Hugo in the tea-coloured river pool. It was warm and clear and Peri felt calmer than she had for months, for years. She had not felt this carefree since playing in the river at Janeane's when she was four years old.

Shaheen sat on her favourite perch, a branch overhanging the water. *Ek-ek-ek-ek*, she said a few times, the sound resonant and harsh, seeming to reprimand them when Hugo's squeals of delight became too shrill. *Where are your fledglings?* said Peri to the falcon. *Did you scold them like that?* Shaheen fluffed out her feathers and dozed in the sun. With the perfect discipline and energy conservation of the hunter, she could spend hours motionless, as if carved in stone.

Peri concentrated on each minute as it passed, feel of sun on her back, water streaming off her oiled feathers, the pleasant ache in her strengthening flight muscles. In her mind every second was the startling knowledge: she was Hugo's mother. His real mother. She was right to care for him, to love him as much as she did. Every few seconds she glanced at him again, measuring what this new distance, or closeness, might be.

And she could feel how she was growing in power and skill with every hour she spent in the air with the Audax fliers. Every moment with them she was becoming more the flier she had hoped to be. The airy lightness she'd always dreamed of was at last unfolding.

How ironic that she should grasp these competing ecstasies of her life here at the same time, with Audax.

There was always that uneasiness; whatever Peri did the other clamoured for her. Mother and flier—both selves had grown stronger, more intense, in her time with Audax, as if she had been a fire, banked and smouldering, and now she blazed, burning high and hot. Wouldn't she burn out all the sooner, be scattered, ashes to the wind? For a second she could understand Avis and Peter's ambivalence towards Hugo. She would not be this torn if Hugo were a fledgling. But he was not and so the things she most loved tore her in opposite directions.

Peri nursed Hugo, then fed him dinner from the cool larder in the river. The sun was still strong and warm on her back but it was starting to lower and Hugo was nodding. He was tired after all the playing with Raf and then with Peri.

Peri wrapped Hugo and took him back to the overhang. Leto was there and said she was about to sleep herself. Peri left Hugo asleep, snuggled into Leto's side, and walked back down the track. Her whole body was coming back to sensual life, surging with energy as her fears dropped away, as the rush of Flight was hers, more and more every day.

When she stepped down to the river pool, Jay was there, changing a dressing on one of his wounds. He straightened up and caught Peri's eye. 'Give me a hand,' he said, indicating a dressing on his back, under his wing. 'I can't reach it.'

'I can't either,' said Peri. 'You're too tall.'

Jay sat down on the sand and Peri sat on the log behind him, straddling his narrow waist with her legs. He leaned back into her and arched out his wing. Peri gently detached the bandage and pad and cleaned the cut and surrounding bruise.

Jay winced.

'What happened?'

He shook his head. 'Doesn't matter.' He handed her a first-aid package.

Peri opened it and smoothed on the new skin and dressing it contained. She ran her hand carefully down his outstretched wing as far as she could reach.

'Let me check your feathers,' she said. 'Make sure there aren't any more broken ones that need fixing.'

Jay turned and looked at her.

'Okay,' he said.

Peri worked over every dark and golden feather on Jay's wings, grooming them until they shone. She leaned in against his back to reach the feathers at the leading edge, along the top. She let her hand run up his neck and felt him shiver.

'Jay,' she whispered, pressed against him.

'Yes?'

'Take the bracelet off me.'

'No.'

She kissed his neck.

Jay stood up and turned to face her. He bent down and helped her up, circling her wrist with his hand. He walked along the river, still holding her wrist. She almost had to run to keep up.

Jay took her along the river to a small private beach. He was all easy confidence taking her in his arms. Jay's mouth was soft on hers, he was taller and far more massive than Peter, his skin smooth and brown and warm, his muscles dense and unyielding.

Jay kissed her. 'What do you want from me?'

'I want to know more about you,' said Peri. 'You're the most mysterious one here. How come you know everything? You know what I went through in the storm. You knew how to fix me and Hugo.'

'Isn't it obvious?' said Jay, looking down at her. Peri's gaze flicked to the dressings on his chest and arms, the tattoos on his upper arms.

Niko said, 'Your six years of rigorous training with the best of the best.'

'Oh my god. You were a Raptor!'

'No,' said Jay. 'I *am* a Raptor.'

So this was a Raptor. He pulled her on top of him and entered her and she sighed, letting herself soften in a way she never could with Peter. That had been all tension and rush, hard exquisite lust, but this was slow bliss and she kissed Jay deeply. Jay held her tight, easing her, slowing her until they barely moved and she was melting like honey in the sinking sun. Minutes, maybe hours, hung suspended in the hush and warmth of the early evening and she wondered if she could pass out with pleasure.

Afterwards, Peri lay pillowed on one of Jay's wings, her head on his arm. Jay shivered when her hand grazed one of the dressings as she stroked him.

'Injuries do it for some girls,' said Jay.

'Oh, come on,' laughed Peri.

'True,' he said. 'I saw the way you looked at me after the raid.'

'You looked even tougher. But in need of loving care. I'll bet you had lots of girls when you were a Raptor.'

'You don't understand,' said Jay. 'When I say I'm still a Raptor, I mean it. Once a Raptor, *always* a Raptor.'

'Really?' said Peri, propping herself up on one elbow. A curved leaf from the tree above them drifted down and she caught it in her hand. She stroked the leaf down his chest. 'What do you mean?'

Jay sighed. 'The treatments and the training are different. More extreme. I can do things you can't.'

'So you have superpowers,' said Peri.

'In a way. But I'll pay the price.'

'What does that mean?'

'I won't live as long as you.'

'Oh.'

'That was the price of leaving my village. You paid a price to leave *your* village.'

'How did you become a Raptor?' said Peri.

'The men of my islands have been an export for generations. We're big and strong and have a warrior history. We *like* to fight, I've been told. So we've always been in demand from the armies of the world.'

'So they came for you?'

'I always knew they would. I wanted to get away, see something of the wider world, but I also knew my own worth. I held out against the recruiters until I was promised Raptor training. You know the saying *Be careful what you wish for, you might get it*? Well, I got my wish alright.'

'What happened?'

Jay closed his eyes as if to remember better. His voice was slow and warm; Peri had never seen him so relaxed. This was not Jay as the rest of Audax usually saw him.

'I can't describe six years of Raptor treatments and training but there were times I thought I was going to lose my mind. It was as if every part of myself, every mental and physical characteristic I thought of as me, was put into a molecular blender and atomised and reconstituted into something else. Military training can be like that at the best of times but this was a thousand times more challenging. I knew only the other Raptors had the slightest idea what I was going through and even then only the ones in my intake. They change the techniques and treatments, refine them, all the time. The comradeship of the Raptors in my unit was the only thing that got me through.'

Peri said, 'I wish I'd had someone who was going through the transition with me. I was so alone and it was the most terrifying thing I've ever done, that and giving birth—but the terror of getting my wings lasted longer.'

'How do you mean?'

'I needed help just to learn how to get my brain to move my wings. They were just heavy, dead things. They felt stuck on, *not-me*. For the first days after the surgery I didn't dare even look in the mirror. I couldn't bear to see what I'd become. It wasn't until I started being able to use them that I could stand to look. Even then I wasn't sure whether I was a monster or not. The wings themselves were beautiful but I wasn't sure about the whole package, whether all the parts of me fitted together anymore.'

Jay opened his eyes and looked at Peri. He put his arm around her waist and pulled her close to him. 'I didn't go through that,' he said after a moment. 'We were up and into rehabilitation and training so quickly. I became a new person but never had time to give it much thought. I'm glad it's over now but I wouldn't have missed it. We did things that make me shake my head now.'

'Like what? What are your superpowers?'

'We used to fly up into the low stratosphere. Our officers said if a bunch of fucking geese could fucking surf the fucking jet stream then so could we. Were we going to let ourselves be shat on by a shit-for-brains goose? Sir, no, sir, we would not. When we started we had thermal suits and oxygen but all that was cut back as the treatments progressed, until we could do it ourselves. Most of us, anyway. The attrition rate was high.' Jay paused. Was he remembering what flying in the jet stream was like? Peri thought of her own instant at the top of the storm, seeing the shining curve of the earth for one moment, then blackness and falling, an eternity of falling. Jay had experienced that. Alone among anyone she was ever likely to meet, he knew what she had seen.

'I remember,' said Jay almost dreamily. 'I remember looking down from that high. If it was clear I could see roads and rivers, just squiggles, like they are on a map. I could see the sea and the white band of surf but no movement. I could see grey and brown, darker green along the coast and over the hills, patches of lighter green around the towns and along roads. And the towns themselves looked like odd-shaped areas of coloured dots scattered among more uniform browns and greys and greens.'

'You must have taken Zefiryn to see like that,' said Peri.

'Of course,' said Jay. 'Zefiryn enabled us to deploy characteristics of eagle vision, among other effects. The higher you fly, the more sharply you see.

'The most amazing thing was flying over mountains, especially around four or five klicks up. You fly along a big valley or the side of a massif. Then head for the highest mountain or plateau and you soar up along the rock face and *just* clear the top. Then swoop over the top and *drop* down into the valley. Gives you vertigo like nothing else. It's dangerous because the weather in high mountains is so unpredictable.'

'What was hardest about your training?'

'One of their favourite things was to take us up blindfolded—like being fucking kidnapped, over and over. They wanted us to focus on bird navigation abilities. Could they release us over unfamiliar territory and could we find our way back to base without instruments? Did we have compass sense? Map sense? We'd circle our release spot and off we'd go. Some we never saw again. I often wondered what happened to them. They kept on, though, our superior officers, they were fucking ruthless, trialling us under different conditions. Night-time. Cloud cover. Rain. Storms. Over water. Over land. You name the terrain and weather and we had to do it.'

Jay sighed and crossed his arms behind his head. 'When we were at the very limit of how high we could fly, we'd develop hypoxia, even with oxygen, and when you do you become euphoric but it's weird because the colours grey out. So coming down was a real rush as the colours flooded back.'

'Wow. That sounds incredible.' Peri ran her hand through Jay's hair. 'These lightning flashes on your wings and hair,' she said. 'Are they to do with your unit?'

Jay shook his head. 'No. It's the kind of thing Raptors do. Adolescent, really.'

'I love them,' said Peri.

'Yes,' said Jay, laughing, 'but then you're so young, even younger than I was when I started training, so that fits.'

Peri dozed in Jay's arms and woke into darkness, to find him kissing her. Her body was still sore from all her bruising in the storm but she eagerly enfolded him. He spread his wings over her and she breathed in the scent of neroli from the oil he used to groom his feathers. It occurred to Peri, as she felt the warm silkiness of her own and Jay's feathers all around her and the heady drifts of scent released whenever they moved, that this was her first time with a flier since acquiring her own wings.

After a while Peri disengaged and splashed herself in the river. Jay stood and stretched himself, then began grooming his ruffled feathers.

'So, about that bracelet?' Peri said, sluicing herself with water.

Jay kept grooming his feathers. 'Answer's still no, sweetheart.'

Later that night Peri woke into darkness. A chill had stolen across all of them sleeping there; she saw Finch shudder in her sleep and burrow down into her feathers. She had puffed them out, the way birds do in winter, to trap air in them to insulate her from the cold.

Peri was hungry. After checking Hugo was still asleep, she padded down the path to the river, to the larder. A bit of far cloud obscured the stars, very high, and she could just make out the outline of a flier bending over the pool in the water. Who could it be? She did not recognise the figure. It was thinner than any of the Audax fliers.

Peri halted, her body knowing instantly she mustn't make a sound, not a leaf crunch, and before thought could form, a wave of horror flooded her. The figure turned and Peri felt a scream rise but shock froze her.

The flier was devouring food, hands and mouth dripping, a ragged, hairy vulture with stringy muscles and a raw, haggard face: the ferocity of its expression beyond or below the human. The shine of its eyes terrible in the dark. A horrible falling blankness. A thing lost.

Peri could hear low breathing, a hissing growl through bared teeth. Something mechanical in its hostility. The automatic rumble of aggression was unfocused. She gagged on its rank, heavy stink. This mixture of human and other was not lovely. It was dire. It was all that had been feared: werewolf, vampire, succubus. The horror had been lurking there for all time; we always feared it. So easy then to lose the human—this thing so much worse than if it had never been human.

It did not look at her. Wild animals don't. She was not part of its world. It melted away along the river towards the cliff edge.

There was a rustling in the bushes and two fliers stepped into the clearing: Jay and Raf.

'Did you see it?' Peri gasped. 'It must have come straight past you!'

'*What?*' said both at once.

Peri tried to describe what she had seen.

Jay whistled. '*Fuck*. I was sure there weren't any around here. You saw a Wild.' The two men sprinted back along the path, crashing through the brush, not caring how much noise they made. Peri heard the rush of air as they took off into the night.

Peri ran back to the overhang, where everyone still slept. She sat up until Raf and Jay reappeared.

'Nothing,' said Jay. 'We redouble our watch from now on.'

Peri moved next to him. 'What does it want?'

'What does anything want? Food. Somewhere to sleep. The real worry is if there's more than one. If there's a group they'll want territory. You saw the country on the way to Diomedea. Most of the land out there wouldn't support them. If we can survive here, so can they. Though we have access to resources they don't have.'

'I don't think I'll be able to sleep,' said Peri. 'Can I watch with you?'

'No,' said Jay. 'I never put you on watch or patrol with me.'

'You think I'll distract you.'

'No,' said Jay. 'I *know* you will. Stay here with Hugo. You need your sleep.'

'Don't you?'

'Not so much. Two or three hours a night will do me and I can go without for periods of time. It's useful to have soldiers who don't need to sleep much. One of the things that shortens our lives. Now get some rest.'

Peri lay down next to Hugo, who was so deeply asleep he didn't move as she nestled him into her feathers. She lay so she could look out of the overhang and watch Jay's outline against the sky until she fell into a shallow, troubled sleep.

17

ZEN ESTATES

By the time I reached the hospital Thomas had been revived. I sat next to him on the bed in the cubicle in Accident and Emergency, holding his damp hand as Lily spoke to Ruokonen. Thomas was pale and breathing heavily.

Lily put her slick away and turned to me, triumphant. 'Ruokonen says the drugs are not responsible for Tom's episode. Still, she says she'll be down in an hour or two to check on him, see if the dosages need finetuning.'

This made no sense. If the drugs were not responsible, why would the dosages need to be altered?

My slick. Now was hardly the time to work but there was Lily, distracted, answering a colleague, and we were all just waiting around. Henryk again. Furtively I read his message. *M's go-see flushed B out. B such an amateur, makes call instant M leaves. Don't know who B called but will soon. Blasts him, says not want anything happen 2 L, want 2 scare her. Stupid prick. In way over his head.*

I replied: *Saw MP in B's office, Harris Waterhouse. Origins. Check him out?* I thought this was worth drawing to Henryk's attention because Brilliant and Waterhouse seemed to have such a weird relationship: friendly in private, hostile in public.

I looked something up, sent another message: *Hermes not just messenger. God of thieves. And fertility. Also crossroads.*

My other hand still held Tom's. 'We're not scared, are we, Dad?' he said. I squeezed his hand.

Neither Richard, Lily nor I had any idea what had caused Tom's incident. '*Post hoc ergo propter hoc*,' said Richard, coming in with cold water for Lily. For Lily! That'd be right. Thomas was the one who'd been unconscious but Lily made damn sure Richard was looking after *her*. 'A common fallacy,' Richard added complacently. He'd recovered his composure with indecent haste.

You can take your Latin tags and shove them up your arse, I thought, turning away from Richard and putting my arm around Thomas. Richard thought I had no idea what he was talking about. That Lily had picked him to replace me was, I felt, a calculated insult.

'We can't stop the treatments now,' Lily said.

'How can you risk his life so casually?' I demanded.

Lily rounded on me. 'He's fine,' she said, quivering with rage that I dared question her concern for Thomas. 'Look at him, he's fine!'

I stared at Lily. Incensed, she said, 'Are you a doctor? What the fuck do *you* know about anything? Going to withdraw your permission? Just you try it, you'll see how far you get.' Passing orderlies and nurses stared at us. Lily wasn't yelling but there was an intensity that alarmed them. Lily had always understood that attack is the best defence. There was no winning a fight here. I'd have to speak to Ruokonen myself.

On Thursday, when Vittorio heard I was going out for dinner, he insisted on babysitting Frisk. Relieved, I accepted and drove to Henryk's, reflecting that I'd become too used to driving around for convenience on this job and as no more fat payments would be coming from Chesshyre, I'd better break myself of the expensive habit.

I'd spent half the day trying to reach Ruokonen and when I'd finally managed to speak to her, her reassurance over Thomas was brusque. 'He's just a little kid!' I wanted to yell at her. But what could I do? Either I let the juggernaut set in motion by my permission continue or I had to bring all my power to bear to stop it in its tracks, and even that might not be enough. To say nothing of earning Tom's undying disappointment, if not outright hatred. No half-measures were possible, Ruokonen informed me crisply. No waiting and seeing. Not now. I wasn't sure if I believed this but my opinion didn't matter; in this, reality was whatever Ruokonen said it was.

Chesshyre was still trying to contact me, so persistently that I wondered if I could threaten him with a restraining order. The constant hounding was intolerable. The fact was, even if I'd wanted to speak to him, there was nothing more to say. Henryk had said there was no result from the initial efforts he'd made to locate Peri and Hugo. I didn't know if they were dead or had just disappeared and it seemed to me that the best I could do for Peri now was to help Henryk nail Luisa's killer.

As the car bumped and clattered through the backstreets, I reflected that tonight was the one oasis in this horrendous week made bearable so far only by the recovery, in both senses, of Frisk. The only other thing looming in my future was SkyNation, hovering on my mental horizon like a comet, fascinating and ominous.

Henryk and Vivienne had moved to a redeveloped neighbourhood within the City called Zen Estates. Shocking to think Henryk moved to the Estates over three years ago and yet this was the first time I'd visited him there. In my busy, middle-aged mind the few years had fallen away with gathering speed.

At the gate of the high-walled compound I waited as guards confirmed I was expected. After running a security sweep on the car, they waved me through to the car park. A low wooden bridge curved over a lotus pond, the path of stepping stones leading away from the bridge lit with stone lanterns.

As I walked along the path I stared at the Japanese gardens on every side, rooms laid out under the cobalt sky of evening. One garden gleamed, gravel raked in waves that ran up against a large irregular rock, island in a sea of pale stones. I passed boulders dark with moss and groves of maples, their shelving tiers of leaves glowing green with their own internal fire in the fading light. A jungle crow flapped onto a maple branch, its wings a fall of autumn night in the summer dusk.

The path led to a reception hall; I approached the concierge and gave her the number of Henryk's house.

The concierge smiled up at me. 'Walk past the temple then follow the middle path as it curves around to your left.'

'The middle path?' *Ah, should've known I'd be following the middle path here.*

'Keep walking for fifteen minutes,' she said, ignoring my implied joke. 'You'll see the houses on your right looking out over the City as you walk.'

I thanked her and set out. The Estates were bigger than I'd expected. I passed the main temple complex, which fronted its own rice paddy, and paused to listen to the monks within chanting the Kannon Sutra, deep voices resonating, the rhythm hypnotic, the chant competing with the evening wall of sound arising from frogs and crickets in the rice paddy. Lantern light glowing through ricepaper walls outlined the silhouettes of the monks and for a moment I wanted to join them in their deep well of chanting.

By the time I arrived at Henryk's house, I'd left the City behind, entered another world. My breathing slowed, my awareness of the crises entangling me blinked out of existence, clearing my mind of guilt and anxiety for, oh, seconds at a time.

Henryk, wrapped in an indigo yukata and looking for all the world like a Buddhist poet rather than a middle-aged cop, stood at his latticed front door. The twins, James and Juliana, rushed out to greet me, then ran into the garden.

'You didn't tell me about this place,' I said as I took off my shoes.

'You would've laughed. You're living the authentic life, apparently, in your crumbling flat with live music and street life all around you.'

'Beautiful,' I said, as Henryk showed me around, pointing out the way views revealed themselves, disappeared, slivered into odd angles with the slip of a door, the raising of a screen, 'but kind of fake, isn't it? Zen kitsch, manufactured, sanitised. Oh, hi, Vivienne,' I said as we passed the kitchen.

'Oh yes,' said Henryk as we headed for the deck at the back of the house where I could see we were high on the side of a hill, looking back towards the centre of the City twenty klicks away. A rare plane descended, lights flashing; as it sank, it revealed the summit of Cloud City, looming over all the other towers. The silver-green up on its prow would shush in the night, lone and wild as if the grasses waved on a distant prairie.

'Maybe it is fake, though the monks are real. I don't give a damn. I'm a middle-aged man with two small kids and I'm getting tired. I deal with reality every day and you know what? It's too fucking real. Broken children, rapes, murders, contract killings. Remember? I just want to come home somewhere calm, and if that calm owes as much to guards and walls as to the monks, well, so be it.'

I nodded. Yes, I knew exactly what he meant, especially after the last few days.

'It's breathtaking,' I said, looking at the view over the City. 'And your tame monks? Are they expensive?'

Henryk smiled. 'No. Zen Estates built the temple and we all chip in for the upkeep as part of our maintenance fees but the monks manage their own living expenses, begging for food, growing rice, teaching meditation. Every home should have one.'

I shook my head, smiling with a mixture of envy and mockery. Envy had the upper hand.

After we shared a noisy dinner with the kids Vivienne withdrew, pleading exhaustion, and since she'd spent dinner jumping up every few minutes to fetch James a cup of water or a tea towel to wipe up a spill of Juliana's, it was understandable.

Henryk handed me a beer and we walked back out onto his deck overlooking the garden and the distantly blinking City. The moon, silver woven through black pine, seemed to flood us with scent from unknown flowers. A bamboo water feature knocked water intermittently into a pool below us, observed by a mossy Buddha.

Henryk handed me a bottle of insect repellent. 'Slap that on,' he said. 'Not safe outside at night anymore. Bloody City's a tropical swamp. Dengue mosquitoes are supposed to bite only in daytime but apparently this new strain didn't get the memo. We still kid ourselves the City is "subtropical". What a joke. Fifty years ago, maybe.' Henryk took the bottle of repellent and put it on the table as he sat down.

I leaned against the railing of the deck, beer cold in my hand.

'So, you said you were going to work fast,' I said. 'Whoever Brilliant was talking to, you think he's the one had Luisa killed?'

'Brilliant certainly seemed to think so.'

'And the information I gave you on the church projects, the stuff from Cam?'

'Well, you won't be surprised to hear Perros *was* a foster child, and thank god her file was one of the ones Cam was able to get hold of.'

I thought of my conversation with Cam the night I got back from RaRA-land. I'd given her Perros's name then. She must have pulled out the file the very next day.

'Not only was Perros fostered like Peri, but this is the really weird bit, Zeke—one guess who took her.'

'No idea,' I said.

'*Origins*.'

'No. No, that's just . . . You have got to be kidding me.' I felt queasy, just as I had when I realised Waterhouse was an Origins MP. 'Who'd let those nutcases foster kids?'

'You'd be surprised. They look after dozens of foster children. Batches of them.'

'They're criminals.'

'*Not guilty*, remember? As if you could ever forget. No, they offer *a wholesome, ordered, stable environment anchored by strong values*. *Strong values* means they beat the crap out of the kids, as you know only too well.'

'So poor Perros is fostered by Origins, has two kids for Brilliant, gets wings.'

'Then ends up dead.'

'Any closer to knowing why?' I set my beer on the railing.

'Well, that's where your information comes in. I've got a forensic accountant looking at the stuff you gave me. As you said, a lot of money is changing hands on these deals.'

'You said Brilliant told whoever he called that he'd just wanted to scare Luisa.' I straightened up from where I leaned against the railing. Something fell, or jumped, into the pond below. Sound of water. Frog, I suppose. The splash seemed to make things fall into place in my mind, like a row of tumblers clicking in a lock. That most pleasurable feeling in all the world now flooded my brain: pieces of a puzzle suddenly resolving into a picture. *I get it.*

'Think I've got something,' I said. 'Peri told me that Luisa saw a girl that she'd known when she was a kid. Said she was all upset because the girl pretended not to know her and that she was going to dig around, try to find out more about what was going on with her. Said there were others. You said she was fostered by Origins. So this girl she knew, Luisa must have known her from when she was with Origins.'

Henryk was staring at me. 'They wanted to scare her off.'

'From digging around about Origins. About Origins sending girls to the City. Those are the *others*, Henryk, the *others* are other girls, the girls being fostered by Origins, then sent to the City. Then handed over to Little Angels for whatever fliers want to use them for. Little Angels gets them their work permits and gives them their cover stories—nannies, maids, whatever. Some of them would be above board. The other stuff is probably only part of their business but the most profitable part. By far.'

'And Little Angels knows all about them,' said Henryk.

'Even worse,' I said, 'I'd bet Little Angels actually decides which girls to target, because they know their backgrounds, including their medical histories.'

'So, this Hermes project of the church's, all this money, you think this is what Luisa was poking her nose into, realising that what she thought was just some deal she made was actually going on with other girls, that she was part of a trade?'

'I think that's what you'll find. You know where to look to find out where the money's ending up. It's *trafficking*, Henryk.'

'Yeah. Suppose they've got to do something to keep Trinity in solar yachts. You said yourself on the Charon case that they've got very deep pockets.'

The Charon case.

'Do you think there's a connection with that case?'

Henryk shrugged. 'No idea. Defending it cost them dearly. I do still wonder why they kidnapped those two girls. Now it occurs to me that perhaps they staged a hunting expedition to the City. Probably done it before, who knows how many times? They didn't know what they were getting into, didn't know whose daughters they were. Just nice-looking girls, you know? Charon was a pretty rough place. They had every reason to think girls hanging around there weren't well protected.'

'So, Origins is getting girls to foster. It gets money from the department to foster them, then as the girls grow up Origins offers them to the Church of the Seraphim and they make even more money out of them that way. This is fucking bizarre. Origins *hates* the church and everything it stands for.'

'Yes. Hates them enough to take them for all the money they can.'

'Seems to me, whoever Brilliant called must be connected to Origins,' I said. 'Always knew Jones was a nasty piece of work. Poor Luisa, she had to endure a whole childhood imprisoned with them, then, even when she thought she'd escaped, she found she was still caught in their web, just one more product making profit for them. No wonder she was upset. And she was going to blow the whistle on them.'

'In a way, she succeeded,' said Henryk. 'Shame it cost her her life.'

'That's Origins. What about Harper?' I said.

'Harper comes into the picture later. She targets them when they're old enough and brokers deals too. Some deals are directly between Origins and the church but many are between Little Angels and the church.'

'Understandable,' I said. 'The church wouldn't want to depend just on Origins.'

'God no,' laughed Henryk. 'Having at least two suppliers, maybe more, would bring a bit of competition into the market.'

'Explains why Peri would have been so attractive to Harper. She's got class in her background, you can tell by looking at her. She's not the usual RaRA-land leftovers.'

'Speaking of Peri,' said Henryk, 'guess what Mick found in RaRA-land? A Raptor. Quite a dead one. Washed onto the coast south of Pandanus.'

I sat down abruptly and held my head in my hands, waiting for my sudden dizziness to pass.

'Are you okay?' said Henryk.

'Sure,' I said, raising my head. A dead Raptor! What did that mean for Peri and Hugo? Was it more or less likely that they were still alive? Wild hope fluttered painfully in my chest like a trapped bird.

'I've told Mick to keep his eyes open for Peri and Hugo,' said Henryk, 'but at least we haven't found their bodies. That has to be a good sign.'

'Yes, I hope so.'

'Peri wasn't fostered by Origins though, was she?' Henryk said.

'No, but she did come to Little Angels through the church. That was mentioned in her Little Angels file. As you say, they'd want a few different suppliers, even if Origins is their biggest one. Henryk, in the stuff I've given you you'll find a project attached to Hermes called Nest Egg. A series of little programs with non-fliers across the regions.'

'I see,' said Henryk. 'Nice. Nest egg—capital, something for a rainy day.'

'Maybe,' I said. 'But nest egg has another meaning. A nest egg can be an egg, real or artificial, that's put into a hen's nest to get it to continue laying, after all its other eggs have been taken away.'

'Jesus. They're spreading their bets.'

'Think so. It'd only take a few people connected to Nest Egg, wouldn't have to be all or even most of them. Just enough to make sure they're not dependent on Origins.'

'So, why is this such a big deal, Zeke? Why so much money changing hands?'

'Couple of reasons,' I said. 'I've spoken to a specialist who said there are some fertility problems for fliers, especially women. Peri told me many flier women don't want to get pregnant, especially if they're going to have more than one. If they're not careful, months or even years go by and they risk never flying again. Imagine putting in all the work and money you need for the transition to Flight and jeopardising all that. Especially when there's such an easy and, let's face it, relatively cheap solution.'

'You told me about that doctor working with Diomedea on the surrogate pregnancies and doing the research; you think they're involved in the trafficking?'

'Haven't seen any evidence of it,' I said. 'Why would they risk it? I don't think they have any involvement with the Church of the Seraphim and they certainly wouldn't with Origins; way too dangerous. No, I think they just sit back and wait for fliers to come to them and they go ahead, keep doing their research. Whatever the fliers do to get themselves their babies is their own business, know what I mean? Can't see Diomedea gambling their reputation on anything to do with that side of it.'

'Why does the church risk it then?'

'That's different. Their whole thing is that this is the way forward for the elect of all humanity. No way forward without children though, without *enough* children, without as many children as fliers want. They want more fliers and more children of fliers; ensuring that not only removes the downside of the treatments and increases the size of their flock but as the broker of these deals, it gives them power. Lots of fliers wouldn't think much of the church—can't imagine someone like Chesshyre going along with their hare-brained theology, for example—but they're not going to stand up to them if they're using them to have kids.'

A temple bell. *Bong*, *bong*, *bong*. Muffled, like the moon now behind cloud, resonance sounding from deep under the sea. One cicada started up, competing.

'Makes me wonder, Zeke—you going ahead with the treatments for Tom or what?'

'Oh god, not you too, Henryk!' I stood up again, paced the deck. 'I can't go more than a few hours without arguing about this with Lily. Well, now I have real news. The treatments have begun, it's too late to turn back no matter what I find out and we've already had our first medical emergency.'

'So you've plunged in, just like that? What happened? Thomas okay?'

'Don't know what happened. He was unconscious, we couldn't rouse him. Seems alright now. His specialist says there's no problem and Lily won't even consider going slow for a while or waiting till he's older.'

'Yes,' said Henryk. 'She thinks it'll give him a better chance in life.'

'Assuming he survives the process. Anyway, how do you know?'

'Because it's what Vivienne thinks.'

'You two cannot be having this discussion. You don't have the money.'

'Vivienne thinks we should have one twin done, if we can't afford both. She says it's the least we can do.'

'You can't be serious.'

'You can talk. You've only got one to worry about. Anyway, I wasn't asking for your approval. I just wanted to know what you thought about it for Thomas.'

'I still don't know, even though the treatments have begun. He's so excited I'm worried he'll blow a fuse. Maybe that's what happened to him in the car. Still, how the hell did we get into this mess? Now we're forced to consider these things because, no matter what *we* want, the bar of what is desirable, or even of what's merely good enough, keeps being raised. Even if you hate the idea, you have to keep up.'

Henryk stared down into his beer. 'The Red Queen. Have to run faster and faster just to stay in the same place.' He was grinding his teeth. 'It's unbearable having to make so many choices. People think you're *eccentric*, some sort of religious nut, if you don't want to choose. I mean, I don't know how tall I want my son to be! Who the hell knows—what's the right height for happiness? A little taller than other men? But we can't *all* be a little taller, or a little smarter or better-looking! Didn't know how lucky we were when we didn't have these choices. Now kids can *really* blame their parents. For everything. Wings are a startling point of difference but even that currency will be devalued eventually.'

'Yes, by people like you and me, Henryk, sacrificing our retirement funds and peace of mind to push our children that extra bit ahead. Should be grateful for Origins, I suppose. Our only reservoir of pure, unaltered genes. Living relics. A bridge to our past.'

'God, how did we get this way so fast? Fliers have only been around for—how long, Zeke? Twenty-five years?'

'Thirty or so I guess. Prototypes've been around for longer. You know, the various defence projects, the ones run by the AIRPA?'

'Well, there's weirder things going on. Mick tells me there are more extreme modifications. If you can *think* it, you can *do* it. That's what Mick says.' Henryk swallowed some beer and slumped down into his chair. 'Glad I'm more than halfway through my three-score years and ten. Things are moving too fast for me.'

'Hate to break it to you, Henryk, but you're not halfway there. You'll live longer than seventy years.'

Henryk sighed. 'I've always been an optimist. *Stolid*, Vivienne says. *Mr Plod* when she's being bitchy. I like my life, mostly, but I can only endure it because I know it's going to end. They'd better not take that certainty away from us too.'

Henryk put down his drink. '*Since time began / the dead alone know peace. / Life is but melting snow*.'

Henryk and I finished our beers and stared out into the night. It grew so quiet, only the *breek breek* of a cricket, that we could hear the chanting from the temple.

'I've saved the best for last, Zeke. We did find out who Brilliant called. It helped that you pointed us in the right direction. It was Waterhouse.'

I turned away from the railing to look at Henryk. A long breath out. Of course. 'I've heard Waterhouse speak in the House. If he meant even half of what he said, killing a flier might not bother him. One less abomination.'

'We'll arrest Brilliant quite soon, as soon as we can get more on Waterhouse, now that we can scan some of their past communications, and as soon as I can get a warrant. We'll scare the crap out of Brilliant. Weak bastard, he'll sell Waterhouse down the river, long as we give him a deal.'

My thoughts drift with the chanting as I look out. A cloud hangs over the City, its silhouette darker than the night. It hovers, ominous. A feeling rises in me, a most unchristian feeling, a most unBuddhist feeling, despite the hypnotic chanting. It is primal.

Winged balancer of life, dark-faced goddess, daughter of Justice.

This goddess is ancient; she is first, before all others. I learned this poem to her as a child. She broods over the City and in the chill breath of her approach, the stasis of my black mood is whirled up, dispelled into a baleful exultation in her dark, cloudy wings. We are her instruments—me, Cam, Henryk. She's the only deity we three truly serve. She is coming. Punisher of hubris. Deliverer of justice. Avenger of crimes.

Nemesis.

18

FLYING HEAVENER

Peri woke suddenly very early in the morning after she saw the Wild. Bending over her, blotting out the stars, was a dark shape and, still half-asleep, she saw the clawed hands reaching for Hugo. Though the creature was ragged, gaunt and Wild, she could see that it was Peter, come to take Hugo back. Come to steal him again, as he'd stolen Hugo from her right from the beginning, from the moment he'd made her pregnant. She grabbed Hugo and scrambled to her feet, the scream dying in her throat as she heard a woman's voice and felt a light touch on her back.

'Don't blame you for being jumpy,' said Finch loudly, seeming not to care that the other Audax fliers still slept around them under the overhang. 'The others should be too but they have no idea what we're up against. Help me wake them,' she added over her shoulder as she stepped over the sleeping bodies. She bent down and grabbed Leto's arm, shaking her awake, half pulling the younger woman to her feet, against her complaints. 'Niko and Jay have been arguing about what to do. Now they're calling a meeting. Starts at civil dawn so shake a tailfeather.'

When all the members of Audax had gathered around the ashes of the fire, Niko and Jay appeared, still arguing in an urgent undertone. Jay was carrying his crossbow and as they moved into the centre of the circle Jay shook his head, as if signalling he would say no more, and sat down, cross-legged. Niko stood, ignoring them all for a moment, looking at something on his slick. Jay broke down his crossbow and cleaned it, checking each part meticulously.

The other fliers observed Jay and Niko expectantly, a few chewing energy strips. Peri gave Hugo a banana and watched Jay as he reassembled the crossbow, noting exactly how he snapped each piece together; behind him Shaheen sat on her perch, following each movement of Jay's as intently as Peri did. The threatening *snick, snick* of the crossbow mechanism clicking into place was the loudest sound in the quiet morning.

Niko flung up his head and stared across the circle at Peri.

'Would you tell all of us exactly what you saw last night, please?' he said.

Peri started. This was the first time Niko had spoken directly to her.

She tried to describe what she'd seen, unsure if she was remembering it all accurately or whether the darkness and her fear had made the creature more monstrous than it really was.

It did not reassure Peri when she saw that those who looked most grave at her description were the older, more experienced fliers. Only the younger ones did not look worried.

'*That* is a description of a Wild,' said Niko, staring at each flier in the circle in turn. 'Definitely Wild. We'll have to move.'

'*What?*' That was Raf. Young, strong Raf. *He* wouldn't want to leave without a fight.

'Wild pose a real danger,' said Niko. 'Unless you want to get serious about fighting over territory with them we have no choice but to leave Heavener. Besides, I'm not risking what we've just gained from the raid in a fight with Wild.'

'I'm not running,' said Raf. 'They can piss off.'

'Did I ask for your opinion?' barked Niko. Peri had never heard him raise his voice before. Raf blinked as if Niko had slapped him. A shirring of feathers whispered around the circle as the other fliers shifted. 'You don't tell Wild to piss off, Rafael. They don't *negotiate*. They *fight* or they *flee*.'

Jay looked up from where he'd been fitting his crossbow into its case and stood up to face Niko. 'That's the question. We don't abandon Heavener until we know whether it, or they, will fight or fly.'

Niko glared at Jay. 'We don't know how many of them there are but if they need territory then they need it more than we do. We've got other ways of getting food. They haven't. Wild fight hard. They could easily kill someone and we will have to kill to make them leave.'

Peri noticed she was not the only one to draw her breath in sharply at that. She put her arms around Hugo. When was Jay intending to let her and Hugo go?

But Jay was staring at Niko with a look that would have terrified Peri if it had been directed at her. She was seeing Jay the Raptor, the trained soldier, survivor, hunter, killer; a creature more altered, more removed from the normal human than any being she had ever met (except the Wild, she reminded herself) and he was in no mood to give up Heavener without a fight.

'Fuck it,' snarled Jay as he paced back and forth. Peri admired his glossy brown wings with their lightning slash gleaming in the level rays of the rising sun. 'Flying conditions here are optimal. We've got ridge-lines, thermals, long-distance flights in all directions without having to worry about being seen, and more glass-offs than anywhere else.'

There was a murmur of agreement at the mention of glass-off.

'I agree with Raf.' Niko bridled visibly at that. 'It's stupid to run away,' Jay continued, 'just because one Wild was scavenging food from us. Besides, we're armed. He's not.'

'Yes, I know we're *armed*,' replied Niko, clearly making an effort to rein in his anger. 'But weapons are useful only if you're prepared to *use* them. How many are *you* willing to kill, Jay? They may not appear human to you but they're still human in the eyes of the law. You aren't a murderer.' He paused, staring at Jay, who returned his stare.

'We should go to the winter roost,' Niko said.

'What's to stop them following us there?' said Jay.

'Nothing,' said Niko. 'But we have to—'

'What's the winter roost?' said Peri. Niko shot her a look of rage and she quailed. In her anxiety—would she be taken further away from the City by Audax, would she be forced to leave and fly to the City alone with who knows what stalking her out there?—the words had been out of her mouth before she could stop them.

'We have more than one camp,' said Raf. 'The winter roost is further north—'

'As I was *saying*,' said Niko, 'we should go to the winter roost, but we need to decide on our strategy first. We're surrounded by enemies. The Wild hate us and want what we have and City fliers fear us because they think *we're* turning Wild. We think we have the edge on everyone when it comes to flying but these Wild know a thing or two. And they're neither willing nor able to let us in on their secrets.'

'In the City they don't believe there are any Wild,' said Raf.

'Officially no. They *start* believing pretty damn quick when they lose a relative.' Niko turned on Raf. 'Is that what this is about? You don't actually think there's any such thing as Wild? Is that your problem?'

Raf's jaw worked but he said nothing.

Niko turned back to the others. 'The official silence is not surprising when no-one knows what turns them Wild, what the warning signs are or who's susceptible. No-one has any idea how many there are out here. Or how long they last.'

'It didn't look in great shape to me,' said Peri.

'Perhaps not,' retorted Niko. 'But that doesn't tell you much about how tough it is.'

Leto shuddered. 'How human *are* they?'

'No-one knows,' said Niko. 'I suspect they've lost language. I don't know what sort of communication they have with each other but I guess they have some.'

'If no-one knows anything,' said Raf, 'how come you're so sure? How do you know so much?'

Niko glanced at Finch, who shook her head slightly.

'Oh come on,' said Jay, still pacing. He'd worn a dark path into the sandy clearing. 'Fucking tell them, Pale Male.'

Niko sighed loudly and opened his wings a little, rattling his feathers. Angry, downturned lines appeared around his thin lips. '*Fine*. You want to know? I'll tell you. Most of you have only been with Audax for six months or so. There've been other cohorts of young fliers before you. You come, learn what you need to know, or what you *think* you need to know, and you go. Finch and I have been part of Audax since the beginning and have stayed out here, on and off, for four years. *Four years*. We've spent months at a time away from here, usually back in the City, and we've been lucky enough to have Jay with us for a year. But Finch and I weren't the only ones with Audax from the beginning. There was one other.'

Finch was staring at Niko, her eyes shiny; she was holding them open as wide as she could, as if trying to stop tears from spilling over the rim.

Raf sat very straight, arms folded across his chest.

'I don't need to say more,' said Niko. 'We lost Hoshi. We *lost* her and we couldn't get her back. We don't know why.'

After a moment Jay said, 'Many Wild are solitary, Niko. It's likely this one is. That could explain why he took the risk of scrounging from us.'

Niko looked down at one of his wings and inspected a feather closely. 'Could be,' he said. Then he raised his head again. 'You don't know what it's like,' he said, looking past the younger fliers. 'You can't begin to imagine. A friend, someone you know so well. And they're just . . . *gone*. Her face, those delicate features, but it's staring at you blankly, filthy matted hair all tangled around her head. She'd been so clean. Fastidious as a cat.'

Jay stopped pacing and looked over at Finch. 'We can agree then,' he said, 'on a plan. It is proposed that we do not abandon Heavener. Not yet. We have three objectives. First, we secure the perimeter of our camp far more tightly; I'll organise the roster of patrols, sweeps and sentries. Second, we need more intelligence. All our training flights from now on are also recon flights. It is critical we find out the status of this Wild; is he alone, was he just passing through and so on. If he's solitary and still hanging around, I will develop the strategy for getting rid of him.'

Jay glanced at Niko. 'I will not *intend* to kill him,' he said. 'But his personal safety is not my primary goal.'

'And our third objective?' said Niko, speaking even more quietly than Jay.

'We prepare to evacuate at a moment's notice. That plan will be triggered the instant we have evidence of more than one Wild.'

A murmur of approval rippled through the fliers and they all turned their faces to Niko. At last, he nodded.

'From now on,' said Jay, sweeping his arm around the circle, 'none of you does anything alone. You want to go for a solo flight, you take someone. You need to get up at night for a piss, you take someone. And we are all armed at all times.'

No-one felt much like flying that morning, Peri sensed. Raf and Niko set out on the first reconnaissance patrol but their faces were hard, with none of their usual enthusiasm. Before Niko left, Peri overheard him say to Jay, *It's all very well doubling the watch but that one got past our lookouts*. Peri didn't hear Jay's reply but both men looked grim.

Peri and Hugo, Phoebe, Wren and Leto stayed on the river flat. Finch sat on her own a little to one side, working on her slick. Jay disappeared on a mission of his own before Peri, desperate to speak with him, could catch his attention. It was clear Jay didn't think his order that they stay together applied to him. He obviously felt that he was more than a match for any Wild on his own.

The fliers talked a little or dozed, close together, conserving their energy. Hugo felt the group's anxiety, or more likely hers, Peri thought, and clung to her. 'Mama 'ug,' he said urgently, raising his arms to be picked up whenever she put him down. '*Mama 'ug*.' Good thing Avis wasn't around to hear him. She'd been obsessed with teaching Hugo to call *her* that. The rare times Avis had spent with him she'd kept up a constant stream of *Look, here's mama, see, mama's bringing you your juice, you love your mama, don't you?* But not only had Hugo not called her that, he'd never called her anything. Now here they were, his first words aside from 'awk!' for bird and 'ooo' for moon, his first sentence, two words he'd heard often but never put together in just that way. His own words. *Mama 'ug.*

Peri held Hugo close till he dozed off.

An hour passed before Peri and the others heard the whirr of wings above them. They froze.

'Relax,' said Finch. 'It's Jay and Griffon.' She turned her attention back to her slick.

They splashed down and then Jay stood for a few moments up to his waist in the pool of clear brown river sliding over leaves and stones, dashing water over his hair, his face, his arms and wings, the drops rolling off his feathers. The river smelled of tea and mud and medicinal leaves, fresh and sharp.

'See anything?' called out Phoebe. Griffon shook his head as he waded towards the group.

Peri walked down to the water's edge, balancing Hugo on his feet. He wanted to walk and she took his hands; they trod the wet sand together. Each step of Hugo's was so tender and deliberate, she felt her heart move each time he planted a tiny foot, five-petalled flower, onto the ground. Peri's cheeks burned; she was conscious of Jay's eyes on her as she circled in the sand with Hugo.

Jay was on his own and she must not miss this opportunity to speak with him. She hesitated, not daring to ask what she most needed to know. The other fliers were still too close, though she doubted they could hear her as long as she kept her voice low.

'You don't seem to have any difficulties with money or supplies,' Peri began, as she watched Jay help himself to food from the larder.

Jay looked back at her, his handsome face austere. 'No,' he said. 'All our people have plenty of money. From well-off families, as you'd expect. Except for me. And you.'

'Aren't their families worried about them?' She glanced sidelong to where Griffon had joined the others further along the river flat.

'Sure, but what can they do? Essence of golden youth, isn't it, to be careless? To have no idea how much you've cost others?'

Oh, wouldn't it be wonderful to have someone, somewhere, who worried about me? Someone who was looking for me—not to kill me, but to make sure I was safe. Someone who'd be thrilled if I showed up on their doorstep. Someone who loved me. What would that be like? It's so easy to hate Leto and Phoebe and Griffon and Rafael, they're all so shining, carefree, loved. They can risk it all. They don't value that love because they've never questioned it, never worried about losing it. They can treat their families as badly as they like, then show up at any time, be welcomed back with love. I wanted to give Hugo that certainty, not to expose him, alone, to the indifference I've known my whole life.

Jay was looking at Peri as if he knew her thoughts. 'We have a lot in common, don't we?' he said in his soft, clipped way, the precision of his speech reminding her a little of the way Havoc talked. Peri looked at him. 'It's something the others will never understand,' he said, 'but we do. What it's like to sacrifice the very stuff of our own lives for wings.'

Peri ducked her head, not wanting Jay to see the tears in her eyes. She led Hugo to a tree and they explored the trunk together, patting the curling bark, stroking the soft leaves. She ran her hands over the tanned skin of Hugo's arms and legs, pausing when she came across a rash of red welts on his leg. Sandflies? A poisonous plant? She sat Hugo down on the sand in front of her and checked him thoroughly, keeping an eye on Jay.

Hugo looked a little taller and leaner since she had taken him away with her, less of a baby, more a child. Peri ran her hands through his hair, looking for ticks. Nothing. She'd picked a leech off him earlier and he scratched at that spot, blood still streaking his leg. She checked his hands and feet. The satiny skin had small scratches, bruises. Hugo crowed with delight as she tickled under his chin gently. He reached out, trying to tickle her chin in return.

Jay waded out of the water, shook himself and unfurled his great wings in a billowing rush of air. They glinted bronze in the strengthening sun and Peri caught her breath. No statue, no towering golden icon, could capture his moving, breathing magnificence. The Raptor was massive, dazzling, the closest she would ever be to a living god.

'I have to talk to you,' said Peri.

Jay turned to her, still shaking water off his wings in the warm light. 'I know. If you want to speak to me right now, you'll have to come with me on a recon flight. I've only searched the south-east sector so far this morning and I need to cover all the other sectors today. Leave Hugo with Finch.'

Jay and Peri flew at the same height a few metres apart. Jay had mentally divided the northern sector they were now searching into a grid and they covered each grid square quickly and methodically. The sky was quiet, clouds sketched monochrome against blue like blots of water-thinned ink.

Jay was carrying his crossbow, drawn and loaded, but Peri's was still clipped into its soft case next to the quiver belted to her waist. Before they'd left Heavener, Jay had taken her aside, well out of Hugo's sight, and given Peri her own crossbow. 'This is self-cocking with a sixty-kilo draw,' he'd said. 'It's good for women and smaller men. You said before that you can use one of these but I want to see for myself. So, we'll do some target practice before we go up.'

'Yours is bigger,' Peri had said, marvelling over the lightness of the lethal little weapon in her hands as she stood facing the targets Jay had set up among the trees.

'Of course it's fucking bigger,' Jay had snapped. 'This is a military rifle crossbow with a hundred-and-fifty-kilo draw, accurate over long distances. It's an offensive semi-automatic weapon with fibre-optic sights and silencer. Yours will get you out of trouble; it's for smaller game, target practice and self-defence. It will wound, even kill, but mine is a serious bastard; it's for hunting *big* game.'

'Like Wild?' said Peri. 'Other Raptors?'

Jay didn't answer. He took Peri's arm and guided her into the correct position.

'Fire,' he said.

Now Peri looked down, scanning the grey-green valleys below them. 'I have to go, Jay,' she said. 'You have to let me go. You can't guarantee my safety or Hugo's here.'

'True. The difficulty is that I can't guarantee your safety if you leave right now either.'

'I don't think I should go with you to the winter roost if you do have to leave.'

'No,' said Jay, who was now spiralling down in a long shallow gyre. 'Definitely not. You have to face your future. Now, follow me. We've done a sector-wide sweep and it all looks good from on high but now we drop down and really hunt. We're looking for any sign of a large animal. Flattened grass, broken branches, discarded kills, big, ragged nests, anything. Wild are messy. They don't keep eyries or home ranges with any kind of discipline.'

Not like us. There's never a scrap of litter around camp. Suddenly it was clear why Jay had forbidden soap except in basins which were tipped out on the ground well away from the river. No telltale foam to dirty the water falling from Heavener's escarpment. From the air Heavener looked untouched. Truly wild.

Jay skimmed fast over the trees and Peri followed, working hard to match Jay's speed.

'*Have* you worked out what you're going to do?' he asked.

Peri sped up, unsure whether the surge of power in her veins and muscles was driven by excitement or fear. Jay was right. She couldn't put off her future any longer.

'I told you, I'm going to kill Peter.'

Jay turned his head to look at her.

He doesn't believe me. Understandable. Do I believe myself or am I just saying this to get him to help me?

'Come on, Peri. I get why you'd want to, after what he's done, but—'

'Jay, you don't understand. It's not about what I *feel*. It's not about revenge. Well, mostly not about revenge. It's practical. You're a soldier. Tell me, what do you do with an enemy?'

'You kill him. You don't frighten him. You don't hurt him. You kill him. First rule of war.'

'Yes. That's it, isn't it?'

'Peter is not just your enemy,' said Jay. 'He's the father of your child. And the City is not a war zone.'

'It's not? Jay, Peter sent a Raptor after me, he tried to dispose of me; *he's* the one who raised the stakes so high and I will not be safe anywhere unless I do one of two things: take action so extreme that Peter will never threaten me again or hand Hugo over, just give him up, forever, and that I cannot do. So help me. How do I deal with Peter so Hugo and I can be safe?'

Jay thought. 'I see why you're frightened,' he said. 'I saw what Peter sent after you. I *know* what Raptors can do. I saved you, dressed your injuries, and I could just about kill Peter myself for what he's done. My concern is not for him; it's for you. You don't comprehend the forces you plan to unleash. I know about violence, I'm the only one here who does; it can be effective, though people love to tell you it's not because that's what they *want* to believe. But it's tricky. Often its results are not what you planned. The important thing is not to be caught. You're no use to Hugo if you're in jail.'

'So, you'll help me?'

'I'll think about it, Peri.'

A ridge to the north of Heavener loomed before them. Jay slowed, dropping below the ridgeline so that they would not be blown over the top. The ridgelift welled beneath them as they flew along the wall of creamy red-gold sandstone striated with dark lines of trees. Jay peered at the rock face, looking for ledges and caves.

After the recon flight Jay brought Peri down into a grassy clearing she'd never seen before. 'Oh,' she said as he laid her down. He took her quickly. 'Jay,' she breathed. 'Oh, oh.' He turned her over and made her spread her wings so he could enter her that way. She held onto the grass underneath her; he gripped her shoulder and bent her back, holding her still as he pushed into her. When he finished he pulled her to her feet. Still raw and quivering, she thought of Jay's fierce arguments with Niko that morning, of the fear coursing through all of them and of how heavy the burden of their security must feel to him now. No wonder he was so much rougher, his mood so much darker, than last night.

Jay pulled Peri close and kissed her hair. He circled her wrist with his thumb and forefinger and lifted her arm. Peri blinked. Jay was unclipping the grey bracelet.

'You're free,' he said.

Oh. Suddenly she was ferociously jealous of Shaheen, linked to Jay every moment by her bells.

A few days after Peri had asked Jay to help her, he lay with her longer than usual after they were together. He rolled to the side a little, sparing her his weight, but kept her pinned beneath him as he looked down at her, studying her face.

'I've thought about what you asked me,' Jay said. 'And I've given you time to think. You still determined to go ahead?'

Peri nodded.

Maybe I've convinced him I would really do this. Do I know myself how far I'm willing to go?

Jay's mouth folded into a straight line.

'Do you have a better strategy?'

'No. Just the obvious. Legal advice, that route.'

'You can't guarantee that will work.'

Jay stared at her. 'Of course not. And killing, you think *that* comes with a guaranteed outcome?'

'You going to help me or not, Jay?'

'I've spoken to Niko about this and there is a way, I think, to be almost sure, as sure as anything can be, that you'd get away with it. SkyNation is coming up in just over a week. You could plan to leave here in time to reach the City for that. By then I should know how things stand here and I could escort you as far as the coast, make sure you and Hugo are safe.'

'What's SkyNation got to do with it?'

'It's the time and the place. The perfect setting, the perfect way for you to escape the consequences of your actions. Things happen at Sky-Nation: chaos, accidents, stupid mishaps or fights, and some incidents that are *not* accidents. There's always risk with this kind of event. People disappear.'

'So you're saying Peter should have an accident at SkyNation?'

'No-one will even know you were there. Everyone's dressed up. No way to link you with what happened. Your weapon will be untraceable. Worst comes to worst, Niko can organise an alibi.'

'How on earth would I get in?'

'That's nothing. Niko can get you in easily.'

Peri was silent. 'Good,' she said after a while. 'Thank you. It's a good plan.'

'I advise you against this,' said Jay. 'The only reason I'm helping you is because you're rash enough to do it without my help and I'd rather make sure you stay safe. Still, if there's one thing a soldier understands it is that sometimes there is no other way.'

It was a relief to know exactly when she was leaving Audax, though it was frightening too. Still, knowing that she had a day marked when she must leave, and that Jay would protect her and Hugo for at least part of her flight, was reassuring.

Often Peri thought of her final flight with Jay. Would he really leave her? She imagined a hundred scenarios in which he decided not to abandon her, in which he came with her to the City. Anything might be possible, nothing would be too difficult, if only Jay would stay with her.

The days on and above Heavener were serene, hushed in the sun of late summer. It was hard to stay vigilant during the still, sun-struck days. Hard in the sunlight to believe in the threat of a lone, dark Wild. Every flight was still a patrol and no Audax member, except for Jay, was ever alone. But they saw nothing. Even Jay, even *Niko*, relaxed a little.

And three times the heat from the valleys below Heavener had risen up all at once into glass-off, lifting them into golden evenings of perfect bliss. Glass-off was the only time Jay permitted Peri to fly with Hugo and she treasured each second floating silently with him on the warm clear sea of air.

Peri was not sure she agreed with Raf that glass-off was better than sex, though the choice was exquisitely hard. Fortunately, she did not have to choose, though with Jay so dedicated to ensuring their security, she had precious few minutes alone with him. He would pull her away into private spaces he'd found away from the others—he knew the bush around them so well—but Peri's joy at being in his arms was tinged by fear; what if they were surprised by a Wild while they were alone and so vulnerable? Jay must have felt pressed by the same fear, for there was none of the leisurely exploration of their first time together; now their sex was urgent and quiet, with Jay's hand fastened over her mouth. Whether he was more concerned that they would be heard by a Wild or by other members of Audax, she didn't know, but it was agonising, exquisite not to be able to make a sound; all her sensations and emotions swelled in her like the pressure of expanding air on a bubble until she could almost burst.

During the days, Peri practised her flying with the group. The appearance of the Wild had drawn them all together and now she felt truly part of Audax. The feeling of extending her body grew exponentially in the group, as if they were one body, immensely larger and more powerful, extending round them in three dimensions.

Peri revelled in the companionship of the other fliers. The sense of belonging accelerated her abilities more than anything else. Except for Havoc, whose expertise she'd paid for, no other fliers had ever flown with her before Audax except, a few times, Luisa.

With the strength of the group buoying her up, Peri began to feel the abilities that Finch had spoken of: her sense of their height from the ground, airspeed, the subtleties of air pressure, changing weather. Even the horizon. She could not have explained, would not have been able to say how high she was or exactly what the air pressure was, but she could feel it and adjust her flying.

Peri flew with Jay and Shaheen as often as possible, though it was hard to study the falcon, she was so swift, her turns and dives so sharp, her wings so long and slender compared to Peri's.

She listened for the watery clink of Shaheen's bells every waking moment, the bells that by their shifting rhythms and volume told her what the falcon was doing: preening, bathing, waiting-on, landing, plucking and eating another bird; most often, by their silence, the activity predators are best at—nothing at all. Many years later Peri would feel the chime of those bells was still imprinted on her being as one of the most intense pleasures of that time, a live thread tying her to the huntress.

'You need to learn pigeon tactics,' said Jay one day. He'd taken Peri, Leto, Raf and Phoebe up and worked them hard, putting them into fast dives and turns, pushing them to the edge of their abilities. Shaheen flew with them, diving so fast she winked in and out of their field of vision, an arrow of night released under the sun.

'Peregrines can stoop on a pigeon at over ninety metres per second. A pigeon can never outfly a peregrine. But often they do escape. Today I'll teach you how.'

High in the cloudless azure above Heavener they flew, the ridge lying so far below them it was just a wrinkle of dark green fringed with tawny stone scored here and there by silver glints of river. That afternoon, the thrill and rush of it, was, Peri often thought later, along with realising she was Hugo's mother, the bright high point of her entire life. Whatever happened to her in future, it could never be surpassed.

She saw, they all saw, Jay as he truly was, in his full glory as a Raptor. He stooped on them out of the sun, like a falcon, and they learned to dip one wing and veer to either side, plunging away from his dive, then fold their wings into a W and drop like stones. Then they soared up and around behind him, trying to gain height. Again he'd arrow above them and again he'd dive and they'd roll and drop, until they perfected it.

'You're rolling away just like a fighter jet peeling off from a formation,' said Jay, 'and you're making your slower speed work for you. If I'm diving faster on you and you use the pigeon roll and drop, then at my greater speed I'll overshoot and you can come around behind me and start gaining height.'

'That pigeon's dead,' Jay would laugh as he swiped them in passing, their dives not sharp or steep enough. 'That pigeon made it. Till the next hunt,' was the highest praise they earned from him. He didn't stop driving them until they had all escaped him several times.

Yes, the days above Heavener were glorious. But the nights were another matter.

Every night, as the gloom solidified between the trees and, after the expansiveness of glass-off or the day's flying, the space collapsed in on them, the fliers were too keyed up to sleep. The threat of the Wild crept closer and they drew in on themselves and each other.

Niko mostly talked politics, describing what he thought had to be done in the City. 'I'll start publishing the Diomedea material soon so people will understand what is really going on. We have to organise our knowledge, refine it, share it. If we don't change what's going on *there*, in the City, then you won't be able to just continue on your chosen path out here. What future will there be in Flight at all?'

Jay was shaking his head. 'You talk about knowledge but they have to feel it for themselves in their bodies. No point talking about it.'

'That's nice for you,' said Niko, looking at the rest of the group, 'but it won't change anything. What exactly is it you think you're becoming?'

'That's the point,' said Jay. '*I don't know yet.* No-one does.'

'It's obvious,' said Leto, 'that our new abilities have nothing to do with language. They must be located in different areas of the brain.'

'That would make sense,' said Niko, 'as they're mostly spatial abilities. We're learning how to deal with three-dimensional space and also with different senses of time and speed. Language gets in the way of that.'

'That's what I've been trying to say,' said Finch. 'Looking at readouts on a watch pulls you out of the state where you can do it yourself. It's like trying to ride a bicycle by following a set of printed instructions: it's impossible. Your body has to learn it and take over.'

'I guess it'll be easier for kids,' said Peri. 'They'll learn it in the same way as learning to walk.'

'Up to a point,' said Niko. 'The basics, yes. But real Flight, what we're doing, is not equivalent to learning to walk; it's more like elite athlete training. What *I* wonder, though, is whether you can just add all these abilities on without paying a price.'

'What do you mean?' said Jay.

'Well, maybe you sacrifice processing power elsewhere.'

'You think we're turning *Wild*?' said Leto.

The discussion petered out and they were quiet for the rest of the evening. Peri lay and looked up at the stars, the words Finch had said days ago—it felt like months ago—running through her mind: *Wings are heavy unless you give something up.*

Every night as Peri lay with Hugo nestled into one wing and tried to banish her fears for long enough to fall asleep, a strange sensation invaded her body; as if she were falling from a long, long way up, just as she had plunged from the height of the storm. The feeling was beyond her control. It was as if she was reliving all the Flight of the day—up, down, around—going over the exact configuration of her flying, reliving it body and mind, the process no more conscious or willed than her blood pressure, the Flight pattern twining itself into the very fibres of her muscles. There it was, whenever she needed it, part of her. The learning was so intense, the repatterning of her mind so deep, it continued even while she slept.

Peri's anxiety over Hugo was a constant white noise in her mind, like the rushing of the water over Heavener's cliff edge. She'd decided what she was going to do. She had rights but rights were no use if she weren't alive to claim them.

Two days before Peri had to leave Heavener, Niko, the Pale Male himself, dropped a bombshell on her. He found her playing in the river with Hugo and beckoned her out onto the sand. Peri felt dizzy with apprehension as she sat down with Hugo, setting him up next to her with a mound of sand and an array of pebbles to play with. What could Niko want? He'd never before sought her out.

'You still planning on leaving us soon?' Niko began.

Peri nodded.

'That is for the best. You must be frightened. You're the only one of us who's actually seen the Wild.'

'Scariest thing I've ever seen.'

Niko picked up a leaf and began shredding it. 'Strange to be so frightened by the existence of a few Wild,' he said. 'But they are terrifying. You wonder, *how does it happen?* Well, I wonder that. All the time. Why do you think I'm so interested in finding out more about Flight research, especially the things they've been hiding from us?'

Niko must be thinking of his friend. *Hoshi*, that was her name, wasn't it?

'What do they become? We don't know which props we're knocking away from our own humanness. We *should* be afraid. We have no idea what we're doing.'

'You went ahead with the treatments,' said Peri.

'I didn't know what I was getting into,' Niko replied. 'I am not sure I'd do it all again, to be honest.'

'But you're here,' said Peri. 'Out of all of us, you're the strategist, the politician.'

'Ha. Well, I'm the one that knows something about it. The rest don't have a clue. They will though. They'll realise soon enough the world has no place for them the way they want to be. They believe they are becoming something other; not ordinary humans but not Wild either.'

'Jay said you couldn't forget what you were. What were you?'

Niko laughed. '*Powerful*. That's what I was.'

'Oh,' said Peri.

'And,' said Niko, 'the reason I'm here is this: now that I'm a flier, I'm going to become a *real* flier. I will not just sit around, like so many in the City do, with wings as my latest executive toy. I'm not going down that road. And I am going to change the way some things are done. Flight is a powerful dream but sometimes dreams should stay dreams. Now it's up to people like me, to the fliers we train out here, to make the reality worth it.'

Niko picked up a slender twig bearing a cluster of leaves and white waxy berries and he handed this to Hugo, whose eyes lit up, his mouth forming a perfect O of astonishment. Peri wanted to laugh and yet tears sprang to her eyes. Hugo was still so easy to amaze. He was surrounded by branches and leaves here on Heavener and yet he reacted to Niko's offered twig as if he'd been given a precious gift. Well, maybe he had.

'What I want,' said Niko, 'is to take the knowledge we're generating here, combine it with proper research and refine it, standardise it, teach it, make Flight Gyms effective. Otherwise we'll lose what we're learning here. There are unscrupulous operators throughout the system—doctors who are not fliers, instructors who've never flown outside the City. Most importantly, if we want to be real fliers, we will be fliers *in the world*. We can't ignore the degradation of the wilderness, the air, the seas. There is no Flight without becoming part of those things. The pressure on our energy reserves, like our dwindling fuels, and on our energy harvesting—that is, renewable energy—is extreme. As a result, what we can do in ourselves, such as flying, is going to grow more and more important. Flight began as an extreme sport and status symbol for the very rich but it's not going to stay that way. It's too useful.'

'You've a lot of work to do.'

'I'm not doing it alone,' said Niko. 'There are a few of us scattered around. These documents we've liberated may help. That's why I've come to speak to you. There are things I've found out about the history of Flight that directly affect you.'

Niko scrolled a document up on the slick, then passed it over to Peri. 'Have a look at that. I only found it in among other material last night.'

Peri read for a moment, shaking her head. Then she froze and read the same few paragraphs over and over. She looked up at Niko, stunned. The sun was behind them and Niko's spiky silver hair was lit up into a corona around his head.

'I see your association with Diomedea goes back some time,' said Niko. 'Your family name is Almond, isn't it?'

Peri nodded.

'Read that passage again. It describes Liam Drake Almond as one of Diomedea's early prototypes, one of their star subjects on the Chenomorphae Project.'

Peri stared at the document but it dissolved into a meaningless swarm of marks. Her eyes refused to focus. She put the slick down. 'Liam Drake Almond was my father?'

'From what I've read here, yes.'

'What happened to him? What is the Chenomorphae Project?'

'You know about AIRPA?'

'No.'

'AIRPA is the defence agency tasked with blue-sky research, the most out-there projects. They fund the weird, cutting-edge stuff, like one of my all-time personal favourites, weaponising bees. Talk about stinger missiles. Chenomorphae was fairly tame, for them. Through AIRPA, the Department of Defence funded Diomedea to undertake the research. Put simply, the subjects enrolled in Chenomorphae were Raptors. The first ones. Project aims were to investigate extreme applications of the first Raptor treatments to enable military fliers to operate in environments and at heights thought impossible for fliers. This included development of true bird navigational abilities. Any and all data harvested during the project were considered valuable.'

'What happened to my father?'

'It was an extremely experimental project that exposed its participants to unprecedented risks.'

I knew only the other Raptors had the slightest idea what I was going through and even then only the ones in my intake. They change the techniques and treatments, refine them, all the time.

'What *happened*, Niko?'

'A number of subjects died early. You know Raptor treatments shorten life. But Almond is not recorded as an early death. He disappeared.'

I'll pay the price.

'Disappeared.'

'After that is recorded in the project notes there is no further mention of him. Raptor treatments include extremely high doses of Zefiryn over the long term. Both Raptor treatments and overuse of Zefiryn are associated with disappearances.'

'Oh god. You mean they turn Wild.'

'Possibly. We just don't know.'

That filthy, stinking creature. Hungry. *Alone*. It could be her father. He could be like that.

'Peri, did you ever try to track down your parents when you came to the City?'

Peri put her head in her hands. Her shoulders trembled. 'I thought about it.'

'But you put it off. Of course you did. Why would you feel bad about that? You were just starting your life.' Niko glanced at Hugo, who was mouthing the branch Niko had given him. 'You were very busy. And you had sound reasons to fear you weren't going to find out anything good. No, what I meant is that you might have found out things about Liam Almond's earlier life, but once he entered the Chenomorphae Project, it was all classified. You wouldn't have discovered a thing about what happened to him.'

Still with her head in her hands, Peri said, 'My mother? Is there anything about her?'

Niko put his hand on her shoulder. 'No mention.'

Closed in by a whirl of feathers, suffocating, bursting above her, a grey storm. Then they flew away. Left her. No proof. Her nightmare didn't mean her mother had been a flier too. Did it matter? Her father had disappeared and her mother had left her. Somewhere unsafe. *Don't move. You'll fall.*

'The real reason I'm telling you this is that Diomedea has been tracking effects of the project on children of participants in Chenomorphae.'

Peri brought her head up. 'Why? Why did they think there would be effects? Did they do germline engineering?'

'Not that I'm aware of. Still, you can see it was the responsible thing for Diomedea to do. Even without germline engineering, you could be affected by the treatments: drug exposure, epigenetic effects and so on.'

'So you think I might be affected? By my father's Raptor treatments?'

I won't live as long as you.

'I think you already have been. Your progress in the short time you've been with Audax is remarkable. Have you noticed? You've learned more in a few days than most Audax fliers grasp in months. Perhaps you're aware that Phoebe and Leto and the others don't like you much. Not because they don't trust you. It's because the only Audax flier better than you is Jay.'

Jay. 'Was Jay part of Chenomorphae?'

'No, but all the Raptor programs are descendants of it, one way or another. Peri, Jay knows he doesn't have all the time in the world. I wish I could reassure you that that won't be a problem for you. I think your chances are much better than Jay's; after all, you were just exposed through your father, you didn't actually undergo Raptor treatments yourself. But the fact is, we don't really know and that's the reason I pushed Audax into doing this raid; if Diomedea knows more about the effects of the treatments and what turns fliers Wild, they must be made to share it.'

Niko put the slick away. 'Are you okay?' he said, watching Peri as she sat silent, biting her lip.

'It's hard to take in, Niko.'

'Think of it this way,' said Niko, getting to his feet, brushing the sand from him. 'It's possible that with you they've found the sweet spot. I mean, think of that. You could be the new breed of flier, enhanced by the after-effects of Raptor treatments combined with regular treatments. They might really be onto something with you.'

After Niko left, Peri paced, Hugo in her arms.

I need to think. I need to be alone, even though, of all the fliers here, I'm the one never allowed an instant to myself, because of Hugo and because Jay has forbidden it. Still, I must risk it.

She found Phoebe, who was now nursing a new injury after their afternoon of learning pigeon tactics and was willing to play with Hugo.

Peri kissed Hugo, then almost ran down the path towards the cliff. She stopped on the river bank, looked over to the scooped hollow of water at the fall's edge, its lip pouring foam into the valley. Her mind was spinning with what Niko had said. She thought about Mama'lena and the trail that led from Mama'lena to the Church of the Seraphim, to Little Angels, to Peter and Avis. She had put one foot in front of the other the whole time, thinking she was driving herself forward, making her hard choices. Perhaps it had not been that simple. Had she always been a flier-in-waiting, a Raptor-in-embryo?

Peri took off her skims and sat naked in the pool, the water surging over her on its way into the sky. She was going back to the City; maybe once she knew what would happen to her and Hugo, she could find out more about her past. Whatever had happened to her mother and father not only affected her future, as Niko had suggested, but also Hugo's.

Peri heard the crackle of leaves and looked to the bank. Jay appeared and beckoned her out of the water. Naked, she stood and walked over to him. Jay took her into his arms. Was this the last time she would be alone with him? She loved to stroke his smooth skin, slide her hand over the silky russet feathers.

'Do you trust me?' Jay whispered into her ear.

Oh. *That* question. Peri felt her stomach contract and a trickle of arousal flow like molten gold between her thighs and upwards, along the central line of her belly, warming her. How could he know to ask her that, of all things, the words that most stirred both terror and desire in her?

Yes. I trust you.

Jay took Peri's hand and led her down to the cliff edge. He could not possibly know the power of the question he had asked. It had been the central question between her and Peter. It was twisted into her memory and her longings, the thrilling along her nerves to her heart, her brain, her muscles, her thighs, her womb. In her most intense memory, the most severe test of her courage, Peter had taken her to the end of a long spar jutting from a communications tower. The spar was slender and he'd held her tight. She'd been three months pregnant with Hugo; nothing showed yet but she tired easily. The flow of hormones in her body made her even more submissive to Peter, if that were possible. At the end of the spar there were a few wires fanned out taut, just enough for Peter to lay her down. The wind sang around them and through the wires. Each time Peter took her he had made it more extreme, more dangerous. As she tensed around him, holding him with her whole body, he slid her a little over the edge. She gasped. He took her through their own catechism, the one he liked to make her repeat whenever they were together.

Do you love me? he demanded.

Yes, she said.

Do you trust me?

Yes, she said.

Would you give me your life?

Yes, oh yes, she said. It was so fatally easy to worship him, abandon herself to him; he wasn't just a man, but another order of life: higher, stronger, resplendent. *Whatever you ask*, she said, *I will do*.

Let yourself fall, he commanded. She shuddered and wept in his arms as he kissed her hair, her mouth, but he was insistent, he would not relent. She said she would die for him; now she must prove it. Sick with terror, she launched herself into the air; she would never know how she made herself do it. The fall was beautiful and terrible beyond reason, the stark lines of the communication tower rushing past her into the sky, the wind snatching her breath away, her heart thundering so it must come right out of her chest, she would die before hitting the ground.

Then she heard a great rush of air through flight feathers and she was caught in that grip she knew so well and he brought her to earth and took her on solid ground. Though she walked on air for three days afterwards, so happy to be alive, she worried about what he would do next. How much further could he go? Perhaps he thought the same way for he didn't approach her until a few months after Hugo's birth, when the cycle began once more, each place more dangerous than the last, and she had been more reluctant, though still in thrall to him.

Once Peri had her wings Peter never touched her again. She had grieved for that but the torrent of feeling had turned, carving a new channel. It wasn't right to risk her life now that she had Hugo to look after. But Peter still believed her life was his, to do with as he wished.

Peri could not allow that any longer. She followed Jay, trusting herself to him. He took her to the edge of the cliff and down its face to where they now stood, he facing her on a narrow ledge, his back to the drop. Peri's back was to the cliff and he shielded her with his outstretched wings, taking her in his arms. Why was she doing this? She caught her breath. Because now she had her wings. That was what was different. Jay was exploring the edge of danger with her, they were both equal to the challenge. She was trusting herself now, not only Jay. She pushed herself back against the cliff. There was just enough room for her feet on the ledge; a centimetre less and she would slide down into the chasm. Jay balanced himself, using his hands against the rock and raising his wings. She wrapped one leg around him so that he could lift her and enter her. He slipped away a fraction, balanced himself, then entered her again. Peri laughed. Having sex in this way was a bit like hard work but she was willing to see where it led. Jay gasped. 'Careful when you laugh,' he said, grinning. 'You've got strong muscles there.'

They were silent, Peri focusing her attention on the pleasure swelling in her like a rising gale, each flurry stronger than the one before. She tightened her grip on Jay, looking past his shoulder into the splendour of the afternoon sky. Never before had she felt the intensity of her wings quivering, beating against another's like this, ruffling her feathers against Jay's, the massive surface of the wings increasing the area of her body shivering with excitement.

Her muscles trembling with effort and delight, Peri withdrew her gaze from the sky to look into Jay's dark eyes.

'Hang onto me,' he whispered.

She nodded.

He pushed his head down onto her shoulder and put his arms around her. He spread his wings as wide as they would stretch and launched them both into the sky.

They plunged towards the valley floor.

The swoop of their falling, coupled together, flooded Peri with ecstasy; for a few seconds it was as if the smooth bliss of glass-off had fused with the rush of outflying a storm or a predator, as she'd fled Jay that afternoon, pigeon to his falcon.

After a few seconds Jay let her go and she soared back to the cliff. She beat her wings, landing at the side of the pool where Jay had found her.

'Well,' she said when Jay joined her and they had caught their breath. 'Have you done that before? I haven't.'

Jay shook his head. 'No,' he said, putting his arm around Peri and stroking her hair. 'You are my first, my only one,' he said warmly, seeming to satirise the romantic words and yet mean them at the same time. 'It was the subject of much wishful thinking and boasting among all the Raptors but I don't think a single one of them actually did it.'

Peri smiled. 'You did say you were here to push Flight to the extremes.' She slid into the pool and floated on her belly, her chin on the lip of rock, her wings held just clear of the water. Her whole body hummed with energy, as if her flesh was made of lightning. 'I want to ask you something.'

'You can ask,' said Jay. 'I don't promise I'll answer.'

'How did you track me in the storm?'

'Oh, that. You'd already been fitted with a tracking device. Clearly you didn't know about that. So I was able to track you myself with the equipment I had.'

'I thought Audax members didn't fly with equipment.'

'We *learn* to fly without equipment. Doesn't mean we don't use it when we need it. And we make damn sure no-one can track us here so we are well aware of any devices other fliers are carrying.'

Peri ducked her head under the foaming water, then surfaced. 'I had no idea.'

'Of course not,' said Jay. 'They're designed so you don't. But you can't be surprised.'

Peri sighed. 'That detective must have done it.'

Jay knelt at the edge of the pool and kissed her. 'Come back to the camp,' he said. 'You shouldn't stay out here on your own.'

'I'll follow you in a minute.'

Jay disappeared into the trees.

Peri was so overwhelmed by all that was happening to her, the rush of feeling about Hugo, Jay, herself, her possible future and past as revealed by Niko, that she was glad to be alone for a moment. The late afternoon was clear and warm, hushed and safe. Nothing was going to ambush her. She stood, balancing herself on the edge of the pool, then allowed herself to fall down, down the cliff face, then powered herself up, rising next to the vertical, falling river, spray surging over her, wash of waterair, higher, body singing with energy, feels so good nothing between her and air, why did they ever wear anything?

Peri had never felt so light, so light she had to stop herself from soaring too high in the first few minutes of her flight. She made herself slow down and then thought, *Why?*

For the first time Peri felt in her bones the knowledge that she had the technical ability to do what she wanted in the air, without thinking about it, without fearing she would miscalculate. She just had to think, I want to fly there, or tumble over myself here or circle swoop sweep up again higher. Grace and freedom, exhilaration of Flight. Hers. Part of her body, as easy and sensuous as swimming. Wings powerful and *hers*. Not stuck on like angel wings in a play. She was new, become something different. Not Peri-with-wings. Now Peri-who-flies. Peri the flier. She rose higher, excitement driving her, she had to move to express her joy.

To truly fly have to let thoughts slide away, not narrate each second into words but fly each moment. Flight an eternal Now, have to be present to each second in the sky.

It's hard. This is what's so hard.

Much harder than the rhythm, breath, angle, muscles working.

Once word-thoughts slide away sky and light slip in, wrap around, clouds and forest and stones coming clearer, three-dimensional, precise curve of leaves, angles of stones, dead branch fallen just there, thrown net of dark twigs, fuzzy grey-white flowers near cliff edge. Dark hollows. Burrow. Most of all, *movement*. Scurry of leaves in wind, sweep of tree, light sliding along branches and water. Birds rocketing just above canopy, parrot swinging upside down. Never truly *seen* anything before. This what the world is like, this what the eagles see every day? Turning under her as she circles.

Flowing, she was, herself, the air, sliding under the clouds, over and in them. Higher, into those hills of cloud. Can feel which way is up, don't need to see it, can fly inside cloud. Fair-weather cumulus; short-lived clouds, only last half an hour. Sometimes five minutes. These ones newly thermal-puffed, can tell by sharp edges. Fun to pretend they're solid, flying over bulges, through holes, over white battlements then tumble fast through ivory ramparts, over and down, falling and falling, suddenly soaring up, sinking sun dyeing crinkled sheets high above rubyfire. Opal vault arching.

High tower, fragile shapes breaking up all around wind streaming walls into banners mandarin sky streaked raspberry all ripe and sweet happier than ever been and lighter, heart singing, I am flying, heavy weight lifted, why so light?

Soaring swooping wildly, push to the limits, fast and agile, turn and brake. Stoop like giant falcon, heart-rocketing dive, screaming down delight, pulling up, thousands of feet high still land below exquisite so textured can feel it, crisp flower spikes, click of pebbles, crackling bark, land music, green shining song, lower tones, browns greys, blue above burning cloud, chiming glass metal notes, bell striking singing. Temptation don't go back. Something warning note down deep. Don't think pause to remember pull back small self not whole sky, can feel to be that cloud over there, petalthin leafing sky, flying with it there as well as here. Spreading across the sky. Seeing all. Remote blissful. Wider and wider.

Feeling into light itself, flaking air gold.

Against pale yellow, black dot.

Look closer.

Shaheen, hunting in last light?

No, too big. Shaheen can't soar like that.

Eagle?

Broad wings.

Eagle!

Big. Very big. Female.

Never flown near eagle keep your distance mind your manners, remember they can and will attack, now try extending over, patterning flying on it. Fly like that, up, down, circling, scanning territory. Now introduced through sharing pattern of flight okay approach a little closer? Fierceness of joy *that* feels like raptor looks also strange sense—courtesy—predators know importance of that—eagle teaching propriety! Feel way into right distance, flying together, creating something, musicians, call respond, you do this I do that, sometimes echo, then do same thing but this way instead, never further away than this, never closer together than that. Not competing, not threatening, creating. Weaving living pattern fleeting and beautiful as notes one after another. Work of art in time and also colours melting and flowing and hardening around them as sun sinks and shapes flying made in those colours.

Never say how long one way forever but every dance has its time finish gracefully most important final flourish rise high together, spiral round each other first time fell like stones. Levelled off flying in different directions. Over.

Goodbye sister. Into the wind.

Pain in belly dropping towards Heavener without thinking. As she fell closer naming the feeling in her belly as hunger, ordinary thought began coming back, swimming up as if from underwater.

She landed in the river and her ordinary thoughts returned almost completely as she splashed into the night-black water, found her skims and dragged them on, cloth sticking to her damp skin. She waded up the shallows of the river to where the others were gathered near the lightstick in the tree, and seeing the gazes turned on her with mixed anxiety and relief, the euphoria of that flight with the eagle still surged through her. It would never entirely leave her. It was part of her, like Hugo.

Peri picked Hugo up from Jay, thanking him, his reprimand over her late return dying on his lips when he saw the exhilaration on her face.

Jay slipped a small slick into her hand. 'Keep it safe. You know what it is. Your fate is in your hands now.'

Peri propped Hugo on one hip as she slipped the slick into her waistband. They walked back towards river's edge, where Peri sat on a log with Hugo to give him his last milk of the day.

'Spill it,' said Jay, standing next to her.

Peri tried to describe her flight. She could see it with exquisite clarity, could see cloud shapes and colours, land unrolling with such voluptuous intensity below, almost remember what it felt like slipping through air silkier than oil, clearer than water, her heart surging as she wheeled, the world slow turning underneath her. But she couldn't say it. The words were in a different place. They were over there, jumbled and colourful but utterly separate from that flight.

Jay placed his hand on Peri's arm. 'I do know some of what you experienced. Do you realise, that was your Initiation? Normally we plan for that. We haven't had time to do it for you. But you did it for yourself. Well done.'

Peri shook her head. She had never felt so purely joyful. Hugo's birth had been overwhelming but mixed with so many powerful emotions, fear and pain and sorrow. Her first flight outside the gym had been exhilarating and scary but Jay was right. This was different, her first real flight. They didn't know about this in the City. Most had never experienced Flight at all. She had to tell them. They had to know or there was no point in having wings at all.

Jay nodded. 'That's right, now you've got it. You understand.'

Peri tried to describe to Jay what had happened with the eagle. Jay stared at her. 'Well, that is different. I haven't heard of that before.'

He took Peri back to the lightstick. Bone-weary, she settled Hugo, listening to the others talk, letting it wash over her. As she drifted, dozing, something deep in her mind sounded, a distant bell.

Clearly, almost as if someone was speaking to her directly, she heard the question: *Is this the first step on the path to Wildness? What if I am not offering a way forward? What if it is a Fall instead?*

Troubled, feeling darkness corrode all the way around the rim of her happiness, Peri fell into a dreamless sleep.

She woke briefly to move with the others back to the overhang. This was where they all slept every night, as they had done ever since Peri's sighting of the Wild. Niko sat up, watching. Other lookouts spent the night stationed around the perimeter of the camp. The sky was cloudy and there would be no moon till early that morning. Peri woke once, resettled herself and Hugo, and saw Niko staring into the trees. She fell back into a doze.

Someone screamed, 'They've torn out Griffon's throat!'

There was a crashing, a terrible high shrieking.

Peri scrambled to her feet. Her waistband was already strapped to her, and now she grabbed Hugo. Hands fumbling, she snatched up her already-cocked crossbow, belting the quiver to her waist.

Rafael and Jay were grappling with dark figures. The screeching went on and on. Peri couldn't think for the horror of that sound rising and falling, like sirens, alarms. Niko circled with his crossbow, trying to get behind Rafael's assailant for a clear shot.

Peri couldn't see Leto. Suddenly Jay twisted free and was down on one knee, raising his crossbow. One of the figures fell, screaming. He raised the bow again. Phoebe and Rafael broke away from their attackers, sprinting out of Jay's line of fire.

There was an agonised bellow and an explosion of red sprayed from the chest of another attacker.

Niko threw fluorescent safety dust over several of the Wild, who, to their increasingly vocal fury, were now spectacularly visible in acid-yellow. Jay fired again and one of the Wild disappeared into the trees.

Finch was at Peri's side. 'That way,' she urged, pushing Peri down the path away from the river. 'Stay on the ground,' she hissed, already turning back towards the overhang. 'Run. If they corner you and Hugo, use your weapon! Don't try to fly. They'll be faster. Go to ground. Hide!'

Peri ran along the path with Hugo, terrified she would fall and injure him. She didn't know the path well, having mostly stayed by the river when not flying. This path was no good, too dangerous in the dark. Finch's warning resounded in her ears; the temptation to get up into the sky and away was agonising. Heart pounding so hard can't *hear* anything. Hugo crying, damn him. How could he be so stupid? 'Shut up!' she hissed. As if that would work. She felt like shaking him, so frightened, knew it wouldn't silence him. Her heart was battering so hard she thought she would be sick. Each beat shook her whole body. Seized by the mad impulse she had playing chasings as a child—stand still, show herself, get it over with. Couldn't bear the suspense. But not now, not with Hugo.

Peri dashed through a dark tunnel of trees. Too close there was that dreadful cry and the rush of wings. A Wild was flying over them, hunting them from above. She and Hugo were protected only by the thinnest screen of twigs and branches.

Peri was running and one of the Wild was tracking her. For a moment she thought she'd lost it but it circled back and came above them again. It knew where she was. A lighter patch in the grey ahead showed her she was sprinting towards a break in the trees. She must not run into the open where the Wild could stoop on them like a giant hawk. They had to get off the track, into rougher country. Turning off the path, she scrambled downhill, forcing her way through the prickly bushes. No further sound of pursuit from above.

Peri was hit by a gust of rancid air, a disgusting smell of old grease and carrion. She swung back frantically, straight into the arms of her pursuer. She screamed and the Wild grappled with her, raking her with its claws. It hit Peri and she went down. The creature grabbed Hugo and ran back uphill towards the gap in the trees.

Peri got up though she was still winded and fumbled with her crossbow. The creature's back and wings glowed yellow; it was one of the Wild that Niko had marked. She had to stop it, now, before it took off. She couldn't risk bringing it down from the sky while it had Hugo.

The creature pushed its way up towards the clearing. Peri was sprinting and now dropped to one knee. The safety dust made the Wild a dazzling target and its back to her made it less likely she would hit Hugo. She had one chance. Steadying herself, she breathed in, held the breath, raised the bow and fired. The Wild shrieked as the bolt hit it in the lower back. *Fuck.* If the bolt had gone in just a little higher, it should have killed the thing.

The Wild took off, downdrafts of foul air washing back from its wings, as Peri raced to the clearing. She was at a disadvantage in the air against the Wild but she had no choice. She could hear Hugo wailing as she took to the air. Oh god. Jay had drilled her in aerial combat but what chance did she have, in this darkness, against that thing with Hugo in its claws?

As Peri powered herself up after the creature, she realised she might have a chance. She had not spent hours and days training with Jay and watching Shaheen hunt her prey for nothing. Her only hope lay in height. She had to get above it. Perhaps she did have the advantage—she'd wounded it. She was younger, lighter, than the Wild she was hunting. The laws of physics were on her side, for now.

And she was more desperate. Of that she was sure.

Up Peri soared; she was crane, eagle, falcon.

Shaheen, swiftest, help me. Eagle, fiercest, help me.

Never had she flown so fast; she had not known she had this in her. The Wild was below, hunting her but they were built to look down. The massive flight muscles across chest and back and shoulders did not make for flexibility in looking up when they were in flight. The creature would expect her to follow it, to get as close as she could to snatch Hugo back. It might not understand right away why she was not coming after it.

Peri looked around her. Were any other Wild coming to join it? Were any Audax fighters in the air? Below her Hugo cried. Proof he was alive. She could see and hear other Wild further to the west, above Heavener, but she and her attacker were alone in this sector of sky. Peri took a deep breath. She'd had one chance and blown it. Here was one more, the very last one. That was all.

Circling higher, Peri centred her gyre on her luminous target—*thank you, Niko*—which was disoriented, perhaps by its wound, perhaps by not being sure where she was, for its flight was curving up, slowly, searching.

Peri altered her angle of attack steeply down, folding her wings into the tight W she'd used while practising her pigeon drop and roll; she was both hunter and prey and she pictured Shaheen, trying to capture the feel and form of the falcon when she stooped.

Peri plunged through the black air, a wedge of hate, a dark avenging arrow.

Shaheen, you would be proud. No mere human could learn from you better than I have.

Murder coursed through Peri's veins. That was no figure of speech. Through her veins was exactly where this strength born of love and rage was surging. She would kill this loathsome non-human, non-animal no-thing.

As she struck the Wild with, Peri felt, the force of a meteor, all the speed of her flight and her falling smashing into it, she shrilled, a savage and angry sound she would never have believed she could make. The Wild shuddered from the impact and spun away with a screech.

Peri plummeted again. The thing had dropped Hugo and Peri powered towards the ground at a speed far beyond anything she knew was safe or even possible. And now she was reaching out for Hugo, a little pale shape tumbling in the air and there, she had him, no, he slid from her grasp and she thrust herself forward again, hardly caring whether she struck the ground, she had to grab Hugo and this time she *had* him and she beat her wings ferociously, putting every shred of muscle power into the downstroke. Save nothing, hold nothing back, use every bit of strength *now*.

The force of Peri's wingbeats slowed them but still she slammed into the ground feet first and then tumbled, her body curved around Hugo, shielding him. Her shoulder and elbow struck a tree trunk and then she was still. She lay there for a second against the tree, panting. For the first time she knew how good the shock-absorbing slips were that Jay had given her. Her feet and legs stung from the impact but without the slips she would have fractured bones.

Peri struggled painfully to her feet, soothing Hugo as she strapped him to her. She had only been holding him in her arms when the Wild attacked them; it was why it had been able to get Hugo away from her. Now she tied Hugo tightly to her. They must get away from here. She pushed further down the hill, into thicker cover.

There was a stream at the bottom of this hill. An awful thought struck as Peri pushed her way through thick scrub. What if they could track her by smell?

She waded up the stream. At any other time the sharp stones underfoot would have made her wince, in spite of the slips she was wearing, but her body was singing with rage and fear and relief, even exhilaration, and she did not notice the pain. As she toiled along the stream her own breathing sounded like a hurricane in her ears. Surely if any Wild were around, they could not fail to hear her? Hugo grew quieter, subsided into a whimpering grizzle. She stopped. Silence.

Carefully, as quietly as possible in the dark, Peri pushed her way into the shelter of a gnarled old tree and settled Hugo, nursing him to sleep. She checked him carefully for injuries, but apart from superficial scratching, he seemed unharmed. The Wild were filthy and she sprayed the scratches with antiseptic new skin.

Peri set herself to watch, her arm curled around her crossbow. No sleep for her tonight. She was surprised to feel wetness on her face and realised it was tears. The shock of the fight, the terror of snatching Hugo in mid-air, her murderous rage was washing out of her. She sat still, as still as she could except her muscles were trembling from the extremes to which she'd pushed them, and the tears slid silently for a long time.

When she woke the next morning Peri did not know where she was. Blankly she stared at the dark grey-green branches in front of her. The world was prickly. She felt a weight on one of her wings. A baby, sleeping on ragged, dusty feathers. A baby. Baby Hugo. Oh. Oh *no*. The memory of the night rushed in on her.

Gently picking Hugo up, Peri struggled out from under the shelter of the old tree. She looked around her. The bush was featureless. Impossible to say exactly which way she had come, in the dark. Down that slope, yes, but this angle? Or that way? How could she know if it was safe to return to the Audax camp? How had the battle ended? Had Audax driven off the Wild? Had the Wild taken over this territory, Finch and Jay and the others fleeing to the winter roost? She had no clue how to find the winter roost. She'd lost them all.

Hugo rubbed his eyes and began his hunger cry. Peri sat on a stone and fed him, aware her milk was not enough. She would have to find food for them both, and soon.

And the worst loss of all, Jay and his promise to fly with her. Her shy hope that he might stay with her looked pathetic now, the brightly coloured longings of a young and stupid girl. For she felt very stupid. Very alone. For a few hours she'd had a future, even a future with Hugo. Jay had no way, now, of finding out what had happened to her, either. *Oh god, it's my own fault. I asked him to take the bracelet off me, the bracelet that would have helped him find me.*

Peri put her head down, lightly, on Hugo's. No point crying. No-one to listen. *I don't know what to do. I don't know what to do. No-one can tell you. Not now.*

Peri raised her head. First things first. Groom wings or we're not going anywhere. She gave Hugo a seed pod that amused him and set about straightening and cleaning her feathers with her fingers as best she could. It was hopeless. She needed a proper preening comb and that was back at the camp. Her gaze fell on a small tree with fine, stiff-needled branches. She wrenched off one of the smaller ones. It wasn't much better than her fingers but after a while she had made progress. Her feathers were smoother, more zipped together. As she worked she crooned rhymes softly to Hugo, trying to convey a calmness she didn't feel.

Two little fledglings
sitting on a wall.
Fly away, Mary.
Fly away, Paul.
Come back, Mary.
Come back, Paul.
Fly home now or not at all.

Peri stood up, shook out her wings, tied Hugo into his sling against her and started up the slope. She had to try to find the camp; she had to know who was there.

After an exhausting hour Peri was forced to admit defeat. She was no closer to the camp and Hugo was restless, struggling away in the sling. He was not happy there.

Peri was lost. All her energies had been directed towards perfecting her skills in the air; she knew nothing about the bush, couldn't read it from the ground. Going up was risky but she had no choice.

Peri headed further up the slope. Up there was an outcrop of rock she did not recognise but which would serve as a take-off point. She made sure Hugo was secure and launched herself into the air. Hugo shrieked with what sounded like terror. She tried to comfort him and rose quickly, watching for anyone above, coming out of the sun.

Hugo wailed. He would not shut up. *Please*, Hugo. This made everything so much harder. She put her arms around him, stroked his hair as she rose higher, seeing nothing. There, she'd been turned around. There was the waterfall, its white thread tangled down the cliff. She circled higher. To find out if anyone remained on Heavener, she'd have to descend. Too dangerous. What if Jay was there? How could she leave, not knowing? And where was Shaheen? No Wild would ever catch *her*.

Peri dropped towards the cliff.

Then, as Peri looked west, she could see three, no four, black dots flying east, still far away but coming towards her. There was something alien about their flying. It was fast and aggressive; had they seen her? Could they hear Hugo, his piercing cry? She realised she knew the flying styles of Jay, Niko, Finch and the others, though she'd never thought about it before. She didn't recognise the way those coming towards her flew.

They'll be faster.

That's what Finch said.

They'll be faster.

Now, with no food to fuel her, and carrying Hugo, Peri had to turn away from the Audax camp, away from Heavener, and fly faster than she ever had in her life. She was heading east, flying towards the sea. The nearest towns would be in that direction. She'd have to rely on the Wild not wanting to follow her towards people. How far away were the nearest towns? That night she and Finch had flown over dark country for hours. How close would the Wild dare to get to the towns? Did they want to catch her or drive her off? And why, why, *why* was Hugo crying? Why wouldn't he stop? Could he feel her fear now, shivering through her wings?

Peri climbed to cruising altitude just below cloudbase and set herself to the task of driving hard through the air, wingbeat after wingbeat, not allowing herself to think of what might be gaining on her from behind. It would be a long time before she could dare look. She had to put distance, hours of it, behind her.

Now there was no-one to help her; she had to carry out her plan on her own. She checked her crossbow. No choice now; she had an appointment with Hugo's father.

After an eternity cleaving air, nothing in her head but the rhythm of her speed, power to her wings, the sun began to sink behind her.

Still she drove on through the sky, into the fast-fading twilight.

PART 3

[O]nce people begin to reshape themselves through biological manipulation, the definition of human begins to drift . . . Altering even a small number of the key genes regulating human growth might change human beings into something quite different . . . But asking whether such changes are 'wise' or 'desirable' misses the essential point that they are largely not a matter of choice; they are the unavoidable product of . . . technological advance . . .

—Gregory Stock,
Director of UCLA's Program on Medicine, Technology and Society

19

SKYNATION

Yuri Gagarin, resplendent in a tailored white uniform so laden with medals it was a wonder he could stand up, was humming *The Motherland hears, the Motherland knows / Where her son flies in the sky*. Wernher von Braun and Orville Wright were peering at his medals. Von Braun wore a dark suit with white handkerchief in the top pocket, a lapel pin and red tie. Orville, a slight woman in a three-piece suit with a high white collar and fake moustache, exclaimed, 'Oh, it's *too* delicious. Wherever did you get this? It's a Gold Star of the Hero of Socialist Labor!'

Next to von Braun stood a cosmonaut sweating in her padded white spacesuit with blue insignia and blue stripes. She was saying to a messenger god wearing a winged helmet and winged boots and little else, 'Valentina Tereshkova was the first woman in space, you know. She orbited the earth for nearly three days. By the time she landed she'd logged more time in space than all the American astronauts to that date combined.'

Hermes yawned. 'You've done *your* homework,' he drawled. 'How amusing.'

Tereshkova turned to Gagarin and said, 'This isn't the correct spacesuit—it's a later model, the Orlan-M. Tereshkova never got to wear one of these.' Gagarin took her hand and the two cosmonauts, wings neatly folded over their costumes, tramped over the Botanic Gardens herb beds to the VIP queue.

Travelling to SkyNation had been more difficult than I'd anticipated, dressed as I was in what I suspected was merely an approximation of a World War II pilot's uniform. The outfit of deep brown leather jacket worn into a pattern of crazed lines like the crackled glaze on a ceramic plate, with its sheepskin cuffs and collar, and the accompanying khaki trousers and mirrored sunglasses, was heavy and hot on this muggy Friday afternoon. After a quick study of my slick, which scrolled up a table of air aces from both World Wars, I decided that I was honouring the memory of Marmaduke Thomas St John 'Pat' Pattle, Royal Air Force; it was just too good a name for an air ace to be ignored.

I'd done well to come up with a costume as good as this. I hadn't looked at my SkyNation pass properly until the previous Wednesday evening; to my horror I saw the event was a fancy-dress ball titled 'Farewell History, Welcome the Future', which summoned an unpleasant echo of Brilliant's phrase, *the human project is over*. An image of Cloud City illuminated the pass, which also stated that this SkyNation would celebrate the opening of Peter Chesshyre's new environment for fliers, the very future itself that this SkyNation was welcoming. *Celebrate the future of Flight by honouring the past*, the invitation commanded.

By the time I arrived at the initial assembly point for SkyNation in the Botanic Gardens late on Friday afternoon, I was in an ambivalent mood, which deteriorated as I plunged into the crush of fliers crowding towards the entrance to the party. Fairies at the bottom of the Botanic Gardens, I thought as I was pushed up against a group of young women decked with ropes of pearls and jewels and nothing more. If I'd thought being peered at sidelong as a lunatic on the light rail on my way here was bad, I now realised things were only going to get worse; I stood out even more as a non-flier at SkyNation. Every time I turned my head I caught a sparkling angel or glowering hawk staring at me with hauteur or astonishment.

I found myself in a queue behind a flier wearing a remarkable dress that belled out in a bubble of deep blue worked in a fret of gold lace below her waist. Below that billowed more lapis blue set with gold lions' heads. Each lion gripped a golden ring in his jaws and through this ring looped a ribbon of cherry velvet. Below this golden eagles spread their wings. The dress narrowed towards the flier's ankles and was bound with another strip of red velvet. The woman greeted another flier, who was costumed in a black V-neck sweater, black pants and black slippers. 'It's the Montgolfiers' balloon,' the woman explained, twirling this way and that as best she could in the press of the crowd. 'Who are you?'

'I'm French too, *chérie*,' said the girl. 'Philippe Petit, greatest funambulist the world has ever seen. Naturally I couldn't bring the pole; it'd put someone's eye out in this crowd.'

The girl turned around to reveal embroidered in white script where her black sweater was tied under her wings the words *I don't believe in God, but I believe in the god of the wire, the winds, the tower.*

'Cool,' said balloon woman.

A strolling mariachi band stopped opposite my queue and began to play.

Behind me a troupe of scantily clad fliers fell against me from the pressure of the crowd. I turned as one of the girls began dusting me down, sweeping her hands over my shoulders and back. 'Sorry,' she laughed indifferently, turning back to her friends. I felt even more conspicuously alone and added to my anger was now a simmering arousal; my body tingled where the girl had negligently brushed her hands. I looked down to where the gold glitter she had perfunctorily tried to dust from me was smeared over my shirt and trousers. The girls, diffusing an aura of delicious powdery scent and tangy sweat, were dressed only in low-cut silky pink leotards edged in gold that swelled over their hips and ended at mid-thigh. Pink and gold feathers nodded on their heads, pink bands circled their wrists and soft pink boots reached halfway up their calves.

I put my jacket over my shoulder and glanced at my SkyNation pass, which showed my position between the orangerie and the orchid atrium. Why were fliers enduring such an earthbound crush to gain admission to this apotheosis of Flight? Armed guards patrolled the line, checking our passes. Now it made sense: no-one would gatecrash this party.

I'd expected to be subjected to particular scrutiny and I was. The guard stalking down our line stopped in front of me and inspected my pass minutely. Finally he raised his head and stared at me. 'How did you get this?'

My blood was starting to boil. I had as much right to be here as any fluttering fairy or angel. I drew myself up. 'This pass was given to me by Halcyon Kohn, senior partner of Kohn Chesshyre Li,' I snapped, raising my voice above the competition from the mariachi band.

The guard glared at me, then decided disdain was the most face-saving reaction. He patted the air patronisingly. 'Keep your hair on, sport,' he hollered over the noise, handing me my pass.

The line inched forwards and up onto a grassed terrace. I glowered at the fliers ahead of me, queued near a magnolia tree where I could see a reader past which they filed. Right now I hated fliers. It was all I could do to force myself to attend SkyNation and rub shoulders with them while they looked down on me. But the reason I had to go to SkyNation was the same reason I hated fliers. Everything I was doing this evening was for Thomas.

Halley Kohn had promised that SkyNation was a laboratory and that one aspect of it was dedicated to working out how fliers and non-fliers could live together. Looking around me, I found this claim frankly unbelievable but I owed it to myself and Thomas to test this idea, to prove I could enter this alien world soon to be my son's.

Montgolfier balloon woman passed the reader and was let onto a path like a stepless escalator spiralling up towards a platform high above us. The path was hard to see but as fliers travelled upwards it glowed pink, a streak against the sunset sky.

My heart thudded. Philippe Petit was next. Almost my turn. What was I thinking? I didn't want to rise into the sky. Pride had led me astray. I'd wanted to be special, encounter something no-one I knew had a hope of experiencing, especially Lily. Now I just wanted to go home. I was out of my league. But what about Thomas? Soon he'd be out of my league too.

Would Thomas ever forgive me, once he found out the true cost of his wings? I'd given my permission in haste and was now repenting at leisure, while Tom's treatments progressed. It had become clear to me that Dr Ruokonen had underplayed the effects of the treatments on fertility; an uncharitable person might even accuse her of lying. From Brilliant's correspondence and in the records of meetings he'd held with researchers, doctors and even Origins representatives, it became plain the treatments had a devastating effect on fertility. These effects were catastrophic whenever germline engineering for Flight was attempted.

The human project is over. Sure it is, you fat dangerous bastard. We don't need *you* but we'll see how far you get without us. While fliers were busy transforming themselves into another species, one that looked down on us, they were still relying on the rest of us to make sure they could reproduce.

I'd recklessly allowed Thomas to begin the treatments without understanding the full picture. I might have robbed myself of ever having grandchildren. Too late, I'd tried to convince Lily and Richard of the dangers but they had waved my fears away; to them I was a dog in the manger. They knew what they were doing: Ruokonen had assured them the fertility problems would be fixed and that she knew many flier families with children. Worst of all, they understood, as did Ruokonen and I, that it was too late to stop the treatments. If I decided to deprive Thomas of wings and the promise of Flight, even though his every waking moment was consumed by the wonder of what was unfolding for him, then I'd better have a damn good reason, Lily informed me. Better than any I'd come up with so far.

The crowd jostled me forward. It was time to leave the ground but the idea of spending the night in the sky with a crowd of fliers on sense-enhancing substances was alarming. Maybe I'd be found dead under a bush in the gardens with a broken neck and Zefiryn poisoning. Previous SkyNation events had claimed lives.

On the other hand, there was Halley, who'd personally invited me, even if only to make up the numbers of non-fliers required by bureaucratic planning permission protocols. Also, I was curious to see Chesshyre unveil his great triumph.

As I moved to the entrance of the escalator, I felt the blood drain from my face and I hoped I wouldn't disgrace or even kill myself by blacking out on my ascent.

Though it was still warm, I put my jacket on as I wanted to keep both my hands free. After slipping my pass into an inside pocket with my slick, I gripped the handrail and found myself drawn upwards by its movement, which skimmed me smoothly along the path. The first moments were the worst, but soon the distance to the ground became purely abstract. My mood lifted as I stared up into a sunset of thunderous, streaming beauty, rising into those violent colours, without anything between me and the sky.

The path swept me up to the platform I'd seen from below. There, beaming at me, stood Halley.

'*Hello*,' I gasped, as she helped me off the path and onto the deck of the platform.

'Hi,' she said. 'So pleased you made it. A climber and a couple of my construction workers have bailed already. Sorry to bother you but could you look at this screen?'

She held out her slick. I looked at it.

'Good,' she said. 'At least I've registered your attendance.'

'You're not registering everybody, I take it,' I said. 'Just non-fliers.' Resentment rose in me again. I was now in a special category of person, one needing a quota.

'Well, everyone has their passes,' Halley said. 'But yes, I actually have to prove a certain number of non-fliers turn up. Such a pain. Sorry, I don't mean it like that. I'm glad you're here. I really do want to know whether what we've done includes non-fliers, makes them comfortable, at least in some parts of SkyNation. I've worked hard on that though I will admit . . .'

'What?'

'It's not an aspect of my work that interests other fliers much, I'm sorry to say.'

I saw two non-fliers, young women, huddled in a corner of the platform. I nodded at them. 'Climbers?'

Halley glanced across. 'One is. Other's a trapeze artist. She'll become a flier herself before too long. You can see they won't lack for company tonight.'

It was true. A circle of four or five male fliers was already forming around them.

'Male fliers seem to like non-fliers,' I commented.

Halley cast me a very sharp look. 'Some do. They have their reasons, as I think you know only too well.'

The view from where I was standing was spectacular. I could see the whole of SkyNation laid out before me, with its fluorescing colours, its spotlights and islands of light, its musicians and dancers, hovering over the City like a vast, brilliant spaceship.

'I like your outfit,' said Halley.

'Yours is breathtaking,' I said. 'What is it?'

'Once upon a time there was an airline called Singapore Airlines,' said Halley. 'This sarong kebaya was one of their air hostess uniforms.'

'They couldn't have worn them quite like that.'

'No,' smiled Halley. 'Not quite.'

For as I peered at Halley more closely I saw she was wearing nothing at all, except brief underpants. From more than a few centimetres away she looked dressed, her body swathed in the illusion of a long-sleeved jacket tight across her hips above a split skirt falling almost to her ankles, both jacket and skirt elaborately figured with intricate paisley leaves and branches and flowers of magenta, orange, blue, white and black on a Chinese red background.

'I was going to wear a copy of the actual uniform,' said Halley, 'but it was too restricting. So I had the colours applied to my skin instead.'

'You look amazing,' I said, enjoying the paradox of being able to look at the swell of her breasts and the muscled curves of her hips and legs and bottom without being able to see much more than if she were covered by cloth instead of these shimmering pigments.

'Thanks.'

'Fabulous party,' said a flier in passing to Halley, who nodded and smiled.

I looked around the platform, which of course had no parapet and was large enough to hold about fifty fliers. Twenty or so were milling around, greeting each other and then flying away. Up here, the crowd of jostling fliers posed a real danger. If one of them was pushed off the platform they could just flutter back up but I'd have to keep my wits about me. I turned back to Halley. The party must have started for her hours ago—her eyes were shining with more joy than was strictly natural—but I could see she was still plugged in to the world around her. Perhaps these new drugs were designed to keep fliers focused enough on physical reality so they wouldn't fall out of the sky.

Halley extended one wing along the small of my back. 'Let me show you around,' she said. 'Even though some of this will be inaccessible to you, there's still more to see and do than you'll ever be able to explore, even if you stayed for the full three days.'

I could hear the pride in Halley's voice; she wanted to show me this temporary wonder of the world she'd helped create, wanted to know whether I could appreciate it as a non-flier, the way she intended. She placed a purple gel into my palm. 'You need to take this to really enjoy it.'

'What is it?' *Jeez, Fowler, do you have to sound quite so uptight?*

Halley smiled. 'Zefiryn. Oh dear, you should see the look on your face. Been listening to the horror stories, have you? This is half the dose fliers take. You'll be fine.'

More fliers came up to congratulate Halley on SkyNation.

I swallowed the tablet. I hadn't come to SkyNation to stay safe.

What happened next I can only describe as if an eagle looked out through my eyes. I removed my aviator glasses and stashed them inside my jacket. My eyes felt as if they'd become telescopes with someone else adjusting the focus. I could see individual hailstones fall from inland clouds, each drop of ice backlit by the sinking sun. I could see each ripple in the waves below, each rivet on the great grey bridge, the grain in the fabric of sails on the boats tacking across the harbour. At first I was dizzy, disoriented. How on earth was I going to make my way around safely when I was staggering drunk on the glory of such godlike seeing?

Surely I would fall as my focus zoomed wildly from the miniature to the grand overview. 'Breathe,' said Halley. 'You'll get it under control.'

As I struggled to master my surging vertigo, I became aware that my hearing was also heightened. Laughter and music sifted down from the clouds; wind whistled through the feathers of the fliers and clanked the rigging on the sailing boats as they whooshed through the water so far below.

Abruptly it was as if a switch had been thrown in my brain which now directed my enhanced perceptions more seamlessly. Exultation overwhelmed me. If a sparrow stirred in a park suburbs away its presence could not escape me. The remaining fog of my bad mood fell away. My resentments and fears were remote, shadows moving high over a mountain far away. They would all keep for another time.

Now I was calm. Even if I died, so what? I would experience the sky.

'Now you're ready, I think,' said Halley. She folded her wing and took my arm. 'See how walkways branch away from this platform? You'll have to use them to explore SkyNation. The rest of us can fly to any part of SkyNation but we also need these walkways and other places to rest.'

Halley guided me to one of the semi-transparent walkways stretching up and away from the platform like gridded catwalks or narrow swaying suspension bridges complete with handrails. Gingerly, I tested my weight. The walkway gave a little but held; it was strong and flexible and I had to grip the handrails tight. In the gathering dusk, the coloured light pulsing along the edges of these walkways and handrails strengthened. The one under my hand winked green. How could I walk along these threads in the air with no fear, in fact with a mounting euphoria? I assumed that was also an effect of the Zefiryn.

Halley and I climbed high above the platform and she paused, sweeping her arm around, indicating one plane of SkyNation below where we stood. 'See down there?' she said. 'From this height you can see the main level of SkyNation, though there are other environments above and below that. Can you see how it's a map of the City on a one-to-one scale? Those bright lines of green and blue and gold are ropes of riverlaminate outlining the contours of the harbour, its bays and beaches, below. We've copied the harbour islands with aerial rooms; some of them look like clouds and others we've set up as ethereal restaurants and bars. There are nests to sleep in too; they're those nets down there suspended from the riverlaminate. They're padded with cushions; you can sleep in them or listen to music while you look down to the harbour. And see those pools of what looks like water?'

'Fantastic,' I said. 'You've got towers of cloud too, right above the real towers they're mimicking. Not really cloud, though, is it?'

'No,' said Halley. 'Except for those faux-cloud towers, all of it, all the nets and catwalks and bars and other structures, is anchored by the riverlaminate lines and *those* join up and finally anchor to the City towers below, which stand around the edges of SkyNation. Most of the space we're using for the party lies directly above the harbour. That means that there's lots of open space for people to fly in.'

Halley showed me how the edges of the catwalks were colour-coded; the colour flickered from green, which denoted safety for non-fliers, to yellow, which demanded extra caution, to red for areas that were strictly fliers-only. A security or first-aid patrol of fliers in fluoro yellow-edged jackets flashed past us and vanished into the gloom below.

Every moment that Halley guided me through this new world that extended around me in three dimensions, my confidence soared. No diver descending into the ocean, no acrobat flying on a trapeze, could traverse such vaults of vertical space as those I now explored. My rising euphoria was probably my enemy up here but I couldn't help enjoying it. I was high on Zefiryn and adrenaline, no doubt about it. High and getting higher all the time. I must be feeling the carefree exuberance of the fliers, able to tumble so easily into the air with no fear of falling.

'What's so funny?' said Halley, smiling; I realised I was grinning like a loon. Here I was, Zeke Fowler, ex-cop and trusted investigator, completely off my face on Zefiryn. My senses were still intensifying their perceptive power. I could effortlessly follow the threads of music from each band and smell the smoky spices of the food in each bar, restaurant and stall throughout the whole of SkyNation.

Across the other side of the harbour from where Halley and I stood, something remarkable was emerging. At first it looked like just another one of the cloud towers, but as dusk deepened and the tower was correspondingly more brightly lit I could see the structure was a castle, complete with moat, crenellated parapets and a cloister, yet it was airy, with great blue holes of night and stars torn into its cloudy substance.

'You said you'd copied the City,' I said, pointing to the castle. 'So what is *that*?'

'A little joke,' said Halley. 'See?'

I did see. The castle was directly above Parliament House and was a satire on it, an elaborated fantasy version of the old building's sandstone battlements and turrets.

A cloud of flashing light and dark burst from the top of the castle and poured up, luminous as fireworks, flickering this way and that, now silver, now blue, as it wheeled and turned. It divided down the middle and swirled above us, stencilling complex whorls and twists against the dark. The cloud, made up of individual fliers as I now realised, swooped together again. Another flock, green and gold, exploded up with a giant *churr*ing of wings from a cloud above the gardens and rose through the first flock. They arced, fell, peeled away and re-formed. The flocks shattered into a spray of fliers, then regrouped, flowing away over the harbour.

The catwalk Halley and I were on intersected below us with another catwalk that led to the castle. I pointed to it and Halley nodded. The castle moat, so high above the City, was filled with sparkling liquid. Shrieks of laughter drifted across the gulfs of air as fliers rode fantastical creatures, mechanical dragons and phoenixes, around and around the moat, knocking each other off.

Astonishing how quickly the miraculous becomes commonplace. Here I was, climbing through the sky, druggedly fearless, suspended on threads of delicately strong stuff as if I were an artificial spider, greeting the fliers we passed, who all complimented Halley on her work.

Then it hit me. Is that what this SkyNation was foreshadowing? Would the notoriously overcrowded, overpriced and underserviced city below be built up into the sky in this gossamer way? There could be vast parks, entertainment platforms and play areas. Halley had said Sky-Nation was a laboratory and I began to wonder. Was this a template for a whole sky city? It had been created by architects after all. Were the fliers trying to escape us?

As we drew near, the castle loomed above, airy yet impressive, and ahead of us I saw a stairway that switchbacked up the outside. Two masked men swooped down past me, leaping, half running, half flying, as I mounted the stairway. They swept past so quickly I only caught a glimpse of them and couldn't tell if their costumes represented super-heroes or acrobats. As I scaled the wall, marvelling at how substantial the 'stones' looked, grained with textures of moss and granite, I heard a warning shout.

'Look out!' A mass of white fell towards me. I just had time to think, *They're defending the castle*, when I was enveloped in something light and cold and buoyant, like the 'snow' I'd seen in Hugo's nursery. I floundered to the top of this powdery dry 'snow' drift. Luckily it was not as dense as real snow or I would have been in trouble.

'Oh dear!' the flier gasped. He launched himself off the parapet and into the night.

'You okay?' Halley said, coming up behind me.

''Tis nothing, madam,' I said carelessly. 'A mere flesh wound.'

I hauled myself over the parapet to stand on the ledge from which my attacker had jumped. It was piled a metre deep in snow. I should've been more alarmed—the falling snow could easily have swept me off the castle—but nothing seemed real at SkyNation. Perhaps the insouciance proper to my character as a fighter ace was affecting me, along with the Zefiryn.

'I can smell food,' I said.

'Yes, I'm starving. This way.'

We climbed higher into the castle, Halley spreading out her wings for balance on the stairs, and then we pushed our way through the crowded cloister out onto a flat roof on the top of the castle's highest tower. Halley led me past rows of tables to one set right at the edge. It was reserved for her.

'Look,' said Halley, 'they're preparing for the opening ceremony for Cloud City later.' She pointed to a darkened tower to the west of us—Cloud City, I realised—and I saw that in the gulf between the castle and Cloud City had been fastened a net, upon which musicians and other performers were now setting up equipment and rehearsing.

Halley turned to me and, lowering her voice, said, 'Speaking of Peter, I just wanted to say how devastated we all were to hear about Hugo. We hoped and hoped it was going to be alright but now . . . ' her voice trailed away. 'Anyway, I just wanted to say how sorry I am.'

I looked at the floor. She laid her hand on my arm.

A chorus of greeting erupted from a crowded table behind us and I turned to look. A portly man dressed in a white astronaut's suit and carrying a space helmet under his arm waddled over to the table.

'Oh god, it's David Brilliant,' I said, turning back to Halley. His boldly striped wings were unmistakable.

I shifted in my seat and took off my leather jacket. I didn't want to start an argument with Halley by telling her that Chesshyre and Brilliant were responsible for what had happened to Peri and Hugo and Luisa, and that her sympathy was wasted on her colleague.

Of course Brilliant had to toddle over and suck up to Halley. 'You've outdone yourself this year, my dear,' he said. I'd just had time to put on my aviator glasses but I needn't have bothered. Brilliant didn't even look at me.

Halley said, 'A lot of this is Peter's work, too. I'll tell him you like it.'

Brilliant stumped back to his table.

Halley's gaze wandered to the table next to us, where four women sat together, all dressed in flying helmets, their goggles hanging by straps from their chairs. One woman looked familiar, with her sleek tin-coloured hair. She wore a khaki military tunic with blue flashings on the collar and over her chair she'd flung a heavy leather flying jacket.

Worn leather gauntlets lay on the table in front of her. Slashings of light in her feathers and skin caught my eye. I was dazzled by the shimmer as she moved. She turned.

'Dr Ruokonen.'

She peered at me. 'Mr Fowler. I *am* surprised to see you here.'

I'll bet. Didn't know I was so well-connected, did you?

'Hello, Aleta,' said Halley. 'You look convincingly warlike.'

'I'm Lilya Litvak,' said Ruokonen. 'This is Beryl Markham,' she waved her hand at the woman next to her, 'and Amelia Earhart. The startling plum satin jumpsuit over there is Harriet Quimby. An early aviatrix known for her indescribable fashion sense, as you can see.'

'Who's Lilya Litvak?' said Halley.

'Why, the white rose of Stalingrad. I was the premier female fighter ace of the Second World War. *Twelve* German kills to my name. Luftwaffe pilots were utterly terrified when they saw my Yak One bearing down on them.'

'Gosh,' said Halley. 'How romantic.'

'Well, not for *her*,' retorted Ruokonen, her mood darkening. 'She was dead at twenty-two and quickly forgotten, like all the other female aces. She got no glory to compensate for her short life. Women like her become invisible to history overnight. Hard to understand why, though. It took *eight* Messerschmitts to shoot her down. Knocks the Red Baron into a cocked hat, if you ask me.'

'Yes,' laughed Halley. 'From now on I never shall think of the Red Baron, only the White Rose.'

I smiled at Halley, impressed by her instincts as a peacemaker. What a likable person she was. It was rare to meet a person as successful as she was who even noticed other people's feelings, let alone bothered to soothe them.

Halley indicated Ruokonen's skin. 'What have you got there?'

'It's new,' Ruokonen said. 'You won't see it on anyone else yet. Take a look.'

We stared at the warm moonlight that made up part of Ruokonen's body.

'Pearl,' said Ruokonen. 'I've grown it. Relatively easy with pearl, which is produced organically anyway.'

'May I?' said Halley and skimmed her hand over the pearl skin. 'Oooh, nice.'

Ruokonen leaned back in her chair, crossing her long legs at the ankles. 'Thomas is coming along quickly,' she said to me. 'Not long till he's flying now.'

'Yes,' I said, not trusting myself to say more.

Halley glanced at me, surprised. 'Your son is having the treatments?'

'The research is advancing all the time,' Ruokonen continued. 'I've been doing work on insects but there's been a setback.' Anger came into her voice. 'There was a raid on a lab where I've been overseeing a project.'

'Diomedea?'

'How did you know? Hard to believe fliers would do such a thing but I guess there are ignorant fanatics and self-styled revolutionaries in every time and place.'

'Could they have been Wild?' I said.

She glanced at me sharply. 'You know my views on that.'

'I do,' I said. 'What I don't know are your views on whether there are any limits on what Diomedea will do to tackle the fertility problems. Are there any limits on what they'll do to track down Peri Almond and her baby, for instance?'

Ruokonen laughed. 'Oh dear,' she said, spluttering into her drink. 'I believe there is someone here tonight who's probably wanting to catch up with you.'

'Well, that's just great,' I said. 'Can't imagine Diomedea wanting you to admit that.'

Ruokonen waved her hand airily. 'No law against putting someone under surveillance. As you know very well. Bit rich you complaining about it.'

'Surveillance is one thing. Break and enter is something else. Especially as my lion was nearly killed. My concern is to ensure this Raptor intends no harm to Peri and Hugo.'

'Don't know anything about a break and enter,' said Ruokonen. 'No doubt you've annoyed any number of people who might want to do that. As for Peri and Hugo, of course no harm will come to them. They're needed for follow-up, as I think you know very well.'

Ruokonen was not telling all she knew, I thought, as Halley and I sat down again. Wine and food had arrived while we'd been talking to Ruokonen and I was grateful to sit quietly, absorbing a little of all that I'd done and seen. The plates in front of us showcased artful constructions, architecture rather than food. I glanced at Halley; she would appreciate this. But she ate quickly, demolishing her highrise of shaved crispy greens, landscaped with its own delicate garden, as if it were nothing more than a toasted sandwich. 'Something I *must* show you,' she said, wiping her mouth and rising to her feet.

'This is the most incredible place I've ever been,' I said.

Halley took my hand. 'Beautiful, isn't it? It's good to get away from everyone for a little while. It's nice being congratulated and everything but I'd just like to enjoy the party without interruptions for a moment.'

We stood in a park of deep forest and rolling meadows floating high above the castle.

We'd climbed a long ladder up to the park and now walked along green airy lanes, past sweet flowering vines. Trees almost met over our heads: avenues of beech, oak, pine and willows shivering down their long strands of leaves like green hail. We walked on paths woven of tangled roots and through small gaps and fissures between the roots we looked down to the glinting lights of the City below, shifting as the park moved in the air currents.

It was fantastic, dreamlike: a walk on a forest path over an abyss. A breeze streamed through the branches with a keening note, something high in its timbre, as if the very sound could tell us we were hundreds of metres in the air. I pulled my flying jacket around me, grateful for its warmth. Heat radiated from Halley's skin and feathers; she did not seem to mind the increasing coolness of the night air.

Stars shone above our heads and below our feet. We walked on a shadowed island of trees floating in a well of light.

A trilling, chirping song running as sweet and clear as a brook fell from the trees over our heads.

'Nightingale,' said Halley.

We paused at the edge of the forest, looking over a rustling meadow bordered at the edge furthest from us by three smooth hills forming the southern boundary of the park. A waterfall splashed down the side of the highest hill into a pool. As we headed towards the waterfall, the meadow gave slightly under our feet. It was unutterably strange to walk on this undulating mat of green and trees and water in the sky and look over the edge and see the City winking below.

'So this is where the fledglings will play,' I said. A rush of anger heaved up like bile in my throat, despite the Zefiryn. These fliers wanted *everything*, no compromises. They wanted all the beauties belonging to the earth—flowers, trees, water, grass—but they wanted it all up here, away from the muck and creatures that generated it. It was all artificial, even though living, but they didn't care because they were the same, they were alive but artificial too. They wanted to be just like these plants, uprooted, purged of dirt. This was the life promised by the Church of the Seraphim, with all the blood and shit and tears left behind for others to suffer through and clean up.

I stared into the waterfall clattering over boulders at its base. This was just showing off. Boulders in the sky! The audacity of it. I looked at Halley, one of the architects of this new world, with a heady mix of admiration and fury.

Next to a pool on the other side of the stream stood a young god, Eros. He was tall, with chopped pale hair and a filmy gold mask covering his eyes and cheeks. His wings swept behind him, luminous warm white, like mother-of-pearl. In one hand dangled a crossbow, held against the white tunic that came to his thighs. He was searching for someone; he looked around him and when his eyes rested on Halley and me, he startled, just the vaguest tremor, suppressed. He turned and began walking away towards the dark lane of trees. I stared after him. Something familiar in that walk; I should have recognised it but I was distracted by Halley.

'Let's find somewhere to sit down.' I wanted to get Halley alone. It seemed fitting we'd run into Eros and now we searched among the hills till we found a bowl scooped into the side of the hill, less than a cave, more than a ledge. We sat and gazed over the falls and forest and past them to the rest of SkyNation, watching fliers darting and dancing in the clouds. Sound pulsed up from the net and spread all around us, vibrating through the whole of SkyNation; it had become the very substance of the air.

'What is that noise?'

'Songs from the Blue,' Halley said. 'Music made from weather, in real time. Waves, storms, earthquakes under the sea, ice cracking, solar wind, meteors, electromagnetic fields.'

Halley leaned into my shoulder, her feathers rustling against me. Perfume was released from the feathers every time she moved. I was intensely curious. What would touching her be like? I took the end of one of her wings in my hands and stroked the great primary feathers. They were softer than I'd imagined. I ran my hand over the broader part of her wing, from the shoulder down, careful not to brush her feathers the wrong way. My watch snagged on one of her feathers and she winced.

I kissed Halley. It was spine-tingling, electric, to feel her sleek feathers against my skin but it was strange. Every time she moved in my arms her feathers released a rush of sensation along my skin, soft and thrilling, along with drifts of warm, rosy scent.

I stopped kissing her after a while. I'd like to think it was the Zefiryn but I was overwhelmed by sensation. I needed to catch my breath. Halley curled up on her side. She yawned and then laughed, putting her hand over her mouth.

'The twenty-hour days leading up to this must be catching up with me. I have to close my eyes for a moment.'

I was relieved. Kissing Halley was great but I needed time to think. I'd never touched a flier before and she wasn't just any flier but Peter's colleague. What did she really want from me?

I must have dozed for about half an hour. Halley was next to me, asleep. She looked lovely, pillowed on one barred wing with the other one covering her. Directly on the edge of the hill in front of me, her burnished chestnut wings with their green undersides shimmering in the darkness, stood Peri. So she *had* come back then, just as she said she would. Clever of her to find me at SkyNation. She held up baby Hugo and I reached for him but as I took him, he slipped into the dark. Peri shrieked and then both were gone. I woke up properly, then. I leaned over Halley and tucked a strand of her dark hair back behind one ear.

A movement caught my attention and I peered upwards. The luminous white Eros was high above me on a narrow walkway. I knew I recognised that flier climbing steeply away from me but who was he? Seized by the need to know, I pulled on my flying jacket and began confidently scaling the almost-vertical incline myself, amazed at how easy it was. The island-park dropped away and there was nothing and no-one near me, no floating bars or netted rooms, no other walkways. We were heading towards one of the cloud towers, far higher than anywhere I'd yet been. Eros didn't seem to be aware of me as, far beneath, I followed him.

Eros disappeared into the cloud tower. Singing fell down from it like rain.

I pushed my way into the cloud tower but could see nothing but the cloud-stuff itself, which parted like mist and yet was springy and bore me up. This was cloud just as I'd dreamed of it as a child, as if the clouds were blissfully springy pillows.

I could see nothing except the glow of colours as they played through the cloud. Was Eros hiding in here? A warm tenor voice floated towards me from a purple mist. A chorus of voices rose to a crescendo around the tenor.

As I made my way through the mist I caught a glimpse of a trailing white wing in front of me. I hurried as much as I dared after him. All the while that song went on and then faded into other songs that poured over me as if the sky itself was singing and still the singing went on and the voices did not pause but drifted, swelled and died away and then gathered strength as a new voice, a bass and then a soprano, took up the main melody and soared above the others. *This* is flying, I thought. *This singing is the truest Flight I ever heard.*

Now I'd stumbled out onto an outcrop of cloud, and stood up to my calves in cloud-stuff like a cherub in a painting, unable to see anything but plum mist on three sides and one starry wall of sky falling to black water—and there in front of me, his back to me, his white wings spread wide, stood Eros.

My vision of Peri flashed across my mind. My dream had been trying to tell me something. I knew where I'd seen that god's walk before. The god was a goddess, her movement too sinuous for a man. The tall girl looked like Peri. But could it really be her? Her hair had been sheared off and dyed and her feathers were the wrong colour but that was nothing; many fliers at SkyNation were more elaborately altered than that.

'Peri!' I yelled.

The figure turned and gasped. Then she spun away and launched herself like a great white bird into the dark.

I crept as close to the edge of the cloud-that-was-not-cloud as I dared, trying to make out where she'd flown, but she'd disappeared. What was she doing here?

Then terror laid its grip on my head and neck and heart. I shivered in the high cold night air. *Where was baby Hugo?* For, if he was gone, what wouldn't Peri do? What desperation and rage and hate was now driving her?

The bridge glided to the right far below me and I realised I was drifting. In one heartstopping instant I saw that my outcrop of cloud was dissolving, its edges breaking up, streaming away into the air. There was no link now to the walkway I'd used to climb up. So this was how I would die. I laughed out loud. Who could have foreseen that though I'd come to SkyNation focused on Thomas, I'd ended up hot on the case instead, still chasing that damn fool girl Peri? I'd made a stupid mistake and would pay with my life.

I am as stubble before the wind, and as chaff that the storm carrieth away.

Well, Marmaduke Thomas St John 'Pat' Pattle, old chap, looks like this is it, eh? I patted my jacket pockets. Might as well go down with my aviator glasses on. As I felt inside my pocket my hand closed around something else—my SkyNation pass. *Christ, you're a flaming clot*, the ghost of Marmaduke said to me. *Nearly bought the farm for no good reason other than LMF. That's lack of moral fibre to you, old son.*

I used the pass to navigate me to the only walkway still connected to my cloud, which had been hidden from me on the other side of the cloud tower. This walkway led me back down to the net I'd seen earlier from the castle. Now it was packed full of performers and partygoers and the music of Songs from the Blue was much louder here.

As I steadied myself on the net, jostled by jugglers and clowns and musicians, I rang Halley. 'Halley, I've seen Peri. She's here and I'm worried she's going to do something crazy. I've got to find her or at least warn someone.'

'Sorry?' replied Halley, her voice breaking up. 'Can't hear you, Zeke. Where are you? Can you hear me?'

'Halley, *listen*. Oh, Christ, I've just realised Peri's actually armed. That crossbow isn't just part of her costume, I'm afraid.' Deep tremors from the music shook my body.

Halley's voice crackled and dropped out in the static burst from some god-knew-what pulse of solar radiation or shuddering from a distant tsunami.

'Who do I speak to about this?' I was almost screaming into my slick. A richly robed man with flowing hair and beard and soft hat sitting on his head like the cap of a large black mushroom bumped into me, then turned back to stare at me as if I were deranged. A pin on his velvet robe proclaimed him to be Leonardo da Vinci.

'I can't hear you,' Halley said, her voice dropping in and out as the Songs from the Blue reverberated through SkyNation. She said something else I couldn't hear, then added, 'Peter's giving his speech soon for the launch of Cloud City. I'm going there now.'

'What's Peter's costume?' I bellowed.

'*What?*'

A group of musicians harmonising with Songs from the Blue on didgeridoos, keyboards and kotos glared at me as I shouted.

'Daedalus!' yelled Halley. Her voice broke up again and I caught through the crackle and hiss the words 'was an architect too'.

I shook my slick and tried one last time. 'Warn Peter and find some security, Halley. I'll do my best to hunt down Peri or find someone to tell. I'll meet you later at your table, okay?'

'Okay,' I thought I heard Halley say as her voice was submerged under the avalanche of blurring, buzzing sound, but I didn't think she'd understood anything of what I'd said. And I had no fucking idea what Chesshyre dressed as Daedalus would actually look like. Draped in some sort of classical robe? He already had the wings.

I rang Chesshyre but only got a message. Of course he wouldn't be answering any calls now, not when he was about to give the biggest speech of his life.

I looked around wildly but couldn't see any security nor any sign of Eros from where I was forcing myself through the crowd. Angry glances and curses were thrown my way as I pushed towards the edge of the net nearest the castle, reasoning that if I could get back up to the top where Halley's table was, I'd have a better view and more chance of seeing either Eros or a security patrol. The greater bulk of all these fliers, thronging like a massed choir of angels, was really hindering me; it was so hard to squeeze by all those wings and every time I snagged a feather I thought I'd get a punch in the face.

Rising ahead of me, about a hundred metres away, gleamed the walkway leading to the castle, but at my current rate of progress I might as well be a kilometre away. Songs from the Blue swelled till I could barely hear myself think: it was as if the sounds had become the molecules of my own body and were vibrating me to their chords; as if I'd been seized by sound and was moving over the face of the earth as a great storm; as if I were part of the earthquake shaking the sea bed; as if I'd been thinned to vapour and flung wide to drift on the atmosphere, part of the planet-sized drama of the weather. How could anyone ever think the weather was boring? To fliers it was fascinating, a matter of life and death.

Two fliers in fluoro jackets, who could have been security but were more likely paramedics, stood at the very edge of the net, looking down. I thought about trying to reach them but decided it was a waste of time.

Finally, near the edge of the net, the densest press of the crowd thinned a little and I escaped up the walkway. The walkway was lined with fliers too, turning their heads towards Cloud City, which, formerly in shadow, was now being lit in a rising tide of light pouring up from its base.

Breathing hard, I forced myself halfway up the catwalk and paused, looking back for a moment. Spotlights converged on the broad prow of Cloud City just as the tide of light reached it and my Zefiryn-enhanced vision could see Chesshyre standing right at the tip of the prow. A mass of people shifted and glittered in the light behind Chesshyre; I could pick out Halley, just behind and to the side of Chesshyre. David Brilliant stood further back, talking to a polished, important-looking woman I vaguely recognised. *Just you wait, buddy. Your turn's coming.*

Truly, I was running out of time. Chesshyre stared out over the crowd towards the castle, readying himself for his speech. As I'd foreseen, he'd draped himself in a white classical robe, which fell over one shoulder, and in his left hand he carried a chisel. Two wide purple bands crossed over his chest and disappeared over his shoulders. I supposed the bands represented the means by which Daedalus had affixed wings to himself and his son.

Halley, I wanted to scream, *get away from Chesshyre!*

I tried to call Halley but there was that sparkling, burring sound that indicated about a hundred other people were also trying to contact her. Not surprising at the climax of this triumphant occasion for Kohn Chesshyre Li.

Furiously, my heart pounding as if it was going to come up into my throat, I thrust myself up the stairway and onto the castle.

As I scrambled up the stairs, Songs from the Blue faded. Chesshyre started to speak. My back was to him and I expected his words to be blown away in the breeze that had sprung up, but every word was clear, as if he were standing next to me.

'Every year since its inception,' Chesshyre said, 'SkyNation has been a marker of our progress. Every year we party, we celebrate, but we also catch our breath and see how far we've come, how far Flight has advanced.' Chesshyre was interrupted briefly by applause. He resumed. 'Every year we push ourselves to redefine what life can mean when we have wings.'

Now I was half running up the stairs, searching the faces of all the fliers I passed and hearing Chesshyre still speaking behind me but only tuning into his words now and then. As long as he was speaking I knew no-one had attacked him yet.

'Flight,' Chesshyre said as I elbowed my way through the cloister, 'is not just flying. We all know this.'

Christ, he was starting to sound a bit like David Brilliant.

I burst out onto the terrace at the top of the tower and made my way towards the edge, towards Halley's still-reserved table. The terrace was busy but not too crowded; many of the VIPs who had reserved tables here were now on the prow of Cloud City with Chesshyre.

'Flight gives us a vision by which we can live the whole of our lives,' intoned Chesshyre. His voice had taken on an incantatory quality; he was becoming entranced by his own rhetoric. 'We yearn for a life freed from constraint, in which we've slipped the *surly bonds of earth*.'

I searched the crowd systematically, dividing the fliers on the net into quadrants and going over it clockwise. An owl-masked goddess among dragons at eight o'clock. Fairies surrounded by gargoyles and vampires at twelve o'clock.

Something moved. The merest flash of white at the corner of my eye made me glance upwards. Of course. Eros was poised high above the crowd, on a wire of the lighting rigging. A good place to hide in plain sight. Even fliers rarely look up, unless gauging the sky for Flight. No-one would notice her there, balancing, intent, her head cocked to one side, listening to Chesshyre.

What did she have to gain by coming here? She had unfinished business with Chesshyre but what could it be here and now, in front of all the fliers in the City?

In prosperity the destroyer shall come upon him.

'Peri! No!' I shouted up at her. For a non-flier there was no way up to where she was standing.

My vision of the cloudy, dark-winged goddess above the City came back to me. *Winged balancer of life, daughter of Justice.* I'd thought that Cam and Henryk and I were her instruments. But here she was. *Nemesis*. All in white.

I searched for Halley in the crowd behind Chesshyre but couldn't see her as he said, 'In this vision, fliers live, work, play, grow, in the air, a truly aerial existence. Flier children are born and fly before they walk, their feet hardly ever touching the ground.'

I looked up again.

At Chesshyre's last words Peri stiffened. I held my breath. Was this the future for Thomas, for his children, if he were fortunate enough to have any?

'I speak of vision,' Chesshyre continued. 'Visions of what Flight can mean. And that is why I stand before you now, costumed as the first great dreamer of Flight that we can put a name to: *Daedalus*. Daedalus the inventor. Daedalus the engineer. Daedalus the architect. It is no accident,' Chesshyre's voice rose in conviction and strength, 'that the designer and builder of the great Labyrinth confining the monstrous hybrid Minotaur, symbol of our beastliness, our viciousness, our eternally and *fatally* conflicted natures, is also the inventor of wings, of the very dream of Flight itself which has been kept alive for thousands of years and which *we* now embody.' A wave of applause drowned him out. Chesshyre raised his hand.

'Since the myth of Daedalus, Flight has been a metaphor. Daedalus has stood for the artist, the scientist, the engineer, for all Promethean and Faustian seekers after knowledge, for all those who push the boundaries. But I claim Daedalus for Flight. We have *done* with Flight as a symbol! We are mastering it in *reality*!' Chesshyre roared the last two sentences and was met by a cheer and an answering roar from the assembled fliers.

Chesshyre bowed his head and an expression of pain and weariness crossed his face. Would he dare to name the price Daedalus paid for his inventiveness? He did not. Instead, he raised his head and flung his arms and his wings wide.

'And so we come to Cloud City!' he cried. 'The first building, the first creation of its type on earth to take Flight and the life that it means seriously.'

I shook my head. I'd fallen into a trance of my own, standing there gawping at Chesshyre and listening to his words.

'Peri! Hey! *Peri!*' I called. But the wind from the sea blew away my words, though not Chesshyre's cleverly amplified speech. Obviously I was not totally inaudible, as some of the other fliers on the terrace shot me nasty looks.

As I prowled the terrace, making my last-ditch attempt to find a single sensible or official-looking flier I could try to warn, Chesshyre began to outline the latest advances and how they were incorporated into Cloud City. He talked about how inspired he was by this new conception, how this was not a building, not even a 'machine for living', but the foundation for a new way of life, the beginning of a true city. Was he talking about secession? Surely the laws of the land still applied a hundred metres in the air? But there was the planning minister, the polished, powerful-looking woman I'd seen earlier and only just recognised, beaming at him. I thought of the documents I'd sent to Sunil. I had only a few pieces of the whole picture but it was clear fliers had all the influence they needed in this City.

Now Chesshyre was saying how proud he was because Cloud City was ready and this SkyNation would celebrate its launch. The

Songs from the Blue swelled again and Cloud City, ablaze with light, emanated a low powerful hum of its own.

High above us, Peri was motionless, her being concentrated on Chesshyre. She looked as if she'd been placed there by SkyNation organisers; a beautiful ornament, the marble image of the god. She reminded me of Frisk, his stillness when he hunted, his body frozen, ready to spring in a split-second.

Then two things happened simultaneously. The top third of Cloud City, the part Chesshyre had said would rotate, lifted away from the rest of the tower at the point where the base of the prow joined the structure. The top of Cloud City was rising into the air above the City. It was flying. Or at least floating slowly, with all those fliers still standing on its prow, lights coursing over its surface and fireworks bursting into the air and gasps and cheers coming from the crowd. Now was the most dangerous moment. I threw my head back to stare up at Peri.

She'd twined herself round the lighting strut.

She raised her crossbow. Aimed it.

'*Peri!*' I yelled.

I would have missed what happened next except that I'd automatically glanced back to Chesshyre. All at once, with shocking swiftness, red had flowered on his white robe and he'd staggered sideways off the prow and was falling, falling away with the speed of a meteor as Cloud City continued to rise. Two fliers on the prow reacted instantly and dived after him. There were a few shrieks of horror but most fliers were too busy *ooh*ing and *ahh*ing at Cloud City dropping its fantastic flowers of light over the CBD to notice.

I looked back at Peri. She lowered her bow and as she turned, someone else, an unusually large flier below on the net, was now taking off, heading for her. I knew those red wings.

Bellowing, 'Peri, over here!' I ran right to the edge of the terrace. A few other fliers turned to stare at me. 'Watch out, Peri,' I yelled.

The Raptor reached Peri as she was halfway to me. Peri twisted and dropped like a stone into the gulf of air just before the castle structure but the huge Raptor clutched at her as she plunged and grasped her wing. They tumbled and fought in mid-air like two giant eagles and then they were falling towards the terrace where I stood, appalled. Without thinking, I grabbed at the Raptor as he swept past me.

The Raptor faltered, Peri still fighting in his grasp. All I could think was that if I added my weight to Peri's, the Raptor would not be able to manage, he would have to let Peri go.

We were a welter of feathers and clawing hands. I caught the Raptor's wing and my weight brought him staggering onto the terrace, Peri writhing to free herself from his grip. The other fliers on the terrace were screaming as they backed away. I seized a chair and smashed it into the Raptor's side. It fell with a crash as he swayed and grunted. Then I grabbed the Raptor from behind, clambering onto his broad back, thinking there was no way he'd take off with my weight on him, but I didn't slow him down enough and to my horror he reeled towards the edge of the terrace, still hanging onto Peri, and lurched into the air again.

Jesus Christ on a bike, I'd really done it now! I was so fucking dead my funeral was just a goddamn formality.

Now we were plunging, the Raptor and Peri and I, down towards the City, as all the fliers and structures of SkyNation streaked past us in a blur.

I hung on for dear life. The Raptor was a giant, the biggest flier I had ever seen. I'd fastened on him like a barnacle, instinctively, and now the idiocy, the sheer certifiable lunacy of climbing onto the back of a flier, was coming home to me.

We were plummeting.

Suddenly—I nearly lost my grip—the Raptor and I shot higher; Peri had twisted herself free and the loss of weight had sent us rebounding. Freed of this weight, the Raptor now powered both of us higher above the City, still pursuing his quarry. How could I describe my feelings? A shrieking vortex of terror and fury but also awe at the beauty of the blue City below us, and around us the spangled shroud of sky.

I clamped onto the Raptor's wings, grim as death, and managed to inch myself a little further up his back. A bit further, and a bit further. Now I was riding him and my weight and position—arms round his massive shoulders, legs straddling his waist—were seriously hampering his flying. He was wallowing, ungainly as a landing albatross, keening with fury like a wild creature. I gripped him so hard my hands began to go numb.

The Raptor climbed higher, twisted and let himself drop, like a fighter plane executing barrel rolls, spiralling downwards.

Sky, City, sky, City spun in a whirl of lights and blue dark.

The Raptor was going to kill me—twist me off in mid-air, slam me into the wall of a tower, scrape me off on a girder—whatever it took.

I leaned into him, into the storm of wind and rage, and screamed at him to stop. The ground loomed nearer, now the Raptor powered up again, wings beating hard, the sound of them immense. I could not hear myself think.

Out of the blue-dark a boneshaking *thud* smashed us so hard I heard something crack, whether in me or in the Raptor I wasn't sure. It must have been him, for I couldn't feel anything. It was incredible I was still hanging on but I couldn't for much longer. Peri swore as she veered away. *Don't try that again, Peri. I won't survive it.*

The Raptor beat up higher, preparing to spiral down. No way could I hold on through another series of rolls. No way could I make it to the ground alive without his help, either.

An image of Frisk, Raptor feather in his mane, flashed across my brain. Halley wincing when I caught her feather. My only chance. I grabbed one of his feathers and pulled. Hard. A violent shudder wrenched his frame.

'*Listen to me*,' I snarled, and pulled out another feather. He shivered again. He was listening. 'You get me down safely,' I hissed, 'or I'll pull your flight feathers out *one—by—one*. You'll be dead in the air too. I'll pluck you like a fucking chicken.'

I grabbed another feather and tugged. He turned, shearing down the wind, gliding as best he could, floundering under my weight. '*Roof*,' he gasped. 'Best can do. Crash any lower.' His strangled words proved how much the flight was costing him. I relaxed my grip on his feathers a fraction, enough to let him know I understood.

The rest of the flight could only have been a few seconds but they were the longest moments of my life, time expanding like the tail of a comet, stars streaking with speed, blue and green and red and white lights smearing, wind slicing me, atoms spread across the sky, part of the very sky, world dropping away.

Even SkyNation was nothing, *nothing*, compared to this whirl, this wild dark falling flight. In spite of the terror and the rage, I understood, in that endless instant, why they loved it so, why they would give up anything for it. In those moments, I too was a flier.

Circling above a clear building shining blue from within, no, it's too high, no, no, not now but now or never, loosening grip, have to let go at the right moment, tumbling through air.

Crunch. Sickening. Waves of pain.

In a rush of wings the Raptor was lost to the sky. I uncurled my body a little, gingerly, from clasping the dome I was lying on and peered around me. I was very high. Right in the middle of the City, on the top of a high building, a cold wind gusting over me.

My ankle burned. Something warm ran down my arm. I inspected it in the cold light beaming from the building. *Blood*. Running purple in the blue light. The thing had scraped me against the castle wall when I'd first grappled with it and shredded my flesh as well as the leather sleeve of the flying jacket. I hadn't felt it grate me but now my flesh throbbed.

My slick. Surprised, I answered.

'Mate!' yelled Henryk. 'What-the-*fuck*-is-going-on? SkyNation security has called in our flying squad, which they *never* do, they never let us near their exclusive little shindig, and now I hear a Raptor's got you. What the hell are *you* doing up there with all the freaks—you okay?'

'I think so but I need someone to pick me up. Soon. Where's Peri?'

'Mick's bringing her in. She's pretty beat up but won't let anyone look at her. We'll take her to my flat. I haven't got tenants in there and I can't think where else is safe. Where are you?'

'No idea.' I realised a blue dome of light surrounded me. 'Henryk, you're not going to believe this. I'm on top of the Church of the Seraphim!'

'Fuck!' barked Henryk. 'The least you could do is not make extra work for us.'

As I drifted in and out of consciousness waiting for Henryk and the rescuers, trying to plaster myself to the church's glassy surface, I was overwhelmed by the physical memory of the blue air, the plunging flight, my falling aeon as a flier. A fragment of that euphoria would always be preserved in me, its beauty and terror as intense as the night Thomas was born. I knew now I couldn't deny Thomas this freedom, this world entire. I'd tasted the sky and glimpsed the dream that was now his inheritance. I could not stand in his way.

Waiting on that slippery roof should have been terrifying but after my time at Cloud City and SkyNation, I could control my vertigo enough to sit tight and watch the great coloured bauble of the top of Cloud City, Chesshyre's triumph—his *final* triumph?—float above the City.

By the time Henryk and the rescue workers clambered out from the neighbouring building onto the roof, I was shaking so violently with cold and shock I could barely speak, and yet as my ankle was bound up, Henryk and I were seized by wild hilarity at being in the one place where our presence was most unwanted. We couldn't stop laughing, though I feared my laughter would shake me free and slide me into the dark. As the rescuers helped me across the access buttress Henryk said, 'Thought you'd like to know we've just arrested David Brilliant for trafficking. And accessory to murder.'

20

LANDFALL

I sat on a chair in Henryk's vacant flat, my foot up on a cushion. Tomorrow new bone would be implanted to help the break heal. 'You're lucky it's the only thing broken,' the rescue workers had said. No-one believed my story of how I came to be there, except Henryk, until I showed them the red feathers I still clutched in my fingers.

Henryk ordered us food and took his leave. 'I've got to get some sleep,' he said. 'I'm starting work in a couple of hours.'

'Are you okay?' I said to Peri. Hugo was asleep in her arms. We'd had to detour via the Jack and Jill child-care centre to pick him up.

'Is this one of those child hotels?' I'd said as we pulled up to the seedy highrise, with its billboard slick outside that made it look like a resort, complete with palm-fringed pool. *From newborns to 12 years old*, the sign said: *24 hour care; weekly rates. Special needs catered for. Separate dormitories for boys and girls. We give them the best holiday so you can have the best holiday.* 'Never seen one of these before.'

'Jack and Jill?' said Henryk. 'Hope that doesn't reflect their standard of care. I recall J and J suffered a distinct lack of trained supervision and sustained notifiable injuries as a result.' He shook his head. 'CaFS workers call these ratholes *kid kennels*. They have to use them, too.'

Frisk was lying next to Peri, his head shoved into her side, rumbling intermittently. The little lion was in a trance of bliss. He so clearly preferred Peri to me that I couldn't help smiling, though I was a bit hurt. *Ungrateful creature. Who tended your injuries so devotedly?*

Some of the white powder caked on Peri's wings had dusted onto Frisk's nose and was drifting down onto the cushions of the sofa where she sat, her arms around Hugo. The flat *crump* of night-time surf drifted in through the slightly open window.

'I'm alright,' Peri said. 'But so sore. Hate to think how much all this'll hurt tomorrow.'

'Peri, *what* is going on? When I saw you at Janeane's you agreed to bring Hugo back. I know you did start to fulfil your promise—'

'The tracking device,' Peri interrupted. 'Yes, I found out about that.'

I shrugged. 'It was the responsible thing to do.'

'I know it was,' said Peri. 'You saved my life with that thing.'

'So what happened? You didn't show in the City when you were supposed to and now you turn up trying to kill Chesshyre. Henryk spoke to the hospital. Peter's stable now so he's lucky to be alive, I guess.'

'*No*,' said Peri. 'It's not luck. If I'd wanted him dead, he would be. It was a warning.'

'Why?'

'Hugo is mine,' Peri said.

And then she told me. She told me about her plan to run away and about her change of heart. *Wow*, I thought as I listened. The vastness of the land and sea had achieved what no merely human argument could: shown Peri her smallness compared to the forces against her.

She told me about the storm and her rescue, her time with Audax, the raid and what happened as a result of the raid. By the time she described the fight with the Wild over Heavener Ridge, I felt like I'd been punched in the heart.

'So you see,' Peri said, 'when Audax made me take part in their raid I thought it was such a cruel thing to do. But it turned out it was one of the most important things anyone's ever done for me. Zeke, if I'd just brought Hugo back to the City like I promised, I'd never have known I was Hugo's mother. Can you imagine how that makes me feel? If I'd done the right thing from the start, *I would never have known*.'

I thought of my conversation with Mira. It would keep.

'So you decided to make it clear when you came back that you would not just let Peter take Hugo from you?' I said. 'Not sure you chose the best tactic, Peri.'

Peri stared at me. 'What would you suggest? He had me chased into that storm. I nearly died. Hugo too.'

I thought of Peter showing me the rose Peri had given him. Even though he'd had an affair with her, dumped her, abused his wealth and power to make her bear his child, even after all that, the worst betrayal was his lies. He *was* lucky to be alive after what he'd done to her.

Peri shivered. She looked so sick her skin took on a greenish tinge.

'Peri, you're not well. I think we need to get someone to take a look at you.'

'I'll be okay.'

'So what did you think—Peri, what on earth!' I gasped. The front of her shirt bloomed red. I just had time to grab Hugo from her before she slumped to the floor.

Peri was in intensive care, and still unconscious, when I visited her in the hospital nearest to Flierville the next day. I'd had treatment there myself on my ankle that morning and then limped up to her ward, Hugo walking next to me, clinging to my hand. I wasn't a family member, but then, who was?

Several of Peri's ribs had been broken, I was told. I thought of the bone-shaking crack when she'd hit the Raptor in mid-flight. Like me, her skin had been badly scraped along her arms and, worse, her belly, from struggling with the Raptor and being dragged along the castle battlements. The skin she'd sprayed on the wounds at first must have held for a little while then given way—that first-aid skin was only meant for minor wounds. She had lost blood and now infection was raging.

I sat by the bed and took Peri's hand. Her skin was hot and dry. 'Look, I've brought Hugo to see you.'

Hugo patted Peri's face. 'Up?' he said to me, his little brow wrinkling with worry. 'Mama 'ug?'

'She has to sleep, Hugo,' I said.

When we got out onto the street I bent down next to Hugo, favouring my good leg.

'What am I going to do with you, Hugo?' I didn't want to be charged with kidnapping either. As I walked Hugo to the light rail, my eye was caught by one of the big slicks on the platform that ran ads, music, news headlines. SCANDAL IN NANNY AGENCY said one headline. BABIES FOR SALE! shrieked another. INVESTIGATION GOES TO HIGHEST ECHELONS OF CHILD AND FAMILY SERVICES said a more sober news service. OPPOSITION CALLS FOR INQUIRY said a fourth. CALLS TO SACK DEPARTMENT HEAD, SECOND IN TWO YEARS. At last, the juggernaut set in motion by me and Cam and Henryk was crashing into public view.

I took Hugo to my flat. Halley rang me. 'Are you alright?'

'I think so,' I said.

I laughed out loud when she told me that Chesshyre was in the same hospital as Peri. That made sense; it was the closest to the SkyNation site.

I rang the Chesshyre-Katon house but, as I expected, there was no answer. So Avis had not returned. I rang Henryk's wife, Vivienne. She didn't mind babysitting Hugo out at Zen Estates for the afternoon.

I found Chesshyre awake, propped up in bed on a pile of pillows, reading.

'You're still alive,' I said, standing in the doorway. 'Lucky you.'

Unlike Peri's crowded intensive care ward, with its green-curtained beds and dark laminated floors, Peter's room was light and hushed, as luxurious as a hotel room, with its pale wooden blinds and pale walls and desk which now bore a profusion of exotic flowers, greenery and fruit.

Chesshyre turned the slick in his hands so I could see it. Of course. Headlines about Brilliant's arrest. 'Seems to be an awful lot of news about at the moment,' he said. 'Anything to do with you?' His skin was the colour of icing sugar, its pallor emphasised by the cream robe wrapped around him. His wings were folded underneath him and looked lustreless, the feathers dry and disordered.

'Yes, it has a lot to do with me. And with you too, for that matter.'

Chesshyre sat up a bit further. 'So, can you tell me anything about this?' he said, indicating one of his wings.

'What?'

'They removed a bolt from my wing,' said Chesshyre. 'Traced to a weapon stolen from an armoury a few years ago. No-one will tell me more than that.'

'SkyNation organisers are less than keen to pursue an investigation. The police won't be motivated to do much more since they're getting so little cooperation from your people, who always insist on their own security anyway.'

Chesshyre sighed. 'They won't want any interference in their affairs, even if it means covering up what happened to me. But you know who's responsible?'

'We both know,' I said. 'But you're the one who brought violence into this case.'

'So I've only myself to blame? She's the one who stole Hugo!'

'You're the one who stole Hugo and you know it.' I thought of the red rose again. Why was I here? To parade my righteous anger at a wounded man? No. I was here to try to make Peri's plan actually work; I was here to make Chesshyre understand that he *had* to negotiate with her, especially as more and more people were going to know the truth about him and Peri and Hugo.

Chesshyre was silent.

'I want to know where Avis is,' I said.

'I told you, she left. What business is it of yours?'

'Well, there's really no-one to look after Hugo at the moment.'

Chesshyre was electrified, as I'd intended. He jerked bolt upright. 'You know where Hugo is? Is he safe?'

'Yes.'

'For god's sake, Fowler, bloody well sit down. You're annoying the crap out of me, hovering like that.' Chesshyre gestured to the visitor's chair at the side of his bed.

I sat.

Chesshyre fixed his gaze on me. 'You have to stop protecting Peri and give Hugo to me. Immediately.'

'How are you going to look after him in here? Besides, I don't work for you anymore. Remember?'

'That has nothing to do with it. Hugo is my son.'

'He's Peri's son too. Disposing of her is not an option, Peter. Brilliant tried that with Luisa Perros and, as you say, that's generated rather a lot of news.' I took a deep breath. 'Peri is very sick. You'd better pray she doesn't die. When she wakes up you will meet with her and decide what arrangements you will make. You can't just take Hugo away from her. Peri's made it clear she won't let you.'

'Nonsense,' Chesshyre snapped. 'Hugo will live with me.' But he looked thoughtful.

'Where *is* Avis?' I said.

'Gone,' said Chesshyre. 'I've told you that.'

'Yes, but where? And *why*?'

'Who knows? Her staff have been calling me morning and night. Her collection's due in three weeks but no word or sign from her.'

'Peter, you *know* why Avis left.'

Chesshyre blinked. 'Yes,' he said. He took a deep breath. 'I do know why. You know that I used to be a non-flier like you. I didn't get my wings till I was seventeen.'

I nodded. He was getting around to answering my question. This was the scenic route. His injury and hospitalisation, the shock of Avis leaving, even hearing that Hugo was almost within reach, meant he had to talk.

'It took me a long time to realise the truth. My twenties were one long decade of euphoria—the exhilaration of Flight, the beginning of my professional career. There was something essential I ignored in my happiness. And that was that I was not attracted to other fliers. All my thoughts were about women who were not fliers. That was who I grew up with; they were real women to me. But mixed marriages don't work. Well, a few do—most fail. I thought I loved Avis, once. I just never desired her. Nor any other flier. Ever.'

Chesshyre broke off as a nurse padded into the room on thickly soled shoes. Discreetly I moved over to the window as she took his temperature or whatever she was supposed to do but inside I was seething. Would Chesshyre keep talking after this interruption? After the nurse left, I resettled myself in the chair and Chesshyre spoke again without looking at me. He wanted to finish what he'd started to say.

'I'd give a lot to know how common this is. I even saw someone about it. I asked him whether other fliers felt the same way and he said we weren't there to talk about other fliers. I could've killed him. That was what I needed to know. He thought it was transitional. That the new generation growing up with wings would know nothing else. Wish I could be so sure.'

It occurred to me that it was a little late in the day to be beginning to worry about this but I held my tongue.

'Fliers are beautiful,' Chesshyre said. 'That's not the problem. But beauty and sexual attractiveness have only a tangential relationship. Lots of beauty in this world doesn't move you in that way.'

I scratched my head. 'So that's why you decided to fuck Peri? Come on, Peter, I don't believe it's anything to do with beauty. It's about power.'

Chesshyre glanced at me sharply. 'You have no idea what you're talking about,' he said. 'You don't have any idea what real intensity is, what real power or control is.'

'Well, I'm not lacking in imagination,' I said. 'I can see that if you make the stakes so high that every sexual encounter becomes a potential love-death it might be hard to settle for anything less extreme. That sort of thing tends to be addictive.' I thought of Ruokonen. Fertility was a casualty of the treatments. *You become a different person when you become a flier. Different things matter to you.*

'So, that's what you finally told Avis, didn't you?' I said. 'That Peri was Hugo's mother? Bit of a miscalculation on your part, wasn't it? Were you so used to the fact you couldn't get Avis pregnant that you forgot it might be easier with someone else? That's why everything started unravelling when you got those test results. You knew

Avis would find out she wasn't even Hugo's genetic mother, which was not what she signed up for. It was all falling apart and you had to tell her why. Jesus, poor Avis. Her baby isn't hers, which she must have felt all along, just like she knew all along you never desired her. Not ever. No wonder she had some problems.'

Peter looked down at the slick still in his hands.

'I knew you were dishonest with me from the beginning but I never imagined you'd denied Peri her own child. You people really are monsters. Freaks.' I was almost spitting at him. 'Did they take out your heart when they gave you your wings?'

'Don't be so naive, Fowler,' Chesshyre said, raising his head to look at me. 'It was kinder not to tell Peri. She had to give him up anyway.'

'And Peri was terrified you were going to send him away and couldn't bear to see how you loved him less because he's not like you,' I retorted. 'I'd say she's got you two pegged pretty well. I'm not surprised Avis pissed off. Though she's no better, is she? Outsourcing pregnancy and labour to a poorer woman. Like Hugo's a pile of washing she can't be bothered to iron herself. I don't suppose she was too sorry to miss out on the whole experience. As long as Hugo's genes were half hers, that's all that mattered.'

Now Chesshyre was angry. He put down the slick and sat right up, away from the heap of pillows, wincing as he moved. 'Fowler, just where do you get off being so fucking self-righteous? You're ignorant, maudlin about pregnancy and birth precisely because you don't have to do it. What's so ennobling about stretch marks and torn perineums and abdominal incisions? It's barbaric. Do you weave your own cloth, grow your own food? It's all about where you draw the line. You sentimentalise pregnancy and birth because your family had no other choices.' Exhausted, Peter leaned back against the pillows.

'I'll tell you something else,' he said after a moment. 'This scandal about Little Angels and the church and the department will do far more harm than good. You think you're some sort of fucking white knight, riding in to rescue helpless girls? Guess what? *They won't thank you.* You've just made it a lot harder for those girls—girls who have *nothing*—

to sell the one thing they do have to offer and get off the bottom rung. Who are you to say they shouldn't? You think Peri would rather not have her wings? Why don't you ask her?'

I glared at him then dropped my gaze to the slick Peter had set down on the bedside table. My attention was drawn into the images fading up, then dissolving away: views of a house as if it were already built.

'You'd better tell me where Hugo is,' Chesshyre said, glancing over to see what I was looking at.

'Of course,' I said, my attention still drifting to the slick. 'As soon as you arrange the meeting with Peri and the lawyers. Peri's lawyer will be in touch with you. At the moment you don't have anyone to look after him.'

'I will,' said Peter.

'Another nanny? Because that's worked out so well.'

Ignoring that, Peter indicated the slick. 'That's where Hugo will live.' He swept his finger across the screen, bringing up more detailed images. 'You don't build this house. You *grow* it; its colours and textures develop from petals, leaves, rind. Each room has its own intrinsic scent—orange, vanilla, hay, thyme. And it's more or less self-repairing.'

'It's fabulous,' I said, impressed in spite of myself. Chesshyre might be a ruthless son of a bitch but he was a *talented* ruthless son of a bitch. How could he show me this work, his true passion, as if all the rest had not happened, was all in the past already? He really was moving on. No more wife, no more clifftop house. No more Frisk. He hadn't mentioned the lion, not even to ask how he was. Too easy to blame the treatments, the alien genes. It was human, after all, to treat the mother of his only child that way. To treat his *child* that way. Don't you understand yet what the real sacrifice is? *It's Hugo.*

A green vertical meadow, sprigged with flowers, formed walls around the house, enclosing a courtyard. I'd like a house like that myself. Peter wanted to give Hugo the best of himself, I could see, but I wanted to say: *the best is not enough, don't you get it?* You have to give *everything*. The house rose up from the earth like a scarlet runner bean on a stake with Peter's rooms at the top. *We* get claustrophobia. *They* get vertigo.

Chesshyre closed his eyes, dismissing me, saying coolly as his parting shot, 'Hugo is ours. Remember that. His birth certificate names Avis and me as his mother and father.'

I visited Peri when I could but each time I did she was still unconscious. I told Henryk the infection was not responding to treatment. *Must be one of those superbugs*, he said. He and Vivienne and I worked out a roster for looking after Hugo for the few days Peter remained in hospital. None of us could bear the idea of returning him to the child hotel. He liked playing with the twins and was overjoyed to see Frisk. The lion, who had started to look old and stiff, was as tolerant as any grandfather, letting the baby pull on his ears and mane and tail. He even let Hugo ride on his back for a few steps at a time, before gently rolling him off his back and onto the floor, to squeals of delight from Hugo.

'I don't like to think what CaFS would say about us looking after Hugo without anyone's permission,' said Henryk one night when I'd gone to his house for dinner. Hugo was sleeping there overnight. 'But you can't talk to anyone there anyway. The whole department is in lockdown.'

'Cam rang me,' I told him. 'Says she's going away after giving evidence at the commission of inquiry. She's been suspended. She said her reward for exposing the most serious breaches of trust and procedure, to say nothing of the law, in the department will be narrowly escaping a prison sentence for breaching security.'

'That sucks,' said Henryk.

A rumble of thunder sounded right over the house.

'I'll have to give evidence at the commission of inquiry too,' I said.

Lightning flashed, rain poured down. Another storm in this long, wet, wild summer.

'Where's she going away to?' said Henryk.

'Buddhist monastery, apparently. Says that in her culture it's the right time of life for her to attend to her spiritual development.'

Henryk rang me a few weeks later. 'You watching the news?'

'I'm *always* watching the news,' I said. 'Especially since you and me and Cam are responsible for making so damn much of it. I particularly enjoyed watching Mrs Harper's arrest and her outraged denials of any wrongdoing. That helmet of hair was looking ruffled.'

'Turn it on now,' said Henryk. 'I'll stay on for a sec. Want to hear your reaction to this.'

'Okay.'

The news came up. The lead story was about a category six hurricane. Fair enough. It did seem, these days, that weather was the beginning of the news, not its end.

'Here it comes,' said Henryk.

'That's one of your guys,' I said, watching a detective head into the Origins compound. 'Fantastic.'

The next thing we saw, with delight and for me an almost hysterical glee, was the arrest of His Incandescence, the Most Serene Trinity Jones.

For a moment I was speechless.

It was blissful seeing Jones finally, *finally*, led away in cuffs from his compound—there were those bloody solar yachts in the background, just where they were when we'd raided him—on a serious array of charges, from trafficking to kidnapping to murder.

He had the stare of true fear, that white mask around the eyes. Now you know how it feels, you bastard. You're not getting off. Not this time. The scandal with Brilliant was being used as a blunt instrument to crack Origins and its secretive ways wide open.

'You know what's really funny?' said Henryk. 'It hasn't come out yet but the charge that's really going to hurt Trinity, the one he's really going to go down for, is *tax evasion*.'

'So your specialist in financial data and tracking came good,' I said.

'Certainly did,' said Henryk. 'All those lovely rivers of undeclared cash from rich fliers. The government's going to settle its scores for the crime that really matters.'

Well, that's what we all thought at the time. But there was one more turn of the screw regarding Trinity I failed to grasp until later . . .

Peri had her own room in the hospital, almost as swish as Peter's. I guessed he was paying for it now, now that he had Hugo.

She was lying on her side, very still, like an angel carved on a tomb.

'Peri,' I said. 'I'm sorry.'

She glanced at me, eyes glittering, but didn't move.

Yet man is born unto trouble, as the sparks fly upward.

'Can you tell me what happened?'

'What did you expect? My lawyer was never going to scare Peter's team.' Peri sighed. 'He did what he could. It was better than nothing. Better than I had any right to hope. They're going to change the birth certificate. I don't get *residence*, as they say. He'll live with Peter. I get *contact*. I get to *visit* him. Supervised at first.'

I started to move over to Peri but she patted the air, motioning me to sit down. She didn't want me to be outraged on her behalf. She was trying to hold herself together but the dam was bursting. 'He's not here. I can't believe they just . . . took him. He cried so hard.' She shook her head. 'Don't say anything. *Please.* I can't bear it. I did the best I could. I have no money, nowhere to live. I have a history of abuse and neglect and foster care so I'm the one who's punished. They're not trying to charge me with kidnapping my own child but there's eight different ways Chesshyre's team can make me look a bad risk.'

Peri sniffled. 'There's one good thing. There's no sign of Avis. Legally Peter and I are Hugo's parents. Actually two good things. The residential parenting order is only temporary. Anyway, I know what'll happen. He'll be thrilled to have Hugo back at first but I know the hours he works, how busy he is, how much he likes it. He'll hire someone to look after Hugo and end up hardly ever seeing him.' Anger seized her. 'Oh, why couldn't they—why couldn't they just give him to me? They might as well have.' She lay face down on the bed and howled as if her heart would break.

I put my hand on her shoulder. 'Peter's angry now. You can't be surprised about that. Things will get easier. You'll see more of Hugo over time.'

Peri sat up, stony-faced. 'I've got what I deserved. The only one who's suffered who didn't deserve it is Hugo.'

'What do you mean?'

'I thought I knew best. That I was helping Hugo. But I'm the one who's harmed him. As if the storm didn't terrify him so that he can't bear to fly at all, he was also seized by the Wild in the fight above Heavener. Can't imagine him ever wanting to fly after that.'

I was silent. No point offering her false comfort. 'I can help you with somewhere to live. Henryk needs a tenant. How would you pay rent?'

Peri rubbed her eyes. I handed her some tissues and she blew her nose. 'I'll go down to Flight Gym for a start. I'm better than any of those instructors.'

I sat with Peri until she fell asleep. As I watched over her, the tear stains drying on her cheeks, her breath slowing until it was low and even, I thought how strange it felt that this case was finally over. Hugo was with his father, parenthood knocked down to the highest bidder. Nothing new about that. Chesshyre thought he'd had it all worked out. Peri would give him and Avis a baby. And what had gone wrong? A natural conception and birth. Because he'd fucked her. Why? Because he wanted to. Because he could. Because he could make her pregnant, even if he wasn't fully aware of that motive. *Nature doesn't care about your happiness*, my father used to say, warning me not to get my first girlfriend pregnant. Nature doesn't care if a baby is what *you* want. A baby is what Nature wants. Nothing personal. We keep acting as if the link between sexuality and fertility can be broken so easily but Peter admitted he wasn't attracted to flier women. Perhaps he just hadn't worked out why.

I met Sunil at Kamchatka Joe's again, hoping he'd summoned me to give me more work. He was already there when I arrived, reading.

'Interesting article,' he said, smiling.

'What is it?'

'An analysis of the Origins scandal. This article explores the idea that the Most Serene Trinity Jones didn't hit on the idea of trading in babies by accident. For a sufferer from Klinefelter's, but one with such a strong will to power that he'd set up his own cult, for a man who felt himself only half a man, with his microorchidism and congenital sterility, controlling a trade in the fertility of others—especially the rich and powerful enemies of all that he claimed to stand for in this world—would be intoxicating indeed. And highly lucrative.'

I nodded. 'Makes sense.'

My arm still hurt where my skin had been shredded, though proper new skin had long since been pasted over the wounds. I rubbed it thoughtfully.

'I suppose,' I said, 'that information I got for you about Brilliant isn't of much use now he's so embroiled in scandal?'

Sunil stared at me. Then he started laughing. He laughed so hard I started laughing too, though I didn't really know why.

'Is that what you think?' said Sunil when he could speak again. 'God, that's fantastic. By all means, don't let *me* disabuse you then.'

'Oh. I've been a bit slow, haven't I?'

'You know, Zeke, for an investigator you aren't *nearly* suspicious enough.'

I stared at him. Wheels turned in my brain.

'Ah, I see now,' I said. 'You never were that interested in Brilliant. The fact he's now been charged as an accessory to murder is just a bonus. Brilliant and the church are collateral damage; it's Trinity you were after all along. You thought there was something suspect between Brilliant and Waterhouse and I proved you spectacularly right. My information and Cam's revelations were useful, they started the deluge, but the storm engulfing Brilliant and the church and then, inevitably, Origins and Trinity—you'd worked towards that from the beginning. It awaited just the right moment to set off the avalanche.'

Sunil smiled. 'Do you think what happened to Brilliant was entirely unforeseen?'

'You mean you knew I'd get Henryk onto it? I'm a good pawn. Well, I guess the financial detective work his people did was very useful to your boss. Whoever the hell *he* is.'

'You see?' said Sunil. 'You can get it if you really think it through.'

'Patronising bastard,' I said.

With a flash of clarity that took my breath away I knew who Trinity's real enemy, and Sunil's boss, was: the ex-cabinet minister, well connected with many powerful friends, whose daughters Origins had kidnapped years ago. The Charon case, the case that had given me whatever notoriety I possessed, was still working its way through the body politic. Revenge is a dish best eaten cold, they say, and this dish was being served at absolute zero.

I was a true servant of Nemesis after all.

'It was well done, Sunil,' I said. 'Congratulations.'

Well done indeed. Watch the masters at work. And each time I had been one of the instruments of retribution, the first time by chance, the second by design. An elegance I could attribute to Sunil's intellect and love of the game.

21

OPERATION

This was the season of spending time in hospital. I'd needed treatment for my ankle, I'd visited Peter, I visited Peri. But this was the moment of truth, the hospital appointment I dreaded most. Now I sat in the waiting room next to Lily and waited for Thomas. Finally, after all the preparatory treatments and therapy, this was the morning scheduled for his surgery. Thomas was whisked away into another country behind those swing doors. When he re-emerged, he'd be transformed.

I'd thought Lily would be jubilant but I'd underestimated her. She was subdued, even frightened. She'd dressed soberly in her perennial grey and brought case files to read but didn't look at them. She just sat on the white plastic chair in the waiting room and stared at the television high on the wall. I fetched us both coffee. She took one sip but didn't touch it again. 'He looked so small,' she said, keeping her face turned up to the TV.

'Yes,' I said. Thomas had looked tiny as they wheeled him into the operating theatre, surrounded by blue sheets and all that silver and matt black equipment. 'Brave Thomas,' I'd whispered to him. I was assailed by the most powerful feeling of guilt I'd ever experienced. Lily and I had delivered him to a torture chamber. Drugs, masks, needles, knives. How could we do this to our little boy? Legally, surgery is assault, a crime mitigated only by consent and necessity. Well, we'd consented, but was it necessary? Would Thomas have consented, if he'd known what he was really in for?

Now I had to sit and hope that nothing went wrong in surgery, that nothing went wrong as he recovered, that nothing went wrong ever again that might be my fault.

Lily chewed at the side of one of her fingers, an old habit I thought she'd disciplined herself out of long ago. Gently I pulled her hand away from her mouth. She let it rest in mine for a moment before twisting both hands together in her lap.

'We're going to be here for a while,' Lily said.

I stood up and started to walk around the room. Along the blue line running down the corridor towards the swing doors at one end of the room, then back towards the windows at the other end. The surgery, while not especially risky, I'd been told, was taxing and time-consuming—all those muscles and nerves to knit up perfectly.

The sun didn't move that morning. Every time I paced up to the window, it stood in the same place in the sky as before. Hospital time. Dead white time that lurches forward only for meals, and not even then if you're not a patient. I insisted on searching for food and returned with soft drinks and plastic-wrapped sandwiches. Lily didn't touch these either.

The afternoon was searing, sky molten white. A woman in blue scrubs splashed with blood—Tom's?—approached us, undoing her mask. 'Thomas is in recovery now,' she told us. 'He's fine. You can see him when they bring him up to the ward.'

Lily sprang to her feet. Now she was excited. After all this waiting, Thomas was a present she'd finally get to unwrap. What would he be like?

Tom's bed was next to a window facing west. Sun poured over him. Lily and I stood looking down at him. Eyes closed, sleeping. Sheet pulled up to his neck.

Lily reached out and picked up the hem of the sheet.

'What are you doing?'

'I have to see.' Slowly, she drew the sheet down to his ankles.

And there they were. I had to admit, Ruokonen had outdone herself.

Tom's white body, thin as a peeled stick, was hidden. He was covered in gorgeous heavy warm wings that lay on him as if carved from pure gold.

Lily wept.

The sun lit up each feather, so perfectly sculpted and detailed, as if etched.

We stood and watched him breathe, wings lifting ever so slightly, as the sun sank behind us, and as the angle of its rays shifted, Tom's feathers flashed hard green.

I bent down and kissed my son.

22

LONG-HAUL

Wind beat the trees till they raked the sky. Keening entered Peri's dreams, that rising note signalling the impending wall of storm. She lay on her back, breathing fast, abandoning herself to voluptuous fear, pleasure as pure and dreadful as her moment of falling with Jay. When she dropped into her breathing, listening to the wind, she could feel her weightlessness at the top of the storm, the second she'd hung there, bright curve of earth below. She often closed her eyes and lived that eternity, that breathlessness before dropping into the dark, its sublime terror the talisman of her soul.

Frisk stretched himself along the end of the bed, his fur tiled dark and light in the pattern of perforated light falling through the window. She leaned over, buried her hands in his mane. Good to feel the rough warmth of his fur. Frisk yawned and turned over, still asleep.

Peri rolled over and shoved her head under a pillow. Hugo wailed for her if he heard thunder. On those nights they slept curled together. Though not frightened of storms herself anymore—so many things no longer frightened her—when she lay asleep, defences down, and howling wind wove through her dreams, she woke distressed when Hugo was not there, hoping someone was comforting him at Peter's house.

She got up and padded to Hugo's room; his absence, his warm sweet smell, filled it. She shut the door and went to the kitchen to pour herself a glass of water. The leaves of the oak outside the kitchen window shed a warm glow over her as they moved.

Peri wished she knew what had become of Avis. Peter had heard nothing. There was an investigation, Peter even coming under suspicion, but there was no evidence she'd met with foul play of any kind. *Fowl play*, fliers remarked sagely to each other. *She's turned Wild. Any fool could work that out. And all they can say is—not proven.* Her disappearance was sensational: she'd been famous, and now that she'd vanished she became more so. Now Peri's fears took the same form, over and over. Avis Wild; ravening, hollow-eyed, shrieking as she snatched Hugo back into the sky.

Peri set her empty glass in the sink. Wind buffeted her flat. Hugo had his own house, the one Peter had decided he should live in. She knew Peter was talented but had thought it was talent for mass, shine, awe. She hadn't known he had it in him to create a house like a cloud, each room grown into its own exquisite tint. Sunset colours: pink, purple-blue, clear red. Walls rolled in waves or unfurled like flowers. They looked none the worse when Hugo splashed paint on them or hit them with his trucks.

Peri sighed, looked out the window. This was going to be one of the bad nights, when the walls closed in. Her ability to bear confinement was diminishing alarmingly. Often she slept in the silvered oak outside, dozing on the wooden platform built by other fliers, listening to the shifting air. It took her back to her time on Heavenier with Audax. That felt right but unsettling. As if the part of her that was Wild arose in those times, grew stronger. She had to make peace with that self, the being she became when she flew.

Back to the bedroom then. She knew when she was beaten. She pulled on her night-flying skims that rasped shreds of light from moon and star to make her faintly visible in the dark.

Peri flew out over the ocean, always where she most liked to fly. Below rocked a scatter of brilliant needles stuck into the sea. A few fishing boats, not enough to justify the word 'fleet'. There were no fishing fleets anymore.

Not long after Peri started working at Flight Gym, Niko had returned, alone, to the City. And was promptly sued by Diomedea for publishing their research papers. Niko was jubilant. Diomedea had made the fatal error of fighting Niko on his own ground. They never dreamed it would go this far, he said. They thought they could scare me. Never, he said to Peri, *never* sue anyone who has nothing to lose. Nothing they can do to me except tell me to stop publishing and everyone's already copied everything.

As the case ground on, Diomedea realised it had made a disastrous mistake from which it could not now extricate itself. The worst part for Diomedea was that every detail of its research, its company operations, its relations with competitors and customers, was dragged through open court and put on the public record. Niko and his associates aired allegations on everything from collusion with MicroRNA/Corvid on drug pricing to falsifying research on treatment side effects.

'There is an odd thing,' said Niko a month or so into the case. 'Even though they're suing me, they sent someone to talk to me about you.'

Peri looked at him.

'They know you'll listen to me.'

'What am I supposed to listen to?'

'Well, they're still interested in you and Hugo, of course.'

Of course. Niko said Diomedea had admitted that in a sense it was responsible for what had happened to Peri's father. 'They're offering you compensation. Without prejudice. They're not calling it compensation but that's what it is. They'll support you in anything you want to do—any studies, any projects of your own—to a very considerable degree.'

'If I let them study me and Hugo,' Peri said.

The thing is, I want to know myself.

'Yes,' said Niko. 'It might be important for your future and Hugo's, to know what effect your father's treatments had on you.'

'Tell them I'll think about it, Niko. I do often wonder if that's why I had such a strong yearning to fly from the start. I'd rather think it was just me, though, not an urge implanted in me by the company that experimented on my father.'

Peri headed east, further away from land. How far could she fly? She had been pushing herself, extending her range. She was in training.

Jay was planning something. They wanted her help. You're becoming well known, Niko had said. In the right circles, among people who know about these things. I hear you're just about the most sought-after Flight instructor in the City.

Niko had also told her, when he first came to see her on his return to the City, that Finch was dead. She'd been cornered that night, forced up and into aerial combat against a Wild. Jay had seen her fall. They couldn't look for her body; they had to save themselves. What a lonely, terrifying death. Peri often saw, out of the corner of her eye, a dark shape falling from the sky into a death spiral. Once the wings were set in the wrong angle there was no way to get them back up, no way to generate forward thrust.

Jay went back to find you, Niko had told Peri. But you were gone. He searched for you, at risk to himself.

Had Jay's search drawn the Wild away from pursuing her?

Jay had brought down quite a few of the Wild, Niko had continued, but there were too many so he organised our retreat. He blamed himself for Finch's death; he believed if he'd prepared us better it wouldn't have happened. I don't agree; those were the risks we were taking. Anyway, he went back for you. I thought you should know that.

'What happened to Shaheen?' Peri asked.

'We don't know. I like to think she's found herself a territory, another mate. Good thing Jay kept her free. Otherwise she'd have been killed that night.'

Ahead of Peri, a cloud-dragon was swallowing stars, its crooked shape blotting out the sky. She set herself to climb above it. It was like seeing a broad path leading ahead of her, higher into the sky. She'd been seeing more and more in that way. Seeing the path and then flying along it; it didn't matter whether the trajectory was straight or curved. In daylight, at least, it might be linked to a dim ability to perceive ultraviolet. She could sense colour gradients in the sky; they altered her patterns of flying, particularly for long flights. Niko and Jay said they'd been exploring that too and wondered why no-one had spoken of it. Too hard to describe. Peri herself couldn't but she also thought City fliers didn't notice it because they didn't need it. They didn't use it. They rarely flew long distance.

Jay did, though. We're thinking about real long-distance flying, he said. We'll head out across the ocean. Like a migration. No-one's ever done it before. Will you come?

Peri flew higher, heading slightly north-east. Will I join them? More than anything, I want to fly with Jay again.

She came about, checking her heading against the rush of stars and the rainstorm of city lights, which she knew well from this direction, from the sea back to the land.

Peri accelerated. Thrilling to skim fast above the City at night; as darkened towers wheeled below her they made her feel so much higher, their spires giving scale to her height. She circled above her favourite buildings, soaring above vents, streams of hot air surfing her up, and then, as always, saving the best for last, she wheeled over the tallest tower, Cloud City, one of the few still lit each night. This was almost as good as glass-off: tumbling down into the ravines formed by its sides, lit walls flying past her, waterfalls of light plunging up into the sky, giving the rush of speed like nothing else.

It would be a year before the migration. Jay was gathering support, working out the logistics. Fliers would join them from each territory and country they flew over. It would be an exploration, a protest, a challenge. It would be the talk of the world.

Peri arrowed up and over the top of Cloud City, testing her speed.

She braked and turned, floating, a seed on the wind. That had done it. Now she was tired. No more fancy moves. Go home.

If you come with us, if we make it, Jay had said, you will be an explorer. A legend. No-one else is doing this, they don't even think it's possible. Maybe it's not. But it hung there, a shimmering possibility. She could see them taking off at sunset, using the polarised light patterned across the sky then to orient themselves, aligning with the earth's magnetic field, then flying through the night, under the moon, straggled into the long, wide V that geese use. The rhythm of Flight for days, breathe in, wings up, breathe out, wings down, till there was nothing but that rhythm and the changing light and clouds flaked like salt, translucent as rice paper, torn into pieces, breaking up, bubbling over and streaming away like boiling milk. No thoughts but the movement of light, the glassy feel of air over her wings.

By the end of it she would be Wild.

Perhaps not. Perhaps they could find a balance.

They'd have to start without her. Only now was she getting to spend more time with Hugo. If she took off for a long migration, with no guarantee she'd be coming back, wouldn't she be like Avis, disappearing into the blue? It would be such a long time for Hugo. And for her. She'd had enough of leaving things behind in her life for now.

Still so much to do, exploring the realm of Flight. They'd hardly begun. She was young. There was time.

When Peri got back to the flat, she took out the letters Zeke had given back to her.

Dear Hugo,

I wrote these for you because I wanted you to know how it was when you were very little. Because you can't remember it yourself. And I was the one who was there with you. Who saw you and listened to you and knew how you were.

Dear Hugo,
You loved the moon. We'd sit up at night when I fed you and if we could see the moon through the eastern windows you'd stare and stare at it. You'd look for it even if you couldn't see it. Do all babies have such a passion for the moon? I'd never heard of such a thing.

Dear Hugo,
You used to wake so early and I sat with you in the deep blue before sunrise. You'd finish nursing and fall back into sleep, as if you were sliding fast away from me into deep clear water. I could see you but you were gone.

Dear Hugo,
I wanted to tell you—

Peri put the letters away and went out to the oak tree. Tonight she would sleep outside.

EPILOGUE

FLYING LESSON

Thomas bounced up and down on his seat inside the light-rail carriage. 'We're going to Sugar Island,' he sang. 'We're going to Sugar Island. We're going to Sugar Island.'

'Settle down, sweetie,' I said, as I buckled him in, tucking his gold wings around the seat. They were still the most beautiful wings I'd ever seen. I guess Lily and I had to count ourselves lucky as Thomas had been one of Ruokonen's last clients. She'd turned her entire attention to research, mostly on cracking the dynamics of insect flight. Insects 'fly by wire', she'd said. They constantly alter the shape and tension of their airfoil and so they can do things birds could only dream about. They can fly upside down and backwards. I hoped those abilities were a long way from being transferable to humans. Bird men were one thing but insect men I didn't want to live to see. Then the human project would be well and truly over.

'I'm not a sweetie,' Thomas said happily. 'I'm a Swift.' He was using his fledgling name more and more. *Swift* was an inaccurate name in one way—swifts are black—but accurate in another way because the slender recurved arc of his wings made him, potentially, incredibly fast and agile. I'd looked up swifts only to read they were capable of the fastest flight of all, excepting the screaming dives of falcons, and lived almost all their lives in the air, drinking on the wing, mating, even sleeping in flight. I didn't find this information reassuring.

I handed Thomas a banana—he was always hungry these days—and settled in for the long ride to Sugar Island. I'd only been there once, as a child, and the image of it had stayed fixed in my mind as the setting of ideal beauty, with its turquoise water and its sand that was indeed as white and fine as sugar; so fine, my awe-struck child self had been told, that the sand had been used to polish the lenses in the great mirrors used in space telescopes.

Thomas bounced up and down as much as the seatbelt allowed and sang around mouthfuls of banana—*Thomas fly round the sun, Thomas fly round the moon, Thomas fly round the chimney pot on a Sunday afternoon.*

Sugar Island was deserted when we arrived. The cost of the ride out there was beyond most people these days. As always, it took forever to unbuckle Thomas and shepherd him away from the light rail. Now with his wings the performance took twice as long, manoeuvring the wings out carefully, making sure no feathers got damaged, smoothing them down. Finally, we walked down the path away from the station and followed its winding white sand into tall green forest. After ten minutes or so we could see blue water and blue sky ahead of us. We were not down at the beach yet but nearing the edge of a cliff about twenty metres above the water. I knelt down and brushed Tom's hair out of his eyes.

'Hello,' I heard a low gentle voice say. Peri. Then, 'Tom! Tom!' a little voice squeaked.

'Hugo, my big man,' I said and turned with my arms out. Hugo ran to me as Peri came up close behind him. 'Can I kiss you?' I said. Hugo nodded solemnly and I kissed his cheek. Hugo and Thomas squatted down and began playing some game they'd invented with stones. I kissed Peri's cheek too.

'You look well,' I said.

'I am,' she said. 'Thanks. How's Halley?'

'Good. She's good. Have you heard anything about Jay and his crew? Where are they?'

'Indian Ocean.'

'Oh. That's something, isn't it? And Hugo? He seems well.'

She hesitated. 'Yes. I have to get him back to Peter's by seven.'

'Thanks for taking Thomas on this flight with you. I don't think he realises how lucky he is, to be taught by such a celebrated flier as yourself. They say no-one can bring out the exhilaration of Flight the way you can.'

'It's a pleasure,' she said. 'It's not that I'm so great. It's just that there are still not many real fliers around.'

I smiled.

'I never did ask you,' said Peri, 'what finally made you decide on wings for Thomas?'

'I told myself all sorts of things,' I said. 'That it would set him up for the future, make him a success, keep him out of places like the Venice. But in the end, I'm not sure any of those things were the real reasons. I think it all came down to one thing: *you* try telling a small child that he or she can't fly. That you won't allow it.'

'Yes,' said Peri, pain crumpling her features for a moment. 'I have that conversation to look forward to.'

'Oh Peri, I'm sorry. Are you sure they can't do anything?'

'Don't know. Peter doesn't want to start the round of specialists yet. Maybe he never will. I don't think Hugo will *want* to fly. My fault. He'll probably end up being a—what do they call them?—someone who explores caves, or something.' She turned to Thomas. 'Hello, Thomas. Do you want to show me your wings? They're the most amazing wings I've ever seen.'

Thomas stood up and arched his wings out, turning round, proudly displaying them, green fire sparking from the undersides in the sun. Hugo kept his head bent, concentrating on his stones.

Peri had stepped forward and was hugging Hugo. 'Now you and Zeke are going to have a great time together and Thomas and I will join you pretty soon. Okay?'

Hugo did not look at her. Peri kissed his cheek, gave him another hug and straightened up. 'He'll be fine,' she whispered. She took Tom's hand and they stepped to the cliff edge. Tom's fearlessness had not ceased to amaze me. *Brave Thomas*. It was one way I could feel him drawing away from me. I was still overcome with dizziness whenever I saw him step into the air.

Up they went, Peri flying wingtip to wingtip with Thomas, then circling below him. The sun struck flashing gold from Thomas's wings. He was bright as a day star, flying up there.

Hugo watched, not looking at me, until they rose into two dots, one dark, one shining.

'Come on, Hugo,' I said. 'Let's have some fun. Let's go down to the beach.'

He put his hand in mine and we walked down the lush path of palms to the sheltered cove.

We swam together under the water and saw fish and jellyfish. A big blue groper came and inspected us. We were intruders in his precinct. We built elaborate sandcastles and dug for pippis and explored rockpools.

After a while we sat and ate our lunch in the shade.

In the safe waters of the cove a meteor landed. It was Thomas, his wings almost too bright to look at in the noon sun. Peri landed near him in a ruffle of water. Lazily, like great swans, they floated in towards us. Hugo jumped up and ran into the water. He and Thomas walked out together, Hugo showing him the sandcastle we'd built. They sat down, ignoring Peri and me.

Peri walked towards me, as awe-inspiring as a statue. The goddess Victory. She looked so much older, more womanly now. My greeting stopped in my throat. I'd forget how breathtaking she was and then moments like this would knock me sideways.

Peri sat down, folding her wings and turning to look at Hugo and Thomas, utterly absorbed in their construction. I handed her a piece of watermelon.

'I hope they'll always be friends,' I said, watching them bicker over a sand rake.

'Yes.' Said with more fervour than I'd expected. 'I hope so too.'

'Look at that,' I said, but Peri had already seen it. 'Did you tell Thomas to do that?'

'No, I'm ashamed to say I never even thought of it myself.'

Thomas had arched one wing above Hugo, sheltering him from the sun.

Peri and I settled down for our afternoon's surveillance on the sand.

This is as good a moment to leave as any. For the rest of my life I could see us on this beach, figures in a painting, transfixed, washed with colour, transparent blue and green, Thomas's wings the gold leaf, blazing against the sky. All stories are tragedies if they end in death, which they all do, and all are comedies if they culminate in the birth of a child. Which, so far in our life as a species, they have. So far as we know, children will keep appearing, in whatever form, and I would like this story to be a comedy so I end it with Thomas and Hugo.

That day was Midsummer. I often dreamed of it later, as if it continued and we were there, always. We celebrated it by crowning Hugo, our youngest, *our faery prince*, Peri said, with flowers. They were weeds we found along the path to the beach: morning glory, jasmine, honeysuckle. Tough, rambling, prolific survivors but they made a blue and white and golden crown, dripping sweetness. Peri carried Hugo on her shoulders, the flowers falling down their backs, unravelling already. Thomas trailed them, an angelic attendant.

You know, Peri said to me as we walked, *Thomas and I are still the, you know*—she lowered her voice—*still the freaks, even though we chose it. Hugo is perfect in every way. He's not missing anything.*

Nice of you to say so, Peri. Maybe you even believe it. But no-one knows yet whether that's true. There's not enough evidence and judgement's not been pronounced. The best we can hope for is a provisional verdict: *not proven.*

Neither guilty nor innocent.

Thomas skipped ahead of us singing *Brave Thomas!*

Unbidden, the response rose in my mind, smoothly as a counter-weight: *we're not scared.*

At the top of a small hill ahead of us he paused, his wings catching the slanting rays of afternoon sun and shining so brightly that he appeared to melt into the sun itself, dissolving without silhouette into its sinking golden orb so that I could no longer see him at all.

ACKNOWLEDGEMENTS

The descriptions of the mechanics of flight in Chapter 9, *The Unforgiving Element*, have been informed by *Taking Wing: Archaeopteryx and the evolution of bird flight* by Pat Shipman (Phoenix, 1999), a brilliantly clear and detailed account of the debates over the evolution of bird flight. Any oversimplifications or misinterpretations are of course my own. *Birds: Their habits and skills* by Gisela Kaplan and Lesley J. Rogers (Allen & Unwin, 2001) was also a valuable source. The quote about raptors from Thomas Bewick's *The History of English Birds* (1797) is taken from the anthology *An Exhilaration of Wings: The literature of birdwatching*, edited by Jen Hill (Penguin Books, 2001).

It takes much hard work to turn a manuscript into a book. First thanks are due to my brilliant and passionate agent, Selwa Anthony, who makes things happen. I am grateful to Katherine Howell and also to Jody Lee.

Thanks to Ali Lavau, a wonderful, sensitive and dedicated editor; you held the book up to the light and showed me new facets. Many thanks to Christa Munns and all at Allen & Unwin who have worked on and believed in the book. Special thanks to Annette Barlow, whose vision for this book is all I could hope for.

Most of all, heartfelt gratitude to my husband, Julian, who has read the book more times than anyone can count and has given more detailed criticism and thought and creative energy to this project than anyone else can ever know, to say nothing of physical, emotional and financial support. Without you, this book would not be what it is.